Searing Surrender

Sancho de Cordoba had taken off his jacket to reveal his magnificent body. Then Lizette felt the strength of his arms as he pulled her against him, slowly, gently, deliberately.

"You—you said you don't rape ladies," she desperately pleaded.

His smile was lazy, insolent. "I don't intend to rape you." He took a deep breath as he gazed into her green eyes, letting them fire the very depths of his soul. "I am going to make love to you," he murmured provocatively, and the hair at the nape of Lizette's neck prickled as it stood on end, while a fear like she'd never known before began to tear her apart.

"Please," she begged. "Don't do this to me. You've taken everything else. Now you'd take this, too?"

"I only want what I know you can give," he said, and as his mouth came down on hers hungrily, Lizette knew it was not only him she had to fight, but herself. . . .

Tides of Passion

- ☐ BELOVED TRAITOR by June Lund Shiplett. (138007—$3.95)
- ☐ SWEET SURRENDER by Cathrine Coulter. (142004—$3.95)
- ☐ FIRE SONG by Cathrine Coulter. (140001—$3.95)
- ☐ THUNDER IN THE WIND by June Lund Shiplett. (135997—$3.95)*
- ☐ DEFY THE SAVAGE WINDS by June Lund Shiplett. (137493—$3.50)*
- ☐ HOLD BACK THE SUN by June Lund Shiplett. (127943—$3.50)*
- ☐ RAGING WINDS OF HEAVEN by June Lund Shiplett. (131355—$3.50)*
- ☐ SATIN EMBRACES by Julia Grice. (132424—$3.50)
- ☐ THE WILD STORMS OF HEAVEN by June Lund Shiplett. (126440—$3.95)*
- ☐ LADY WILDCAT by June Lund Shiplett. (400267—$3.95)*
- ☐ WILD WINDS CALLING by June Lund Shiplett. (129539—$3.50)

*Prices slightly higher in Canada

Winds
of
Betrayal

by

June Lund Shiplett

A SIGNET BOOK

NEW AMERICAN LIBRARY

NAL BOOKS ARE AVAILABLE AT QUANTITY DISCOUNTS
WHEN USED TO PROMOTE PRODUCTS OR SERVICES.
FOR INFORMATION PLEASE WRITE TO PREMIUM MARKETING DIVISION,
NEW AMERICAN LIBRARY, 1633 BROADWAY,
NEW YORK, NEW YORK 10019.

SIGNET TRADEMARK REG. U.S. PAT. OFF. AND FOREIGN COUNTRIES
REGISTERED TRADEMARK—MARCA REGISTRADA
HECHO EN CHICAGO, U.S.A.

SIGNET, SIGNET CLASSIC, MENTOR, ONYX, PLUME, MERIDIAN
and NAL BOOKS are published by NAL PENGUIN INC.,
1633 Broadway, New York, New York 10019

First Printing, October, 1987

1 2 3 4 5 6 7 8 9

PRINTED IN THE UNITED STATES OF AMERICA

*This book is dedicated to
my wonderful grandchildren, Grant,
Brittany, Braxton, Vincent and little Erica
who always wonder why grandma spends
so much time shut up in her office,
but still seem to understand and
know that I love them all.*

Chapter 1

The Island of Barlovento: June 17, 1821

IT WAS ONE of those lovely nights often seen in the world, with the stars hanging so low in the sky it was as if one could touch them, and the moon so brilliant it seemed more like day, while the gentle breeze rustling the leaves on the trees carried the soft scent of the sea across the island to mingle with the perfume from exotic flowers blowing amid the ruins, and one man stood there alone, his clothes a mixture of military and civilian, staring into the silvery shadows. His dark flashing eyes were searching for something, anything that would tell him it was all a mistake. That he was living through a nightmare instead of reality.

Emilio Sancho de Córdoba, otherwise known as Sancho el Sangriento or Sancho the Bloody to his fellow pirates, stood for a long time on the blackened terrace of what had once been his father's hacienda, anger beginning to replace the pain and sorrow that had first gripped him when he'd waded ashore from the landing boat only moments before. What had once been an island paradise with lovely gardens and a beautiful stucco house had been reduced to a crumbling mass of rubble that would soon be reclaimed by the tropical foliage that grew in abundance on the island that was adjacent to the mangrove swamps at the southwestern tip of the Florida territories. He felt sick inside as well as angry, and the wide scar across his right temple had begun to throb, his fists clenching.

Suddenly he turned at the sound of footsteps behind him. Some of his men were coming up from the beach, with Jigger in the lead. Jigger was a short, stocky man, nothing like his captain. He had a pockmarked face, eyes that were

7

always bloodshot from too much ale, and his speech was rough, uneducated.

"What d'you think happened, Cap'n?" Jigger asked when the men reached him.

Sancho's jaw tightened beneath the heavy black beard that covered his chin, and his handsomely chiseled features were like granite in the moonlight.

"Is it not obvious?" he answered in English. "Somehow Kearney discovered who my father is." He straightened anxiously and looked at the rest of the men. "See what you can find." He pointed toward what remained of the stables, then waved his arm toward the far end of the island, which was some ten miles long and close to four miles wide. "I want the whole place searched, then get back as soon as you can."

The men behind Jigger moved off, melting into the moonlit surroundings, and Sancho once more turned his attention to what was left of the house. He took a deep breath and stepped inside, with Jigger close at his heels. The place was a shambles, the rank smell of charred wood strong in the air. Skeletons of what had once been elaborate furnishings were scattered about, and he bent down, picking up a cracked vase that had once held flowers on a stand in what had been the parlor. Brushing the vase off, he tensed, then looked around more carefully before turning again to Jigger.

"Go see if there are any graves, *amigo*," he ordered curtly. "If my family is dead, someone will pay."

Jigger nodded, and slipped from the room, welcoming the clean fresh air away from the burned-out house. When he returned some ten minutes later, Sancho was no longer inside, but pacing the terrace briskly, one hand resting on the hilt of his sword.

"Well?" he asked.

"There's a place down near the stables. Could be a grave, could be somethin' else. Only if it's a grave, I think you'll find more'n one body in it."

"How long ago, you think?"

Jigger shrugged. "Three, maybe four days. It's hard to say."

"I will kill them. I swear on my sainted mother's grave, and my father's too if he is dead, that I will find the bastards and kill them all."

"And how do you find out for sure if your father's dead?"

"You know the answer to that. When the others get back, they will start digging."

An hour later, Sancho once more stood on the blackened terrace and stared off into the night, watching the moon play on the water where his ship, *La Piranha,* was anchored. The ship looked unreal beneath the star-filled sky, its sails furled, the masts like silvery shrouds. A night like this was the kind to spend somewhere with a woman, not digging up your family's grave. Only it hadn't been his whole family. Only his father was buried there, along with some of the servants. So where were his sister Elena, Tía Isabella, and his young brother Mario? Prisoners?

His eyes hardened. By hell, wherever they were, he'd find them. The island had been searched and there wasn't a sign of them anywhere. That meant there was a good chance they were still alive.

Sancho turned, gazing off toward the stables, where his men were putting the last shovelfuls of dirt back into the grave where his father's body lay. His father had been born Don Luis de Córdoba, youngest son of a Spanish baron, and he'd always said he'd never leave his island. It had been given to him in lieu of money because of favors done for the crown, and now it was his grave. Sancho's eyes narrowed. Damn them all to hell!

"Come, men, we go!" he called hurriedly. "There is nothing more for us here," and he started down the flagstone walk that led to the beach where they'd pulled the longboat ashore; then when he reached it he turned back to get one last glimpse of the island home his father had called Barlovento, or Windward in English. A place where Sancho and his men had found safety so often over the past few years. It wasn't fair. His family didn't deserve this. Someone would pay, and pay dearly—he'd see to that.

The place was full of moonlight, shadows, and memories as he stared at it while his men joined him; then he straightened, filling his lungs with the warm night air, and hoping to clear his nostrils of the stench that had clung to them ever since he'd been inside the burned-out house. What hell had taken place here? One way or the other he vowed to get to the bottom of it, and a grim determination filled him as he turned back to the boat, climbed in behind his men, and they shoved off, moving out across the water toward the ship where the rest of the crew were preparing to weigh anchor.

Once on board, he stood on the deck, his eyes again scanning the horizon toward Barlovento, and his heart was heavy. For a long time he stood there while the ship got under way, continuing to stay at the rail as they sailed along the coast, away from the island, plying the familiar waters of the western coast of Florida like a ghost ship, silvery pale in the moonlight. However, after a while, weary and restless, anger at what he'd found back at Barlovento gnawing at him inside, and sore at heart, yet not wanting his men to see the pain in his eyes and start thinking he was soft, he left the rail and went belowdecks to his cabin, to grieve in private, the way he'd done all his life.

He had wanted to sleep when he reached the cabin, but sleep wouldn't come, so instead he paced the floor for a while, then finally sat at his desk staring at a small enamel portrait of his parents. His mother had been dead for so long it was hard to remember her, and now it'd be the same someday with his father. As the years rolled along, the memories would fade more and more until finally it'd be hard to conjure up his father's face too, just like it was with his mother. Only right now, the memories of his father were still far too strong, and he cursed softly as he thought back to his first sight of what had once been his father's home.

It was well after three in the morning when he finally straightened at the sound of scuffling overhead; then a few minutes later he stood up in response to a knock on the cabin door.

"Come in."

It was Jigger. "We've spotted a fire at the cove, Cap'n," he said hurriedly. "You don't suppose . . . ?"

Sancho stared at Jigger for a brief moment; then his eyes narrowed shrewdly. "Tell the helmsman to take her in," he said thoughtfully. "But tell him to take it slow and easy. I do not wish to be caught in a trap."

Jigger nodded. "Right!" and he left, closing the door behind him.

Only the door didn't stay closed for long as Sancho put away the portrait of his parents, then slipped into the purloined British captain's uniform jacket he always wore, grabbed his broad-brimmed hat, and followed Jigger up on deck, where once more he stood at the rail while the helmsman brought the ship around, turning inland, and headed toward a natural inlet that opened up along the coast.

High on a hill to the left of the entrance to the cove, a fire was burning, and Sancho's eyes found it easily. The flames were low, barely flickering, but it was there like a weary beacon, and Sancho never let it out of his sight as the ship cleared the channel and moved far into the cove where it was sheltered from the gulf by high sandy cliffs.

The moon was lower in the sky now, but still bathing the land in its eerie glow, and as the men began to furl the sails, Sancho leaned farther over the rail, then called for the longboat as he saw a slim figure move out away from a grove of trees at the top of the hill where the fire was and start down its side.

Elena de Córdoba stopped when she reached the foot of the hill; then she moved slowly forward, her eyes on the ship, watching eagerly as the men on board lowered the longboat, the moonlight so bright that she easily recognized them. Thank God her prayers had been answered. Mother of God, how hard she'd prayed. Her bare toes scrunched the sand at her feet, and she sighed watching the longboat draw near; then she moved forward, waiting for her brother, tears glistening in her warm, dark eyes. Elena was just twenty-one, but suddenly felt old as she thought back over the past few days. She rubbed her hands together, feeling the broken blisters on the palms. They'd needed more wood for the fire, and since she was the only one who could handle the ax, it had been up to her. Ah well, her hands would heal.

Biting her lips anxiously, she watched Sancho step from the boat; then she let out a cry and ran toward him, trying not to trip over the skirt of her tattered blue silk dress.

"Sancho! Oh, Sancho!"

The swarthy pirate captain folded her into his arms, letting them tighten around her hard for a brief moment; then he took a deep breath and stepped back, disengaging her arms from around his waist, and he held her so he could look into her face. It was dirty and tear-streaked, a wild, haunted look in her dark eyes that normally shone soft and warm.

"The others?" he asked hesitantly in Spanish.

"Up on the hill by the fire," she answered breathlessly, in the same language, since she spoke very little English. "You were at the house?"

"*Sí*, and I saw father's grave."

"They took some of the servants prisoners, Sancho, but we managed to get away in the swamp."

"We?"

"Tía Isabella and Mario are with me. Paco and Rosa wanted to come too, but the soldiers were too quick and they were cut off between the swamp and the house."

Sancho frowned. "How long have you been here?"

"It seems like forever, but it's been only three days. I've been hoping and praying. That's why I kept the signal fire going. Tía Isabella's sick, we've no food, and Mario was hurt during the shelling. His wound is healing but he can't do much to help."

"Let's go take a look." He put his arm around his sister's shoulder and they started toward the hill where the signal fire was still smoldering; then he turned back to his men and called to them, in English this time. "Come, *amigos,*' I may need help." And he did.

His aunt was worse off than he'd expected. The attack on the island had brought on some sort of seizure and weakness, making her short of breath, and her hands were trembling terribly as she welcomed him, her eyes feverish. Luis de Córdoba's sister, Isabella, was in her late fifties, a bit plump, and she'd never been a strong woman. Elena had managed to get her to the top of the hill that overlooked the cove, though, and into a makeshift hut that had been built there years before, only there was nothing to cover her with. And although the days had been hot, the nights balmy and warm, Isabella had stayed chilly most of the time, so that when Sancho ordered his men to make a stretcher and put blankets over her, she thanked both him and his men with a graciousness she'd never before shown to them.

Isabella had always loved her nephew, but hated the life he led and the part her brother played in it, and whenever the pirate ship came in to replenish supplies and drop off booty, or pick up salvage from ships that had been wrecked on the rocky southern shore of Barlovento, she'd always made certain Sancho knew her feelings in the matter. However, tonight those feelings were quickly forgotten as Jigger tucked the blanket beneath her chin and watched her smile gratefully, the big dimples in her cheeks deepening.

"But you, young man," Sancho said in Spanish again as he stared down at his young brother Mario, while his men started toward the ship with Tía Isabella. "Why the hell didn't you stay out of the way?"

"I thought I could help," Mario answered when he saw the look on his older brother's face. "Besides, it's healing," and he too looked down at his leg that was bandaged with strips of cloth from Elena's petticoat.

"And you could have lost it too, you know." Sancho reached out and Mario took his hand, letting Sancho pull him from the ground, even though he was unable to put much weight on the leg.

Mario was fifteen now, and already threatening to be as tall as his brother, although it would be years before he filled out fully. He was lean and wiry, his dark curly hair and emerging classic features resembling remarkably those of Sancho, making it impossible not to realize they were related.

"You saved nothing from the house?" Sancho asked his sister as all three stepped from the hut, Mario limping badly.

"There wasn't time. We were just finishing dinner when they came, and everything seemed to fall apart all at once." She tossed her head, flinging her long dark hair behind her shoulder and wiping a stray hair from her face. "At first, when the ship anchored, we thought maybe they were just curious, and when the boatload of men rowed ashore, Father was really puzzled, but it didn't take long for us to learn what they really wanted."

Sancho followed her to the fire and they began kicking sand on it to put it out, while Mario watched from the top of the hill.

"They had orders from the ship's captain for Father to surrender himself and everything on the island. It seems that some men reported to the authorities that they'd once been shipwrecked off Barlovento, then turned over to you and sold as slaves in Martinique, and the captain and his men were sent to arrest us."

"They had these men with them?"

"No, not that I know of."

"Then how do you know they really existed? The men who rowed ashore could have been lying."

"How else would they have learned about Barlovento?"

Sancho's eyes darkened, and there was a puzzled look on his face. "But it just doesn't make sense, little sister," he said, frowning. "Even if some of the men we took from the ship-wrecks were to report us to the authorities, they'd have no way of knowing that Barlovento was the island they'd been on. Their ships had always been blown off course and wrecked during storms. There was no way they could pinpoint our particular island."

"Then how did they know?"

He glanced over at her, and his eyes sparked dangerously. The flames in the fire were no longer burning, but the moon was still beaming down just as brightly as it had earlier, and it shone full on her face.

"Domino," he answered softly, but Elena shook her head, her eyes suddenly filling with tears.

"Oh no! He'd never tell. Not Domino."

"It had to be him. Don't you see, Elena, he's the only one who could have." His jaw tightened angrily. "You know damn well what the papers said. Bain Kolter's an American agent. He was purposely sent here to help clean up the gulf and the Caribbean and get rid of the lot of us, so why would he bother to keep a promise to you after he was gone, especially since he lied to you in the first place about what his ship was really doing here in the gulf when it was wrecked?"

"But he had to lie to us, Sancho," she argued. "If he hadn't, you and Father'd have killed him instead of taking him home. But he cared, Sancho. I know he did."

"He was married."

"That didn't mean he didn't care!" Her eyes saddened. "He'd have stayed, but for his wife."

"He told you that?"

"Not in so many words, no, but a woman can tell."

"Even one who's let love blind her?" He searched her face intently. "Elena, he was with Lafitte at Galvez Island and now Lafitte's gone because of Kearney and his warships. Rumor has it that back in January they gave Lafitte sixty days to get out, and he burned the place down when he finally left in March, rather than let the ships blow it to pieces. They were probably the same ships that destroyed Barlovento."

"You don't know that for sure."

"It had to be the *Enterprise*. And where else would Kearney get his information but from Kolter?"

"Not Domino!"

"Yes, Domino!"

"Then why didn't they come here to the cove to waylay you, or take us prisoner? Surely if he'd told them about

Barlovento, he'd have told them about this place too, but they haven't been near here."

"There wasn't any need. Don't you see?" They walked over, joining Mario again. "You think I'm right, don't you, Mario?" he asked.

"What's that?"

"I think all this is Kolter's doing."

Mario's eyes narrowed as he remembered the newspaper Sancho had brought to them a year ago last Christmas. It had been worn, tattered, and written in English, and he and Elena had been thankful they knew just enough English to translate it, for it told all about Señor Bain Kolter, otherwise known to the de Córdoba family as Domino. A man who had told them he was a pirate. A man who'd had amnesia when they'd found him unconscious and half-dead, fastened onto the back of his horse. A man who'd stolen his sister's heart, then, after getting his memory back, had persuaded Elena to talk Sancho into taking him back to his wife and family in South Carolina. Would he have betrayed them? Mario ran the thought over in his mind as he tried to remember the man himself; after all, that had been almost two years ago.

"Well, little brother?" Sancho urged.

"It's possible, naturally. But . . . what do you say?" he asked Elena.

She opened her mouth to answer, but Sancho cut her off. "She's listening to her heart instead of her head, little brother," he said. "So pay no attention to her. It had to be Domino, I just know it, and I warned him that if he ever betrayed any of us in any way whatsoever, I'd hunt him down and he'd pay." He turned to look at his sister again, trying to ignore the misty tears in her eyes that were clearly visible in the moonlight. "Forget him, Elena," he said angrily. "Because when I get through with him, Bain Kolter'll wish he'd never set foot on Barlovento. Now, come on, let's get the two of you aboard so you can get some food in your bellies and decent clothes on, then get out of here before someone does show up." He put an arm around each of them and they started down the hill to where the men had returned in the longboat after taking Tía Isabella out to the ship. Jigger jumped out of the longboat hurriedly and waited for them as Sancho ushered Elena and Mario ahead of him, and within minutes they were on their way out to the pirate ship, the only sound that of the oars rhythmically dipping in and out of the quiet waters of the cove.

Once aboard, before going belowdecks to clean up some and find something more suitable to wear, Elena stood at the rail and watched the sails unfurling in the moonlight, then felt the ship heave beneath her bare feet, and she frowned. She'd forgotten and left her shoes up in the hut after taking them off because they kept filling with sand. Oh well, there was little about her tonight that made her look like a lady anyway, so what difference did it make.

She stared at the cliff as they sailed by, the fire out now, only the moon lighting up the sandy hill, and she remembered another night almost two years ago when she had been sitting in the sand on that very cliff with Domino, keeping the signal fire alight and waiting for her brother's ship. She had offered herself to Domino that night, an offer he'd refused. Not because he didn't want her, because somehow she felt in her heart that he did. But because he already belonged to someone else, and he was not a man to whom betrayal came lightly.

No, it wasn't Domino who had betrayed them, she was sure of it, but there was no way on this earth she was ever going to convince Sancho that she was right, and she glanced over at her brother, who was talking with Mario and one of his men, and for the first time in a long time a strange tingling fear began to grip her. The same fear she knew must have seized others over the years who had come up against such a formidable opponent. For suddenly she realized that regardless of all the love and loyalty her brother felt for his family, Sancho de Córdoba was still a man to be reckoned with, and she began to understand why even Domino had feared him. Sancho was her brother, yes, but he was also capable of killing a man without the slightest remorse, and she knew it. Had always known it, even though she'd tried to pretend over the years that it wasn't true, and now she shivered slightly as the ship's full sail slapped into the wind and *La Piranha* cleared the inlet, heading out to sea.

Miles away, under the same moonlit sky, Bain Kolter, the man Sancho de Córdoba had threatened to roast over a spit the night they parted if he were ever betrayed, stood on the back terrace of the Château, his wife's grandparents' plantation in Port Royal, South Carolina, and stared hard at the woman he loved.

Lizette was standing only a few feet away, her back to him, the brilliant moonlight highlighting her dark hair, and a warm glow spread through Bain as he watched her tilt her head toward the stars and he sighed. He was going to miss her terribly, he knew, and his eyes sifted over the rest of her, loving every soft rounded curve, remembering, as he always did when he knew he was going to have to be without her for a while, how warm and soft she always felt in his arms. Only tonight for some strange reason it seemed harder than usual for him to get up the courage to tell her what he knew he couldn't put off any longer. Maybe it was the dress that matched her emerald-green eyes, making her look so lovely and youthful, reminding him that at twenty-two she was still eight years his junior. Or it could be the way she'd smiled at him when she'd plunged the knife into her birthday cake earlier and made the first cut, letting him know that just for tonight she was going to forget all about her constant obsession over losing weight and was going to enjoy the luscious treat as much as anyone else. Or maybe it was the way her emerald eyes had lit up when he'd winked back at her, letting her know again, as he had so often, that he didn't care if she wasn't thin. Whatever it was, for some strange reason he was having a harder time getting around to it than usual. Maybe it was simply because he knew she always made such a fuss. Ah well, he couldn't put it off any longer.

Straightening hesitantly, he took a deep breath, then stepped up behind her, his arms enfolding her as his head of dark russet hair nestled against hers, his lips close to her ear, his clipped beard and mustache touching it lightly.

"Happy?" he asked.

"Ecstatic," she answered softly, and leaned back against him, her voluptuous body molding to his. "I have everything I've ever wanted. A wonderful husband, two adorable children." She turned in his arms, her eyes resting lovingly on his face, and was just about to say something more, when suddenly she caught the look in his eyes. A look she knew only too well. "Oh no. Not again," she exclaimed unhappily.

He frowned, bewildered. "How do you always know?"

She shrugged. "Because I love you so much, I guess." Her

jaw clenched irritably. "Where to this time, and for how long?"

"It isn't as bad as it sounds." He reached up, brushing a stray hair back so it could be with the rest of the dark curls on her head, then let his fingers caress her shoulder just above the lace ruffles that adorned her dress. "It'll only be for a few days." He was hoping to reassure her. "My books don't tally with the figures Anson's been sending me from Pittsburgh the past few months, and if I don't find out now just what's going on up there, we could be in real trouble."

"I wish you could sell the place."

"I don't dare. Not if we intend to stay out of debt. I'm not a farmer, like your father, Liz, and I'd never do any good at law like the rest of my family, you know that. I like to run things, build them up, see them grow from an idea to a reality. But I need something solid to depend on when the going gets rough, and the ironworks is the only really solid thing we've got left now that I've sold the freight line in St. Louis and all my other investments that aren't right here near home. That and the two ships. Don't you see, I have to investigate it."

"You could send someone else first."

"I did. And he sent back word that I'd better get up there myself and take a look because it was more than he could handle."

"You said a few days?"

"The *Raven*'s in port so I'll sail up the coast and it won't take as long."

"Why is it that whenever you have to go to Pittsburgh I always get such a strange scared feeling? It never happens when you go to Charleston."

"Because Charleston doesn't hold any bad memories, I suppose." He pulled her close, his gray eyes searching her face. "I didn't want to lie to you back then, Liz," he went on softly. "You know that. But I had no choice. If Lafitte or his brother, or anyone else for that matter, had run into you during those months I was away when everyone thought I'd turned pirate, your life would've been in danger too if you'd known the truth. And making up the story about one of the forges exploding was the only way I could think of to get away at the time. I'm only sorry the whole damn escapade turned out to be for nothing."

"Nothing? Lafitte's gone, isn't he?"

"But we could have run him out sooner if things had been different."

Lizette ran her hand along the lapel of his dark brown frock coat, then straightened his creamy silk cravat. "Well, just make sure you don't fabricate any more stories about exploding forges that haven't really exploded, understand?"

"Liz, there really is trouble in Pittsburgh."

"There'd better be."

"Won't you ever trust me again?"

"I trust you."

"If you trusted me you wouldn't get so upset every time I leave."

"You think it's because I don't trust you?"

"I think you're afraid maybe the same thing'll happen again, but I've told you over and over that it won't. I'm through working for the government. Never again, I promise."

"Then I guess I'll have to believe you."

"I'm glad." Bain's eyes darkened passionately. "I love you, Liz," he said, the timbre in his voice deepening. "I only wish you really understood how much."

"I think I do." Her eyes filled with warmth. "We've been through too much together, Bain, for me not to know. It's just that I miss you so when you're gone." She sighed. "When do you have to leave?"

"I should've left yesterday, only I wasn't about to spoil your birthday. But I'll have to go tomorrow. It'd be foolish to put it off any longer."

"Then I'll just stay here at the Château. We'll spend the night like we planned, and when you go get your clothes in the morning, you can have Pretty come out with the children and have her bring my things with her. She'll know what I need."

"Have it all thought out, haven't you?" He smiled. "Just make sure you behave yourself while I'm gone, understand?"

She smiled back at him. "Are you telling me what to do, Mr. Kolter?"

"Shut up and kiss me, Mrs. Kolter," and as Bain's mouth covered hers, Lizette fought valiantly to squelch the gnawing apprehension that always began to fill her when she knew he'd be going away.

Her one consolation, however, was that Grandma Dicia and Grandpa Roth always let her stay at the Château whenever Bain was gone, and she loved it here. And that's right where she found herself almost two weeks later, still waiting impatiently for Bain's return.

Sancho de Córdoba, using every deception he could think of so he wouldn't be caught, since the Florida territories now belonged to the United States instead of Spain, had managed to sneak his aunt, sister, and young brother ashore not far from the city of St. Augustine, and there they were taken into the home of an old friend of their father's, where he hoped they could stay for a while and blend into the life of the village without too many questions being asked until he came back for them. After being satisfied that they'd be all right, he'd quickly returned to his ship and continued sailing north again, pondering all the way just how he was going to go about getting even with Bain Kolter, since he knew so little about the northern coasts of the United States. He'd always avoided them as much as possible over the years, keeping his activities mostly in the gulf and the Caribbean, usually preferring to attack ships far out to sea. The problem was a new one for him, and one that was going to take a great deal of thought.

He sat in his cabin now on board ship as the month of July neared, feeling the steady roll from the waves and listening to the creaking timbers. The wind had been strong all day and he was pleased. Inhaling sharply, he reached out, opened the desk drawer in front of him, and took out the worn, yellowed newspaper he'd been keeping for so long. After spreading it out on the desk before him, he leaned forward and once more read about the exoneration of Bain Hadley Kolter, former pirate, exposed now to the world as an agent of the United States government. For almost two years he'd read the newspaper over and over again until he knew the story almost by heart, and every time he'd read it he'd hoped and prayed that his sister was right, and the man they'd known as Domino wouldn't betray them. Only now, after what had happened at Barlovento, he knew she hadn't been, and he cursed angrily to himself for letting her talk him into making such a blunder by taking him home. But he wasn't going to let her talk him out of this. In spite of her pleading, he was going to carry out his vendetta. The only question was, how?

His eyes scanned the paper again, carefully. Although he'd never been a master at reading the English language,

his travels had broadened what he'd learned from his tutors
as a boy, and he could read it well enough to know that
Kolter's home was in the city of Beaufort on Port Royal
Sound along the coast of South Carolina. A city his pirate
ship could never think of approaching without someone rec-
ognizing her for what she was. Not even at night.

Then he remembered the night he'd taken Bain home to
his family. It had been a rainy night, and they'd gone in after
dark. Kolter'd had him sail the ship up the Broad River
instead of going into the harbor at Beaufort; then he'd asked
to be put overboard near what he said was his wife's grandparents' home.

"Hmm," Sancho thought aloud, then looked up in response to a knock on the cabin door. "Jigger?"

The door opened. "Right here, Cap'n."

"Sit down, *mi amigo*," Sancho said quickly, and pointed
toward the chair at the other side of his desk. "You remember when we took Señor Kolter home?" he asked thoughtfully.

Jigger smiled. "Ain't many places I ever forget."

"*Bueno*." Sancho straightened. "Think you could help
Drego find his way in there again without me around?"

"Whatcha got in mind?"

"A way to reach Kolter and get out without being hanged."

"Sounds interesting."

"*Sí*, it is. Look." He reached over and pulled a map off
the other end of the desk, unrolling it, then spread it over
the newspaper. "Here," he said, shoving his finger at a spot
along the South Carolina coast. "See this city? This is where
Señor Kolter lives. His wife's grandparents here," and he
moved his finger across the map to a spot along the Broad
River. "How many miles between, do you think?" he asked,
frowning.

Jigger squinted. The light wasn't any too good in the
cabin, even though the sun was up and the day clear. He
leaned closer.

"Fifteen, twenty, maybe more. All depends on whether
you keep to the roads or go as the crow flies. Why?"

"Because we will do this, *amigo*." He pointed to the
southern tip of Port Royal Island. "We will sail into the
sound here, as close to this point as we can, then put a
longboat over the side and I will have some of the men row
me ashore. Then after the longboat is back on board *La
Piranha*, you will have Drego take her out again and lose

yourselves somewhere along the coast for the next two days, while I make my way to this city of Beaufort, find out where Señor Kolter lives, do what I have to do, then meet you at midnight the end of the second day near the same spot upriver where we dropped him off two years ago. It will be simple, *sí?*"

"Why don't we just pick you up where we put you off?"

"No. It is no good. Too much in the open, and with Señor Kolter dead the authorities will be all over the place. But if you sail upriver the ship will be close enough to the land for me to swim out, and once I'm aboard, we can make a run for the open sea."

"What if someone recognizes you before you get out of Beaufort?"

Sancho's eyes hardened. "Don't worry, they won't." He snatched the map off the desk and rolled it up, his jaw tightening stubbornly. "Except for the man I'm after, no one else in Beaufort will even know Sancho de Córdoba was near the place. Remember that ship we took a while back when you thought I was crazy making those priests change clothes before turning them over to the slave block?"

"You gonna dress like a priest?"

"*Sí.* Why not? With the Florida territories part of the United States now, no one will pay any attention to the fact that I don't speak English very well." He rubbed his chin thoughtfully. "I suppose I will have to clip my beard a bit shorter." His hand moved to his head. "And it won't hurt to have my hair trimmed either." He set the map aside and glanced down again at the newspaper. "Do not worry, *amigo,* I too can play at Señor Kolter's game of masquerade."

Jigger studied the gleam in his captain's dark eyes. "You sure you don't want me along?" he asked.

"Positive." Sancho reached down and picked up the newspaper, then folded it and put it back in the desk drawer, his eyes hesitating momentarily as they fell on the enamel portrait of his parents beside it. "This I have to do myself, Jigger," he said slowly, then quickly closed the drawer. "I swore I would make him pay, and I will. This is my vendetta, *amigo.* Mine alone." He clenched his fists, then turned, walking over to the cabin window, where he stood staring out, his eyes on the distant horizon.

A few days later, on the second of July, shortly before the hour of midnight, an unidentifiable ship, using as few sails as possible and flying no flag, sailed quietly into the waters of Port Royal Sound, lowered one of its longboats over the side, waited for its return, then after taking it back on board, slipped out again through the inland harbor without anyone having known it had been there except the one man it had left behind, who stood now on the narrow beach, a lone figure dressed in the black garb of a priest, the white collar about his neck threatening to rub it raw.

Sancho reached up and loosened the collar, then sighed. He'd warned Jigger not to pull it so tight. The stupid idiot. Pleased now that it was no longer twisting against his skin, Sancho checked to make sure he hadn't left anything behind. Let's see. His pistol and cutlass were hidden inside the bedroll he was carrying, along with his regular clothes, and a purse with some money in it hung around his neck from a silver chain that was hidden beneath his priest's robe, only the long chain with the crucifix on it visible on the outside. He hadn't forgotten a thing except perhaps some food. After all, he had no idea how long it'd be before he could get hold of any. But then, what he did find should be far better than anything he could have brought from the ship. He'd get along.

He slung the bedroll over his shoulder, resting it comfortably on his back with the straps beneath his arms, then set the priest's broad-brimmed black hat on top of his newly trimmed mass of dark curly hair. If only Tía Isabella could see him now, he thought. The silly woman had always wanted him to be a priest. So had his mother. He took a deep breath, squinting, gazing off into the night, and watched the vague outline of *La Piranha*'s sails as she melted into the darkness; then he turned toward the woods, where he remembered that Bain Kolter told him there was an old stone building. Rumor said it had once been used by Captain Teach and his men, according to Kolter.

"And somewhere along here," Sancho whispered softly to himself as he walked along cautiously, "Señor Kolter also said there was a small stream that led straight to a bridge and a road that traversed the island north to south," and within ten minutes of searching, he was on his way, following the stream Bain had told him about two years before, his broad shoulders and muscular body beneath the priest's robes easily traversing the uneven ground even in the darkness, as if he had the eyes of a cat.

It was late the next afternoon when he finally arrived at Beaufort, nodding congenially to people he passed, and smiling, pretending he belonged. Earlier, during the night, when he'd reached the road Bain told him about, he'd caught a quick nap in a place where he wouldn't be spotted, then moved on again just before daybreak, knowing that to go without sleep would have been foolish. To be at full strength, a man had to have a clear head with his body alert, and as he strolled down the street now, he was glad he'd rested, because the walk to Beaufort had been a long one and unfortunately no one in any of the carriages that passed him had offered him a ride. In a way he thought it rather strange, since he was posing as a priest and people were usually a little kinder to a man of the cloth than they were an ordinary traveler. Ah well, *americanos* were a weird lot.

He straightened, hefting the bedroll into a better position where it didn't hit his shoulder blade, then stepped up next to a bakery and stopped, gazing about. Beaufort was an old city, and a busy one. The bakery he was standing in front of was only a few blocks from the harbor and he could see the masts from at least three ships above the rooftops. Hmmm, maybe he'd better go take a look. He'd been hoping there would be only one or two in port. Casually, without bringing attention to himself, he sauntered from in front of the building and moved down the street until he was close enough to the waterfront so he could see them. There were three ships, all right. One French frigate, and what looked like two private merchantmen. Good, they shouldn't give *La Piranha* any trouble. Her guns could blow the whole lot of them out of the water.

Satisfied, he retraced his steps, this time entering the bakery, where he bought a large hard roll that he began to munch as soon as he was back on the street. Surprising how hunger seemed to disappear when a man's mind was absorbed in other things, he thought as he swallowed the dry roll, wishing he had something to wash it down with. He didn't even want the roll, really, but knew it wouldn't be good to go too long without something. Not if he wanted to get done what he had to do.

He began to move slowly along the street, studying the buildings, trying to decide which one would be the most logical one where he could inquire about the Kolters. The banker would probably know, but bankers were ordinarily suspicious and he didn't want to have to try to avoid answering uncomfortable questions. No, not the banker.

There was a tavern a few doors down, but dressed as he was, the patrons might think it strange if he went inside. He straightened, a sly smile tilting the corner of his mouth. Funny, he'd never thought about it before, but how the devil did a priest ever have any fun without being found out? It would be hell having everyone think you were a saint just because you wore your collar backward and dressed in stupid black robes. And God help him, he knew they weren't saints. Ah well, he'd think of something, and he felt an exhilaration surge through him at the thought of being so close to his quarry.

By the time he'd swallowed the last of the roll, he'd made up his mind not to ask any of the merchants. Instead, he was going to stop the very next person who passed. That is, if he or she looked at all likely to know. He glanced down the street. Aha! He was in luck, and he brushed the crumbs from his hands, smoothing his neatly clipped beard, the thick scar at his temple pulsating while he watched a young woman approach.

"*Señorita, por favor,* please," he asked, confronting her hesitantly, yet trying to be charming, something new to him. "If I might have *un momento?*"

The young woman, who was probably in her early twenties, was hesitant at first, but when Sancho smiled, pretending a humility new to him, she smiled back, shyly losing her reluctance at being accosted by a stranger.

"Is something the matter, Father?" she asked, frowning.

Sancho cleared his throat, trying to remember how a priest would act. It had been so long since he'd had any close contact with any that weren't either dead or in chains.

"No, child, nothing's wrong," he answered quickly, his heavy accent making her listen more carefully. "But I was wondering if maybe you could tell me where I might find an old friend of mine named Kolter. Señor Bain Kolter. I was told he made his home here in Beaufort."

He saw recognition light her eyes. "The Kolters? You're in luck, Father. His sister Felicia Benedict's a close friend of mine," and she not only told him exactly where the Kolters lived, but offered to show him. An offer he quickly declined.

So it was that, half an hour later, he stood contemplating a lovely stone house near the edge of town, trying to decide

whether to wait until after dark or perhaps knock on the
door now. After all, he had no idea whether Kolter was
home during the day or maybe working in some sort of
shop. The place did look rather quiet.

Suddenly he tensed at a movement near the side of the
house close to what looked like a carriage house and stables,
and he watched furtively, trying to keep some bushes between himself and the house as a young black woman stepped
into the open. She was carrying a washbasket from the
backyard and he watched her disappear inside, then made
his decision. You didn't sneak up on a man when he could
see you coming. He'd come back after dark, and with revenge so close at hand now, he decided that it wouldn't hurt
in the least if the newly anointed Father de Córdoba enjoyed
a nice hearty meal with one glass of good red wine, and he
left his hiding place, heading back toward a small inn he'd
passed earlier, where he'd be able to eat and get a room so
he could rest some before facing the man he'd come to kill.

Chapter 2

IT HAD BEEN dark for well over an hour when Sancho finally came down from his room at the inn, deciding that it was time he got on with his plans. They were simple, really. Señor Kolter was going to die slowly and that meant he had to get the man away from his family. Of course, he could just kill the whole lot of them, but something like that would be foolish for him to even attempt alone, especially since the house where Kolter lived was so big and probably had a number of servants as well as his wife and *niños*. No. It'd be too risky. But he'd make sure Kolter was alone first. So before leaving the inn, he walked over and made a quick bargain with the innkeeper's son, a pudgy lad not quite full grown. He had to tell the young man he was playing a joke on a friend, and a few minutes later the duo left, heading back toward the stone house at the edge of town.

Sancho was edgy, yet anxious as they approached the place, but it was so hard to see in the dark, and at first he thought maybe they had the wrong house, since there was only a dim light on in one of the downstairs rooms. However, the innkeeper's son assured him that he knew Mr. Kolter and that this was the right place, so after giving him a folded message he'd written earlier in his room at the inn, Sancho once more stepped close to the bushes, into the shadows, and watched as the lad went to the door.

The minutes seemed to drag by, and Sancho took a deep breath, wishing he could hear what was being said as he watched the young man talking to someone at the door, but it was useless, he was too far away. Then suddenly he saw the lad turn and start back, without Bain Kolter, and still carrying the message.

A scowl narrowed Sancho's eyes. "*Madre de Dios!*" he

growled when the lad reached him, forgetting momentarily that he was supposed to be a priest. "What the devil are you doing? Why didn't you at least leave the message?"

The young man winced as he handed the note back to the man he thought was a priest. "He weren't there, Father," he answered hesitantly. "The black girl at the house said as how Mr. Kolter's up north somewheres on business and won't be back until after the Fourth of July sometime, and Mrs. Kolter and the children's stayin' out at the Château."

"The Château? Her grandparents' place?"

"You know where it is?" the kid asked.

Sancho's jaw tightened. "*Sí,* I know where it is." He'd passed the Château on his walk to Beaufort earlier today, but the knowledge wasn't much help. Not now. He couldn't kill a man who wasn't here.

"You need me anymore, Father?" the kid asked nervously. "I promised Pa I wouldn't be gone too long."

Sancho shook his head. "Not tonight, *muchacho. Gracias.*" He'd taken a coin from his purse while he'd been waiting, and handed it to the lad. "Here, for your trouble."

"Thanks, Father, and if you need anything else, just stop by the inn."

Sancho assured him he would if he found it necessary, and the lad took off at a run, passing the other houses along the way, until he quickly vanished into the shadows and was lost from sight. Sancho's eyes mirrored his disappointment, hardening his features, and his fists clenched. What now? He'd told Jigger to bring the ship in to pick him up on the day of the *americanos'* Fourth of July, shortly before midnight. That meant he had all day tomorrow. But for what? He had planned to lure Kolter away from his house on the pretense that Elena was here, in the remains of that old building Kolter had told him about, the one he'd found just before he'd reached the road last night shortly after being set ashore. Once there, he'd planned to call him out, then run him through, making sure the bastard suffered with every thrust of his cutlass, suffering just the way his father must have suffered before dying. Now all that was gone.

He gazed off toward the stone house, staring at the faint light in the downstairs window, and suddenly an idea began to work its way into his thoughts. There was more than one way to make a man suffer. In fact, sometimes death was the easy way. He tossed the thought back and forth in his mind. It could work if he managed it right.

Let's see, today was the third and he had all day tomorrow to do what he had to do, and he began to walk back toward the inn, making new plans, and hoping nothing would spoil them this time.

It seemed like the sun was always hotter than usual on the Fourth of July, and today was no exception as Lizette slowly stirred in the big bed where she and Bain always slept when they stayed over. Only Bain still wasn't home. She'd gotten a letter from him the end of the first week he'd been gone. It had been posted the day after he arrived in Pittsburgh, and in it he had told her that he'd found a much worse mess than he'd dreamed it'd be. Anson Harwell, who was supposed to be in charge, had not only been embezzling money from them, but had bought inferior machinery when he'd had to replace anything. The whole place had to be gone over very carefully and checked out against the invoices, and Harwell had to be brought to trial. It was a matter Bain hated, but one that had to be done if they were to have any hopes of recovering any of the stolen funds. So there was nothing she could do now except wait, and the letter she'd gotten from him the day before yesterday had said he'd definitely make it by the end of this week.

She stretched, then tucked the pillow under her head again, hoping to catch a few more winks of sleep before the twins came in as they did every morning. Her eyes had barely shut, however, when she heard the door click, followed by a giggle.

"All right, come ahead," she said cheerfully, and rolled over onto her back. When she opened her eyes, the first thing she saw were two beautiful faces wreathed in smiles as they hurried to the bed, slipping in with her, one on each side to rest with their heads on her arms. She hugged them close, still marveling at how she could have two such adorable children who were so unlike either her or Bain.

Braxton and Blythe were almost three and a half years old already and they talked incessantly. Both had pale blond hair like Lizette's mother, Rebel, perhaps a shade lighter even, especially after being in the sun, and their sparkling eyes were a beautiful shade of gray, like their father's, Blythe's already fringed with the longest lashes Lizette had ever seen. The two of them smiled up at her, dimples denting both their cheeks. They were so alike.

"Is Daddy really coming home soon?" Blythe asked as she stared at her mother, and Liz sighed.

"That's what he said, only not today."

"But we can still go to the cela . . . cela . . ." Braxton began, having a time with the word, and Lizette finished for him.

"Yes, we can go to the Fourth of July celebration anyway," she said. "Now, give me a kiss, then scoot and go downstairs and tell Mattie I'm coming down, and I'll see you at the breakfast table."

They hugged and kissed her, and she watched them leave; then as soon as they were gone, she started to get up when a frown suddenly creased her forehead and she ended up sitting on the edge of the bed instead. Not again, she thought, and could feel the churning beginning to start in the pit of her stomach and quickly gulped back. My God, she was dizzy, and her insides felt horrid. She had to be pregnant. She couldn't see how it could be anything else. And it had gotten much worse since Bain left. She sat on the bed for a few minutes, holding her head down as low as she could between her legs, hoping it'd help the nausea go away.

Wait until Bain found out, she thought. He was going to be ecstatic. And she wasn't going to let anyone else know, either. Not until she could tell him first. Not even Grandma Dicia. After a few minutes she lifted her head and took a deep breath, wondering about how far along she was. Her menses had been due even before Bain left, and had never shown up, now this. It was the fourth time in the past week. Well, it was a long way off yet, and she'd have to try not to get too excited and give it away before he came home. Reaching over, she took a sip from the glass beside her bed. The water helped her dry mouth, but it was warm and tasted terrible, upsetting her stomach again, so she sat for a few minutes longer, then with her head finally clear again, the nausea began to subside a little, and she took a deep breath.

Ah well, she thought as she stood up, reached for her red silk wrapper, and slipped it on over her nightdress, I might as well get used to it, and she headed for the door to go downstairs to join the twins, but ran into Grandma Dicia out in the hallway and smiled as she realized her grandmother was dressed already in a purple silk that matched her violet eyes and brought out the few dark highlights left in her silvery hair.

"Don't tell me the twins woke you up too," Lizette said, joining her at the head of the stairs.

Loedicia Chapman smiled back at her granddaughter. "Nonsense," she answered. "Your grandfather woke me. I've never known him to sleep in on the Fourth of July yet. He's downstairs already, pestering Mattie."

"That figures."

They started down the stairs and Loedicia, much shorter than Lizette, glanced over at her granddaughter. Liz had been looking a bit peaked lately and Loedicia didn't like it. She'd be glad when Bain was home again.

"You didn't say, is Bain going to have the *Raven* dock at the Château's landing when he gets back, or just tie up at the pier in Beaufort?" she asked.

"Neither," Lizette answered. "He took Amigo with him. The *Raven*'s going on to Europe and he's riding down, so it'd be silly for him to go to our place first."

"Well, I certainly hope for your sake that he won't have to leave again for a while, Liz." Loedicia's eyes were full of concern. "He's been gone so much the past few years." She saw Lizette frown. "Oh, I know, he's been straightening out his business affairs. It's just that I know how much you miss him."

"Don't worry, Grandma, when he gets back this time the farthest he'll have to go for a while is Charleston, and I intend to go with him."

Loedicia winked as they reached the bottom of the stairs. "Good," she said firmly, and they headed for the dining room, where Lizette's grandfather was helping the twins decide what they'd have for breakfast, while Mattie, the black cook who'd been at the Château for years, shook her head, reminding him how much he was spoiling them.

Roth only laughed, his deep voice echoing through the place. He was a tall, distinguished man with pure white hair, dark eyes, and an engaging smile that had set hearts aflutter when he was younger, as well as being an asset when he had been a congressman. Even now he was never completely out of politics, keeping up on all the issues, and often active as adviser to some of the younger men in office.

He glanced over as Lizette and Loedicia came in.

"Did you see the sky this morning, Dicia?" he asked his wife.

She eyed him skeptically and headed for her chair. "Yes, but I'm not going to pay any attention to it." She ruffled the top of Braxton's head. "Besides," she said, "the children don't care if it rains or not, do you?"

But Lizette cared. "Oh no!" she sighed as she sat down next to Blythe. "It can't rain today. They might cancel the picnic."

"No, they can't, Mama, please!" Blythe cried anxiously. "I wanna go! I wanna go!"

"Hush!" Lizette quieted her, then glanced at her grandfather. "Did you have to, Grandpa?" she said, looking disgusted. "Now they're going to cry all morning unless I can promise them it won't rain."

"And if you do, you'll be lying to them, Liz," he said. "But don't worry. I doubt it'll rain till late afternoon or evening, and by that time we'll have had the best of the day."

She sighed. "I certainly hope so. That's all they've been talking about all week, and, oh yes, there's something else. It also seems that somebody—and I have my suspicions as to who it was—told them there's supposed to be a traveling troupe of tumblers at the picnic this year."

Roth's dark eyes twinkled. "I wonder who could have said that?"

"Yes, I wonder," Loedicia piped in, her eyes on her husband. "And I wonder how he knew."

"The priest from St. Helena's in Beaufort," Roth answered. "The children and I ran into him in Port Royal last week when they went with me to post some letters, and he said some of the politicians are really trying to outdo each other this year. Besides the traveling tumblers, he said they're bringing a troupe of actors down from Charleston to a marionette show. I'm glad it's not an election year. I can just about imagine what they'd end up doing just to get attention and a vote."

Loedicia smiled, pleased. "Well now, I think it's delightful. But why didn't you tell us sooner?"

"They made me promise." He winked at his great-grandchildren. "Said it'd be our secret. Now, I couldn't betray a trust like that, could I?"

Lizette and Loedicia both looked at the children, who were beaming at their great-grandfather. No, one didn't break a trust like that, they both thought, then suddenly Lizette glanced toward the doorway, where her Uncle Heath had just entered, escorting Aunt Darcy.

Heath Chapman was a younger replica of Roth, although his dark curly hair, just starting to frost at the temples, and the closely clipped beard and mustache he wore, as well as the small gold earring in his right ear, left over from his years as a privateer, made him appear far more rugged and aloof than his father. But he shared the same fascinating smile as he greeted everyone warmly. As he pulled his wife's chair out for her, his gaze fell on the back of her head, and he marveled as he always did at the sight of her gorgeous red hair, the color a dramatic contrast to her pale green eyes, and he wished their daughter, Heather, had eyes like Darcy's instead of the violet ones she'd inherited from his mother. Thinking of his daughter suddenly made him feel strange. She was grown up, married, and he was a grandfather already, and he frowned as he sat down beside Darcy.

"What did the letter you got yesterday from Cole and Heather say, Uncle Heath?" Lizette asked when they were both settled at the table. "I didn't have a chance to ask you last night before you and Aunt Darcy went out."

He shook his head. "Only that they're still camped just north of what your brother says is the Red River. It seems the Mexican government's really determined to keep Americans out."

"But they're searching for their son," Loedicia protested. "They don't plan to settle there."

Heath looked dismayed. "According to Cole, whenever they find an American where he doesn't belong, they arrest him first, then ask questions later, whenever they happen to get around to it, and he says he's not going to take a chance on rotting in a jail in Santa Fe."

"Santa Fe?" Lizette asked. "Is that in Mexico?"

"It's in the northern Texas territories, about three or four hundred miles from where they are now, according to Cole's letter. So far, though, through the Comanche friends he has, he's managed to trace Case to a war party that was heading for the plains area of Texas, just south of a river called the Colorado. His Comanche friends have promised to take him into Mexican territory with them, only Cole's been reluctant to leave Heather and the others behind. He said in the letter that he'll probably have to make a decision one way or the other before long, though."

Lizette couldn't help feeling sorry for her brother because she knew how she'd feel if one of the twins was ever taken from her, and while Mattie and the kitchen help brought the food in so they could start eating, she hoped and prayed things would work out for him and Heather.

"Has Cole ever mentioned a man named Austin?" Roth asked his son a few minutes later, when the servants were gone and they'd all started eating.

Heath nodded. "He wrote about him in this last letter."

Loedicia looked at Roth in surprise. "Who's Austin?" she asked.

"Bain was telling me about him before he left," Roth answered. "Word's gotten around that he's getting about three or four hundred settlers together and has permission from the Mexican government to settle them in the Texas territories. Bain got wind of it when he was out in St. Louis selling that freight company of his. I guess this man Austin is originally from there and Bain knows him."

"Why, that'd be ideal," Loedicia said, her eyes brightening. "Cole and Heather could settle in Texas and keep on searching while they tried to build a home to bring him back to."

Heath straightened, hating to dash water on their new spark of hope. "It sounds well and good, I know," he said unhappily. "And I thought the same thing myself when I first heard Bain talking about it, but unfortunately, from what Cole's found out, in order to go with Austin, they'd have to turn Catholic and give up their American citizenship, and he says he won't do either. His friend Eli talked to Austin the end of January when he was in Missouri, after they'd heard what he was planning, and there'll be no exceptions."

Roth sighed. "Well, it was a thought."

"And a good one." Heath studied his father's face. "I only wish there was some way I could help."

Roth glanced at his daughter-in-law and saw the movement of her eyes as her jaw tensed.

"You don't really want to go out there, Heath," he said, hoping to dampen any spark of wanderlust that may have been ignited by Cole's predicament. "Cole should be able to handle it himself. After all, he's part Indian, and looks more Indian than his father. He can ride into Texas with his Comanche friends and the Mexicans won't even suspect he's a white man."

"And I could ride into Texas and pass for a Mexican too. After all, I speak Spanish fluently, and I've done it before."

"That was years ago, Heath," Roth countered. "Besides, you wouldn't have any Mexican papers. There'd be too much risk."

"Your father's right, Heath," Darcy finally added, joining the conversation as if it were a continuation of one she and her husband were having earlier. "It'd be ridiculous for you to even attempt something so foolhardy."

"But Case is our grandson."

"And I'm sure Cole knows what he's doing. After all, he is Beau's son. He has a great deal of his father in him. Besides, he's young and resourceful."

Heath frowned. "I'm not that old."

"Well, I'd like you to grow a little older. If you went chasing out there, who knows if you'd even make it back."

"She's right, Heath," Loedicia said, hoping to divert a major crisis. "Let Cole be the man his father brought him up to be. Don't worry, he'll find his son and he'll take good care of Heather, and the new baby too. It seems strange, you know, to think that the new little one they have is over two already and none of us have even seen her."

Darcy silently thanked her mother-in-law with her eyes. "Cole wrote that she's walking and talking now. Not as well as the twins, naturally," and she glanced at Braxton and Blythe. "Teffin was just two last December, but he said she's even learning to ride a horse already."

Loedicia sighed and looked over at her husband. "We're getting old, Roth," she said. "Four great-grandchildren already."

"Nonsense," he said, smiling as his eyes caught hers. "We'll never be old. A little worn around the edges maybe, but never old, huh, kids?" he asked, turning his attention to the twins, and Loedicia smiled, suddenly letting the years slip away, and she did feel young again. But then, Roth always made her feel young.

Cole's search for his son was soon tucked away to be talked about later as the subject once more centered on the Fourth of July doings held every year in a huge parklike picnic grove along the sound between the cities of Beaufort and Port Royal. A special day that had started out years before as a political rally and picnic, but had now grown into a full-fledged celebration with dancing and fireworks.

It was well past two in the afternoon and they had all been at the picnic for hours already. Lizette, dressed in an afternoon dress of pale lavender with a small flowered straw hat perched atop her high-piled curls, stood by herself near the steps to the platform where the speeches had been made earlier and watched her grandfather, Braxton holding his right hand and Blythe his left, as he headed toward the huge tent where the marionette show was set up. The children had already seen it once, but they had begged him to take them again, and as usual, he couldn't say no. It hadn't rained as yet, and she was grateful, although the sky had become overcast earlier, and dark clouds were still rumbling off in the distance. After gazing up at the sky once more, hoping the rain would keep holding off, she had just decided that she'd watch the show again too, when she was interrupted by Bain's sister, and whirled around, surprised to see her.

"Felicia!"

The two of them hugged affectionately, then stood back looking at each other. They'd been close friends for years, but the last Lizette had heard from Felicia she'd been in Columbia visiting her other brother Stuart, who was a senator. Lizette studied Felicia carefully. She had put on a little weight, the dark blue dress she was wearing tight at the seams, and for some reason her amber eyes didn't have quite the luster everyone was used to seeing in them. But her toffee-colored hair was neatly coiffed and she was smiling widely, although the color of her dress did make her look a little pale.

"Are you all right, Felicia?" Lizette asked instinctively.

Felicia's smile softened. "Does it show that much?"

"What?"

"We're going to have a baby, Liz," she blurted happily.

"You are?" Lizette was ecstatic. It had been two years last May since Felicia's marriage to Alex Benedict, and Lizette knew she'd almost given up hope of ever having a child. "That's wonderful," she said. "When?"

"Near Christmas, as far as we can calculate."

"Alex is pleased?"

"He couldn't be happier."

Lizette hugged Bain's sister again, then frowned momentarily before releasing her, wishing she could tell Felicia about her own pregnancy, but remembering that she wasn't planning to let anyone know until after she'd first told Bain.

"I didn't know you'd come back from Columbia," Lizette said as their embrace ended and they started heading for the shade of an old oak tree near the edge of the crowd.

"We got back on Sunday, but I've been too tired to do any visiting. I did see Angie, though. She stopped by the house late yesterday afternoon."

"How is she?"

"As well as can be expected, I guess. She still doesn't like living with her in-laws." Felicia frowned. "She did have one bit of news that was strange, though."

"What was that?"

"It was about you and Bain."

"Oh?" Lizette's attention, which had been wandering through the crowd watching for the different people she knew, suddenly focused full on her sister-in-law. "What about us?"

"Well." Felicia watched Lizette closely. "It seems she was stopped while walking in town yesterday afternoon by a priest who asked if she knew where the two of you lived. No, rather where Bain lived," she corrected herself.

"A priest? From St. Helena's?"

St. Helena's was the oldest church in Beaufort, with lovely gardens that often attracted visitors.

"No." Felicia frowned. "That's the strange part about it. She said he was foreign and had a heavy Spanish accent. At least Angie thought he sounded Spanish."

"That is strange." Lizette pondered thoughtfully. "Did she tell him where we lived?"

"She even offered to show him, but he said there wasn't any need, that he'd find the place himself. When I told her neither of you were at the house right now, she was surprised. I guess not too many people know Bain went to Pittsburgh."

"It's none of their business, really," Lizette replied, then shifted the conversation back to the priest. "I wonder what the priest looked like."

"She said he looked rather rough and unpleasant, although he wasn't really bad-looking. But he had a big scar near his right temple, and I remember she remarked on how intense his eyes were. Almost frightening. Yet she said he seemed pleasant enough."

Lizette drew her eyes from Felicia and looked out over the crowd again; then suddenly a shiver went through her as she spotted a man in black standing a short distance away, trying to look like part of the crowd, only his dark clothes among all the women's pastel dresses and men's colorful frock coats was too much of a contrast.

Earlier when she'd caught glimpses of the man out of the corner of her eyes she'd thought it was the priest from St. Helena's, then realized he was too tall, his stature too muscular and broad beneath the cassock; however, the broad-brimmed hat he was wearing shaded his face and she couldn't see if he had a scar.

"I wonder what he wants?" she mused, and Felicia, who'd followed her gaze, stiffened.

"That's him, isn't it? It has to be, Liz." She touched her sister-in-law's arm. "What are you going to do?"

Lizette stood her ground, staring, yet trying not to let the man know she'd seen him. "Nothing," she said softly, cautioning Felicia by covering Felicia's hand where it lay on her arm. "If he wants to see Bain bad enough, he'll either come to me or wait until Bain gets home, then come to the house. After all, he's due home the end of this week."

"In the meantime, you're just going to keep wondering?"

"Unless it gets the better of me, but for now, I don't want to spoil the day." She looked at the sky that was slowly darkening with huge gray clouds. "The rain's going to do it soon enough anyway, I'm afraid. Now, tell me, how are things in the capital of our fair state?" and they continued to stand under the tree talking, while Sancho, standing in the midst of the crowd, tried to think of a way to carry out the plan that had started forming in his mind the night before.

He stood quietly, trying to be inconspicuous as his eyes continued to study Señora Kolter. So, that's the woman Bain Kolter couldn't wait to return to, he thought as he stared across the crowded picnic grounds, watching her talking with another woman while they stood beneath a huge oak tree. He'd been surprised she was so fleshy. Why, she'd make two of Elena. He had to admit, though, that in spite of the extra pounds, there was a sensuality about her that was intriguing. Her eyes were alive, vibrant, and there was a subtle fullness to her mouth that was provocative. Although voluptuous, her figure was well-proportioned, and he could almost understand how a man could prefer her rounded curves to those of a more slender woman. Evidently Señor Kolter did, and the thought pleased him.

He took a deep breath, then gazed about the picnic grounds. Right now, however, Señora Kolter's charms were the least of his worries. What bothered him now was how he was going to do what he had to do. Unless . . . He gazed up at the sky, realizing the thunder that had been keeping its distance had started to get closer. That meant the rain wouldn't be too far behind.

He straightened, glanced back toward Señora Kolter, then suddenly moved off, realizing she'd been staring at him, and he wondered if perhaps she'd known who he was. After all, he had no guarantee that Bain Kolter hadn't told his wife about Sancho de Córdoba right down to the description. If so, then his task was going to be even harder.

It was later in the evening, shortly after dark, and the rain that had been threatening all afternoon had finally blown over, although rumbles could still be heard off in the distance, warning that another storm might be imminent. The marionette show had been deemed a great success, as had the tumblers. And now that the speeches were over, games won, and most of the food consumed, a number of couples were dancing in a roped-off area, while slaves from one of the nearby plantations furnished the music. The dancing would go on until almost midnight, when the fireworks went off.

Lizette stood among the spectators, watching her parents enjoying themselves dancing. She couldn't help but admire them as they moved among the other dancers, Rebel's gauze dress of pale pink like a frothy cloud against Beau's usual black frock coat, and she wished Bain were here so she wouldn't feel so alone.

Oh, she'd danced a few dances with her father and grandfather, but it just wasn't the same. Nor did dancing with her father-in-law help. All it did was remind her that she should be dancing with Bain. Bain's parents had lived in Beaufort for years, and his father, Randolph, a lawyer, had often helped Lizette's father with legal matters. Because of this, the two had become close friends, as had their wives, and now, as Lizette turned her gaze from the dancers, she was surprised to see her mother-in-law, Madeline Kolter, heading toward her.

Madeline was an attractive woman somewhat older than Rebel, with hair the same dark amber color as her daughter Felicia's, and gold-flecked brown eyes that at the moment were moving from Lizette to the bench beside her, where Pretty sat with the twins, then back to Lizette again.

"I see the children have had a long day," Madeline said when she reached Lizette, and they both turned to the bench now where Blythe sat leaning against Pretty, her eyes drooping, while Braxton, his arms around Pretty's neck, was shuffling his feet to the music.

"They'll no doubt fall asleep on the way home," Lizette replied, then glanced about to see if her grandparents were around anywhere. "I was just thinking a few minutes ago that maybe I'll head for the Château now, since it's already after nine."

Madeline glanced at the sky. "It might be a good idea at that. The rain may not hold off too much longer." She looked back at her daughter-in-law. "And besides, it'll be late enough by the time you get them home. Why, it's almost a two-hour ride."

"I'd have left already," Lizette said as the music stopped and the couples started clearing the area until the next dance. "Only I didn't want Grandpa Roth and Grandma Dicia or any of the others to think they had to leave with me. It's early yet for grown-ups, and the Fourth does come only once a year." She turned toward her parents as they joined her and Madeline. "Father, do you think you could find Luther for me?" she asked. "The twins are so tired, and I think I'll start heading back for the Château."

Beau nodded, smiling as he glanced at his grandchildren. "Had a hard day, huh, mister?" he said, touching Braxton's cheek; then he shook his head, his eyes falling on Blythe. Their best clothes that had looked so elegant earlier in the day were rumpled, dirty, and limp, but they looked completely happy and oblivious of the dirt and disarray. He turned back to his daughter. "I think I saw Luther down at the other end of the picnic grounds a short while ago," he said quickly. "I'll be right back," and he left, heading toward the lanterns strung in the trees over the refreshment tables.

Lizette turned to Pretty. "We'll go wait by the carriage, Pretty," she said. "I'll take Braxton, and you bring Blythe."

"But they're going to miss the fireworks," Rebel said, interrupting her, and Braxton, picking up on the word "fireworks," started to whine.

"Braxton, be quiet," Lizette warned. "It's just too late and your sister can't even keep her eyes open."

"But I's not tired," he argued fiercely. "And you said we could," and for the next few minutes they sparred back and forth, mother and son, while Blythe, who was totally disinterested, continued to lean against Pretty, her eyes completely closed now, oblivious of everything that was going on around her.

Finally the matter was resolved when Loedicia and Roth arrived and promised to keep Braxton with them so he could see the fireworks, while Lizette and Pretty would have Luther drive them home. Luther had also been staying at the Château so that Lizette could come and go as she pleased while Bain was gone. Now, as he joined them, taking the sleeping Blythe from Pretty so the little girl could rest on his shoulder, Lizette kissed her son good-bye, urging him to behave himself, hugged her parents, promising to take a ride up to Tonnerre the next afternoon, assured her mother-in-law that she'd have Bain get in touch the minute he got home, thanked her grandparents for letting Braxton stay with them, then headed toward where the carriages were, with the two servants following.

While the family had been talking, none of them, including Lizette, had noticed the priest Lizette had seen earlier standing only a short distance away. Now that it was dark, he was inconspicuous, the priest's robes making him blend easily into the shadows of a nearby tree, while he desperately tried to think of a way to get Bain's wife off somewhere alone. Now, suddenly, here was the opportunity being practically handed to him, and he was elated. There'd be the driver to contend with, *sí*, but he looked easy enough to take. His only problem now was that he had to get rid of the priest's robes, and there were just too many people around who might ask questions. As it was, he'd been dodging that other priest all day. The one he assumed was from one of the churches in either Beaufort or Port Royal. All another priest would have to do is talk to him for five minutes to know he wasn't the real thing.

Quickly making a decision, Sancho left his shadowy hiding place and began to make his way toward where all the horses were tethered, not far from the carriages near the main road that led to the picnic grounds. People were still nodding to him occasionally, and he'd nod back, smiling. Other than that, no one seemed to be paying any particular attention to him. Nor had they all day, and it had given him the opportunity to watch Señora Kolter quite closely, so he could make preparations, just in case.

He finally reached the horses, then stood for a moment gazing about. It seemed deserted enough at the moment. So after quickly taking one last look around, he moved off, closer toward the sound, until he reached the edge of the water, then searched furtively in the dark until he finally found the bush where he'd hidden his bedroll earlier in the day when he'd first arrived. Once he had the bedroll, he moved even farther away from the picnic grounds and into a small wood, where he hurriedly took off the cassock and discarded it, along with the rest of the priest's paraphernalia, keeping with him only the broad-brimmed hat. Then he strapped on his cutlass, made sure the pistol he was carrying was loaded, and crept back to where the horses were, making certain the darkness kept him hidden.

The carriages were parked just beyond where the horses were tethered, and as he pressed himself against a tree looking the area over, he could see Señora Kolter's manservant hitching up a buggy while she and her maid stood waiting, and he knew he was going to have to be as quiet as possible, yet he couldn't lose any time. Not if he wanted to get on the road ahead of them. Cautiously he slipped from against the tree and made his way to the line of horses. He didn't like it, but he was going to have to just take the first one he came to and hope that it wouldn't be some farmer's old nag.

There was no moon tonight because of the clouds, and it was so dark he could hardly see as he reached the first horse, rubbed its nose to quiet it, then felt to make sure it wasn't wearing a sidesaddle. All he would need was to get the wrong horse and end up with some stupid *señora*'s skittish mare.

He knew he was in luck as soon as he ran his hand down the horse's neck, then across its withers. This wasn't just any old nag, it was exactly what he needed. Straightening carefully, he looked down the line of horses again to where Bain Kolter's wife was still waiting. He could just barely make out her figure sitting in the carriage holding her daughter while the black was making doubly sure everything was hitched up right, since it was hard to see just what he was doing in the dark. And the black woman who'd been with Señora Kolter had a flint and was lighting the running lights.

Bueno, with the lights on the carriage he'd be able to see them easier on the road. He ran his hand down the horse's neck again, then reached down and deftly loosened its reins from the hitch line and began to lead it away. Once clear of the other horses, he lifted himself into the saddle, realizing that to try sneaking off would only look suspicious. Instead he'd just ride out as if he belonged on it. So, digging the horse he'd stolen in the ribs, he reined away as casually as he could, keeping in the shadows as much as possible, and started down the lane that led from the picnic grove. Then, once out on the main road, he set the horse into a free gallop and rode like the devil until he was well past the fork that joined this road with the one that led to Beaufort. Then, two miles farther on, he pulled off, reining into a densely wooded area, to wait.

Some distance behind him on the same road, Lizette sat in the buggy, cuddling Blythe while Blythe slept. The roads were really deserted tonight, she thought, and felt rather sad knowing that the others were back at the picnic grounds still enjoying themselves. She tightened her hold on Blythe as the carriage reached the fork in the road and headed across Port Royal island toward the crossroads that led to the Château, over an hour's ride away yet.

As the carriage moved on down the road, neither the occupants nor the driver noticed a lone figure that had begun to follow it some miles back. However, all of them did notice the storm that had finally started to move in again as the wind increased and the air began to cool considerably.

"It's gwine rain this time for sure, Miz Kolter," Luther called back from his perch on the driver's seat.

Lizette didn't want to wake Blythe, and she turned to Pretty on the seat beside her. "Tell him to go a little faster but to be careful if the rain starts," she whispered, and Pretty moved forward in the seat, giving the message to Luther; then she settled back down again as the carriage began to pick up speed.

Sancho, trailing only a short distance behind now, also felt
the fresh wind and heard the crack of lightning not too far
off. Then the carriage started to pick up speed and he knew
he couldn't wait any longer because his job would be harder
to accomplish in the rain. Spurring his horse into a gallop,
he began to close the distance between him and the carriage,
hoping to reach it before it reached the plantation house he
could see off to the right, its outline visible during the
lightning flashes. It wouldn't do to have them try to turn in
there for help, he thought, and his eyes were unyielding, his
jaw set firm as he neared the carriage.

Luther, who'd been concentrating on urging the horse to
go faster, felt the first few drops of rain on his face, but
didn't even notice the rider until suddenly Sancho drew up
alongside and called to him.

"*Hola!*" Sancho yelled, trying to get him to pull over by
pointing and motioning toward the side of the road. "*Por
favor,* I must talk with Señora Kolter!"

Lizette leaned sideways toward Pretty. "Tell Luther to
stop," she said, keeping her voice low, hoping not to wake
Blythe.

Pretty leaned forward to tell Luther, and the slave straightened, then brought the carriage to a halt.

Lizette saw the vague outline of the rider, then recognized
the black broad-brimmed hat he was wearing, only she could
tell that the rest of his clothes were not the clothes of a
priest anymore. It was raining harder how, and Lizette kept
her head beneath the hood of the buggy, leaning toward
Pretty again.

"Ask him what he wants, Pretty," she instructed her, and
Pretty nodded.

"Miz Kolter wants to know what you want," she said
apprehensively.

Sancho straightened, pulling the hat farther down in front
to keep the rain from his eyes, then pointed a pistol directly
at Pretty.

"I want Señora Kolter," he said firmly, and Lizette, who'd
been watching the interchange of words and realized what
was going on, without even weighing the consequences hugged
Blythe closer, then leaned forward, yelling at Luther.

"Go, Luther! Go!" she shouted frantically, and Luther,
who'd been skeptical about stopping in the first place, brought
the reins down in a hard slap as he yelled to the horse, and

the carriage lurched forward, taking Sancho completely by surprise.

His horse shied, pawing the ground, and Sancho cursed, then finally got the animal under control again. He couldn't let them get away. This wasn't supposed to happen.

"*Hijo de puta!*" he cursed savagely to himself as the carriage began disappearing down the road, and he shoved the pistol back in its holster, then took off after it, his head low against the horse's neck.

The road had been dry and dusty earlier, but now the rain was quickly turning it into a quagmire and Luther was having a hard time keeping the carriage from sliding all over the place. Bad enough it was so dark out, and now with the rain, he could barely see, yet he kept the horse moving, knowing the road was a straight line from here to the crossroads.

He leaned back a little and called over his shoulder, "I could pull into Palmerston Grove, Miz Kolter!"

"No!" Lizette shouted back, having no reason to be quiet anymore since Blythe was awake now and clinging to her desperately. "They'd never help!"

Luther nodded, and slapped the reins again, even harder this time, trying to get more speed out of the carriage horse; then he took a quick glance behind them. There was nothing to see except the rain, but he knew the horse and rider were still there from the thud of the pounding hooves overriding the splash of the heavy downpour as it hit the carriage and splattered off the ground. If only he could see.

He turned once more to the road ahead. They'd be near the crossroads soon, and he tried to squint into the deluge, wishing he could pull over and wait out the storm, yet knowing he couldn't, while inside the buggy, Lizette and Pretty were huddled close, Blythe pressed between them, both women trying to soothe the girl's fears.

Behind them, Sancho was drawing closer by the minute, and suddenly Luther sensed him coming up on his left, and he was furious. He glanced over quickly, then with all his strength began slashing at the blurred figure alongside while continuing to yell at the carriage horse to go even faster, but it did little good. The poor animal was going as fast as he could, and Luther cursed silently to himself, while lightning cracked the sky and thunder echoed through the woods on each side of them. Then, as if he'd willed it, the rain began to let up a bit, and the whip Luther was wielding suddenly

started reaching its target and Sancho swore, crouching low
now. He tried to duck it, but couldn't, so instead, eased his
mount from alongside, pulling away slightly, yet keeping up
with the carriage, hoping he'd still get a chance. Then suddenly, as another streak of lightning split through the rain,
once more lighting the whole world around them for a brief
second, Sancho heard the driver let out an agonized scream,
only it was too late, and as Sancho reined his horse even
farther away from the buggy, slowing his mount slightly and
straightening in the saddle, he watched with mixed feelings
as the carriage careened toward the crossroad, the driver
unsuccessfully trying to control it as it began to slide sideways around the corner; then it flew through the air before
crashing down against a rail fence, its wheels still spinning
frantically as it settled on its side.

Without wanting to lose his advantage, Sancho quickly
dug his horse in the ribs and reached the buggy while the
wheels were still turning. The running light on the side that
was facing up was still lit, casting weird shadows in the rain
and darkness, and he dismounted hurriedly, rushing to the
overturned buggy, his pistol once more in his hand.

Although she had tried to hang on to Blythe, Lizette had
been thrown into Pretty as the carriage flew through the air,
and when it smashed into the fence, the impact had been too
much for her. Blythe was wrenched from her arms, thrown
from the buggy, and now she lay whimpering and half-
unconscious, while Lizette, sobbing hysterically, was groping
around in the darkness, trying to find her.

"I found her, Miss Lizzy, I found her," Pretty gasped
breathlessly, her own eyes wet with tears. "Don't worry,
she's here, see, over here," and Pretty's hands reached
Blythe before Lizette's did; then both of them suddenly
looked up as Sancho reached down and grabbed Lizette's
arm, starting to pull her away.

"No! God, no! Leave me alone!" Lizette screamed. "My
baby's hurt," and she tried to wrench free, but Sancho's
fingers tightened on her arm, which was slippery now from
the rain.

"Come, I haven't got all night!" he yelled fiercely. "She
will live," and he started to drag Lizette away, only she
continued to fight.

She was still weak from the shock of the accident, but
didn't care as she swung at him, her fist hitting him in the

face, almost knocking his hat off, and he growled angrily, shoving her free arm aside as he kept on dragging her to her feet, still fighting him; then he shoved the pistol he still had in his other hand against her head.

"One more move and I pull the trigger," he snarled viciously.

Lizette's arm froze in midair and she stared into his face, trying hard to see his eyes, to see if he really meant it or not, but it was impossible. She continued to stare at him as the rain washed down her face, the dye from the flowers in her straw hat streaking in with her tears and coloring her cheeks, while behind her, Pretty tried talking softly to Blythe to see if she was all right.

"Now, you are coming with me," Sancho said firmly. "Move!" His fingers once more tightened on her arm and he forced her away from the wreckage of the buggy toward his horse, only a few feet away.

Lizette let her eyes wander from his shadowed face toward the wreckage and now she could make out the faint outline of Luther's big frame crumpled on the ground only a few feet from the fallen horse. Neither Luther nor the horse was moving. Lord, there was no one to help her. And Blythe . . .

"Mount, *señora*," Sancho ordered when they reached his horse, and Lizette, the pistol still pointed toward her face, glanced back toward Pretty for a brief second, then, still trembling inside, lifted the skirt of her afternoon dress as best she could, put her foot in the stirrup, and landed in the saddle. Her hopes of snatching the reins and breaking free of this strange cruel man, however, were quickly dashed when he grabbed them himself and held them tightly, then leapt on behind her, the rain not even slowing his progress.

Her heart was beating wildly, her tears mingling with the rain as he whirled the horse around and drew closer to the wreckage, where Lizette could vaguely make out Pretty's kneeling form in the faint light from the damaged running light that was almost out now, its whale oil seeping away from the wick.

"You!" Sancho shouted to the black girl, his voice ringing in Lizette's ears like a pistol shot. "Tell Señor Kolter that Sancho de Córdoba has avenged Barlovento! Do you understand?"

Pretty stared up at him through the cold rain, her face

puzzled, tear-filled eyes questioning as she held on to Blythe's hand, hoping to give her some comfort.

"*Comprende?*" he yelled, this time in Spanish. Pretty still stared at him, but didn't answer. "Tell him this is for Barlovento!" he yelled in English again.

This time Pretty nodded. "Yes, sir!" she called back, her voice breaking, and Sancho grinned, his white teeth the only thing visible on his shadowed face, his beard dripping water.

"*Bueno!*" he said briskly, then reined his horse back toward the road.

Lizette, clenching her fists, feeling his arm tighten around her waist like a vise, knowing the pistol was still in the hand at the end of that arm, sat rigidly in front of him, fear gripping every nerve in her body while Pretty watched them ride down the road, then melt into the rain and darkness.

Chapter 3

THE RAINY NIGHT was quiet now except for Blythe's soft whimpering, a sound that tore at Pretty's heart and brought new tears to her eyes.

"Hush, little one," Pretty whispered, crooning to her. "We gonna have help, you see." She glanced over to Luther's still form, then set Blythe's hand down gently as she thought she saw a movement just before the running light on the buggy sputtered, then went out.

"Luther?" she called, stumbling toward him in the dark, trying to see.

He was moaning and shaking his head by the time she reached him, and the relief that he was still alive almost overwhelmed her.

"Thank God," she cried quickly. "I thought you was dead."

Luther moved hesitantly, pushing himself up, the world around him spinning in a dizzying frenzy; then he closed his eyes, trying to clear his head enough so he could at least see her.

"Miz Kolter!" he asked, his voice breaking with emotion.

"She's gone," Pretty answered hurriedly. "That man on the horse took her away. Didn't even let her see if the baby was hurt or not. Just made her ride off with him."

Luther shook his head for a second longer, then tried to stand up, but his knees were shaky and Pretty moved closer, letting him lean on her shoulder until he felt the strength return a little more to his legs. After a minute or so he straightened and looked down at her in the darkness. He couldn't see her face, but just knowing she was there helped.

"You say he took her?" he asked, making sure he'd heard right.

"Said I was to tell Mista Kolter it was for Barlovento. Only I don't know what that means."

"Neither do I." He glanced around. "Where's the baby?"

"Over here."

Pretty led him to where Blythe still lay on the ground. The rain was beginning to let up again, and within a few minutes it almost stopped as Pretty and Luther knelt down beside Blythe.

"She ain't moved?" he asked, his dark eyes questioning.

"I don't think she can, Luther." Pretty reached out and took the young girl's hand again, feeling the small fingers tightening on hers.

"I hurt, Pretty. I hurt," Blythe cried softly, her words almost lost to the night, and Pretty looked over at Luther.

She could just about see him now that it wasn't raining so hard, at least she could see the vague outline of his sturdy chin and familiar face.

"You're gonna have to go for help, Luther," she said quickly. "There's nobody at the Château and the closest place is Palmerston Grove."

"You don't think they's gonna help, do ya?" he asked. " 'Sides, I saw the Palmers at the picnic too." He stood up and moved off toward the horse. Luther's legs were still weak and his head a bit fuzzy yet, but it didn't take much to see that the animal's neck was broken.

"Damn!" he murmured under his breath, then came back to where Pretty was sitting on the ground now, trying to keep Blythe quiet.

"I'm gonna have to walk it," he said disgustedly. "And that could take hours, 'lesson the rain's scared 'em all away from the picnic and I meet 'em on the way comin' home."

He gazed off down the dark road they'd just traveled, watching lightning crashing off in the distance, the uneven rumble of the thunder far away now, and he knelt down again.

"She still ain't moved?" he asked.

"I think she's hurt too bad to move, Luther," Pretty said, tears welling up in her eyes again. "Please, we can't help Miss Lizzie 'lesson we gets help ourselves. You gotta hurry."

Luther took a deep breath and stood up. She was right. If he could reach help in time, maybe they could help Miz Kolter too, and he glanced down at Pretty one more time, then turned the collar of his frock coat up against the night air that had cooled down with the rain. "I'll be back soon's I can," he said anxiously. "You stay with the baby," and he started back toward Port Royal and Beaufort, while Pretty leaned over staring off into the darkness, hugging Blythe's head as close as she could without moving her and she began to hum a silly little tune and talk to her, trying to still the child's fears, and at the same time calm her own pounding heart.

Liz wanted more than anything to elbow her kidnapper right in the gut, only she knew as they rode along that it'd be futile. His grip was like iron around her waist, the pistol still in his hand, and they were moving too fast. She reached up, wiping the rain from her face, and realized that it had started to let up some, and she opened her eyes wider, trying to look around to see what direction they were taking. They were heading right down the road that went past the Château.

Her insides were trembling, her arm and leg hurt where they'd been bruised in the accident, and the constant jostling of the horse wasn't making matters any better. Then, quite unexpectedly, the limp straw hat on her head began to fall down over her eyes, and she reached up, pushing it back into place before glancing over her shoulder at her captor.

"My daughter!" she protested tearfully.

"She'll live."

"You can't know that!" she yelled. "She was hurt."

"*Muchachos* have a miraculous way of surviving," he answered quickly.

She tried to see his face clearly now that it wasn't raining so hard, but it was still too dark.

"Who are you?" she asked abruptly.

He laughed. "You already heard, *señora,* the name is Emilio Sancho de Córdoba, but most men call me Sancho."

He dug his horse harder in the ribs and Lizette felt the sudden jolt as the horse lengthened its stride.

"*Hai!*" Sancho yelled boisterously, and Lizette turned her eyes back to the road ahead, trying to gain a measure of dignity, tears still filling her eyes. "Faster, you damned devil," Sancho continued yelling at the horse. "We have a ship to meet," and Lizette knew there was no use trying to find the answers now.

Past the Château the horse flew, galloping headlong down the road, its hoofbeats partially muffled by the splattering mud, while Lizette strained her eyes into the darkness ahead, hoping and praying they'd meet someone, anyone, on the lonely road tonight, yet knowing that practically everyone on the island was back at the picnic.

It was some half-hour later that Sancho finally slowed the horse just enough to rein him off the road and into a swampy field, where he began following the fence that ran along it. It was one of the lower fields of the Château and Lizette frowned, wondering where he could be headed. The answer came as a surprise a short time later when he slowed the animal, then reined up not far from an old work shed near the banks of the Broad River and dismounted.

Lizette kept her seat astride the horse and stared down at him as he continued to hold the reins, and for a moment Sancho wanted to laugh. She looked so ridiculously funny with her ebony hair all askew, the wet straw hat drooping down over her left eye and the lavender dress soaked and sticking to her, its once billowy sleeves plastered to her arms, while thick mud covered her kid shoes and clung to her stockings that had fallen and were bunched around her ankles, leaving her legs bare and mud-splattered.

"Come, get down," he said roughly, but she didn't move. "I said down, *pronto!*" he repeated, and once more his pistol was pointing directly at her.

Lizette's jaw tightened, her emerald eyes blazing as she slowly slid from the saddle, then stood looking up at him.

"Now what?" she asked stubbornly.

Sancho straightened arrogantly, his eyes narrowing as he stared down at her.

"Now we wait," he answered. "Sit," and while still keeping his eyes on her, he led the horse to a small tree and tethered him, then turned back to his captive . "I said sit."

Lizette looked around. "Where?" she asked angrily. "Everything's wet and cold, and besides, I want to know why you're doing this."

"Like I say before, this is for Barlovento," he answered. "Surely your husband told you of Barlovento, *señora.*"

Lizette studied him curiously. Barlovento? Ah yes, the island where Bain was when he had amnesia. But they were his friends, and that was almost two years ago. She wished it wasn't dark so she could see him better, but there was no hope for that. The rain had stopped altogether now, but clouds still hung low, and even if they weren't there, the moon was waning and would only be a slim crescent. Besides, there were all the trees along the riverbank; moonlight would do little good. She squinted, straining her eyes, the smell of the river strong in her nostrils, the musty smell from the soaked earth mingling with it. Water still dripped from the trees as she walked over to the river's edge and stared across toward the opposite bank, only faint dots of light showing that there was an end to the long expanse of water in front of her. It must be close to midnight, she thought unhappily, then remembered Blythe's still figure lying on the ground and winced.

"Please," she said, turning once more to plead with him. "I don't know why you're doing this . . . I've done nothing to you. Please, let me go see if my daughter's all right."

"There is no way I can do that, *señora,*" he answered, and pointed off downriver. "*La Piranha* is on time, see," and Lizette turned back toward the river, then straightened, an empty feeling gripping the pit of her stomach as the shadowy sails of a ship began to emerge on the horizon, and within minutes a full three-master sailed in close enough for Sancho to call to it, and the anchor was dropped.

"I will not be swimming, send the longboat," Sancho called to the men on board once the ship had been secured, and the sails furled. "I have a captive."

Lizette shivered. "Oh no, you're not taking me on there!" she yelled, and started to make a break for the woods, but he was too quick for her, and his fingers clamped on her arm.

"*Caramba,* but you are a stubborn one, are you not, *señora?*" he said, amused, then leaned close, his eyes searching her face, the pistol pointing at her head again. "Do not make me use it, señora," he went on, his voice deepening ominously. "Now, come, my men are on their way," and he led her back to the riverbank, the pistol hard against her ribs while they stood waiting for the longboat.

"Kolter's dead?" Jigger asked as the longboat landed and he leapt from the bow, slipping slightly in the mud, but catching himself.

Sancho's eyes hardened. "Kolter was not to be had," he answered. "But Señora Kolter will do for now." His voice held a note of malice. "It is one thing to kill a man and end his suffering, Jigger," he went on as he pushed Lizette ahead of him, making her climb into the boat. "However, sometimes the revenge is even sweeter when he dies a thousand times over, *sí?*"

Jigger's eyes sifted over Lizette from head to toe. "I think I see," he said, then frowned. "You think taking her will make him suffer?" he asked. "She don't look like much."

Sancho grinned as he shoved her down into the longboat between the men who were holding the oars. "*Sí*, I think it will," he answered. "You see, *amigo*, before the rain . . ." He hesitated and his eyes fell on Lizette again. She straightened angrily, her back rigid as she tried to control her frustration and tears. "Before the rain," he went on, "she was, *muy bella*, very pretty. Now, hurry, I want to clear the sound before she is missed," and he helped his first mate shove off toward the waiting ship anchored only a short distance from the riverbank; then he sat down beside Lizette, the gun once more pressed to her midsection.

Tears still rolled down Lizette's cheeks as she silently wept. This wasn't happening. It couldn't be. She closed her eyes for a few minutes, then opened them again, the sound of the oars as the man rowed against the swift current breaking the quiet of the night, while off in the distance the low rumbling of the thunder was joined by the faint sound of another explosion carried along on the cool night air, and she knew they had probably started shooting off the fireworks and the picnic would soon be officially over.

Back on the road to Beaufort and Port Royal, Luther was making good time. His head was clear now, the strength back in his legs, although the cut on his forehead was bleeding, and he wiped the blood away with the back of his hand. Strange he hadn't noticed the cut earlier, but then he'd been so concerned for Pretty and Miz Kolter. And the baby! Remembering how still the young girl lay, he picked up his pace, trying to go even faster.

There were few places along the way where he could have stopped for help even if the owners hadn't all been at the picnic, and he cursed softly, wishing to God the horse hadn't died so he could make better time. Well, the rain had stopped anyway. That was one good thing, but now as he strode along, he suddenly realized he'd even left the mud behind. Evidently the storm had hit only the western half of the island before blowing off toward the northeast, and it must have missed the picnic grove altogether. That meant the fireworks would go on as usual and everyone would stay late. Of all the luck.

He stopped for a minute, straining his ears, certain now he could hear the faint explosions from the fireworks mingling with the thunder that was rumbling as lightning split the sky occasionally off in the direction of Beaufort, farther to the north. His jaw clenched in determination again, and he turned the wet collar of his coat down away from his neck and started up again, the empty road in front of him like a dark tunnel, the trees on each side, laden with leaves, making the shadows around him even darker, and he began to hum a sprightly tune to keep his legs moving faster.

He'd been walking for what seemed like hours already, and now suddenly he stopped, the distant sounds of a wagon approaching like music to his ears. Thank God. Someone was comin'. Anxious to get any help he could, he quickened his pace and was running by the time he reached the wagon; then he stopped abruptly as he recognized some of the slaves from Tonnerre.

"Where's Mista Beau?" he asked Job, who was driving, but Aaron, Beau's overseer, rode up beside them before Job could answer.

"What's the matter, Luther?" he asked anxiously. The big black Watusi had been with the Dantes for years and was a freeman now, but with nowhere else to go, like many others, he'd stayed. "You been hurt or somethin'?" he went on, leaning over in the saddle to get a good look at the other man. "What happened?"

"It's Miz Kolter. He took her, and the baby's been hurt," Luther blurted quickly. "You gotta ride back and get Mista Beau and the others, Aaron. Hurry, you gotta!"

Aaron's horse moved restlessly. "Hold steady, old girl," Aaron said as he gently quieted her, then turned his attention once more to Luther. "Where are they?" he asked.

"At the crossroads," Luther answered hurriedly. "We was bein' chased and the buggy turned over. Now, hurry, there ain't no time."

Aaron took one look at the panic on Luther's face, then, without arguing any further, whirled his horse around, heading back toward the picnic grounds, while Luther climbed onto the wagon that was full of men, women, and children. Slaves from Tonnerre on their way home from the picnic. Although both Roth Chapman and Beau Dante bought slaves for their plantations, neither kept them slaves for long, but gave them a wage, then let them work off their original

price, eventually becoming freemen. It was a practice most
of their neighbors condemned; however, for them it was well
worth it for their slaves were not only treated well, but
became more a part of the plantation, their loyalty an asset
to their owners.

Both Job, who was driving the buckboard, and his wife,
Liza, had been at Tonnerre longer even than Aaron. And
Liza, a plump woman who'd been head cook there for years,
made room for Luther on the seat beside her and her husband, while everyone started asking questions at once; then
Job flicked the reins, moving the wagon at a faster pace than
they'd been going since leaving the picnic grounds, and they
continued toward the crossroad.

Aaron rode like the devil, passing buggies, wagons, and
other riders on the way, now that the picnic was over; then
he reined up short as he spotted the Tonnerre coach. The
Dantes had used a closed carriage for the ride to the picnic
grounds earlier in the day because of the expected rain, and
when Aaron called to the driver, the carriage quickly slowed,
pulling over to the side of the road so others could pass.

"What's going on, Aaron?" Beau asked as he stuck his
head out the open window in the door.

Aaron was breathing heavily from the hard ride, his horse
lathered and panting. "It's Miss Lizzie," he said hurriedly,
having known Bain Kolter's wife while she was growing up
on her father's plantation. "Ran into Luther up the road a
piece. There's been an accident at the crossroads, and he
said to hurry!"

"Oh, God, not Liz," Rebel gasped.

Beau leaned his head out farther, calling to the driver.
"Follow Aaron," he yelled anxiously. "And hurry, but be
careful." Then he ducked his head back inside and reached
out in the darkness to take his wife's hand as the driver
flicked the reins and hollered to the matched team. The
closed carriage eased back to the middle of the road again,
and the driver expertly maneuvered his way through the
other traffic that was leaving the picnic grounds, until the
road was finally clear ahead; then he whipped the horses
into a gallop, trying to make up time, while up ahead a
couple of miles, Luther kept looking back as the farm wagon
ambled along as fast as it could, and he watched for the big
Watusi bringing Miz Kolter's parents. As soon as the closed

carriage was in sight, Luther had Job slow the buckboard so he could jump down, and he waited at the side of the road.

"Slow down and pick up Luther," Aaron called to the Dantes' driver, and the carriage drew quickly to a stop. Luther, who had been following at a run beside it, opened the door, and Beau, seeing who it was, and hoping he could find some answers, reached out, helping him in, then signaled to the driver and they were off again, passing the farm wagon with the slaves in it, while Luther sat inside explaining to Miz Kolter's parents just what had gone on. Outside the carriage, the driver had to slow down a bit when the roadway became too muddy where the storm clouds had cut loose before moving on toward the city of Beaufort, and by the time they passed Palmerston Grove, Luther had told Rebel and Beau the whole story as he knew it. Rebel was in tears, urging Beau to have the driver move even faster.

"We can't," he told her, his own voice strained. "The road's too slippery from the rain and we could end up in a ditch ourselves." His arm went around her shoulder as he held her close, trying to comfort her, while up ahead, Pretty still sat with Blythe, her head bent down against the child's cheek, whispering softly to her and helping her as best she could. Blythe still hadn't moved.

Suddenly Pretty tensed, then got up slowly, gazing off into the darkness. It was coming! Someone was coming! A short time later she breathed a sigh of relief as she recognized Aaron, his massive height and build quickly discernible against the night sky.

"Over here!" Pretty shouted and Aaron reined up, then dismounted, while behind him, the carriage quickly drew to a stop and Beau leapt from it with Luther following. Both men helped Rebel out.

"Where is she?" Rebel asked breathlessly.

Pretty pointed to the ground near where the front of the smashed carriage lay against the fence. "Over here, come."

Rebel picked up her skirts, letting Beau help her step over what was left of the tongue and traces; then she practically fell to the ground beside her small granddaughter, her hand fumbling in the dark for the girl's forehead, while she talked softly, letting her know she was there.

Rebel had been forced to do a great deal of nursing when she was younger, and it had often come in handy over the years when any of the slaves had been hurt, and now as she began running her hands over Blythe's sturdy body, she felt a sickening nausea begin to sweep over her, and she bit her lip, trying to hold back a sob.

"It feels like her hip's broken, and maybe her back," she said tearfully as she looked over at Beau, who was kneeling down now on the other side of Blythe. "Oh God, Beau, what do we do?"

"Can she be moved?"

"She can't stay here. We're going to have to move her, but we're going to need a board and some laudanum. The pain must be unbearable."

As Rebel and Beau talked, trying to decide what to do first, the wagon with the slaves from Tonnerre in it arrived, and one of the slaves, sensing the trouble, brought over a lantern they'd been carrying, so Rebel and Beau could see. Rebel thanked him, then turned her attention once more to the road, where more slaves, this time from the Château, River Oaks, and one of the plantations farther down on the left past the Château, began to gather, followed a few minutes later by a carriage with the River Oaks crest on its side.

"Good Lord, what happened?" Rachel Grantham asked as she stepped away from her carriage and saw the wreckage. Her hazel eyes widened. "Can I help?" she asked quickly, forgetting for a moment that she and the Dantes didn't get along too well.

"You can stay out of the way," Rebel snapped as she stood up, then called to Aaron. "Aaron, go find the doctor." She was looking past the owner of River Oaks as if she weren't even there. "And if you see Mother's carriage on the road, tell her what happened. And for God's sake, tell her to hurry, please," she instructed him. "I don't think we can handle this alone."

Aaron nodded that he'd heard, and found his horse amid the crowd that was gathering, then leapt into the saddle and maneuvered him on down the road, melting into the darkness like a phantom.

Rebel suddenly looked at Rachel, the light from the lantern the slave had given her casting shadows on the older woman's face. Rachel had been Rebel's first husband's aunt by marriage, and there was little love between the two women. "If you really want to do something, Rachel," Rebel said, her voice brisk and to the point, "perhaps you and your gentleman friend," and she nodded to a paunchy middle-

aged gentleman standing behind their neighbor, "can keep all
these people back. It's only frightening Blythe all the more,
and the poor child's in enough misery as it is."

Rachel stared at Rebel for a moment, not saying a word.
Just like her mother, she thought irritably, her full mouth
twisting into a sneer, and she reached up, wiping a stray hair
back from her forehead, wishing it was still the deep chestnut color it used to be instead of such a dull gray. Ah well,
she had one consolation: Loedicia had aged too. She turned
abruptly, and surprising Rebel, motioned toward her gentleman friend to follow, and, hoping to show Roth when he
and Loedicia arrived that she wasn't as heartless as Loedicia
made her out to be, she, with the help of her friend, her
driver, as well as the Dantes' driver, managed to keep the
rest of the slaves and curiosity seekers back, away from the
wreckage.

Rebel sighed as she knelt back down beside her granddaughter and handed Pretty the lantern to hold, then glanced
back up, seeing that Rachel had taken what she said to
heart, and she was glad that for once Rachel was acting like
a human being.

Once Rachel was occupied elsewhere so she wouldn't bother
them, Beau, anxious to do something, anything, to help
until the doctor could arrive, took Luther with him and left
for the Château to get some laudanum, blankets, and something they could use for a stretcher so they could get Blythe
back to the house, knowing it was going to be hard to move
her. Just as soon as the two of them left, Rebel, tears still
brimming her eyes, once more took up her vigil beside
Pretty, both of them talking softly to Blythe, trying as best
they could to comfort her, even though they knew she kept
drifting in and out of consciousness, and knowing full well
there were moments when Blythe had no idea where she
was, what was going on, or that her grandmother and Pretty
were even there. Occasionally Blythe would call her mother's name, and every time she did, the faint cry would tug at
Rebel's heart, reminding her all too well that Blythe wasn't
their only concern tonight, and she'd start wondering where
Liz was, and what could be happening to her. All Pretty had
told them was that the man who rode off with Liz yelled for
her to tell Señor Kolter—"that's just what he called him,"
she said—"that this was for Barlovento." The whole thing
was so crazy and mixed up.

To Rebel, the wait for her mother and stepfather to come along to help give her strength seemed endless, and by the time they finally did arrive, bringing Heath and Darcy with them, as well as Braxton, who was so tired he'd fallen asleep as soon as the carriage left the picnic grounds, she was so upset it seemed like no one would be able to calm her down. But Loedicia managed to, with Roth's help, while Heath and Darcy, after learning what had happened, let Braxton keep right on sleeping, and drove on with him to the Château, deciding there was no reason to try to explain anything to him tonight, when in reality, not even Rebel and Beau knew what kind of an explanation they were going to be able to give him.

Rebel watched the coach disappear down the road carrying Blythe's twin brother back to the Château, and her throat constricted as she held back the tears. How were they going to tell him? How did you tell a little boy that his mother was gone and his sister was badly hurt? She could feel the water from the wet, muddy grass. It had already soaked through the skirt of her flimsy dress where she'd been kneeling but it didn't seem to matter, nor did the mud that covered the top of her kid shoes. All she cared about now was the small girl whose twisted body lay sprawled on the ground in the darkness before her, broken and bent, and she gripped her mother's head tightly as Loedicia knelt beside her, both women exchanging a glance of acknowledged sorrow in the dim light from the lantern that Pretty was still holding.

Beau and Luther returned from the Château only a few minutes after the carriage with Heath, Darcy, and Braxton had left, and the next few hours were a nightmare for all of them. Aaron still hadn't arrived with the doctor, and both Rebel and Loedicia knew something had to be done. While Beau was at the Château, he'd had Mattie dissolve the laudanum he wanted to bring in a cup of cider, then put it into a bottle, so he uncorked it now, handing it to Rebel, who managed to get enough of it into Blythe to make her sleep. Then, once she was completely out, and being as careful as they could, Roth and Beau, with the help of their wives and Pretty, managed to transfer the girl from the wet ground to an old door they had padded with a light blanket, covering her with another blanket, and Beau, with Luther helping, and the rest of them walking alongside, trudged the last two miles to the Château on foot. They would have used a carriage, but were afraid she'd be jostled too much and dislodge any bones that were broken, so that it would be impossible to set them. When they finally reached the plantation house, she was quickly taken to the room on the immediate left at the top of the stairs, the room that had once been Rebel's room when she was younger, and was now the bedroom where Blythe's parents slept when they stayed over, and she was gently lifted onto the bed, where the doctor, whom Aaron finally managed to locate and bring out to the Château, was able to examine her, his prognosis being that three-and-a-half-year-old Blythe would never walk again.

"How are we going to tell Bain?" Rebel asked, trying to keep the tears from coming again by wiping her nose vigorously with a handkerchief as they all gathered in the parlor after the doctor was gone. "Liz expected him home this coming weekend."

"Why? Why would anyone do something like this. And taking Liz too?" Loedicia exclaimed, her own eyes red from crying. "The whole thing just doesn't make sense."

Roth was sitting next to Loedicia on the brocade sofa, holding her hand. He squeezed it, frowning. While the doctor had been taking care of Blythe, he, Beau, and Heath had saddled horses and searched in the direction Pretty said the man had ridden, combing the whole area, including part of the Engler property down near the tip of Port Royal Island, but all they'd found was a horse that didn't belong to the Château's stables tied to a tree near the riverbank, and what was left of Liz's straw hat, but not a sign of Liz.

"We'll take another look in the morning, love," he told Loedicia, then glanced over to where Beau was standing staring out the front window into the night.

The storm that had threatened the picnickers earlier, and managed to half-drown this side of the island, had moved on far to the northeast now, leaving only a soft cool breeze in its wake. A breeze that ruffled the long line of trees on the drive out front and carried the sweet scent of the flowers in the pots that lined the Château's front steps in through the open window with it as it blew against the sheer curtains. Beau's face was hard, unsmiling, his fists clenched, and Roth knew the frustration of being able to do nothing was gnawing at his insides.

"Don't worry, we'll find Liz, Beau," he said, hoping to help his step-son-in-law accept what was happening. "I'm sure Bain'll know what it's all about. What we have to do now is pray that the doctor's wrong. That Blythe will walk again, and that wherever Liz is, she's safe."

Beau whirled around. "But it's so senseless!" His green eyes were blazing. "Even if Bain does know what it's about, it can't have anything to do with that child up there! Why should she have to suffer? And Liz! Pretty said the man shouted that it was revenge for something. Why should my daughter and granddaughter pay for what Bain should be paying for?"

"You think he won't pay?" Heath asked incredulously. "My God, Beau, he's going to pay every minute until he gets Liz back, and every time he looks at Blythe. Don't blame Bain for this, because if I know him, he'd gladly take their place."

"Amen," echoed Roth.

Beau ran a hand through his dark hair, the blue-black sheen dulled in the flickering lamplight in the room; then he glanced over at his wife, her eyes still red and swollen, her pale hair untidy, the dark stains from the wet ground dried on the front of her dress.

"I'm sorry," he said huskily, then turned to Loedicia and Roth. "Heath's right, I know. It's just that it's so frustrating when you have no control over what's happening. I feel so helpless."

Rebel moved to her husband and entered his arms, resting her head on his shoulder. She was so tired. "I know," she whispered softly. "That's how we all feel. Why should you be any different?" She drew her head back, the lamplight deepening the violet highlights in her eyes to a lovely shade of indigo, and she studied his face, so unlike his Indian ancestors' faces. Only the high cheekbones and smooth tawny skin gave his heritage away. His arms moved to her waist and she sighed. "I think we should go home now," she went on, her voice weary and strained. "There's nothing more we can do here. Pretty's watching over the baby, and when the others went on up to Tonnerre, Hizzie stayed and said she'd take care of Brax tomorrow. You know she loves the little ones. We can come back in the morning."

"Why don't you just stay the night?" Heath suggested,

and his arm went around Darcy. He knew she was tired too. "After all, it's only a few hours till dawn."

Rebel turned. "Mother?" she asked hesitantly.

"You know you're welcome," Loedicia answered without hesitation. "I should have mentioned it myself. It's just that I can't seem to gather my thoughts together tonight, I guess, that's all." Roth was still holding her hand and she looked at her husband. His white hair was lightly shadowed in the dimly lit room, and for a moment he looked much younger. "I was so hoping Cole would find his son, and all would be well again," she said, and a tear ran down her cheek. "And now this. Will the bitterness never end?"

Roth's dark eyes softened as they met hers. His heart was filled with a mixture of anger and frustration because he couldn't make the world right for her no matter how hard he tried, and it hurt. "Would it really be living, my love," he finally answered, his voice husky with emotion, "if we hid ourselves away from the rest of the world just so we wouldn't ever have to cry?" He squeezed her hand, shaking his head. "That's the coward's way out, and you know it, Dicia," he went on while they all stood listening. "And there isn't one of your children, grandchildren, or great-grandchildren who could ever be a coward, and you know that too. Only how would the rest of the world ever know it, or even God for that matter, if nothing ever went wrong and there was nothing for them ever to stand up to?"

He drew his eyes from hers and gazed around the room at Rebel and Beau, and Heath and Darcy, remembering the impossible odds they'd conquered to be together; then he thought of the small child upstairs and her parents, and what they were all going to have to go through now.

"Don't worry, Dicia, my love," he said, turning to her again as he also thought back over the problems they had overcome when they were younger. "Maybe someday we'll be able to just sit back enjoying life, and watching the sunrise and sunset without having to worry about what happens in between. But you know you don't want to stop living just yet in order to do it, now, do you?"

They all stared at Roth for a minute, the age lines in his face seeming to disappear as he looked directly into his wife's eyes; then he turned back once more to Heath and Beau. The sun would be coming up in another hour or two. "Now, I think we should all go up and see if we can get at least a little sleep," he said, and he stood up, pulling Loedicia from the sofa with him. "We're going to need all we can get if we intend to start searching for Liz again in the morning," and nodding in agreement, they all left the parlor and headed for the stairs.

Rebel and Beau always stayed in the room at the right at the top of the winding staircase that ascended from the huge foyer, when they were at the Château. The room across the hall from where their granddaughter was now, and as they lay in bed, weary and troubled, Beau turned onto his stomach and looked down at his wife, brushing a pale gold strand of hair back off her forehead. The lamp beside the bed was still lit and he studied her face. She looked so worn out.

"I wish I had all the answers, Reb," he said, her warm flesh soft against his dusky skin.

"The doctor has to be wrong, Beau," she said unhappily. "He just has to. Blythe's going to be all right. I know she is."

"And if she isn't?"

"Then life isn't fair."

"No one said it was." He frowned, moving into a different position so he could rest his head close to hers on the pillow. "I only wish we knew where Liz was and what was happening to her," he murmured softly, and felt Rebel tense.

"I've been trying not to think of that all evening," she answered, then sighed. "Oh, Beau, how are we going to get any rest, there's so much—"

"Shhh," he whispered huskily, then pulled her close, kissing her deeply before easing up just far enough to stretch his hand out and cup the chimney, then blow out the light. "I shouldn't have reminded you," he said. "Now, close your eyes and let me hold you, and don't think of anything else except that I love you." As she closed her eyes, cuddling close in his arms as he settled back on the pillow, she tried as hard as she could to think of everything else except the tragedy that had ended the day for them. A Fourth of July they'd never forget, while far out to sea, Lizette sat on the side of a bunk in a cabin aboard the *Piranha* and stared at Sancho de Córdoba, waiting for him to explain his actions.

For hours, ever since being dragged on board the ship back on the Broad River, Lizette had been waiting for some sort of explanation from this strange man, but all he'd say was, "Later, *señora*."

Well, it was later, and she wanted the answer. She'd been kept in a dark cabin all by herself up until a few minutes ago, wondering and crying and hitting her fists against the walls, door, hoping someone would hear and help, but no one did. He wouldn't even let her stand on deck when they sailed through the sound, but she was sure she'd heard the fireworks being shot off at the picnic grounds, or maybe it was just the thunder and lightning from the storm that had hit them earlier. If she'd been allowed to stay on deck, she'd have seen for herself.

Her eyes narrowed as she continued staring at the man who'd kidnapped her. She could see him well now in the light from the lamps that were lit in the cabin, and she knew now for sure that he was the same man who'd been in the priest's clothes earlier at the picnic. The one Felicia said had asked her friend Angie about Bain.

Only he wasn't wearing priest's clothes anymore. His coat was the remains of what looked like a fancy military uniform jacket, and he took it off, tossing it onto the chair by his desk. Beneath it he wore a faded dark red pullover shirt cut low in front to reveal a thick mass of curling hair the same ebony color of the hair on his head that was trimmed to touch his broad shoulders. His beard and mustache were so heavy they'd have hid his lips if his mouth weren't so generous, and a large scar near his right temple pulled the corner of his eye, giving it almost an Oriental slant. He stared down his aquiline nose at her, then straightened, one hand on the butt of his pistol in the holster on his right hip, the other on the hilt of his cutlass that was in the sheath at his left hip, and she realized he was not only a big man, but an exceptionally strong one. His looks were rather frightening in a weird way, and yet he was almost handsome. Maybe it was the eyes. They seemed to look right through her.

He took a deep breath. "You are quite a sight, *señora*," he said, surprising her, his mouth twisting into an amused grin.

"That, sir, is your fault," she reminded him crisply. "Now, what am I doing here?"

He studied her for a moment longer, his eyes moving from her mud-caked shoes and stockings to her disheveled dark hair that was curling riotously about her head. Somewhere along the way she'd lost that ridiculous straw hat she'd been wearing, he thought, then strolled over and turned one of the whale-oil lamps up brighter, before turning to face her again.

"Your husband told you of Barlovento, *señora?*" he asked.

"He said he stayed there for a short time two years ago after he'd been shipwrecked," she answered.

"*Sí.*" His eyes hardened. "Today there is no more Barlovento."

"And you blame him for that?"

"Your husband was the only one who knew of it."

"You can't be sure of that."

"You want facts, *señora?* I give you facts," he said as he stared down at her, his dark eyes intense. "Bain Kolter was at Galvez Island with Jean Lafitte, and he is no longer there. He was at Barlovento with my family. Barlovento is no longer there. What better proof?"

"That's ridiculous." She looked up at him stubbornly. "Bain wouldn't do something like that."

"He was a government agent!"

"He's an honorable man!"

"Ha! He is a bastard! Because of him *mi padre es muerto, y los otros de mi familia*—"

"I haven't the faintest idea what you're talking about," Lizette cut in abruptly. "Bain knows Spanish, I don't."

"Then I translate for you, *señora,*" Sancho said sarcastically. "Because of him, your husband, my father is dead and the rest of my family was almost killed. And I swore that if he ever betrayed us, I would make him suffer as we have suffered. *Comprende?* You understand?"

"That's why you kidnapped me? Because you think he betrayed you?"

"Because I know he betrayed us. I should never have let Elena talk me into letting him go."

"Elena?"

"*Sí, mi hermana.* My sister, *señora.* She swear Domino is good man and I listen. I not too good at your English, you understand, but she say he will never betray us. Bah! He should be dead man. First he break her heart, then try to kill her."

Lizette tensed, frowning as she caught the drift of what he was saying. "What do you mean he broke her heart?" she asked apprehensively.

"Just what I say. She was in love with him and told me he would stay but for you. That he cared for her."

"That's a lie!"

His eyebrows raised. "The honorable man is not so honorable anymore, eh?"

"I didn't say that."

"He told you about Elena?"

"A little." Lizette suddenly felt uncomfortable before Sancho's scrutiny. Bain had told her only that Elena and her aunt had helped nurse him back to health. "Evidently he didn't consider her worth talking about, that's all."

"Perhaps. Or maybe he decided what you don't know don't hurt you."

"What are you trying to say?"

"I say when Bain Kolter kiss my sister good-bye before boarding *La Piranha*, it was not the kiss of the innocent, *señora*. They were together many months, and much can happen when a man and woman are together for so long a time."

"Not Bain."

"Your husband is a saint, *señora?*"

Lizette flushed. "He may not be a saint, but he's not the devil you make him out to be."

"You don't believe me, ask my men, they tell you how it was between Elena and Domino." His eyes sparked knowingly. "A man does not have to sleep with a woman to love her, *señora*," he said.

"I know that."

His eyes hardened again. "Then don't tell me he did not break her heart."

Lizette was at a loss. Bain had told her very little about Elena, and now suddenly small shreds of doubt began to filter into her thoughts and she wished she could shove them aside, but couldn't.

"How old is Elena?" she asked hesitantly.

Sancho stared at her for a moment, seeing the doubt spring to her eyes.

"About your age. Twenty-one."

"She's pretty?"

"Ah, *sí*. To me. Perhaps to others, maybe. Like me, she has the dark eyes and hair, only she is small. My hands span her waist," and he pretended to hold something in his huge hands, the tips of his fingers touching. "She is like a little flower, *señora*, but do not worry, you shall meet her as soon as we reach St. Augustine."

Lizette didn't answer. She couldn't because as she thought

back over Bain's description of Elena, all she could remember him saying was that she was rather wild at times and often ran around barefoot, and that she and her aunt could both be rigid and unbending when it came to nursing him and they could be very obstinate if he crossed them or did anything he wasn't supposed to do. But he'd never even mentioned her age, or what she looked like, although he had mentioned her younger brother, Mario. Since Mario was in his early teens, Lizette had misguidedly assumed that Elena was younger too. More a child. It was hard to remember everything after so long a time, but this she did remember. Now suddenly she felt a hurt begin to gnaw at her breastbone. Bain had seemed so glad to see her that she hadn't even thought he might have left part of his heart behind.

She bit her lip, her jaw tightening, and glanced down at herself. No man's hands had been able to span her waist for years. It always seemed like there was way too much of her to even put into a dress right, and she was always bulging out of her bodices even though she tried hard not to eat too much. She ran a hand over her waist, then across the skirt of her dress, feeling the extra flesh on her thigh beneath the soft material and petticoats. She was anything but slim, and hadn't been for years. Not since she was sixteen. Bain had never seemed to mind, though. In fact he'd often comment on how luxuriously soft she felt and how exhilarating it was to make love to her, knowing every inch of her was his. Had he really meant it? Or was it just something he felt he had to accept now that he was stuck with her?

Lizette was staring at Sancho's hands as they finished spanning his sister's imaginary waist; then she watched him clench them deliberately, and he flexed his fists for a moment before turning and walking to the cabin window to stare out into the night.

"I have much to pay your husband back for, *señora*," he finally said, then turned again to face her. "Since he was not there, I start with you. When he comes for you, then I will end my vendetta. Meanwhile, your presence here will remind me of what I have lost and you will keep me from getting lonely."

Lizette's eyes narrowed as she stood up, his last remark sending fear back into her once again, as she suddenly remembered the name Bain told her Sancho de Córdoba was known by in the Caribbean. Sancho the Bloody!

"I'd rather die than let you touch me," she cried breathlessly.

Sancho laughed. "Ha. You think that's what I want? In the first place, I do not rape ladies, *señora*, only whores, and besides, you are too fat for my liking."

"Fat?" she gasped, her voice breaking. "Why, you arrogant pig!"

"Aha, you still have a fight in you, eh, *señora*? But do not worry, if you really want, my men are not as choosy, so I could turn you over to them."

"Don't you dare!"

"Then hold your tongue or I will forget that my father brought me up to respect ladies."

"I thought I was too fat," she snapped insolently.

His eyes swept over her arrogantly from head to toe, then locked on her face, their intensity frightening. "Perhaps I could get used to it," he remarked. "But for now I will send someone with a tub and some clothes so we can see what we have beneath all the mud and dirt. Then, *quién sabe*, who knows . . . ?" He turned abruptly and left the cabin, closing the door firmly behind him.

Lizette stared after him, not knowing quite what to do. She didn't want to cry, yet felt tears near the surface, and her legs suddenly felt weak. Slowly, unable to keep up the angry defense she'd been hiding behind, she once more sat down on the edge of the bunk and sighed, her eyes fixed on the jacket he'd tossed onto the chair, and she shivered, wondering what was going to happen next, how she was going to get out of this horrible mess, and praying that back at Port Royal, her daughter was all right, and maybe, just maybe, someone might be coming after her. A thought she was certain was only wishful thinking, but a thought that was going to have to become a part of her from here on if she was going to get through this.

With a strength she'd forgotten she ever had, Lizette slowly stood up again, walked over to the captain's desk, and started rummaging around in his things, hoping that perhaps she could find a knife, letter opener, anything she could use to defend herself with, because she had a strange foreboding that before all this was over, she was going to need a weapon of some kind.

Chapter 4

IT WAS SATURDAY, July 7. Bain stood next to the bed where
Blythe lay and stared down at his daughter, tears flooding
his eyes. Evening shadows were filtering into the room already, but he paid no attention as Pretty moved from her
chair at the girl's bedside, lit the lamp on the dresser, then
came back to the chair to resume her vigil. He had eyes only
for the small, pale child in the bed. Her platinum hair,
dampened from perspiration, was clinging to her forehead,
where a frown etched itself as she tried to sleep through the
pain.

Finally he drew his eyes from the still form, all wrapped
and bandaged, and turned to the black woman in the chair,
her quiet presence reassuring.

"You say the man who took Liz said he did it for
Barlovento?" he asked, making sure there'd been no mistake.

Pretty nodded. "Yes, Mista Bain. He yell that his name
was Sancho somethin', and he say to tell you he avenged
Barlovento."

Bain frowned, then rubbed a hand over the clipped beard
at his chin, his gray eyes taking on a faraway look. When
he'd arrived at the Château late this afternoon he'd never
dreamed he'd be facing anything even remotely like this.
He'd been riding hard for the past few days, anxious to
reach home, and so anxious to see Liz and the children he
hadn't even gone to Beaufort first, but had ridden down,
using the Coosaw ferry north of the island, then riding down
past Tonnerre and River Oaks, calling only a quick hello
with a wave to everyone he passed, not even bothering to
stop and talk. Now he knew why so many of them had tried
to delay him. They no doubt knew what had happened and

had wanted to find out how Blythe was and if he'd heard anything about Liz.

He cursed silently to himself as he remembered the stricken look on Grandma Dicia's face when he'd strolled into the parlor all smiles looking for Liz. There'd been no way she could ease the blow for him, and he was glad now that she was the one who'd told him. Somehow, maybe because of all she'd been through over the years, coming from her he'd been able to accept it without losing his mind completely.

That had been hours ago, though, and he still felt as if he was in a mild state of shock. The flickering lamplight fell on his hair, highlighting the russet waves and deepening it so it was almost as dark as his beard.

"I just wanted to make sure again, Pretty," he said softly, then glanced over at Blythe. "Do you want me to send someone else up to relieve you?"

"No, sir." Pretty looked over at Blythe, then reached up, wiping the damp hair from the girl's forehead. "I don't need any relief. I got my sewing and a cool drink." She eyed a tall glass on the stand beside the bed. " 'Sides, I can't leave her, she needs me."

"Thank you, Pretty," he said, and reached out.

She took his hand and he smiled as best he could while fighting back the tears.

"I'll be up again later," he said, then dropped Pretty's hand and turned, leaving the room so she wouldn't see him crying.

It was almost an hour later when Bain stood in the library with his father-in-law and Grandpa Roth, both men shaking their heads in unison.

"You don't even know where they went," Beau argued.

"And where would you start?" Roth added. "Besides, you have no ship. The *Raven* isn't due back for two months yet, and the *Sparrow* just left for Charleston last Saturday."

"Don't worry, I'll have a ship," Bain answered quickly. "If I ride fast, I can reach Charleston before the *Sparrow* leaves again, and as far as where to start . . . Barlovento's as good a place as any."

Beau's green eyes hardened. "Then let me go with you. And Heath too."

"No!" Bain was determined. "This is my fight, not yours."

"She's my daughter."

"And my wife."

"Be reasonable, Bain," Roth said anxiously. "What if you do find out where she is, how can you possibly cross swords with someone like de Córdoba? Even I know what a ruthless man he is. Why, his reputation's known all over. You wouldn't have a chance."

Bain straightened and stared at both men, knowing they were as concerned as he was, yet knowing he couldn't just sit doing nothing while Liz was out there with God knows what happening to her.

"Please, I have to do this myself," he said, the timbre in his voice deepening. "All I ask is that you both promise to watch over the twins while I'm gone, and if neither Liz nor I . . . if neither of us comes back, I want you to promise that you'll take care of them and see that they never forget that we both loved them very much. Will you do that for me?"

Roth frowned. "Then you're determined to go?"

"I have no other choice." He looked at Beau Dante. There were tears in his father-in-law's eyes, and he was reminded that this quiet man once rode the seas as a privateer. Did he understand? Could he? "If it were your wife, what would you do?" he asked, and saw Roth and Beau exchange glances.

"We'd do the same thing," Beau finally answered, remembering the past all too well. "You have my blessing, Bain. Bring her back to all of us, but please, be careful. I'm too old to raise the twins, and so is Roth. Besides, they need you and Liz."

"And for heaven's sake, let us be the ones to tell the women and Heath, otherwise you'll be another two days trying to convince them."

Bain exhaled, relieved, and the next morning, early, after saying a reluctant good-bye to Blythe and Braxton, praying they'd understand someday, and promising everyone else that somehow he'd try to keep in touch, Bain rode away from the Château on Amigo, heading north again, this time across the swamps toward Charleston, where he hoped to catch the *Sparrow* before it sailed for Europe with its usual cargo of trade goods.

It was early Monday afternoon, hot and humid, when Bain rode into Charleston and reined Amigo through the crowded streets, heading straight toward the wharf where he knew the *Sparrow* was docked. The harbor was always full of ships, and today was no exception. Bain had had three ships when the war ended, the *Dragonfly*, the *Raven*, and the *Sparrow*, and all three had been used to run the British blockades at one time. Built for speed and well-armed, all three ships had been able to outrun almost anything afloat, but unfortunately the *Dragonfly* had been the ship Bain had been using when they'd been shipwrecked off the coast of Barlovento, and it was no more.

Although Bain had liked all three ships, his favorite had been the *Dragonfly*, and now as he rode along the wharf, looking for the *Sparrow*, he felt a sense of loss at not being able to have the *Dragonfly*'s decks beneath his feet again. Ah well, he'd learned long ago that life was unpredictable.

He straightened in the saddle, smoothing the long tail of his dark green frock coat, then set his beaver hat at a better angle to keep the sun from his eyes before taking a handkerchief out and flicking some of the dust from his face. The weather was sweltering here in Charleston, much worse than it had been on the road, the smell of the waterfront, with its pungent odors, making his nose twitch. His eyes scanned each ship as he rode along; then suddenly their gray depths deepened as he caught sight of the *Sparrow*.

She was moored between two other merchant ships, her crew busily trying to get cargo on board, and Bain dug Amigo in the ribs, urging him a little faster; then he reined up and dismounted, fastening him to a hitching post near one of the buildings along the waterfront.

Bain stood looking around, taking in all the activity, then moved aside abruptly for some men pulling a cart with crates on it toward one of the ships. When they were out of the way, he hurried toward the *Sparrow*'s gangplank, meeting one of the crew who was on his way down it.

"Afternoon, Waggs," he said, surprising the sailor, who stopped abruptly halfway down the gangplank to stare at him.

"Mr. Kolter?"

"I haven't changed that much, have I?" Bain asked. It had been almost a year since he'd seen the crew of the *Sparrow*.

The sailor flushed. "It isn't that, sir," he answered. "I just didn't expect to see you here. When we left Beaufort the other day, they said they were expecting you there."

"Where's Eric?" Bain asked.

Waggs was sturdy and square-jawed, about an inch shorter

than Bain, with light brown hair that waved slightly over his ears and a crooked nose that had obviously been broken more than once, and the clothes he wore, black boots, full-sleeved shirt, and baggy pants with a wide buckled belt at the waist, were the usual nondescript clothes worn aboard ship. He nodded behind him, his pale blue eyes rolling back toward the ship.

"He's in his cabin."

Bain thanked him, then moved in, and the sailor stood for some time watching him, a frown on his face as he wondered why the devil Bain Kolter had turned up in Charleston.

Captain Eric Edelman was at his desk going over some bills of lading for the cargo that was being put on board when Bain reached the main cabin, and the owner of the *Sparrow* stood in the doorway with his hat in his hand for some time scrutinizing him.

Eric was tall, lean, and in his mid-thirties, with blond hair made lighter by the summer sun, and it fell onto his forehead over a pair of deep-set bright blue eyes. The cabin door was open, only he was so engrossed in what he was doing that he didn't hear Bain until he spoke.

"How long will it take you to unload the paying cargo?" Bain asked.

Eric looked up, startled. "What the devil are you doing here?" he asked incredulously.

Bain's eyes, usually friendly and smiling, mirrored the sadness and anxiety he was feeling.

"We're not taking this cargo, Eric," he said as he stepped inside. "My wife's been kidnapped and I need the *Sparrow* to go after her."

Eric was still staring at Bain, a scowl creasing his forehead. They'd been friends since before the war back in 1812, and Eric had been glad to see Bain finally settle down.

"When?" he asked simply.

"I had to go to Pittsburgh. When I got back, she was gone."

"You know where she is?"

"Not exactly." Bain told him what had happened while Eric listened intently.

"How do you plan to handle it?" Eric asked when Bain had finished.

"That's just the trouble," Bain answered. "Right now I don't know what to do except start at the beginning, and that means sailing to Barlovento. Since the *Raven*'s halfway across the Atlantic by now, that leaves only the *Sparrow*."

"You want to captain her?" Eric asked, and stood up.

"Not this time." Bain frowned. "At least not right now. I doubt I'd be much help to the crew, in the state I'm in." He tossed his hat onto the bunk where Eric slept. "Like I asked before, how long will it take to unload her?"

"How soon do you want to leave?"

"As soon as we can."

Eric nodded. "Then grab your hat again and let's go see what we can do. If the men aren't too far along, we might be able to leave by tomorrow morning."

Bain reached over, grabbed his hat off the bunk where he'd thrown it, and the two men left the cabin, heading toward the hold.

Early the next morning, with a fair breeze catching its sails, the *Sparrow,* riding high in the water without its usual cargo, slipped its moorings and sailed out of the harbor at Charleston, South Carolina, heading down the coast for the southern tip of the Florida territories.

It was hot, only a slight breeze blowing a few days later as the *Sparrow* sailed cautiously through the keys, then rounded the tip of Florida before heading further inland, with the island of Barlovento dead ahead.

Bain stood at the rail. He was wearing a white shirt with buff pants and Wellington boots, but the shirt was open to his waist and the sleeves rolled up in the heat. The sun glinted off his russet hair as he squinted, one hand over his eyes, trying to see the outline of the island.

"Want my spyglass?" Eric asked, stepping up behind him.

Bain looked back at the *Sparrow*'s captain, then took the long cylindrical spyglass from his outstretched hand.

"That would help, wouldn't it!" he said, then put it to his eye to get a better look, but what he saw, he didn't like.

"How close can we get?" Eric asked from beside him now.

"Tell the helmsman that I want to come in at the northern end of the island, and we'll have to drop anchor at least five to six hundred feet out, then take a longboat in."

"Right," Eric answered, and turned, heading toward the wheel, while Bain continued scanning the island. Suddenly the spyglass stopped when he saw movement as the ship sailed in closer, and he steadied the spyglass, trying to see better. As he strained his eyes, he saw an Indian scurry from one of the burned-out buildings and head farther inland, where he was met by two more, their colorful clothes familiar to him, and he watched them disappear again into some brush beyond the buildings. Only he knew they'd be gone by the time the anchor was dropped. Sancho's young brother Mario had been friends with the swamp Indians, and it was obvious they had probably taken over the island now with the de Córdobas gone, disappearing into the swamps again as they always did when confronted with strangers.

He lowered the spyglass and stood waiting, watching quietly as the helmsman brought the sleek ship in and she dropped anchor; then he joined Eric and some of the men as the longboat was put over the side and they rowed in to shore.

"Is it what you expected?" Eric asked a few minutes later as he and Bain left the men waiting with the longboat and made their way up from the beach to the edge of the sand where it met the flagstone path that led to what once had been a house with a veranda.

"It's worse than I thought," Bain answered, and Eric glanced over at him.

Bain had smiled little on the whole trip down, and his mind was often miles away, as it was now. No one could blame him, though, with his daughter lying in a sickbed back in Port Royal and his wife God knows where. Eric wished somehow he could help ease the man's pain, but even an old friend wasn't much help at a time like this.

"There used to be a beautiful house up there," Bain announced suddenly as he stopped halfway up the flagstone walk. "With stables off there." He pointed toward some rubble some yards to the right. "Farther inland is a road, with fields where they grew their own food. Beyond is the swamp."

"You think the authorities did this?" Eric asked as he glanced toward the ruins of the house, now overgrown with plants and vegetation.

"Who else?" Bain straightened stubbornly. "I had to make sure." He turned to Eric. "He thinks I told them," he said, frowning, then headed toward what had once been the stables, where he'd caught sight of a crude cross sticking out of the ground. New grass had crept up over a mound of earth where he knew there'd been a garden before, and Bain noticed it right away.

Eric followed close behind and watched as Bain reached the plot of ground, then bent down, reading some crude writing carved into the wooden cross.

"Luis de Córdoba, Sancho's father," Bain said as he stood back up; then he began looking around again. There was another mound of dirt that looked like perhaps more than one grave, but no more crosses, and he frowned. "Elena and the boy must not have been killed," he said after a few minutes of searching, and he sighed. "At least that might give us another place to start."

"What's that?"

"If I can figure out where she and the boy might be, there's just a chance they might know where de Córdoba spends his time when he wants to hole up."

"You think she'd tell you?"

Bain glanced at him sharply. "What's that supposed to mean?"

"I just meant, she wouldn't betray her brother, would she?"

Bain's eyes hardened. "Given the right incentive, she might. I'll do almost anything to get Liz back."

Eric watched the hard gleam in Bain's eyes. "Let's hope it won't come to that, Bain, because I don't think Liz'd understand, do you?"

"Don't be a fool," Bain shot back irritably. "That's one thing I won't do, Eric, and you know it. So does she, but finding Elena's the only answer I have right now." He stood for some time gazing off toward the swamps, then walked about the place, the remembrance of how vitally beautiful it had once been haunting him like a bad dream.

Eric followed behind, watching as Bain moved from one place to the next; then Bain stood behind what had once been the house and stared off down the road that ran the length of the island. The trees were hung with Spanish moss shading the road from the sun, and once more he was reminded of the Château. Suddenly he turned, his eyes alert.

"St. Augustine," he murmured half under his breath, and Eric looked bewildered.

"You think she'd be there?"

"Sancho's father once had friends there. One family moved

back to Spain when we took over, but there may be others.
And if she's not there, they may know where the de Córdobas
were from in Spain. At least we could try. It's better than
just going back home and doing nothing."

"Then it's St. Augustine?" Eric asked.

Bain nodded, and they headed back toward the longboat,
where the men waited to row them back to the ship. Before
climbing in, Bain turned back, taking one last look and
hoping that when and if he did manage to track down de
Córdoba, he'd be able to convince the man that this had
been none of his doing, yet he knew it was going to take some
talking.

A little over three days later, shortly before dark, with the
sails still dripping from a storm that had accompanied them
part of the way, the *Sparrow* sailed into the harbor at St.
Augustine and dropped anchor. Bain had brought Amigo
aboard when they'd left Charleston, and now, after putting
the animal ashore, he set out to see if he could find out
where the de Vacas had once lived. He'd remembered that
the de Vacas had visited Barlovento when he'd been there,
and they'd been from St. Augustine. And he also remembered talking to Señor de Vaca about the home he'd left
behind in St. Augustine. Strange now how things seemed to
pop back into his memory from time to time. The Plaza de
la Constitución, and St. George Street, as well as the Matanzas River. And it was here, not far from the river, that he
had mentioned their hacienda stood, with an iron gate,
between two stone columns, a wrought-iron V decorating
the gate. He had no trouble finding the place at all.

However, all Bain learned from the present tenants was
the name of the family who lived at the next hacienda
downriver, and the fact that they had lived there for a
number of years. Well, it was worth a try, and a short while
later, with purple shadows quickly turning his surroundings
into only vague outlines as he moved along, he rode Amigo
up the drive of a low stucco house close to the river's edge,
the trees surrounding it hung heavy with Spanish moss that
still held some of the cool rain and formed mists as the warm
night air swirled around it.

At first he thought the place was deserted, but as he
neared the house, a dog barked and he saw the flicker of
lights beyond some flowering bushes. Reining Amigo to a
halt, he dismounted, tied him to the hitch rail near the steps,

and strolled up the walk to the door, studying the place closely. It wasn't as ostentatious as the de Vacas' hacienda, but neither was it the home of poor peasants, and he was even more certain of it when the door was opened by a young woman who was undoubtedly a servant.

"Good evening, is Señora Martínez in?" he asked in English, his hat in his hand.

The young Spanish woman stared at him curiously. She wore a simple yellow blouse with a full skirt and her feet were bare, reminding him of the last time he'd seen Elena.

"You are expected?" she asked in faltering English, and Bain tried to be more friendly.

"I'm afraid not," he answered, in Spanish this time, and the girl looked relieved. "But I'd like to talk to the *señora* if I may. It's quite important."

"Your name?"

"Kolter, Bain Kolter."

The girl nodded. "You wait here," she said, and closed the door, making him wait outside. She wasn't gone long, however, and a few minutes later Bain was ushered into the presence of a formidable lady who appeared to be in her early forties.

"You wished to see me?" she asked from where she was seated as Bain was ushered into what had to be the parlor, the carved furniture with its plush cushions aglow from the light of a number of wall sconces arranged about the room.

"I thank you for seeing me," he said in Spanish, trying his best to be friendly. "Your neighbor to the north said you'd been here a number of years, and lived here when the de Vacas were in residence. Is that true, *señora?*"

Her eyes brightened. "Ah, *sí*, Don Hernando de Vaca is my brother, *señor*."

Bain's eyes must have given away his surprise.

"Did I say something you did not know, *senor?*" she asked.

"I didn't know he was your brother," Bain replied, still surprised, yet pleased. "Then do you also know the de Córdobas?" he asked, and suddenly wished he hadn't jumped right into the problem feetfirst, as he saw the hesitation in her eyes.

"You know the de Córdobas?" she asked warily, her fat fingers clenching the carved arm of the chair she was sitting in.

There wasn't much he could do except admit it, and he was just about to tell Señora Martínez the whole story, when he turned at a noise in the doorway behind him and found himself staring straight into the eyes of Isabella de Córdoba, whose first instinct was to run, but who was rooted to the spot.

"Domino!" she gasped, her face turning white, and she looked like she was going to swoon.

Bain hurried to her side, grabbed her arm, and began ushering her into the room, hoping the shock of seeing him hadn't been too much for her.

"What . . . how did you find this place?" she asked, her voice unsteady as she leaned back in the chair he'd helped her reach, and Bain straightened, gazing down at her.

"Are you all right, Tía Isabella?" he asked.

"*Sí* . . . *sí,*" she murmured, waving away his concern. "But you . . . how . . . ?"

"I have a good memory," Bain answered, and Isabella covered her mouth as if holding it so she wouldn't say any more as she just stared at him.

"Well, this is strange," Señora Martínez said as she studied the two of them; then she addressed Bain. "Since it seems you do know the de Córdobas, what is it you want of them?" she asked. "After all, Isabella is my guest . . . if you mean them any harm . . ."

"Where's Sancho?" Bain asked Isabella, ignoring the other woman, but Isabella shook her head.

"I don't know."

"Elena's here with you?"

"No."

He studied her thoughtfully. "But she was?"

"You betrayed her, Domino," Isabella blurted, composing herself somewhat, although her face was still pale, and Bain could see she'd lost weight.

"I never betrayed Sancho, Luis, or any of you," he answered. "I made a promise, Tía Isabella. A promise to all of you. No, if you were found out, it was none of my doing."

Isabella de Córdoba stared up into Bain's eyes, her own wary, unsettled. "But you were the only one."

"Was I? What of the others who'd survived being wrecked on Barlovento? What of them?"

"What on earth are you both *talking* about?" Señora

Martínez asked, interrupting, and as they both remembered she was there, Isabella flushed.

"Do you mind if I talk to Señor Kolter alone, Margarita?" Isabella asked.

Her hostess frowned. "You will be all right?"

"*Sí*, I'll be all right," Isabella assured her. "But this is a family affair."

Margarita Martínez stared at the two of them for a moment, then stood up, straightening the skirt of her dress, and moved gracefully to the door, then turned back.

"If you need me, Isabella, just pull the bell cord," she said, but Isabella assured her again that there was no need to worry.

Once Señora Martínez was gone, Sancho's aunt turned to Bain again, and her face grew somber.

"How do I know you tell the truth, Domino?" she said bitterly as she brushed a gray hair from her cheek to join the others at the nape of her neck.

He knelt down in front of the elderly woman. She'd not only helped Elena nurse him when he'd been hurt after the shipwreck, but they'd spent a good deal of time talking and getting to know each other long before Bain had ever regained his memory.

"Tía Isabella, remember when we used to sit and talk, and you asked me once why I didn't return Elena's love?" he asked.

She nodded. "*Sí.*"

"Do you remember what I said?"

"You said that deep down somewhere inside, you had a strange feeling that your love was already taken, that the promises had already been given, and you couldn't break those promises because you also knew you were a man who kept promises."

"And that was before I even knew who I really was." He took her hands in his, his gray eyes pleading with her. "I gave my promise to Luis, to you, to Elena, and to Sancho that I'd never tell anyone about Barlovento, Tía Isabella, and I didn't . . . believe me, I didn't. Not after what all of you did for me. But now Sancho has my wife, and my daughter is lying in bed back in South Carolina, and may never walk again. . . . Tía Isabella, where's Sancho?"

She shook her head, tears glistening in her eyes, and her

face grew tense, flickering light from the wall sconces shading it, while deepening the hollows in her cheeks.

"I don't know," she answered softly. "He never tells me where he goes."

"Elena?" he asked anxiously.

"Elena is gone too. Sancho came for her a few days ago, and she and Mario went with him."

Bain exhaled angrily. If he'd only known, he could have stopped here first and been waiting.

"He had my wife with him?" Bain asked.

"No, not when he came here to the house, but she may have been on the ship. He didn't say. He sailed up the Matanzas River rather than dock right at St. Augustine, but he said nothing about having your wife, only that you hadn't been at Beaufort." She frowned. "Why would he take your wife, Domino? His quarrel is with you, not her."

"Because Sancho is Sancho." Bain stood up and began to pace the floor for a few minutes, then stopped again to face Luiz de Córdoba's sister. "Was Elena planning to become a pirate too?" he asked, surprising her.

Isabella's eyes widened. "*Madre de Dios, no!* But no, *señor.* Not my Elena, nor Mario either. Never!"

"Then why did they leave with Sancho?"

"He said he was taking them to Cuba, where their uncle is with the Spanish government."

"Their uncle?"

"Luis' dead wife's brother. Sancho was named after him. His real name is Emilio Sancho, but we've always called him Sancho. His uncle is Don Emilio Pérez. He owns land in Cuba, near Havana somewhere."

"I see," Bain said thoughtfully, then made his decision. "Thank you, Tía Isabella," he said, kneeling down once more to hold the woman's hands. Then he frowned. "You were there when the authorities came?" he asked.

"*Sí.*" She nodded and tears filled her eyes. "It was horrible, Domino. If it weren't for Mario and Elena, I too would be with Luis right now, but they know the swamp, and we waited at the cove for *La Piranha.*"

"Then that should prove to you that I'm innocent, Tía Isabella. If I had told, do you think I would have forgotten to tell them about the cove? After all, it was really Sancho they were out to stop."

"I have thought of that many times, and so had Elena, but Sancho was so sure."

"And now he has my wife."

"He won't hurt her, Domino." She squeezed his hands affectionately. "He is cruel, yes, and would just as soon kill a man as look at him if he's been crossed, but he was brought up a gentleman when it comes to women. Surely some of his breeding in the days before he turned to piracy has stayed with him. For all he's done, he's still my nephew, *señor*."

"And his men?"

"Of them I cannot say, all I can do is pray."

"Then keep praying, Tía Isabella," Bain urged her, and his jaw tightened savagely. "Because if anything happens to my Liz, I won't rest until I too have wreaked my vengeance." He lifted her hands to his lips and kissed them affectionately. "Now, I must go, but I thank you, Tía Isabella, for believing me, and I only hope that you're right as far as Sancho is concerned, and that this whole mess can be cleared up without any bloodshed or any more injury to anyone, but I have my doubts. One victim is one too many already." He stood up.

"You say your daughter is crippled? Sancho would not cripple a child, Domino."

"He chased the carriage my wife and daughter were in and it crashed."

"I will pray for her then, and for Sancho and you too, *señor*."

Bain stared at her for a moment. She looked tired and worn. "Perhaps you should also go to Cuba," he said after a moment of silence.

A faint smile crossed her lips, and her eyes softened. "There's no need now," she answered softly. "Consuelo de Vaca passed away shortly after she and Hernando returned to Spain, and now that his year of mourning is up, he's on his way to get me. The years have been many, *señor*, but now we will finally be together, the way we should have been years ago."

Bain took a deep breath, remembering the way Tía Isabella and Don Hernando de Vaca had reacted toward each other during the de Vacas' visit at the hacienda, and his eyes steadied on hers. "Then I wish you well. Now I must say good-bye, and again, thank you for your help."

Isabella reached for the bell cord.

"No need, I can let myself out," he said quickly, and headed for the door, but Isabella had already pulled the cord and he met Margarita in the doorway.

"*Señora,*" he said, nodding to her. "*Buenas noches,*" and before she even had time to answer, he was in the foyer opening the door, then closed it deftly behind him after stepping outside.

"Well!" Margarita said as she joined her houseguest. "Now, what was that all about, Isabella?"

Isabella looked over at her friend, the woman who'd soon be her sister-in-law, and she frowned.

"I'm not really sure, Margarita," she murmured softly. "I only hope and pray now that I did the right thing," and as the room suddenly grew quiet, the only sound was that of hoofbeats echoing through the open window as Bain rode hurriedly into the warm night, heading back toward the heart of St. Augustine, where the captain and crew of the *Sparrow* waited for his return.

Lizette, dressed in men's breeches and an old shirt, with a strip of rag tied around her hair to hold it back, stood on the deck of the *Piranha,* staring off toward the morning sunrise on the horizon. It had been four days since she'd been kidnapped, and anger still smoldered inside her. Not only anger at being here, but anger at not knowing what might have happened to Blythe. The poor baby had looked so still just lying there on the ground, and at least once a night Lizette had nightmares about it, waking up in a cold sweat. If only Sancho had waited until she knew whether Blythe was all right or not before just dragging her off like that. And to make matters even worse, there wasn't a day went by that the constant rolling of the ship hadn't played havoc with her stomach. Ordinarily the sea never bothered her, but for some reason, this pregnancy was different and these few days they'd been at sea, she'd lost not only her breakfast but also her other meals. Yesterday was the first time she'd kept anything down, and even that had been a fight.

Now, to top it all off, Jigger had told her this morning that the night before, while she'd been asleep, the ship had slipped into shore between Anastasia Island and the mainland along the Florida coast and Sancho had brought his sister and young brother on board. She hadn't seen either of them yet, and certainly wasn't in any hurry to. Especially after the things Sancho had been insinuating about his sister and Bain.

Lizette frowned. She hadn't said anything to Sancho about being pregnant and had let him think she'd been suffering strictly from seasickness, and she was glad now that it had seemed to lessen. It wasn't that he wasn't treating her all right because, surprisingly, he was, and she couldn't figure that out either. He just didn't seem the type to care much about a woman's virtue. Yet, true to his word, he hadn't touched her, even that first night when he'd walked into the cabin while she was still in the tub trying to scrub off the grime and dirt. All he'd done was watch her for a few minutes rather curiously, then take her filthy dress and other things, explaining that he'd see if they could be cleaned. Then he'd left, leaving behind the clothes she was wearing now, and she'd assumed he'd relegated her dress, shoes, stockings, and other things to the deep long ago, since she hadn't seen them since.

Gazing down at her unkempt clothes, she felt a growing weariness, then suddenly glanced up as she saw a woman appear from belowdecks, followed closely by a young dark-haired man who, even without a beard, bore a striking resemblance to her captor, who was following close on their heels.

Her first instinct was to turn and look away, but as Grandma Dicia would say, that never solved anything, you had to face life head-on, so instead she straightened, brushing some dark curls back off her forehead as her green eyes settled on the woman Sancho was ushering toward her.

The morning sun was full on the woman now, and Lizette, knowing it had to be Elena, wished with all her might that circumstances could be different, knowing at the moment that her disheveled frumpy appearance was in such contrast to the other woman's femininity. Sancho's sister was wearing a dress of deep burgundy gauze with huge puff sleeves. Matching velvet ribbons trimmed the bodice, a wide velvet sash tied the waist, and Elena's dark hair, twisted into a fat braid, was coiled at the nape of her neck, emphasizing her slim figure. As Elena walked toward her, for a moment Lizette just couldn't equate this lovely, poised woman with the young barefoot girl Bain had told her about. But then she had to remember, that was two years ago. Still . . .

Elena had really been upset when Sancho told her what he'd done at Port Royal Island, yet her relief in knowing Bain was still alive overshadowed her anger, and now she was about to meet Señora Kolter face-to-face. The thought was frightening in a way. Lizette Kolter had been watching the sunrise and it was behind her now as they walked toward her, and all Elena could see was her silhouette. Then, as they drew nearer, a twinge of resentment began to worm its way into Elena's heart as the dark apparition before them moved sideways just enough so the daylight threw her into relief, and Elena found herself looking directly into Señora Kolter's face.

Lizette Kolter, in spite of the sailor's cast-off clothes, was beautiful. Elena's own hair was dark, yet Lizette's looked even darker, with an iridescent blue-black cast to it, and it was curling haphazardly in the morning breeze as it tried to escape the strip of frayed cloth tied around it, while her large green eyes, the color of the sea when it was clear and flecked with foam, stared at them defiantly. And although the clothes Lizette was wearing were tight, revealing the fact that she was far from being thin, they also revealed the fact that the extra pounds only seemed to make her look more voluptuous and sensual, and Elena suddenly felt very inadequate as a woman.

"Señora Kolter," Sancho said, smiling. "I would like you to meet my family." His smile faded. "The ones who survived Barlovento, that is."

Lizette's eyes were still on Elena, who, she realized, was staring back at her rather intensely, her eyes cold and aloof.

Sancho went on. "My sister, Elena, and my brother, Mario," he said, gesturing to them, and both nodded. "Elena, Mario, Señora Lizette Kolter."

"How do you do," Elena said, her accent heavy, and Mario echoed the words. "I am sorry, I don't speak English too well," Elena went on when Mario had finished greeting Lizette. "But Sancho say you no speak Spanish, *si?*"

Lizette flushed. "Sancho's right." She looked from one to the other. "I can't really say I'm glad to meet you, now, can I?" she said sarcastically. "Since I don't really want to be here. But I guess I can say hello."

Elena frowned. "I have talked to Sancho about your . . . what you say . . . predicament, but he feel it is necessary."

"He would." Lizette glared at Sancho. His eyes mocked

her, amused. "Your brother seems to think a lot of things are necessary," she said bitterly. "As far as I'm concerned, he can go to hell."

Elena's eyes narrowed and she looked over at Sancho, expecting retaliation for the insult, but instead saw only amusement on his face.

"I imagine he will end up there eventually, *señora,*" she said as she looked once more at Lizette, and for some reason, the resentment she'd been feeling at the first sight of this woman suddenly began to become more than just resentment. She was suddenly so overwhelmingly jealous of Lizette Kolter that she wished she could scratch her eyes out. This was the woman Bain preferred over her, the woman he'd refused to betray even though Elena knew he'd have enjoyed every moment with her, and slowly she began to hate Lizette Kolter. She stared into Lizette's face, trying to see what Bain saw in her. Why was this woman so special to him? "Tell me, *señora,*" she continued, her eyes studying Lizette coldly. "Sancho say that you have told him Domino did not . . . how you say . . . betray us? How do you know this?"

"Because I know my husband."

"But how well?" Elena ran her hand back over her hair to the braid at the back of her neck; then her fingers began to toy with the fancy earring dangling from her pierced ear.

"As well as any woman knows her husband, *señorita,*" Lizette countered arrogantly. "It is *'señorita,'* right? That is what they call a woman who's not married, isn't it? And you aren't married, are you?"

"*Sí.*" Elena suddenly smiled, her eyes gleaming wickedly. Aha, so Sancho was right, she thought, and Bain had not told his wife all there was to tell about his stay at Barlovento. Her smile broadened. "Does it worry you I am not married, *señora?*" she asked impishly.

Lizette shrugged, trying to be nonchalant. "Why should it?"

"No reason, I guess. It is only that I thought Domino would have told you all about me, but then perhaps you would not have understood."

"Will you quit calling him Domino," Lizette said irritably. "His name's Bain. When you call him Domino it's as if you're talking about a different person."

"Perhaps we are," Elena answered. "But then you see, he will always be Domino to me."

"Even though your brother wants to kill him?"

"I have tried to tell Sancho he is wrong." Elena glanced at Sancho again, suddenly realizing he was enjoying watching her and Lizette size each other up, and she straightened angrily. "I have told him that Domino would never do anything to hurt me . . . that he would keep his promise to me, but I am afraid my brother is not ruled by his heart, *señora,* only by logic." She turned once more to Lizette, then looked past her to the horizon as she walked to the ship's rail and looked out over the sea. "So you see, all I can do is hope I am right and he is wrong, and that Domino does not discover where Sancho is taking you, although I do not think he will just accept your disappearance and do nothing. No, *señora,* I do not want my brother to kill him. I think Sancho has made the mistake, and perhaps someday we will find out I am right, *quién sabe?*"

Suddenly she turned and said something to her brother in Spanish that Lizette couldn't understand, then walked away, heading toward the other side of the ship, calling to her brother Mario, also in Spanish, and he followed her, his long lanky body looking awkward as he limped along.

"His leg still bother him from the shelling," Sancho explained when he saw Lizette's eyes following Mario.

"How old is he?" Lizette asked.

"Fifteen."

"He's going to be as tall as you someday."

"*Sí.*" Sancho smiled. "Only not as handsome, you think?"

"Conceited ass, aren't you?" Lizette shot back. Then, "What did she say to you?" she asked abruptly.

"Just now?"

"No, last week. Certainly just now."

"I think you would rather not know, *señora,*" he answered, and his eyes darkened, the warmth gone from them. "As I tell you, she and your husband . . . it was not innocent, believe me."

"Damn you!" Lizette had never felt so frustrated in her life. At least not this kind of frustration, because this time there was no one to turn to. No one to share the anger and bitterness with. Two years ago when the world had thought Bain had become a pirate, and she knew he hadn't, she'd had Stuart to turn to. Stuart to help gentle her anger and soothe her when the going got rough. Now there was no one. No one to say: They're wrong, Lizette, they're lying, Lizette. Bain would never betray you ever, no matter what. She stared hard at Sancho de Córdoba. "Your sister and brother are joining your crew?" she asked, her eyes snapping.

"No," he answered, watching her curiously, as if knowing what she was thinking. "I am taking them to my uncle in Cuba. This life is not for them."

"I see."

"No, you do not see. For me I do not mind," he said, trying to explain. "It is what I want, but for them, Elena is a lady, and perhaps she will meet someone there who will make her forget her Domino. As for Mario, there are universities in Havana, maybe someday he will become the man I never could be, who knows?" His eyes caught hers and held. "They will be with us only until we reach Cuba, *señora*, and until then, because of Elena I will tolerate your insolence. After that you will learn what it is to truly be the prisoner of Sancho de Córdoba." As he said it, Lizette could almost feel the violence behind those eyes, and she shivered. "In the meantime, *mi querida*, I suggest you enjoy the trip," and he turned, walking away, leaving her standing by the ship's rail, staring after him, and she knew as she felt her stomach churn that she was going to be sick again.

Chapter 5

AS THE DAYS went by, Lizette tried to avoid Elena de Córdoba as much as possible, only it wasn't always easy. Sancho insisted they all eat together in his cabin every evening; then afterward he'd excuse his sister and Mario, letting them sleep in their own cabins while making Lizette stay in his cabin all night. It was an arrangement she detested but could do nothing about.

Before Elena's and Mario's arrival aboard, Lizette didn't really mind so much because although he made her sleep on the floor, she was afraid of the rest of the crew and knew in his cabin she'd be safe. But now, every morning when she finally came up on deck, Elena would give her the strangest looks. Right from the start Lizette knew what the other woman was thinking, and her heart sank, yet there was no way she could talk Sancho into letting her sleep somewhere else.

"Don't be ridiculous," he said the first night Elena was aboard and they were getting ready to go to sleep.

Lizette was over near his desk, lying on the floor with a blanket under her and another wrapped around her. Even though she slept in her clothes, she felt more secure beneath an extra blanket, and she watched him standing, ready to blow out the last light before climbing into his bunk, bare-chested, barefoot, and wearing only his breeches.

"Let her think anything she wants," he went on. "Who cares?"

"I care!" Lizette yelled.

"Why? Why should you care what my sister thinks?" he asked, wiping a hand across his beard, which was losing its trimness now that it wasn't being clipped regularly.

"Because she thinks I'm sleeping with you, and she's in love with my husband."

"Aha! So you finally admit there was something between them."

She raised up on her elbows. "I said she's in love with him, not that he's in love with her."

"And you think she cares whether you give yourself to me or not?"

"I don't want her thinking that. Please, Sancho. Let me sleep somewhere else. It wouldn't hurt."

"You stay here," he said roughly, his eyes suddenly unyielding. "What she thinks is her business, what I do is mine."

"You bastard!"

He smiled, his eyes blazing as he stared at her for a moment; then he reached over and blew out the light. *"Buenas noches, señora,"* he said abruptly, and Lizette heard the creaking and muttered sounds as he climbed into the bunk; then she shoved her head down on the pillow, moved into a better position on the dirty cabin floor, and tried again to get some sleep, hoping and praying as she did every night that there'd be no more nightmares.

The next couple of days went along quite well, although Lizette cringed every morning at the look on Elena's face when she'd appear on deck. Then one morning a strange thing happened. Sancho surprised Lizette by bringing her dress, shoes, stockings, and underthings in, all cleaned and ready for her to put on, then ordered her to take a bath.

"In what?" Lizette asked.

"In the tub Jigger will bring down," he answered, and sure enough, within the hour she was bathed, her hair washed, and was once more wearing the lavender dress she'd been wearing when Sancho kidnapped her, with the kid shoes on her feet. Only she left off the stockings since the weather had gotten so warm.

She had to admit she felt somewhat better, even though all of the mud stains hadn't come out of the dress. They were mostly near the hem of the skirt, however, and she tried not to notice them. Nor had the dress been pressed. Only she wasn't about to complain. It was better than what she'd been wearing, and she wondered which of the seamen had gotten the task of washing everything for her. The thought was amusing, because Sancho's men were all as cruel and vicious as he was, and she smiled to think that one of them had been forced to do a lady's wash. Especially the camisole and drawers.

She was just ready to go up on deck and tell Jigger to have someone remove the tub of water when the door suddenly opened and Elena strolled in.

"There is rain today," she said in her broken English, and Lizette stared at her for a minute, then frowned.

"Is it raining hard?"

"*Sí.*" Elena's eyes mocked her. "You do know that *sí* means 'yes,' do you not?" she asked.

Lizette tensed. "I know what it means."

The ship rolled a little harder than usual and they watched as the water in the tub slopped over the side, spilling onto the floor.

"I'd better go tell Jigger to get the tub," Lizette said.

"You do that," Elena agreed, and Lizette glanced at her curiously, then left the cabin, running into Jigger in the passageway just outside.

"I'll send someone down to get it right away," he said when she told him what she wanted, and she returned to the cabin to find Elena standing with her back to the door, one hand holding back the curtain as she stared out the cabin window at the sea that was whitecapping now.

Elena's dark hair was loose today and reached to her waist, held back on each side by tortoiseshell combs, and she was wearing the same dress she'd had on the first time Lizette met her. While they were talking one evening, Sancho had remarked that his sister had lost all her clothes during the attack on Barlovento, and the few she had now, a dark blue cambric, gold silk, and the burgundy she was wearing, had been gifts from the family friends where she and Mario had been staying before joining him again on board ship.

This was the second time Elena had worn the burgundy, and for some reason Lizette felt intimidated by her appearance in it. Maybe because she'd formed her first impressions of the woman while Elena was wearing it. Impressions she hadn't liked.

Lizette avoided the tub, skirting it as she moved over and sat on the captain's bunk, her legs curled up beneath her, a position she'd assumed a great deal during the voyage so far, only she'd been wearing the sailor's clothes before, and she settled the dress about her, tucking it in against her legs.

Elena turned, then stood quietly studying Lizette. "You look at home in my brother's bed," she said after a few moments.

Lizette's eyes snapped dangerously. "I don't sleep with him!" she shot back.

"So you say."

"So your brother'll say too, if you ask him."

"I did."

"And?"

"He only smile, wink, then like this under the chin," and Elena flipped one hand beneath her chin to demonstrate, while Lizette fumed.

"Your brother's a liar!"

"Perhaps," Elena retorted, and her eyes slowly sifted over Lizette, the jealousy she felt toward this woman growing even stronger at the sight of her in a dress, even a stained and rumpled one. She could just imagine how captivating Lizette Kolter could be if she were properly dressed, only she tried to ignore the thought. "Sancho said he has a deck of cards in his desk," she said, walking toward it, and she began opening drawers, searching.

"They're in the bottom drawer on the right," Lizette snapped.

Elena opened the bottom drawer, took out the cards, then straightened and turned, smiling provocatively. "Since we cannot go on deck because of the rain, Sancho thought perhaps we would . . . how you say . . . while away the time with these," and she held up the well-used deck of cards. "You know how to play casino?" she asked.

Lizette was still staring at the other woman, wondering just what she was up to. "I might."

"You don't have to." Elena shrugged. "It was only an idea." She walked to the table where they usually ate and sat down, glad both table and chair were anchored to the floor, and she began to shuffle the cards.

Lizette kept watching her for a few minutes, then sighed. "All right. I guess it's better than sitting here twiddling my thumbs," she said, and left the bunk, joining Elena at the table and Elena began to deal the cards.

Close to half an hour went by while they played, few words said between them. Two of the men came and removed the tub, Mario ducked in for a minute to tell them it was still raining, and they continued to play several hands, with Elena winning most of them. Elena had begun stacking sevens during this hand, and now Lizette smiled inwardly, pleased as she used the seven she'd been dealt only a short time before, and picked up the four piles of stacked cards with it, placing them facedown in front of her; then she glanced over at Elena before discarding her last card, which was a three.

"Three, four, five," Elena said quite happily as she picked up the three Lizette had discarded, put it on a deuce, then took a five from her hand, her last card, and scooped up the pile she had just built, plus all the rest of the cards on the table, since it was the last trick in the deal. Her eyes glistened impishly. "Looks like I win again, *sí?*"

"But you were stacking sevens," Lizette protested.

"I know." Elena smiled. "Just a little trick of the game, *señora,*" and she began counting her points, just to make sure she hadn't bragged prematurely.

Lizette counted her own points, which weren't many, then tossed her cards across the table, since it was Elena's deal again.

"You're just full of tricks, aren't you?" Lizette said as Elena shuffled the cards, then began dealing.

"Tell me," Elena said as she dealt a fourth card to Lizette, put another faceup on the table, then set the pack facedown again before picking up her own hand. "Just what did your husband tell you about me, *señora?*"

Lizette glanced over at Elena, then frowned as she started her play. "That you and your aunt nursed him back to health," she answered, discarding the three of hearts.

"That's all?"

"That's all there was to tell, and you know it." Lizette watched Elena closely.

"You honestly believe that?" Elena laughed softly, shaking her head. "*Cielos!* But you are naive, *señora.*"

"All right, what did happen?" Lizette asked, ignoring the fact that it was her turn again, and realizing a discussion of Bain was probably what Elena had wanted in the first place, the cards being only a decoy. "You've been making nasty remarks ever since your brother brought you on board, Elena," she went on irritably. "Just what are you getting at?"

"You mean you don't know?"

"Are you trying to tell me my husband made love to you?"

Elena's eyes warmed as she remembered the kiss Domino had bestowed on her the night they'd waited on the cliffs for Sancho's ship, and the taste of wonder that his hands had given her during that kiss. She had imagined, so many times since, how wonderful it would have been if she could have had it all. And now, ever since setting eyes on this woman who'd kept her from experiencing what she knew would have been heaven, she'd wanted to get even with her for it. Now she could.

"Why should he not?" she said, her voice husky with emotion. "*Sí*, he made love to me."

The cards tightened in Lizette's hands. "You're lying!"

"Why should I do that, *señora?*"

"To hurt me." Lizette's eyes darkened. "Besides, even your brother said Bain only kissed you."

"Sancho believes what I tell him to believe." She fingered her cards assertively. "You see, if I had told him the truth, he would have killed Domino."

"Quit calling him that!" Lizette yelled angrily, and stood up, throwing her cards all over the table. "His name's Bain, and besides, he had amnesia and didn't even know I existed."

Elena began gathering up the scattered cards. "It was after the amnesia was over, *señora,*" she said, and Lizette stared at her for a minute, then leaned across the table, her eyes flashing, as she looked directly at Elena.

"No! Not Bain. He wouldn't do that to me," she cried angrily. "I won't believe it!"

"You had better, Lizette Kolter," Elena answered, her voice sharp, more vindictive, as she looked up into Lizette's eyes, seeing a slight doubt mirrored there. "He may have gone home to you, true, but believe me, part of his heart was still on Barlovento with me. Did you think I tried to talk Sancho out of this horrible vendetta of his simply because it seemed the ladylike thing to do?" She shook her head. "No, *señora*, it was because I knew Domino would never let the authorities learn about Barlovento. A man does not make love to a woman the way Bain Kolter made love to me, then betray her."

Lizette felt her knees weaken as she looked deeply into Elena's dark eyes, and a lump worked its way into her throat, making it hard to breathe. She was looking for something, anything, in the other woman's eyes that would indicate she was lying, but there was no way she could read them. They were steady, unfaltering, with a strength of determination that was intimidating, and the tears that had been swimming in the corner of Lizette's eyes started rolling down her cheeks and she shuddered involuntarily.

"Ah, *sí*, so you finally believe. *Bueno*," Elena said as she saw the tears as well as the stricken look on Lizette's face. "Now perhaps you will understand why I have not been able to make friends with you, *señora*. You see, you and your children are the only reason Domino finally decided to leave Barlovento, so it is natural I should dislike you."

Lizette straightened, still staring at her, unable to answer, and she suddenly remembered how casually Bain had spoken of the island and the family that took care of him. And although he'd told her what really went on on the island, and that he'd promised the de Córdobas not to betray them, he'd told her very little about the people themselves, and she'd never thought to ask. Her eyes narrowed as she began to remember something else. Bain had been so quick to accuse her of having an affair with Stuart. Why? To cover his own infidelity? If that were true . . .

Lizette stood for another full minute staring hard at Elena, who had nonchalantly begun shuffling the cards again; then, "Damn you!" she yelled hysterically. "Damn you!" and she turned abruptly, heading for the door.

"*Señora!* Lizette! It is still raining!" Elena called after her, but Lizette didn't care as she left the cabin, slamming the door behind her, then made her way along the passageway until she reached the stairs.

Tears blurred her vision and she grabbed the rail, pulling herself up the steps, forcing her legs to hold her up until she reached the door, then she leaned against it for a few seconds before yanking it open. The rain hit her full in the face, but Lizette didn't care. All she wanted was to get away where she could try to soothe the hurt that was tearing her apart inside.

Although it had been raining all day, with heavy waves and a strong wind that fought the sails savagely, there was no lightning or thunder. However, the gray sky, bleak and overcast, had held the temperature down and cold air hung low against the warm water, bringing foggy mist with it. Lizette made her way to the nearest rail, then inched her way along it, hoping to disappear behind boxes, ropes, cannon, anything so no one would see her while she fought for composure.

Would Bain? Could he? she kept asking herself over and over again. Were all the soft words and declarations of love a farce? Or was Elena de Córdoba trying to get even with her for being what she could never be, Bain's wife? If only there were an answer.

She lifted her head, letting the rain wash the tears from her face, oblivious of its cold, the heat of her anger and frustration keeping her from chilling, and she didn't hear Sancho approach until he was beside her.

"You were to stay in the cabin," he said.

She froze, then wiped the rain from her face and looked at him.

"Why? So your sister can have her fun?"

"What do you mean?"

Lizette was holding her hand over her eyes now, trying to shield her face from the rain and wind. "You said he'd only kissed her."

Sancho frowned, the scar at his temple paling as fury began to dance in his eyes. "She said he did more?"

"She said he made love to her."

"There is making love, and there is making love, *señora.*"

"You know very well what I mean," Lizette said, and saw his mouth tighten cruelly.

"I will talk with Elena. But come." He took her arm. "This is no place for you."

"I won't stay in that cabin with her."

"Then she shall leave. Come," and his fingers tightened on her arm, forcing her to leave the rail, and they headed belowdecks.

Sancho's ship was not as sleek as Bain's ships had been and the passageways were dark and narrow, the few cabins small and uncomfortable, with only Sancho's cabin truly livable, and Lizette knew Elena was going to raise a fuss if she had to spend the rest of the day in the cabin where she slept. It was really Jigger's cabin and he'd given it up for her while he bunked with Mario.

Water dripped from Lizette's lavender dress and ran in streams from her hair as they made their way toward the cabin, Sancho's hand still holding her arm securely. He too was wet, but wore a hat and cape of canvas that had been oiled so the rain wouldn't penetrate.

He took off his hat, then opened the cabin door and ushered Lizette inside. Elena was still sitting at the table, playing a game of solitaire, and he said something to her in Spanish that Lizette didn't understand. For a few minutes they conversed rather heatedly; then the other woman stood up, leaving the cards on the table, and started for the door.

"Try to dry off some," Sancho said as he released Lizette's arm. "I will be back," and he turned, following his sister from the cabin, shutting the door firmly behind them.

"Now," he said to his sister in Spanish again once the door was shut. "We'll go to your cabin and talk."

Elena's head tilted haughtily. "There's nothing to talk about," but he grabbed her arm and shoved her toward Jigger's cabin, then opened the door and pushed her inside, shutting the door after them.

"Why?" he asked, his eyes intense as he stared at her. "Why did you tell her that?"

"I don't know what you're talking about."

"Oh no?" They were both using their mother tongue now, and the words came readily. "You're my sister and I love you, Elena, but by God, this is my ship, and you'll answer when I ask you something, understand?"

"Why? Why should I answer? What does it matter what I said to her anyway?"

"That's for me to know. Now, I asked you, did you tell her that Domino made love to you?"

"So what if I did?"

"Is it the truth?"

Her eyes faltered beneath his gaze, and she looked away.

"I asked, is it the truth?" He grabbed her chin and forced her dark eyes up so that she couldn't avoid looking at him. "You said all he did was kiss you, and I believed it. Now, should I have run him through right then and there, or not?"

How should she answer? He hadn't actually made love to her, no, but what he had done was so close and she was sure her feelings had been much like the real thing. Still . . .

"Elena?"

"No," she answered softly. "He did not make love to me . . . at least not the way he would to his wife. His hands . . . For God's sake, Sancho, isn't anything in my life sacred? Must you know it all?"

His hand dropped from her arm as he suddenly understood, and his eyes narrowed viciously. "But you told her he violated you."

"Violated? What's the difference?" She was furious as she rubbed her arm where he'd held it. "It probably felt the same."

"You go right on believing that, dear sister," Sancho said briskly. "Only don't confuse the two, because they can't be compared. Now, what I want to know is why you tried to make Señora Kolter think her husband had really made love to you."

"You know why."

"Because you still love him?"

She sighed and her lower lip formed into a pout. "So what if I do."

"That was two years ago, Elena, and he only used you."

"He did not!" She moved to the small window in the dingy cabin and pulled back the curtain that covered it. It was still raining. "A woman knows when she's being used, Sancho, even this woman," she said, then turned back to stare at her brother for a moment.

He was so big and gruff, and his face, once ruggedly handsome, was like chiseled granite, the withered skin at his temple not the only scar left from his years of piracy. There was a hardness about him, and a reckless abandon that often scared her. How different he was from the way she remembered him years ago when their mother was still alive. Even his eyes were so cold and unfeeling. Suddenly she remembered something, and a frown creased her forehead as she stared at him.

"Why are you so concerned about what I told Señora Kolter anyway?" she asked her brother curiously.

Sancho straightened. "What do you mean?"

"You heard me." It was dim in the cabin because of the rain outside, and she moved closer, where she could see him better. "Why are you so concerned about her, Sancho? And what does it matter what she does or doesn't think?"

Elena watched Sancho's eyes grow wary. "What are you getting at?"

"Simply this, my dear brother," she said smugly. "I've watched the way you look at Señora Kolter, and if I didn't know better, Sancho de Córdoba, I'd say you were falling in love with her."

"Don't be ridiculous."

"Aha! That's it, isn't it," she exclaimed, ignoring the dangerous glint in his eyes. "That's why you don't want me to say anything. You don't like seeing her hurt." She stopped smiling and leaned close to him, her eyes suddenly alive. "You're a fool, Sancho," she went on, her dark eyes studying her brother closely, and she knew she'd guessed right. "Did it ever occur to you that if she thinks her husband betrayed her, it might make her all the more willing to turn to you for comfort?"

"Now I know you've lost your head," Sancho said, and shook his disgustedly. "Even if it were true, she's a lady and nothing could come of it. Besides, I vowed long ago never to let any woman get under my skin, and that includes Bain Kolter's wife, so whether she comes to me willingly or not makes little difference. I take my women where and when I want, and to hell with your stupid love and sentiment."

"I see." Elena smiled. "Have it your way, dear brother, but I think you're missing such a grand opportunity. Just think of all the fun you could have if word got back to Bain Kolter that his precious wife had become your willing mistress."

He stared at her hard for a moment, letting the idea run rampant in his head. It would sweeten the vengeance. "You think it would work?" he asked, frowning.

"Why not? And we could both have our revenge."

He continued to stare at her; then the tense lines around his mouth suddenly softened. "All right, I'll go along with you," he answered hesitantly. "But not because I have any special feelings for the lady, understand that, but because of the vendetta. Only one thing."

"*Si?*"

"When you get to Havana, you're to see a priest, an honest one, do you understand, and you're to confess the lies and deceit, and purge the devil from your soul, Elena de Córdoba, just as our mother and father would have wanted you to, because one de Córdoba in hell will be more than enough." He turned abruptly, opened the door, and left.

Once outside in the corridor, Sancho stood for a long time, the oiled canvas hat in his hand, and felt the rise and fall of the ship at his feet, and for a brief moment he thought of hell and eternity and wondered if there still wasn't some way to redeem the path his life had taken. Then, realizing he couldn't go back, only forward, he jammed the hat on his head and went back up on deck to help his men weather the storm.

That evening, dinner on board ship was rather strained. Lizette had changed back to the sailor's old clothes and hung her dress in a corner of the cabin to dry, and although Bain's name wasn't mentioned once during the meal, all three knew he was uppermost in the others' minds. The only one who had no idea what was going on was Mario, but then he'd been too busy on deck most of the day. Ever since boarding the *Piranha* he'd been fascinated by it all. Even while they were still on Barlovento, he'd begged Sancho to let him join his crew, only his brother had always refused. Now, this was his opportunity, and Mario had joined with the men more and more every day, learning all about the rigging and all that went along with being a sailor.

Lizette glanced over, watching Mario's eyes as he talked now about the rain and wind, and how exhilarating it had been to be a part of it, his dark curly hair, still wet and kinked into curls, struggling to stay off his forehead as he shoveled the biscuits, honey, and mutton stew into his lean body that still had a great deal of filling out to do.

He was so enthusiastic. She glanced over at Sancho. He too was watching his young brother, only Lizette could tell he didn't like what he saw.

So far, most of the conversation at the table tonight had been in English, but now suddenly Sancho set down the spoon he was using and spoke to his brother in Spanish.

"Well, little brother, it seems you're really enjoying your trip aboard my ship, aren't you?" he said, and Lizette found herself at a loss as she furtively watched Mario stop shoveling the food in his mouth so he could answer. She was hoping he'd answer in English, only he answered in Spanish too.

"So?" he said.

"So it doesn't take long for the sea to get into a man's blood," Sancho went on, and the conversation continued in Spanish as Lizette glanced from one to the other, frowning while Mario answered.

"What's wrong with that?"

"What's wrong with it?" Sancho exhaled furiously. "You're not going to join my crew, that's what's wrong with it." He leaned forward to emphasize what he was saying. "You're going to do like father would have wanted and go to the university in Havana, that's what.''

"But I don't want to be a priest!"

"Nor do I want you to be one. But you could study law, physics, science, become a doctor if that's what you want, but don't ever take to the sea!"

Mario's eyes bristled. "You did."

"And look what it got me . . . a ticket to hell!"

"Don't be ridiculous, Sancho," Elena cut in as the conversation continued in Spanish. "There's no law says you have to go to hell. Confession's for all sinners, not just a few."

"Confession's for the good of the soul, Elena," Sancho answered bitterly. "I have no more soul, and no conscience either. I've run men through simply because they were breathing, and you know it, and I've closed my eyes to sights that'd turn your stomach. You think I could wash all that away in a confessional? I can't even purge it from my dreams, and I won't let Mario face the same fate." His eyes darkened. "For me there's no going back, Mario, but for you, for both of you, there's more to life than what this ship or any other ship can offer."

"But—" Mario began.

"Do you want to spend the rest of the trip in your cabin?" Sancho asked.

"No."

"Then listen to me, and listen well. Since father's dead too now, I'm the boss, and don't you forget it. What I say, you do. You can go on deck, and you can talk to the men, I don't care, but the next time I see you in the rigging or at the helm or any of the other things you find so fascinating to do, I'll have you flogged, understand?"

"Sancho!" Elena gasped.

Sancho's eyes were blazing as he looked at his sister. "Better his body than his soul!"

Elena's eyes faltered under her older brother's tense gaze, and Mario too became silent.

Lizette sensed that the conversation was over, and looked first at Mario, then Elena, then Sancho, who slowly turned, looking directly at her.

"Well, what was that all about? Or shouldn't I ask?" she said hesitantly, but it was Elena who spoke, in English this time, her voice rather subdued.

"Sancho was just playing *padre*," she said, then glanced

over at her younger brother. "Don't worry, Mario, you will like the university, I am sure, and just think, you can be anything you want."

"Can I?" he asked, and looked over at Sancho, who drew his eyes from Lizette. "That's your opinion."

"Someday you will thank me, little brother," Sancho said. "But here, we interrupt Señora Kolter's dinner with our family talk," and for the rest of the meal the heated conversation in Spanish seemed to have been forgotten.

Later that evening, Lizette stood in the cabin with the curtains pulled back and stared out into the night. The rain had stopped shortly before dark, and although the sea was still quite choppy and wild, the sky had cleared and now stars began to twinkle above the horizon. She was still wearing the men's clothes, only with the rain gone, the temperature had risen and she'd rolled up the sleeves of the shirt and pulled her hair back, tying it in a queue.

She'd been up on deck earlier, shortly after the rain stopped, but preferred it down here because Sancho's men made her nervous. True, Jigger didn't seem to be too bad, but the looks she often got from the others gave her the shivers. And even though she assumed Sancho had evidently ordered them to keep their distance, she was always afraid there'd be one stupid idiot who wouldn't listen. So she spent most of her days here where there was too much time to think and speculate on the future, while trying to sort out the past.

She glanced at the clock behind Sancho's desk. It was almost eleven. No wonder she was tired. Sometimes she'd curl up in her corner on the cabin floor long before Sancho came in, and other times he'd come down early, they'd talk a little, then both retire.

What a strange man he was. With his brother and sister he was warm, often loving, but with his men he was harsh, rough, and ruthlessly unfeeling. Why, he'd never even shown any sign of compassion or sympathy earlier when one of his men had been caught stealing from his shipmates. It had been the day after Lizette was brought aboard. The man had sailed on the *Piranha* for two years, yet Sancho stood by and watched him hang from the yardarm without even flinching, then let the body hang there for the rest of the day to show the crew that to sail with him was to obey orders, and one of those orders was that once a ship was taken and the booty distributed among the men, there'd be no thievery. They had to be able to trust each other in order to stay alive, he'd told her later that day, and a man who'd steal from his own shipmates would have no qualms about knifing them in the back either. "How else do you think I stay alive?" he'd asked her, and after seeing some of the men who sailed with him, she could understand his reasoning. Still, it seemed cruel, and unusually harsh.

So the man was hanged and life aboard the ship had gone on. Still, Sancho was an enigma, because he also treated her much differently from what she'd expected, although he did make remarks now and then that things were going to change when his sister and brother were no longer aboard.

Lizette stared out the window once more and became so engrossed in her thoughts that she didn't hear the door open and Sancho come in. He closed it quietly behind him and stood for a long time watching her, a frown creasing his forehead as his eyes sifted over her and he remembered the accusation Elena had thrown at him that afternoon. She'd said he didn't want this woman hurt, and it suddenly struck him that Elena was right. He didn't want Lizette Kolter hurt. Not anymore, but why?

When he'd first watched her the day of the picnic, he'd been detached, able to be objective in his appraisal of her, but from the moment he'd set her on his horse, then climbed up behind her, the indifference he'd relegated to the deed he was performing had suddenly vanished, replaced by a concern for her that was new to him.

At first he'd tried to ignore it. She was just another woman to warm his bed for a while if he wanted, as well as being a means to an end. At least that's what he'd thought. Then he'd stood here in the cabin and watched her, dirty and disheveled, sitting on his bunk with her muddy feet and soiled dress, her damp hair framing her face, and a pair of deep green eyes, like fiery emeralds, accusing him, and for some reason he knew she wasn't just another woman.

She was the woman he wished he'd met years ago, and he watched her now, wondering what she was thinking, and for the first time in his life he wished to God his life had been different.

"I thought you would be asleep already," he said in his heavily accented English, startling her, and Lizette turned abruptly.

"I didn't hear you come in."

"I know." He strolled over and peeled off the unkempt uniform jacket, throwing it on the chair, then reached for a decanter of wine on a shelf over the desk. "Join me?" he asked.

She shook her head. "I like a clear head."

"And wine makes it fuzzy?"

"Let's just say we don't get along."

She watched him pour himself a drink, the dim light in the cabin casting shadows on his face, and for a moment she thought he looked tired.

"How long before we get to Cuba?" she asked.

He took a sip of the wine, then wiped his mouth with the back of his hand. "Another day if the wind stays with us."

"I see." She turned back to the window again, remembering what he'd said about what would happen after they left Cuba.

"No, I don't think you do see," he said as he set the glass down, then walked up to stand behind her, and she turned, facing him again. The smell of the wine was strong, and it mingled with the saltwater odor that seemed to permeate everything on board, including his clothes, and she stared at him curiously.

"What don't I see?" she asked.

His eyes caught hers and held, their boldness making her apprehensive. "I told you that when we leave Cuba, you will know what it is to belong to Sancho de Córdoba," he whispered huskily. "Now I will give you a taste of what that will be," and he reached out to pull her toward him.

Lizette tried to slip away, but he caught her arm.

"You're hurting me!"

"No," he answered, his voice low and resonant. "*You* are hurting you. Relax." He was holding the flesh on her upper arm and drew her closer to him as he leaned toward her, and Lizette found herself neatly pinned against the wall, with the cabin window over her left shoulder.

"I thought you didn't like fat women," she gasped breathlessly.

He chuckled, amused. "Yes, you would say that," he said, his eyes softening as he stared at her; then she felt his other hand on her waist. "But you are not fat, not really."

"Oh, but I am. I'm terribly fat," she blurted hurriedly. "And I've got stretch marks from the twins."

"Stretch marks?"

"Yes, you know," she went on, her heart pounding wildly. "You don't want me . . . you want someone young and pretty."

"You are young and pretty."

"No, no I'm not." She pressed hard against the wall behind her. "I'm not pretty at all. I'm fat and ugly."

His hand left her arm and moved into her hair, unfastening the strip of cloth that held it back in place, and he captured her dark tresses, entwining the curls through his fingers as he cupped the back of her neck.

"What a strange woman you are, Señora Kolter," he said softly, and his dark eyes, still searching hers, seemed so alive, so vibrant, the scar at his temple even more prominent. "No wonder your husband was so anxious to come home to you." His eyes fell to her lips and Lizette inhaled sharply as she realized he was going to kiss her.

"Please," she begged, her voice strained, faltering. "You don't want to do this."

"*Sí,* I do," he answered, and without giving her any more chance to protest, his mouth touched hers, lightly at first, then gradually pressing harder, moving sensuously, and Lizette wanted to die.

She'd been so scared when he'd first kidnapped her. Then, when he hadn't forced himself on her right away, she'd let herself build up a false security that was quickly crumbling all around her now as the kiss deepened and he pulled her harder against him. Lizette had been touched by only two men in her life, Stuart and Bain, and the two were so alike. How could she live through this?

Her first thought was to struggle; then reason took over, and she realized that if she struggled, not only would it be useless, but he might even enjoy it more, so instead she just froze, letting him kiss her, but not responding.

After a few minutes he drew his head back, and as his eyes found hers again, she knew he'd guessed what she was doing.

"You pretend well, *señora,*" he said, and his tongue ran the length of his upper lip.

"I'm not pretending," she replied. Her voice was unsteady as she tried to find courage. "I don't want you to kiss me. Not now, or ever."

"We shall see." He pulled her head toward him, only this time his lips touched her neck just below the ear and he felt her stiffen again. "You can fight a thing just so long, *señora*," he whispered, against her ear this time. "But the day will come. You'll see. After all, why should you keep marriage vows that your husband disregards?"

Lizette pushed against him with all her might, forcing him to straighten, and her face was flushed. "You talked to Elena?" she asked.

"And learned the truth this time."

"No . . ."

"I told you your husband was a bastard."

"I don't believe it."

"Then you are a fool, Lizette Kolter."

"A fool?"

"*Sí*, to believe that a man, any man, would be faithful to you or any other woman."

"What do you know of love?" she asked testily. "To you the word probably doesn't even exist. All women are to you is something to warm your bed. So don't go telling me there's no such thing as fidelity. When, and if, you ever learn of love, Sancho de Córdoba, then, and only then, will you have a right to call me a fool."

He stared at her for a long time, the memory of her lips beneath his, stiff and unyielding, piercing his heart like a knife, and he suddenly realized he wanted Lizette Kolter more than he'd ever wanted any other woman before, only he didn't want to force her, not Lizette. She had to come to him willingly or it would mean nothing.

"Someday you will learn that I know more about love than you give me credit for, *señora*," he answered softly. "But for now it's late and I suggest we both get some rest, for tomorrow brings us within sight of Cuba." His arms dropped from around her and he walked to his bunk and began stripping the shirt from his back, then sat down to take off his boots. "And don't forget to blow out the light before you settle down," he ordered her matter-of-factly, then stretched out on his bed with his back to her as if going to sleep.

Lizette stayed by the window, staring at his back for a long time, then went to a chest in the corner and took out the blankets she used, spreading them out on the floor; then, after a quick look around, she walked to the wall sconce and blew out the whale-oil lamp, plunging the cabin into darkness. This done, she made her way back to her blankets and settled down on the floor, the darkness giving her more time to think than she wanted, and she clenched her jaw stubbornly, promising herself she wasn't going to believe Elena.

Then suddenly Sancho's deep voice echoed across the dark cabin. "*Buenas noches*, Lizette Kolter," he offered. "And may you have sweet dreams."

Lizette couldn't answer for a moment, the words caught in her throat, tears rimming her eyes. Then finally, "Good night, Sancho de Córdoba," she called back furiously. "And may you rot in hell!" and as she closed her eyes, the only answer she heard was a low, rolling chuckle from the direction of his bunk.

The next day, true to her captain's word, the *Piranha* closed the last few hundred miles between her and the coastline of Cuba, arriving in a quiet inland cove late in the afternoon, only a few hours before dark.

"This is Havana?" Lizette asked as she stood at the rail wearing her rumpled lavender dress again, with Sancho beside her as they watched the sails slacken.

"No, this is some forty miles east of Havana," he answered, his eyes scanning the small bay. "You see, Sancho de Córdoba is not welcome in Spanish ports either."

"Oh." She glanced over at him, surprised to see that his hair and beard were neatly trimmed again, as they had been when she'd first seen him at Port Royal, and she wondered why. She looked off again toward the land, the sight of trees and grass making her homesick. "You said your uncle lives here?"

"*Sí*. He has a *rancho* not far from here, only he is not always there, since the governor keeps him in Havana a great deal to advise him."

"He's an adviser to the governor?"

"Why not? After all, he was once emissary to the king, and a court magistrate."

"With a pirate as his nephew?"

"We choose our friends, not our relatives, *señora*."

"How true."

His eyes darkened briefly as they caught hers; then he turned away as Elena and Mario joined them on deck, carrying the small bags they'd brought with them the night they'd boarded.

Elena was wearing the blue cambric, much plainer than the other two dresses, and although she was wearing a small straw hat, Lizette could see that once again her hair was braided and twisted neatly at the nape of her neck. Mario too was cleaned up and wearing dark brown trousers with a light brown frock coat and silk cravat, a stylish beaver hat in his other hand. They set down the bags they were carrying and Sancho walked over to meet them. Lizette studied the three of them closely for a few minutes while they talked, then turned back, watching the land getting closer, and suddenly an idea struck her. If she were to move forward just a little bit more, so the helmsman was between her and the others, she might be able to slip overboard, swim to shore, and get away.

But where would she go? At first the thought of freedom was exhilarating and she began to hope. But then, as she let the thought penetrate, she realized she knew nothing about this place, including the language. Even if she did get ashore, by herself it'd be just as bad as being on this ship, and could maybe be worse. Still, maybe she'd find someone who could speak English or who'd take her to the authorities, and maybe they'd know what she could do.

The more she pondered her dilemma, the more she realized that it'd be worth it to take the chance, and she started to take a step farther along the rail when Sancho's voice cut her off.

"Don't even think it, *mi querida*," he said bluntly, and she whirled about. "I know what you were comtemplating, *señora*," he went on, and she saw the cold, calculating look in his dark eyes. "Even if you did make it to shore, there would be no place where you could hide from me. As you can see, the land is better suited to my abilities than yours."

Frustration began to sweep over Lizette again. Oh how she hated this arrogant man, and tears welled up in her eyes. She fought them back, trying to stay calm so he wouldn't guess how close he'd come to guessing the truth.

"I'm not stupid, Sancho," she said, trying as hard as she could to keep her voice steady. "Don't worry, before I try to leave you and your friends behind, I'm going to be absolutely sure there's no way you could ever follow me, even if I have to make sure you're all dead first in order to do it."

She saw him relax, and he smiled, amused. "And how will you do that, *señora*, since I am so much bigger than you?"

Her jaw tightened with determination. "Just don't turn your back, Señor de Córdoba."

"Oh, I see, you would like to swing from the yardarm too, is that it?"

"The yardarm would be better than your arms, *señor.*"

His eyes narrowed, and he glared at her. "I will remember what you say, *señora,* only let me warn you of one thing: if you ever do decide to do this thing, make sure that you strike true the first time, *mi querida,* you understand? Because if you ever try what you have threatened, you'll never have a second try. Now"—he looked down at her dress—"go put on the men's clothes again and put something on your feet. I'm taking Mario and Elena ashore and you will go with me. I'm afraid I do not trust my men alone with you this time, nor you with them. This way, I will know that when we sail from Cuba again, you will still belong to Sancho de Córdoba."

Lizette gave him a nasty look as she left him and went back down to the cabin to change her clothes. Just before going back on deck, however, as the sunset deepened, turning the sky red gold, she glanced out the cabin window toward the land and made a vow that if there was any way possible to make a break and get away from Sancho de Córdoba while they were on shore, she'd take it, and to hell with whether she could speak Spanish or not. With this determination at the back of her mind, she left the cabin to join Sancho as he prepared to leave the ship to take Elena and Mario to their uncle.

Chapter 6

AT FIRST, it was so good to feel the land at her feet again that for a while as they walked down the dusty road Lizette had forgotten how upset she'd been just a short time before, but now, as they all moved further along under the darkening sky, she began to remember her vow, only this wasn't the place to try. It was too open here, and besides, it wasn't dark enough yet. They had reached the road only a few yards up from the beach where they'd anchored the ship, and the land was comparatively flat here, with only a few small hills. It was beautiful country, but mostly pasture, with only occasional trees, and it seemed like she could see for miles.

The day wore on and as darkness continued to descend, the heat that had dampened their clothes with perspiration earlier, dried their throats as well, and they had to stop now and then for a drink from the flask Sancho had brought with him.

There were four of them escorting Elena and Mario inland. Sancho, Lizette, and two of the crew. Sancho had left Jigger with the ship as a precaution and had brought Mosely and Kidder. Lizette didn't mind Mosely too much. He was lean and hawk-faced, his hair graying already, the lines in his face deeper than those in most men his age. She guessed he was in his early forties, and he was always talking about the children he had someplace back in England. But Kidder she could have done without. He was built more like Sancho but not as tall, with a deep scar on his left eyelid that made it droop, and a broken tooth in front, and every time he looked at her and grinned, she shivered. There was just something slimy about him, and to make matters worse, he always kept his dark brown hair greased down with something that smelled terrible, then combed it back, with a soiled red band that kept it off his forehead.

Yes, Lizette would much rather have had Jigger along in his place, and she trudged along the country road disgustedly now in the heat, realizing that the darker it got, the closer Sancho stayed to her. At this rate she'd never get a chance to slip away unnoticed.

Sancho was carrying Elena's bag with her things in it for her, and he stared ahead to where his sister was walking. She was so slim and graceful, and he hoped Havana would be good for her so she'd forget Domino, then he glanced beside him to Lizette. He had seen her eyes scanning the terrain more than once since they'd started walking, and knew instinctively what she was thinking. Well, he wasn't about to let her get away, and he moved a little closer as the night shadows began deepening around them; then he let his thoughts wander to what lay ahead.

Tío Emilio was going to be upset by their arrival, he knew, but then maybe they'd be in luck and he'd be in the city, he thought. Only he wasn't, and a few hours later, when they finally reached the Pérez hacienda, they were greeted in the parlor by Don Emilio. Lizette was quite surprised. He was a big man like Sancho, but more genteel and soft-spoken, dressed in the tight pants and embroidered bolero of the Spanish aristocrat, and it was obvious his nephew's profession was an embarrassment to him, since from the moment his servant ushered all of them into the room, he left orders not to be disturbed by anyone.

The Pérez ranch, being on one of the main roads that traversed the island, was often forced to play host to a number of unusual visitors, but none quite so unusual as the ones standing in the parlor this evening. Mosely and Kidder had been left out by the main road to make sure there'd be no unexpected company, and now the rest of them faced Señor Pérez, who looked anything but pleased.

"So, to what do I owe this visit, Sancho?" he asked briskly in Spanish, the pain of seeing his sister's son wearing the ragtag clothes of a pirate showing in his dark eyes.

Lizette had recognized none of the words except Sancho's name, so she just listened to the conversation uneasily.

"Father's dead now too, Tío Emilio," Sancho answered his uncle. "And Elena and Mario had to have somewhere to go."

"I see." Emilio Pérez thought for a moment. "How did Luis die?" he asked.

Sancho told him, and again Don Emilio grew quiet, then walked over toward the open French doors beyond the fancy stucco fireplace and gazed out.

"There was no place else for me to take them," Sancho continued, hating to have to ask his uncle for help. "But if they can't stay here, their only other alternative would be to join me, and I don't think even you would want that, would you?"

Don Emilio turned, his eyes resting first on Elena, then Mario, and Lizette wished she knew what was being said.

"If they stay here, they will do as I say," Don Emilio insisted firmly.

"They know that."

"I have been a widower many years, and I'm not used to young people around the house."

"Please, Tío Emilio," Elena cut in. "We will be no trouble, I promise you. I'm not a child anymore, and perhaps I can help, and Mario's planning to attend the university."

"Oh? But I thought your father lost everything."

"I'll pay for his studies," Sancho answered.

Emilio looked displeased. "Blood money?"

"No more bloody than the money that bought this ranch for you, Tío," Sancho countered testily. "What difference does it make if you lie to put a man to death legally in order to gain his wealth, or I run him through during a raid? My way is messier and more risky, I agree, but piracy is piracy no matter how hard you try to make it look respectable."

Emilio Pérez straightened, his eyes resting uncomfortably on Sancho's face. So his father had told him about Rosario. He'd hoped that part of his life had been forgotten.

"They may stay," he finally said. "But I warn you, Sancho, I won't be a haven for you and your men as your father was. My own past may not be faultless, but I am no longer the man I was then, and I have made peace with God for my earlier failings."

"Then I congratulate you, Tío," Sancho replied. "I only wish penance was as easy for all men as it was for you," and he reached into the pocket of his worn uniform jacket, pulling out a small leather pouch. "Here's enough gold coins to buy them clothes and get Mario started at the university as well as pay you for their keep for a while," he said, tossing it to his uncle, who caught it deftly. "When I feel it necessary, I will stop by again to supplement their monies."

"And if you fail to return?"

"Then I ask you to watch over them as best you can and pray for my soul."

"That I always do, Sancho," Emilio said, his eyes steady on those of his nephew; then he straightened, taking a deep breath. "Now, you have not said"—Lizette felt his eyes settle on her, and she flushed—"who is this woman? It *is* a woman?"

"*Sí*," Sancho answered. "But she does not speak or understand our language, Tío Emilio. She's an American."

"Hmmm, so what is she doing with you?"

"She's part of his vendetta," Elena cut in before Sancho had a chance.

Emilio scowled. "She's here against her will?"

"She is my problem, not yours," Sancho replied, his eyes warning Elena to keep her mouth shut. "And now, since our transaction is settled, I'll be leaving."

"I asked you, Sancho," Emilio said, his voice deepening with authority, "the woman, what of her?"

"She's the wife of the man who betrayed my family and Barlovento," Sancho offered viciously. "And as such she's my responsibility. That's all you need know. I live my life, Tío Emilio, you live yours. As for Elena and Mario, for them I thank you. As for myself, I am still the master of my own soul, and what I do is my business, and only mine!" He turned to Elena and Mario. "*Adiós*, little sister and brother, and just remember," he said, cautioning them, "I'll be back in a while to make sure all goes well with you."

"Meantime you'll be where?" Elena asked.

He shrugged. "Who knows—wherever the wind takes me." He leaned over and hugged Elena, a gesture that surprised Lizette, then shook hands with Mario. "Both of you remember," he warned them solemnly, "while I am not here, you will do as Tío Emilio says. Agreed?"

They both agreed.

"*Bueno*," he said, then thanked his uncle again and turned to Lizette. "Come," he said, in English this time, "our job here is done." As he began to usher her from the room, moving off through the open French doors instead of heading for the door where they'd come in, then stepped on outside into the dark night, Lizette quickly glanced back, her last sight that of Elena and Mario standing in the flickering light with their bags at their feet staring after them while their uncle came over and put an arm about each of their shoulders.

"So what was that all about?" she asked as she drew her eyes from the room and let him guide her through the walkways of a garden and on toward the front gate some five hundred feet away, where she knew Mosely and Kidder were waiting.

"I told you before that they were going to stay with our uncle."

"He didn't look very happy."

"He is not very happy, but he is family, and to honor his sister he will accept what has to be."

"Or you'd have killed him?"

"Perhaps yes, perhaps no. We will never know, will we?" She couldn't see his face in the dark, but his voice was low, mocking. "Now, hurry, we have a long way to walk yet tonight and I want *La Piranha* to clear the shores of Cuba before daybreak," and he grabbed her arm, hurrying her along.

Mosely and Kidder were waiting right where they'd left them, in a patch of bushes not far from the main gate, and before long they were all four well on their way down the road again, heading back toward the quiet cove where the ship was anchored and waiting, and Lizette's heart sank. There was no way she was going to be able to get away now.

It wasn't until the wee hours of the morning that Lizette finally smelled the fresh sea air and knew that it wouldn't be long until they reached the ship. She was tired and weary and had been hoping and praying all the way back that something would happen, anything so that she'd get a chance to make a break for it, but it hadn't done any good. Even back at the hacienda when they'd first arrived, she had used the excuse of having to relieve herself, only he'd followed her to the privy and waited outside, embarrassing her.

She glanced over at Sancho as they left the road and started down the slight incline toward the small bay where the ship lay waiting. Now her stomach was beginning to be upset. Probably because she was hungry. They reached the spot where the longboat was hidden, and as Lizette watched the three men pull, then push it off the bank into the water, she suddenly felt another surge of strength as a new idea hit her.

She gazed about, trying to remember the lay of the land as it had been when they'd arrived late that afternoon. It had been daylight then, and if she remembered right, off to their

right as she'd faced the land were a lot of bushes and rocks
at the edge of the water, and in this darkness there was no
way they'd be able to see her if she hid in them.

"Come, *señora*," Sancho said abruptly as he grabbed her
arm, and Lizette drew her eyes away from the direction
where she thought the huge rocks were, and climbed into
the boat, sitting down quickly in the bow, where she waited
for Sancho to join her. He sat down beside her and the men
shoved off, then hopped in themselves and grabbed the oars.
The longboat began to move.

Lizette had decided to wait until they were at least fifty
feet or more from shore before going over the side of the
boat, and now her hands became clammy with sweat as the
moment neared. Well, it was now or never, she told herself
silently, and as the oars came out of the water one more
time, she glanced over to make sure Sancho was preoccu-
pied with what his men were doing, then jumped up, gulping
a huge breath of air as she did, and went over the side of the
boat before Sancho had a chance to even grab at her.

Once beneath the water, she began to swim swiftly away
from the longboat, trying to head in the direction where she
thought the rocks were, yet keeping beneath the surface as
long as she could. Her lungs began to hurt so she pretended
she was back on Tonnerre with her brother Cole, swimming
in the old swimming hole and trying to hide from him; then
slowly, a little at a time, she began to let the air out of her
lungs, each long stroke and kick taking her farther and
farther from the longboat. Finally, with no air left in her
lungs, when there was nothing more to do except swallow
water, she moved her arms, heading toward the surface, and
broke the water, beginning to tread with her feet, trying to
see where she was while she caught her breath.

Straight ahead she could vaguely see the pile of rocks and
bushes, and she sighed, then took a good deep breath, filled
her lungs with air again, and looked back in the direction of
the longboat, where Sancho was both cursing his men and
calling her name heatedly as his eyes searched the surface of
the water, to no avail.

She was going to get away. She was sure of it, and as
softly as she could, Lizette eased toward the bank and pulled
herself from the water, slipping into the bushes as silently as
she could, then leaned back against the rocks to rest for a

minute. She'd stay here all night if she had to. Anything to be free again, even in this strange place.

Back in the boat, Sancho glared at the two men with him, then cursed the darkness as the longboat headed back toward shore.

"Wait here," he ordered as he left the boat.

"You don't want us to help?" asked Mosely.

"If I wanted your help I would ask for it," he snapped viciously, and both men exchanged glances, then watched as their captain headed up the small incline again and stood for a long time studying his surroundings while rubbing his beard thoughtfully.

She couldn't have gone far, he reasoned as he looked around carefully. Even if she knew how to swim, which she'd never mentioned, to stay underwater long enough to reach clear to the other side of the bay would be impossible, so she had to be on this side yet, and since there were few trees or bushes up here, that meant she'd use the cover of darkness to hide close to the water. His eyes moved to some rocks and bushes a short distance away, at the edge of the water. There were only a few places close enough to the water's edge where a person could hide. He took a deep breath, mumbled a curse on all women, then started down the hill again.

Lizette was so scared she was shaking. Now that it was over, she wasn't so sure it had been such a good idea after all. What if he found her? What would she do? More than that, what would Sancho do? But then it wouldn't be any worse than what he'd already threatened to do, would it? She'd had to try something. There was no way she was going to just sit back and let him do whatever he wanted with her.

She took a deep breath and tried to stop trembling, then straightened and rose a little, looking over the rocks and trying to see what had happened to Sancho and his men. She could barely make out the vague outline of the boat with two of the men standing near it, and her heart began to pound. He was back on shore. That meant he was searching for her.

Now that she could breathe easily again, she moved onto her haunches and looked around. Wherever he was, she couldn't see him. She glanced farther up the incline, off some distance to her right, and was sure she could barely make out the outline of more bushes and a few trees. If she could make it to the road, she had at least two hours before daylight for the darkness to hide her, and who knows, some-one might come along to help by then.

With all the courage she could muster, she moved slowly away from the security of the bushes, staying hunched over, and headed for the dark mass of shrubs halfway up the small hill. There was only a bare sliver of moon tonight, and since it was close to morning it was so low on the horizon that it gave little light, and she felt a confident elation as she reached the cover and quickly fell to the ground, burrowing beneath the leaves. She was panting now, her breathing erratic, and she tried to calm herself, being as quiet as she could.

Just a few more yards up the hill and she could reach the road and be out of sight in no time, she told herself silently. But where to next? There was no cover between here and the road. Suddenly she heard a twig snap close by, and her heart leapt into her throat.

"It won't do you any good to hide, *señora*," Sancho called from only a short distance away. "I intend to search every bush and tree on the hillside until I find you, so it will do little good to prolong this any further."

Bastard! she thought bitterly, and raised her head from the ground, straining her eyes as she stared into the dark-ness, trying to spot him, but she couldn't see a thing.

"Two can play at this game, *mi querida*," Sancho called out again, his voice sounding like it was somewhere near the rocks and bushes she'd just left, and her jaw tightened angrily. "I can wait until sunup if need be, or you can come out now. Which shall it be?"

Lizette lowered her head again. This time she'd make certain he couldn't see her, and staying on her stomach, she slithered out from beneath the bush like a snake, inching along on her belly toward the road. Dirt clung to her wet shirt and pants, and more than once she had to bite her lip to keep from crying out as twigs and gravel poked and scraped her stomach and legs, but still she moved on, stopping only once because of a large rock in her path. After maneuvering around it, she continued to crawl, covering ground as fast as she could and hoping with all her might that it was going to work because she had only a short way left to go.

She was almost at the crest of the small hill when she suddenly froze, the hair on the back of her neck prickling at the sound of Sancho's voice from only a few feet behind her.

"You've got to do better than that, *señora*," he said, then started to laugh softly.

Fury welled up inside Lizette as she looked over her shoulder and saw him standing so close, and without thinking of what he might do, her only thought to get away, she rose up, half-stumbling, and began to run toward the road as fast as she could, hoping beyond hope that there'd be someplace to hide before he reached her. But she was tired, her body weary from the long swim and the dread that filled her, and within seconds he was on top of her. His arms went around her, trying to catch her to him, to stop her forward progress, and with one last lunging effort she almost broke loose, only to end up with both of them down, rolling in the dusty grass at the side of the road.

Sancho rolled her onto her back, pinning her arms to the ground, and stared down at her, his breath heavy to match hers, and they were both panting as they gasped for air.

"That was a foolish thing to do, *señora*," he whispered breathlessly. "Now you will pay."

"I'll pay anyway, either way!" she shot back, and her eyes filled with tears. "Go on, go ahead, rape me! You bastard!" she yelled. "You might as well get it over with, it's what you've been threatening to do for days."

His face was so close to hers she could feel his breath, yet Sancho didn't move. He wanted to see her face so badly, but it was too dark.

"I told you before, I rape whores," he said softly. "You, *señora*, are not a whore."

"But you still intend to rape me."

"I intend to make love to you."

"Never!"

"Never is a long time, *mi querida*," he replied, and his mouth found hers in the darkness, then covered it hungrily, and there was nothing Lizette could do except lie there and submit.

At first the kiss was hard and demanding; then after a few seconds Sancho's lips began to soften, he eased up on her mouth a bit, and instead began brushing her lips with his in a sensuous way that brought a response from her that was frightening because it reminded her of Bain and the intimate moments they'd shared together. She tried to push him away, but he was just too strong, so instead she relaxed, trying to ignore what he was doing, and waited for him to stop.

He finally drew his head back and looked down at her, still unable to see her face, but he sensed she was silently crying.

"Don't try it again, *señora*," he cautioned her huskily. "Or I may decide to forget you are not a whore," and with that he moved off her, then reached out, pulling her up with him so they were both on their feet.

Water still dripped from her clothes and now, even though the air was warm, Lizette suddenly felt cold. He saw her tremble.

"Here, take my coat," he said as he peeled the uniform jacket off, but she shook her head.

"Keep your damn coat."

"Have it your way." He started putting it back on again. "If you do not care about my men seeing you with your clothes plastered to your body, that is up to you."

She reached out and grabbed at the jacket quickly before he had a chance to get it all the way on again. "I've changed my mind," she snapped belligerently. "I am cold." He let her take it from him, then watched as she put it on, pulling it close together in front.

A frown creased his forehead as he stared at her, the scar at his temple standing out paler than the rest of his face. What was it about this woman that made him want to forget what he was, what he'd become over the years, and for a brief moment he almost felt as if he should still be that young gallant cavalier again who had once enjoyed the ladies at court, and favors from the crown.

But that was before . . . Ah well. He shook his head slightly, clearing it of the past, and quickly returned to reality, then gestured for her to precede him to the longboat.

"We will try again, *señora*," he said, his voice warning her with its intensity. "As I said before, I intend to be far from these shores when the sun comes up."

Lizette sighed. There was nothing she could do now except go with him, and she trudged back down the hill with tears in her eyes, glad it was too dark for Mosely and Kidder to see them, and once again she climbed into the longboat so they could head out to the ship.

Her heart was heavy, a physical pain knifing through it as the longboat left the shore behind, and later, aboard ship once more, a sense of complete loss began to sweep over her as she watched the sails unfurl and felt the big ship heave in

the water, catching the wind that filled its sails. She had no
idea where they were headed or what was going to happen
next, and an emptiness gnawed at her insides.

She was alone, all alone, and whether she lived or died
was up to her now. There was no one else to help her. Her
one chance for freedom was behind her, and tears rolled
down her cheeks. Well, she was going to survive, dammit,
she'd always been a survivor, even when things seemed the
worst. She clenched her fist angrily, and as the ship began to
plow the waves, heading farther and farther away from the
cove and out to sea, as the last sight of the island of Cuba
disappeared on the horizon and the first few rays of the
morning sun began to light the sky to the east, Lizette made
up her mind that in spite of everything she was going to live,
and so was the child within her, and someday, no matter
how long it took, she was going to get back home.

Bain paced the deck of the *Sparrow* feverishly, his thoughts
in a turmoil. It had been days since they'd sailed out of St.
Augustine headed for Havana. Days he didn't even want to
think of. Days that Lizette was being subjected to God
knows what at the hands of that madman de Córdoba,
Sancho the Bloody! Bain's only hope was that Sancho wasn't
living up to his name, and his fists clenched as the man in
the crow's nest suddenly shouted down that he'd sighted
land. A short time later as they neared the entrance to the
channel that led to the harbor at Havana, Bain was like a
coiled spring ready to snap.

"You think we'll have any trouble?" Eric asked, joining
him on deck.

Bain shrugged. "No more than normal, I hope. The Spanish have had their ports open to American shipping for only
a short time now and there are bound to be a few disgruntled sea captains who'll think we're coming in to spoil their
trade."

Eric sighed and looked up as they sailed past the fortress
of El Morro on the hill overlooking this part of the approach; then he turned to face the Punta on the opposite
shore. Both forts had been built years before to guard the
harbor, as had been the Fortaleza de la Cabaña, an even
larger fortification farther into the channel, and just a few
years back, because they were an American ship, they'd
have been stopped before getting this far. As it was, both

Eric and Bain could feel a dozen spyglasses trained on them as their ship passed beneath the heavily armed fortresses, and it gave them a feeling of apprehension, as did another massive stone fort, the Castillo de la Fuerza, set at a vantage point right at the mouth of the harbor where it could guard the walled city even better than the others.

Havana was certainly well-guarded, thought Eric as he gave orders to cut sail, and already they were moving slower, since there was always a chance of meeting other ships in the channel that led to the harbor, only today most of the ships were either docked already, waiting to leave in the morning, or still loading or unloading. And most of them flew the flag of Spain.

Eric had the helmsman bring the *Sparrow* in at an empty berth, then let Bain handle the rest, since Eric wasn't all that adept with the language. He could speak it a little, but barely well enough to keep him out of trouble.

"How do you intend to start your search?" he asked when Bain had come back on board ship after making sure the pier where they were docked was available for their use.

Bain smiled. "I've already started," he said as Eric followed him belowdecks to the cabin he was using. "The man I asked about docking here said Don Emilio Pérez has a cattle ranch about forty miles or so east of the city, and a house here in town, and he gave me directions. According to him, everyone knows Señor Pérez."

"You want me to come with you?" Eric asked.

Bain shook his head. "I'd better go alone. As it is, I'm not even sure I'll be able to see the man. From what the fellow said, he's rather hard to get an audience with."

"Then I'll just wait here for you?"

"Unless I send word otherwise."

Eric wasn't sure he liked Bain going off alone. True, Bain was more than proficient in the language, but it was always risky to explore a new place alone, especially a city like Havana, and he wished he could have talked him into letting him go along. However, Bain wasn't letting anyone talk him into anything this trip, and a few minutes later, as Eric stood on deck, leaning against the rail watching the owner of the *Sparrow* disappear into the crowds, his russet hair glinting in the afternoon sun seconds before hiding it beneath his beaver hat, Eric said a prayer for him, hoping everything would go all right because Bain cut a fine figure, just the sort that thieves and ruffians often made their targets.

He watched only a brief second longer, then quickly called Waggs over. "You see where Kolter went?" he asked hurriedly.

Waggs nodded. "Yup."

"Think you could find him again and keep him in sight?" he asked.

"You want me to follow him?"

Eric nodded. "See that he stays in one piece."

Waggs grinned. "Righto, Cap'n," he answered briskly, and took off down the gangplank, disappearing into the crowd as quickly as Bain had, and Eric breathed a sigh of relief. He felt a little better now anyway. Waggs was almost as proficient in Spanish as Bain, with the instincts of a bloodhound. Pleased that he'd decided to send him, Eric headed for the hold to see if they'd have to pick up any new supplies while they were here.

Havana was a walled city with only two gates leading out of the main section, one not far from the Castillo de la Punta, one of the forts they had passed earlier that protected the approach to the harbor on the western side of the channel, and the other inland, midway along the wall, with access from the main street that split the city in two. It took only a few minutes for Waggs to spot Bain strolling down the main street of the city, his plain clothes in distinct contrast to the tight-fitting pants, boleros, and fancily decorated clothes of the Spanish nobility, as well as the more casual, yet distinctive and colorful costumes of the less fortunate. Beaver hats and frock coats, with buff trousers and Wellington boots, were quite out of place in a city born and bred to a Spanish culture, and Bain stood out quite easily.

Bain had no idea he was being followed as he strolled along, taking a mental note of the places he was passing, while trying to ignore the occasional strange looks he was receiving. Havana was an old city, with tight ties to Spain, and if he hadn't still been in such a turmoil over why he was here, he might have enjoyed just looking at some of the old buildings. As it was, however, he kept at a brisk pace, and after quite some time he turned down one of the side streets and headed toward a formidable-looking house near the end of the street with sculptured lions on each side of the stone steps and a balcony above the entrance, the door a massive

barrier of thick oak with a door knocker the size of his fist
and shaped like the head of a lion. He mounted the steps
and used the knocker, then waited. No one came. He lifted
it again, letting it fall more briskly this time, and a few
minutes later heard the doorknob begin to turn. The door
opened a wee crack.

"Excuse me," he said in Spanish, as graciously as he
could. "Is this the home of Don Emilio Pérez?"

He was looking into the stern face of an elderly woman,
her eyes narrowing curiously. "*Sí,*" she answered.

"Then may I have a word with him?" Bain asked.

She shook her head. "He's not here, *señor*. He is at a
meeting."

"Where might that be?"

"At the home of his excellency, Señor Nicholas De Mahy,
governor of Cuba, *señor.*"

Well, Tía Isabella was right, he thought, Don Emilio does
move in high circles.

"Would you kindly give me directions?" he asked.

The woman stared at him thoughtfully for a moment, then
told him which way to go before shutting the door again.

Bain turned, set the hat on his head again, and gazed
about. It was a beautiful afternoon. The streets were crowded
and although the directions sounded like the place was quite
some distance away, he decided to walk. Besides, he didn't
see any hack he might wave down, and he wasn't about to
stand around waiting. So he set off again, backtracking part
of the way he'd already come.

Bain had been walking for some time, when suddenly he
slowed, his steps faltering slightly. He had the strangest
feeling he was being followed. He stopped beneath a
streetlamp, pretending to ponder directions while he tried to
see if he could spot anything out of the ordinary, but everything looked all right. Shrugging, figuring it must be his
imagination, he set off again and arrived a few minutes later
at what looked like a town square. After gazing over toward
a tall impressive cathedral the woman back at the Pérez
house had mentioned, and realizing his directions had to be
right, he began to walk again, and turned left from the
square, then walked a couple more blocks and took a right
turn this time. A few minutes later, he avoided some ladies
who were out strolling with their duennas, tipping his hat to
them respectfully, then continued on, but still the sense of

being followed stayed with him. Another right turn a short while later, and he stopped again, the feeling of being followed so strong now that the hair at the nape of his neck stood on end.

Then he saw Waggs and a smile touched the corner of his mouth. He might have known Eric wouldn't let him venture out alone. Since it was only Waggs, he breathed a sigh, and began walking again, unaware that Waggs wasn't the only man following him. On the opposite side of the narrow street, two officers in the uniform of the Spanish Navy were slowly strolling along in the same direction, pretending to be talking about their latest voyages. They'd been doing just that only a few minutes before while they'd walked in the opposite direction when Captain Carlos de las Torres, the one on the right, had spotted Bain, and they'd quickly reversed directions, making sure the man they were following, who was definitely a foreigner to Havana, was still in sight.

"I know it's the same man," the captain said anxiously. "I always said I'd never forget that face."

"But that doesn't make sense, *amigo*," the other man protested. "What would he be doing in Havana? Besides, that was over two years ago. You could be mistaken."

"Two, ten! I don't care if it's twenty," the captain said to his friend. "I say that man is the pirate they call Captain Gallant, and he and his men stole my ship from me and my crew, then set us adrift in a boat."

"But we heard he was dead," his friend argued. "That pirate who was hanged a short time later, the Frenchman, captain of . . . what was it? The *Golden Rose?* You remember—anyway, he said Captain Gallant's ship was wrecked and he drowned in the same storm that crippled the *Golden Rose.* Now, why would the Frenchman lie with a noose around his neck?"

"Maybe he didn't know he was lying," Captain de las Torres answered. "Perhaps no one knows Gallant survived."

Captain Antonio Sánchez, longtime friend of de las Torres, glanced over at his companion furtively. Carlos could be right. After all, he was known to have a remarkable memory. Once more Antonio's eyes rested on the man they were following, and both officers were surprised as Bain, after reaching the Plaza de Armas, headed straight for the governor's palace.

"What do you suppose he's up to?" Captain Sánchez asked.

De las Torres shook his head as both men hesitated for a moment, watching Bain, who had also hesitated at the steps to the palace, trying to figure out which would be best, to say he was a friend of Pérez's and maybe have Pérez deny it, or just tell them that he was looking for Pérez's niece and be sure of being put off. Either way he was sure he was going to have to do some fast talking before getting to see Señor Pérez, and to top it off, he'd probably be interrupting an important meeting. That in itself might irritate the man enough that he'd refuse to see him.

He took off his hat, grabbed a handkerchief from his pocket, and wiped his brow. The long walk had done him good, but the heat he could do without. Well, only one way he was going to learn anything and that was to ask, and with his hat still in his hand, he faced the door and knocked.

The door opened and a tall dark servant stood quietly looking down at Bain.

"*Sí?*" he asked, his equally dark eyes studying Bain curiously.

"Good day," Bain said, then began hurriedly. "I don't mean to interrupt the governor, but I stopped by Señor Pérez's home a short time ago, and the housekeeper said he was here with the governor. Is there any possible way I might get to talk to Señor Pérez?" he asked. "It is quite important."

The servant continued to study Bain for a moment longer, then gestured for him to come in.

"Follow me," he said, and led Bain to a room off the main hall, telling him to wait, then started to go in the opposite direction down the hall toward a set of large closed double doors, when there was another knock at the front door.

Bain stood quietly, paying little attention to the mumble of voices coming from the hallway; then he walked over and stared out the side window, admiring the palace grounds.

Suddenly he turned at a strange shuffling noise behind him, just in time to see the servant hurry past the open doorway, at a run, and seconds later two men filled the arched doorway, their uniforms easily recognizable in the afternoon sun that was streaming in at the window.

"Well, so we meet again," the taller of the officers said, and Bain stared at them bewildered, only they couldn't see his face too clearly since the sun was behind him, throwing his face into shadows while his figure was silhouetted in front of the window.

"*Por favor,* I beg your pardon?" Bain questioned. He hadn't the faintest idea who the man was or what was going on.

"Come now, *señor,*" Captain de las Torres said as they continued blocking the doorway. "Surely you haven't forgotten our first and only meeting, have you? I know I haven't."

Now Bain was really confused.

"You look perplexed, Captain Gallant," de las Torres went on, and his dark eyes snapped viciously. "But then perhaps I have more reason to remember you than you do me. After all, the *Maravilla* was my ship before you took her from me, wasn't she?"

The color drained from Bain's face as he stared at the man, and suddenly he remembered where he'd seen him before. The *Maravilla.* My God! What a hell of a time to run into something like this.

"I'm sorry," Bain said, trying to keep his voice steady and feign innocence. "I don't believe I understand."

"Oh, you understand, all right, *señor,*" de las Torres said as he and his companion stepped a bit further into the room. "I always swore I'd never forget your face, Captain Bain Kolter, and *por Dios,* I haven't."

"Now, look here. There's been a mistake," Bain began, shaking his head in frustration, only before he could say any more, the governor's servant returned with not only the governor, following curiously behind him, but also two soldiers, their guns drawn, and Bain stared at them all furiously, knowing there wasn't any way he was going to talk his way out of this one.

Only one thing to do, he told himself hurriedly, and that was take them by surprise. The windows of the palace were too high up to exit that way, so his only other alternative was the doorway. He held out his hand as if in supplication, as if he were going to try to appeal to them for mercy, then instead, he lunged forward and knocked the two officers into the two soldiers, whose guns went off, just missing Bain's head.

The governor began yelling frantically, the soldiers were shouting and cursing, and only the naval officers seemed to keep their wits about them as Bain shoved them aside and made a break for the front door, brushing past the startled

servant. However, Captain de las Torres, anger and determination now driving him, got his footing quickly and gave
chase, moving with a speed he hadn't realized he possessed,
managing to reach Bain just before Bain reached the front
door. Tackling Bain successfully, de las Torres dragged Bain
with him, and they both hit the floor.

The cords in Bain's neck bulged as he fought, trying to get
away from the man, only de las Torres hung on like a leech,
and within seconds the others were on top of Bain too, and
he knew there was no use even trying to fight anymore.

"All right, all right, so I'm Bain Kolter," he gasped breathlessly, finally giving in as the soldiers grabbed him, their
hands tightening on his arms as they pulled him to his feet.
"But I wasn't a pirate, Captain, believe me. Not in the sense
that you call me one. I was working for the American
government as an undercover agent, and I was exonerated
of the charge of piracy. Didn't you read the papers?"

"Papers?" the captain questioned as his friend helped him
straighten his uniform, and he ran his hand across his lower
lip where Bain had kicked him while they were struggling on
the floor. There was blood on his finger. "What papers,
señor?" he asked.

"The American papers," Bain answered, and tried to
stand up straighter, but the soldiers wouldn't let him, their
hands tightening even more, pulling his arms back until they
hurt. Bain grimaced uncomfortably. "They explained the whole
damn thing," he went on, trying to make them understand. "I
was working for naval intelligence. I've been exonerated."

"Not by me," de las Torres snarled angrily. "We don't
read American papers in Havana."

Captain de las Torres straightened and turned, as did his
companion, and Bain stared at the man who was coming
toward him. He was obviously the governor. The man's eyes
were hard and unyielding as they stared back at Bain.

"Forgive me, Nicholas, I'm sorry for the disturbance,"
Captain de las Torres began. "But as you no doubt heard,
this man is the American pirate Captain Bain Kolter, also
known as Captain Gallant. A man who raided a number of
Spanish ships some years back, and mine was one of them."

The governor raised a hand for the captain to be quiet.
"That's enough, Carlos, I'll handle it," he said, his eyes still
on Bain. "Is what my friend Carlos says right, *señor?*"
Governor De Mahy asked Bain, and Bain laughed ironically.

"Your friend?" he asked.

"Sí, my friend," the governor answered confidently. "Carlos and I have known each other for a number of years. But I asked you, señor, is it true? Are you Captain Bain Kolter?"

Bain sighed. "Yes, I'm Bain Kolter," he answered, and he could already see his head in a noose. "But like I told your friend the captain, I'm not guilty of piracy, your excellency. I was working as an agent for the American government, and I still have friends in high places. So before you do anything foolish that you might regret later, I suggest you check with the United States government."

"I see." The governor continued to stare at Bain, then looked at Captain de las Torres. "Perhaps we'd better," he said. "I'll let you handle that, Carlos, since it was your ship that the captain ran off with, only in the meantime, just to be on the safe side, I think while you're away checking on his story, we'd better put Captain Kolter in irons, just to make sure he's still around when you return."

Bain began to protest, and started to tell them that Señor Pérez could help straighten out the matter, but they didn't give him a chance as de las Torres' fist snaked out, splatting across the side of Bain's face.

"Take him to the dungeons," De Mahy ordered firmly, then turned and started to walk away. Suddenly he stopped and turned back to Captain de las Torres. "By the way, you didn't say, Carlos, had you come for a visit, or what?" he asked.

"Not today, Nicholas," de las Torres said as he watched the soldiers open the door and start dragging Bain out. "We were following Kolter, and he happened to come here."

"Here?" The governor's eyebrows raised. "Hmmm! I wonder why?" he said thoughtfully, then shrugged. "Ah well, who knows, maybe I'll ask him later, after you return from the United States." He headed back toward the huge double doors at the end of the hallway, while Bain still shook his head, trying to clear it from the force of de las Torres' blow.

Outside, Waggs had been loitering around the square, watching the door where Bain had disappeared, and wondering if maybe he should ask one of the passersby what the place was. It certainly was impressive enough, only it didn't look like an ordinary house. Some sort of government building maybe, or maybe one of those Spanish nobles lived in it.

He watched the place for a long time, then was just about

ready to ask someone about the name of the square he was in, and what the building was, since he'd never been to Havana, when the door suddenly opened and two soldiers began backing out, followed by the two naval officers he'd seen go in after Bain had entered, and as the soldiers turned, facing the street, Waggs could see that they were dragging someone between them. It was Bain Kolter and the side of his mouth was bleeding.

Instinctively he started toward them, then suddenly stopped when it occurred to him that whatever they were to do with Kolter could possibly happen to him too if they discovered they knew each other. So instead of hurrying over, he sauntered over slowly with the rest of the crowd that was starting to congregate, and kept his ears strained to see if he could hear any of what was going on.

It took a few minutes for him to make his way near enough to the front row of spectators where he wouldn't be as likely to be seen, yet could hear everything, and by that time a carriage was on its way down the drive next to the building.

Bain seemed to be in a bit of a daze, evidently from the blow that had split his lip, and Waggs watched the soldiers trying to get him to step back so the carriage could reach them, while moving the crowd back at the same time.

Waggs, still having a hard time hearing with all the noise, and catching only a word or two here and there, such as "pirate," "die," and "prison," made his way around the back of the carriage, elbowing his way through the onlookers until he was directly behind the two naval officers, who seemed to be extremely interested in Bain and were offering to accompany the soldiers if needed.

"What happened, Capitan?" Waggs urged in Spanish, his voice carrying over de las Torres' left shoulder, and Carlos de las Torres straightened arrogantly.

"Nothing to worry about, really," he said, more to the crowd than directly to Waggs. "We've just captured one of those bloodthirsty American pirates, Captain Gallant, that's all." He leaned closer to the soldiers as the carriage pulled up to the walk and they started putting Bain inside. "Are you sure you don't want us to go with you, Sergeant?" de las Torres asked, but the sergeant who seemed to be in charge shook his head.

"We can handle it, sir," he said, and drew his sword from

its sheath, brandishing it dramatically, and the crowd moved back some. He hadn't had time to reload his pistol after missing the shot earlier, nor had his companion. With a great deal of ceremony he climbed into the carriage, sitting opposite Bain and the other soldier, then motioned to the driver, giving him orders to head for the waterfront.

"We'll see how Kolter likes the dungeons at El Morro," de las Torres mused to his friend.

Antonio scowled. "You don't suppose he has friends here in Havana, do you?" he asked. "After all, how did he get here? Maybe he's not the only one who should be in prison."

"You think we should check out the harbor?"

"It might save you a trip. You heard the governor. He isn't going to hang Kolter until you bring back word as to whether he's lying or not. If we find his ship and men right here, we won't need any other proof."

"And a trip to the United States could take two, maybe three weeks. Hmmm . . ."

While de las Torres was pondering whether to go to the port authority and get permission to search every ship in the harbor, Waggs took the opportunity to slip away so he could head back toward the ship.

Jesus, wait till the captain hears about this, he thought as he worked his way through the crowded streets, trying to get his bearings and remember which way the harbor was; then it dawned on him. Damn, all he had to do was follow the carriage Bain was in. The sergeant had told the driver to head for the waterfront. Quickly, before it could get out of sight, he headed in the same direction; however, as soon as he caught sight of the first ship's mast, Waggs took off at a dead run, zigzagging in and out among the confusion of carriages, carts, and people, hoping to get to the *Sparrow* before the soldiers could reach a boat to take Bain across the bay to the dungeons of El Morro.

Eric was in his cabin going over a list of the supplies they'd just put on board when Waggs burst in without bothering to knock.

"Sorry, Cap'n," he panted, winded from the last few hundred yards he'd run. "But we got trouble. That is, Kolter does."

"What happened?"

"Some stupid captain evidently recognized him from when he was workin' for the navy pretendin' to be a pirate, and they've arrested him."

"Arrested him?"

Waggs gestured with his thumb. "They're down at the end of the wharf now, puttin' him into a boat to row him across to El Morro."

Eric frowned. "I've heard stories about the dungeons at El Morro," he said slowly, and rubbed his chin. "Now what the hell do we do?"

"We could see that they don't reach the other side of the bay."

"And we'd never get out of the channel."

"We would if we left right away. After all, the only ones who know he's arrested is us, them soldiers, and the Spanish naval officers I left back at that big fancy buildin' they dragged Kolter out of."

"Those navy officers the ones who spotted him?"

"From what I could hear, they were talkin' about checkin' the ships in the harbor to see if he has any friends."

"Oh my God." Eric stood up and walked to the cabin window, staring out, trying to figure out the best thing to do.

Life had been so simple the past few years. Except for an occasional skirmish with the likes of men like Sancho the Bloody, and getting caught in a few local wars and uprisings now and then in some of the countries they sailed to where they had to try to stay neutral, and the usual drunken sailors to worry about, he'd had little taste of intrigue and danger since running the British blockades back during the war, and that had ended six years ago. Now he had to make a decision and make it fast.

If they waited until the soldiers were halfway across the bay and rescued Bain, then took off, Bain would probably get mad because then he'd never be able to find the people he was looking for, since they'd never get back inside the harbor past the guns on those forts again. Yet, if he let them take Bain to the prison, there was every chance Bain might never get back out again. He turned to Waggs.

"Did you hear anything else?"

Waggs frowned. "Yeah, come to think of it. One of them Spanish captains said somethin' about the governor not hangin' Kolter till the other one got back from the United States. Somethin' about gettin' proof."

"Aha, that sounds better. Now, look," he said hurriedly, "go get the men together and get ready to cast off. We're gonna sail out of here and lie off the coast for a day or two until your Spanish captain simmers down; then we'll sail back in, and this time you and I are gonna go see this Señor Pérez or whatever the heck his name is, and if this lady Bain's been looking for, this Elena de Córdoba, is with him, she should be able to clear Bain. After all, if Sancho de Córdoba thought Bain was the one who gave the information about him to the authorities, then the de Córdobas had to know he wasn't a pirate, but was really working for the government."

Waggs nodded, his eyes alive, anxious. "Nice goin', Cap'n," he agreed quickly. "Kolter sure as hell can't expect more'n that. I'll go tell the crew so we can get under way."

A few minutes later, as the afternoon sun began to dip down toward the walls of the city of Havana, and the bustle of traffic on the wharf began to slow some in the midday heat, the *Sparrow* relinquished her berth at the docks, slipped from her moorings, and let the breeze blowing across the bay catch her sails, then headed back across the harbor toward the channel that led to the sea. While in a small dinghy only a short distance away, his hands tied securely behind him, his tongue slowly caressing the cut at the side of his lip, Bain Kolter watched apprehensively as the *Sparrow* drew near; then he frowned as it sailed right past them. He'd been hoping they were coming to his rescue. It'd be so easy to swamp the dinghy and take him aboard. But they didn't, and as he saw the ship pick up speed and move into the channel, his only hope was that Waggs had kept right on following him, seen what happened, and Eric knew what he was doing. But even as Bain drew his eyes from the disappearing ship and gazed off toward the distant hill where El Morro stood, he began to wonder if Eric might be deserting him, and an empty feeling began to gnaw at his insides.

Chapter 7

TWO DAYS HAD passed since Eric had taken the *Sparrow* back out to sea, and now once more they approached the narrow channel, then rode under the guns of the forts, heading back in. Eric was on deck making sure nothing went wrong, and after entering the harbor itself and sailing past the last fort, he had the helmsman maneuver the ship as far away from the place where they had just docked as they could before tying up, hoping all the while that none of the chandlers or other shopkeepers along the waterfront would recognize the *Sparrow* with its distinctive sleek lines. After all, he had no idea whether the Spanish captains had been nosying around or not, but wasn't about to take chances. He wanted to help Bain, not make things worse for him, and the *Sparrow* had been built on the same lines as the ship Bain had used during his brief sojourn as a pirate.

Eric took Waggs with him when he checked to make sure they could stay at the pier where they were docked, and once they were sure everything was all right, he left one of the other men in charge and he and Waggs headed into the city to see if Waggs could remember the route Bain had taken the first day they'd arrived.

Eric was glad he had Waggs with him, even though the man was a bit rough around the edges, because Waggs not only spoke Spanish fluently, but had a good memory, and he was the one who had followed Bain that first day. It had started to rain a thin drizzle shortly after they had left the ship, so consequently the streets weren't as crowded as they had been only a few days before.

"Maybe we oughta hail a hack," Waggs suggested as the rain started coming down harder and he saw Eric pull his hat down farther over his eyes and turn the collar of his coat up.

"Sounds good to me," Eric said. "Only where do we tell

him to go? Bain had the address, I don't, and if I know you, you didn't take time to see what street the Pérez house was on."

Waggs flushed. "You know me too well, Cap'n," he answered. "Only, can't we just tell him to take us to where the gent lives and give him the name?"

"That might work. But what if it doesn't?"

"It's worth a try, ain't it?"

Eric couldn't argue with that, so after hailing the next hack that went by, they ended up riding the rest of the way, and a short while later found themselves standing in front of a heavy oak door with an iron lion's head for a knocker.

"Well, this is it," Eric said. "Now I just hope I remember enough Spanish to get things across."

It was fairly early in the day yet, and Eric wasn't surprised at all when the housekeeper opened the door only a crack and looked at them suspiciously.

"*Por favor*, please, *señora*," Eric began as cordially as he could in stilted Spanish. "Is Señor Pérez at home? We'd like a word with him if we may."

"He is at home, *sí*," she said warily. "But he's not receiving guests."

"Please, *señora*," Eric pleaded. "It's a matter of life and death."

"Oh?" Her eyes widened. "Whose, *señor*? Yours?"

"A friend." Eric had changed from his workclothes to the clothes he wore when he had to handle business transactions, and although they were soaked, they were still presentable. "Will you do me a favor, *señora*," he went on as he slipped the toe of his boot furtively between the door and the doorjamb. "Just go to Señor Pérez and tell him I have an important message for him regarding his niece Elena de Córdoba, and that a man's life depends on it."

She eyed him for a few minutes as if contemplating.

"Please?" he begged. "There's no one else I can turn to for help."

She sighed. "I will see," she said, and started to shut the door, catching his foot in it.

"I'm sorry, *señora*," he said in his faltering Spanish, his face flushing slightly. "But it is quite wet out here. Would it be possible to wait just inside the door?"

She glanced down at his foot, then up into Eric's blue eyes that were twinkling warmly. "All right, *sí*, come in," she finally said, opening the door wider, and was rewarded by big smiles from both Eric and Waggs as they stepped into the elaborate foyer.

"*Gracias,*" Eric said, thanking her, but she straightened to her full height, which wasn't too tall, and tried to look stern. "Just see you don't put a foot any farther than that rug," she said, pointing down at the small reed mat they were standing on; then she hurried away, glancing back at them once just to make sure they were staying put.

A few minutes later she was back again and ushered them into a room off to the side of the foyer, then told them Don Emilio should be with them in a moment.

To Eric it seemed like the man was taking forever. He fidgeted about, examining some of the furnishings, his tall muscular frame feeling out of place in such elaborate surroundings, since he was more used to his ship's small cabin, and this place wreaked of wealth; then he sighed in relief as they finally heard the clicking of heels in the hall just outside the room.

"So, and what might I do for you, *señores?*" Don Emilio said as he entered and stood staring at them. "And what have you to do with my niece?"

Eric introduced himself and Waggs, whose real name was Ulysses Waggoner, then tried to explain.

"It's rather a strange story, *señor,*" he began, "but you see, we happen to know that you are the uncle of the notorious pirate Sancho de Córdoba—"

"Now, just a minute," Don Emilio interrupted. "What do you think you're—"

"Please, *señor,* let me finish," Eric pleaded. "Then you may throw us out if you wish, but I must finish."

Emilio Pérez stared at him hard for a moment, then finally nodded. "All right, go on."

"*Gracias,*" Eric thanked him, then continued. "We also know that Sancho de Córdoba, after kidnapping the wife of my employer, Bain Kolter, had her here with him when he brought his sister, Elena de Córdoba, and her brother Mario to Havana to stay with you."

Señor Pérez's swarthy complexion suddenly paled, but Eric went on.

"Bain Kolter and I sailed into Havana two days ago, Señor Pérez, looking for you and Elena de Córdoba and hoping the two of you could help us find her brother Sancho and put an end to this whole stupid mistake, but unfortunately, Bain ran into some trouble and they've taken him over to the dungeons at El Morro."

Don Emilio looked confused. "Now, just wait, *señores*," he cautioned Eric slowly. "Do you mean to say that the gentleman who was apprehended in the governor's palace the other day, the one Captain de las Torres accused of being this pirate, Captain Gallant, that he is the husband of the woman who was at my hacienda with Sancho?"

"If she was about so high with dark hair and green eyes," Eric answered, measuring as close to Lizette Kolter's height as he could remember, "*sí*, she's his wife."

Emilio Pérez straightened authoritatively. He didn't like the way this conversation was going. Not at all. "Well, now, *señores*, I'll tell you," he said, his face troubled. "Before I go any further with this conversation, I'm afraid I must ask a favor of you, and one you may not want to grant."

Eric eyed him curiously. "What's that?"

"Regarding Sancho de Córdoba. I have no idea how you or this man in El Morro prison . . . what's his name?"

"Bain Kolter."

"*Sí*, this Señor Kolter . . . I don't know how you discovered that Sancho is my nephew, *señores*, but I must warn you, both of you, that no one on this island of Cuba, or anywhere else for that matter, has the same knowledge, and that's the way I want it to stay. Do you understand?"

Eric thought as much. "I guess I can't blame you there, *señor*," he answered. "But at the same time, I did come here to help Bain Kolter, and I intend to help him, no matter what it takes."

"Even if it were to destroy my life here, *señor?*"

"I doubt it would come to that."

"You do not know the people of Havana, *señores*. No, they must never know of Sancho's relationship to me."

Eric glanced over at Waggs, then back to the Spaniard, his eyes steady on the man's face. "All right, then, let's put it this way, shall we? If you will cooperate with us, *señor,* and help us secure Bain Kolter's release, then I don't see why we can't cooperate with you, and no one in Havana need know anything about de Córdoba. How's that?"

"I see." Don Emilio studied Eric for a moment. The young man was shrewd. Although his command of the Spanish language left much to be desired, it was apparent by the forthright way he presented himself that he was used to being in charge. "You are a sea captain, Señor . . . ?"

"Edelman, Eric Edelman, Señor Pérez," Eric reminded him. "And, yes, *sí,* I captain one of Bain Kolter's ships, the *Sparrow.* Normally we trade between the United States and some of the Scandinavian countries, France, occasionally Spain or Portugal. But at the moment the ship is docked in Havana's harbor. And now, since I think perhaps we both understand each other, Señor Pérez, do you think maybe it's possible you could help us secure Señor Kolter's release and help us locate Elena de Córdoba?"

Emilio inhaled as he looked from the captain's bright blue eyes staring back at him from his tanned face, to the other man's hazel eyes, also staring at him intently from above a nose that had obviously been broken at one time or another.

It was obvious neither man was comfortable in these surroundings, yet it was also obvious that they must have a deep loyalty to their employer. A sign of integrity, he was sure.

"The latter, I can do for you easily, *señores,"* he finally said, making a quick decision, and one he hoped he wouldn't regret. "My niece Elena arrived here in Havana from my hacienda farther inland only yesterday afternoon, but as for Señor Kolter . . ." He shook his head. "I'm afraid that will not be so easy."

Eric frowned. "Why?"

"Because Bain Kolter is accused of piracy, *señor.* How can I possibly help him? I don't even know the man, I only heard his name the day he was arrested."

"Your niece knows him." Eric was tense, determined. "She knows he wasn't really a pirate, that he was a government agent and was forced to attack several ships during the time he was posing as a pirate to cover his real purpose in being there. She could tell the authorities."

"And reveal how she knows him? I'm not a fool, Capitán Edelman. No, Elena will say nothing."

"Elena will say nothing about what?" a soft feminine voice cut in, and all three men turned toward the doorway where Elena de Córdoba stood.

She was wearing a dress of pale pink silk that emphasized her tawny skin and dark hair that was twisted into a chignon at the nape of her neck, and her dark eyes moved from her uncle to the two men, then back to her uncle again as she entered the room and walked toward him.

"Well, Tío Emilio," she said, her voice low and husky, "I'll ask you again: what is it I'm not supposed to say?"

Emilio Pérez ignored the question and instead took her arm, turning her to face Eric and Waggs, and introduced them.

"That's fine and well," she said after acknowledging the introduction. "But you still haven't answered my question."

"And I don't intend to."

"Then maybe the *capitán* and his friend will," she said, turning to Eric, and her eyes were bristling with annoyance. "Well, *capitán*? It's obvious, since my uncle was talking to you, that you know what it is I'm not supposed to say to God knows whom. Maybe you'll give me an answer."

Eric glanced at Don Emilio. "She's bound to learn about him eventually, *señor*," he said. "You can't keep something like this a secret."

"She'll say nothing to the authorities!" Don Emilio insisted angrily. "It would ruin everything for her, me, her brother Mario."

"Don't you think she won't realize that?" Eric looked at Elena for a moment, then back to her uncle. "But maybe with her help we can think of something—some way to get him out of that place."

Elena frowned. "What place? What are you talking about?" Suddenly she paled. "*Madre de Dios!* Has Sancho been arrested?"

"Not Sancho, no," her uncle answered, and saw the relief in her eyes.

"But Bain Kolter has," Eric added deliberately, and Elena gasped, her hand covering her breast.

"Bain? Where?" was all she could murmur.

"Here in Havana," Eric answered before Don Emilio had a chance to try lying to her. "He was arrested the other day when he came looking for your uncle here, and they threw him in prison."

"You had him arrested?" she asked incredulously.

Don Emilio shook his head. "No . . . no, don't be ridiculous. I was at a meeting with the governor when he arrived and I guess he must have come there to see me, and Captain de las Torres recognized him. It seems that Señor Kolter, whom he claims is a pirate named Captain Gallant, raided his ship some years back and left him and his crew adrift while they sailed off with the *Maravilla*, which de las Torres never saw again. And now, from what these gentlemen have told me, and from what you haven't told me and I've managed to piece together since their arrival, I've come to the conclusion that Señor Bain Kolter, or Captain Gallant, if you will, is obviously this man Domino you've been talking about and whom your brother Sancho has taken up a vendetta against. Am I right?"

"Where is he?" she asked softly.

"There's nothing you can do about it, Elena." Don Emilio's face was somber, his eyes cold, unfeeling. "If you were to speak even one word in his defense, you would have to explain how you came to know him, and it could jeopardize everything we have here."

Her eyes narrowed stubbornly. "Where is he?"

Don Emilio's shoulders drooped in defeat. "In the dungeons of El Morro. It's an old fort that protects our harbor from men like your brother."

Elena didn't answer, but instead turned and walked to the window, staring out. It had stopped raining now and the sun was trying to break through the clouds. Tío Emilio was right, she thought. If she told them how she knew Bain Kolter was a government agent, Tío Emilio would have to admit he was Sancho's uncle and he could lose everything. Then where would she be? Yet, she had to think of something. Bain was here, in Havana. The thought brought butterflies to her stomach and an ache to her breast.

Eric had been watching Elena de Córdoba, and now he frowned as he looked over at Don Emilio.

"I don't mean to be nosy, *señor*," he began in his hesitant Spanish. "But how did you explain your niece and nephew's sudden appearance here to your friends? And how did Sancho manage it without being caught? You said she arrived in Havana yesterday?"

"I have a cattle ranch to the east, not far from the sea," he explained. "Sancho brought *La Piranha* into a small cove nearby and brought her and Mario there, where they've been for some days, then yesterday they joined me here."

"I see." Eric was still curious. "So you haven't introduced her to your friends yet?"

"No."

"Then they have no idea who she is or where she's from?"

"Oh, I have told them that, *señor*. I told them they were my sister's children from St. Augustine, in the Florida territories, and that their father died a short time ago, only they were so upset when they first arrived that I took them out to the hacienda for a short time until they got over the shock of his passing. Which is basically true."

"They believe you?"

"I have lived on this island for fifty years, *señor,* and my word is never questioned. Besides, there are those who knew me in Spain, and knew my sister lived in the Florida territories before her death, and that her husband and family still live there. All but the oldest son, that is. They were told long ago that my namesake, Emilio de Córdoba—or Sancho, to you—was dead."

"And none of your old friends ever visited them at Barlovento?"

He glanced over at his niece. "Elena?"

She turned slowly, only from the look on her face it was obvious her thoughts weren't with them completely.

"Did you hear the *capitán,* Elena?" Don Emilio asked.

She nodded, the faraway look leaving her eyes. "The only ones from home who ever came were the de Vacas, and they're in Spain now." She looked right at her uncle, frowning. "Why didn't you tell me about Señor Kolter yesterday afternoon when I arrived?" she asked.

"Yesterday?" His eyebrows raised. "Did I know yesterday that he was this Domino you've been talking about? Even Sancho never said whose wife the woman was who was with him, only that what he did was his business. And you and Mario"—Don Emilio's eyes glistened irritably—"even you two never said his real name was Bain Kolter. How was I to know? Besides, it still wouldn't have helped, even if I had known. I can't tell the authorities anything about the man without telling them about Sancho."

"Why not?" Elena's eyes suddenly came alive. "Why can't you?" she said eagerly. "Rather, why can't I? They don't know what Barlovento was, or that I even lived there. They think I'm from St. Augustine. Well, fine, I am, and for all purposes I met Bain Kolter there also. They don't have to know otherwise."

Eric was interested. "What do you have in mind?"

Elena was determined. "Just this," she answered. "We can say that Bain and I were keeping company back in St. Augustine, only shortly after my father's death we had a lovers' quarrel, then I came here."

"That's well and good," Waggs interrupted. He'd been listening silently to the whole conversation, and finally decided it was time to speak up. "Only what are you gonna do when the Spanish *capitán* your governor sent to America gets back and tells everybody Bain Kolter's already married?"

"But de las Torres hasn't left yet," Don Emilio offered hurriedly.

"He hasn't?"

"No. He's to leave the day after tomorrow."

Waggs relaxed and looked over at Eric. "Then it just might work," he said, and Eric agreed.

"In fact," Eric said, "if she can convince the authorities that Bain isn't really a pirate, the governor probably wouldn't even send de las Torres." He looked over at Don Emilio. "What do you think?"

"I think perhaps you're right, *señor.*"

"But I think I'd better go talk to Bain alone first," Elena suggested, and all three looked at her curiously. "Well, someone has to tell him what we're planning," she explained. "So he doesn't inadvertently give the whole thing away. Besides, Tío Emilio, I have to make sure he really is Bain Kolter, don't I? We can't ask them to release the wrong man."

"Then you think you can convince the authorities that he should be released?" her uncle asked.

Elena smiled warmly, her eyes shining. "With you attesting to my honesty and integrity, I don't see how they can't believe me," she answered. "After all, I am the niece of Don Emilio Pérez. They wouldn't dare call me a liar, now, would they?"

"It's plausible," Eric said hesitantly. "But what if Bain won't go along with it?"

Emilio frowned. "What do you mean?"

"He's a determined man, *señor,* and very much in love with his wife. What if she can't talk him into pretending there's something between the two of them, what then?"

Elena's mouth twitched provocatively, and her eyes were smoldering. "Ah now, don't worry about that part of the plan, Capitán Edelman," she purred enticingly. "That's one thing I don't expect to have to worry about. He'll go along with it, you'll see." She turned to her uncle. "Now, Tío Emilio, I suggest that while I go find Mario and fill him in on what's happening, you go see some of your friends to see what can be done, and if all goes well, *señores*," she said to Eric and Waggs, "Bain Kolter may be out of El Morro before nightfall. How does that sound?" and as she left the room smiling, Don Emilio watched her closely, and suddenly it dawned on him that she was in love with the man. His niece was in love with Bain Kolter, and as he saw Capitán Edelman and his first mate to the door, promising to get in touch as soon as there was anything definite, he couldn't forget the look on Elena's face and wished there was some other way out of this mess, because he had a strange feeling that if the authorities didn't believe her, Elena would find some other way to get the man out of prison, and he hated to think what that way might be.

Bain was as uncomfortable as all hell, and so hungry his stomach actually hurt. He glanced across the corridor and winced. At least he was better off than those poor wretches, and he drew his eyes quickly away from the two men who were chained to the wall, unable to sit, unable to stand erect. All they could do was hang between floor and ceiling, their wrists bloody from the irons that held them, their muscles, once strong and sinewy, now weak and flaccid, and he wondered how long they'd been here and what their crimes might have been.

So far he hadn't been treated too badly if you could call watered soup and wormy biscuits food, and lice-filled straw on the floor a bed. He scratched at his beard. Two days . . . no, this was the third. He looked down at his hands, the filth and grime turning his stomach. Even the smell here was foul. A mixture of urine, excrement, and the putrid smell of rotting flesh. He'd heard rumors of the torture and brutality here in El Morro, but had never believed it could be so bad.

Suddenly the haunting cry of a man in pain echoed through the place and Bain shuddered. They were torturing some poor soul again, and he covered his ears, trying to block it out, while he wondered, as he often had over the years, why men had to be so cruel to each other.

After a while his hands eased on his ears and he lifted them off. The screaming had stopped as quickly as it had started and he prayed there'd be no more today. Strange they hadn't picked on him yet, but then maybe his time was coming. After all, he hadn't been here all that long. He was sitting on the floor and shifted into a more comfortable position against the side of the cell he was in, glad they had at least let him keep his clothes and boots, even though his pants and coat were a mess and his boots covered with filth.

Leaning his head back against the wall, he watched a spot across the cell where there was a small hole. He'd put a tiny piece from the wormy biscuit brought around this morning near the hole just to see what would happen, and sure enough, two pairs of eyes shone red from the darkness inside, light from the fire in the corridor reflecting off them. The dungeons were deep underground, their only light coming from lanterns in the corridors or fires the guards used for cooking their food. And unlike the temperature aboveground, it was always damp and cold, the heavy scent of must and mildew in the air.

He had just become engrossed in watching the two rats begin to sneak toward the piece of biscuit when there was a commotion in the corridor, and one of the guards stopped, starting to unlock the door to his cell. Bain strained his eyes to see better, wondering if they'd finally decided it was his turn on the racks or if he was getting a cellmate, when he caught the outline of a slight figure directly behind the guard, and whoever it was, was shrouded in a long cape. He tensed, alert now as he sat up a little straighter so he could see better.

"There he is, other side of the cell, *señorita*," the guard was saying as he swung the door open all the way. Then he called in to Bain, "Someone to see you, *amigo*," and he chuckled as the hooded figure entered, the cell door clanging shut behind it.

Bain rose to his feet now, and stared at the caped figure moving hesitantly toward him. It stopped a few feet away, and he frowned.

Elena was watching Bain closely. It had been two years since she'd seen him. Two years that seemed like forever, and as she stared now, trying to see him in the dimly lit cell, her heart was pounding erratically.

"Well?" Bain said sarcastically, his mouth parched from the lack of water, lips dry and cracked. "Are you part of this horrible nightmare I've been having, or death coming to take me?" he asked.

Elena swallowed, then took a deep breath as she reached up and lifted the hood from her hair, letting it fall back onto her shoulders.

"Neither," she whispered softly, and Bain's frown deepened at the sight of her silken hair, the light from outside the cell flickering over part of her face.

"Elena?" he gasped, startled. He couldn't believe his eyes. "It is Elena, isn't it?"

She smiled. "I thought maybe you'd forget, yet I was hoping . . ."

He shook his head. "I don't believe it."

"Why? You were trying to find me, weren't you?"

"Yes, but . . ."

She took a step closer and looked up at him, her heart in her eyes. "Now, why don't you greet an old friend the way you should?" she whispered, and started to lift her hands up to his head, only he grabbed them quickly.

"No!" he snapped abruptly, his hands tightening around her fingers. "I'm dirty . . . filthy. Don't touch me or you'll be full of every kind of vermin there is."

"I don't care."

"I do."

"Are you sure that's the only reason?"

He released one of her hands and took hold of her chin, turning her face more so he could look into her eyes. "You've changed," he said, ignoring her question.

"Not inside. I'm still the same inside, Domino."

His hand dropped from her chin. "I left Domino back in Barlovento two years ago, Elena."

"And never looked back?"

"Why should I? I had Liz." He was still holding her other hand, and released it too.

She bit back the tears. "When you kissed me good-bye that day, did you think of Liz then?" she asked, watching him closely.

He sighed. "I thought of you, then, Elena," he answered huskily. "I thought of everything you'd given me, and I wanted to give you something in return. No, for that moment I thought of you, but to me it meant nothing."

"Your Liz was waiting for you?" she asked.

He thought back for a moment to the turmoil he'd faced when he'd first returned to Liz, and the anger and hurt; then his heart warmed, remembering the past few years since then.

"Yes, she was waiting," he answered. "And my life was good until your brother decided I'd betrayed him and your family." His eyes grew intense. "I had nothing to do with what happened at Barlovento, Elena," he said angrily. "I swear to you."

"Sancho thinks you did."

"And you?"

"I know you didn't, but then, I'm not my brother, am I?"

"And you couldn't talk him out of this?"

"No one talks Sancho out of anything," Elena said, her eyes darkening. "It's possible to talk him into things, but once he's made up his mind—my brother's a stubborn man, Domino, and I'm afraid at times not a very nice one."

"If he's hurt Liz, I'll . . ."

"Don't worry, your wife's all right. At least she was the last time I saw her."

"That's right, I'd forgotten for a minute. You did see her, didn't you?" he said, suddenly remembering that Elena had been on Sancho's ship with him.

"*Sí,* I met your Liz, as you call her."

"Why do you say it like that?"

"Not here, please, Domino," she protested uncomfortably. "There'll be time later to talk. Right now we have to concentrate on getting you out of here," and for the next few minutes she told him about Eric's visit and the plans they'd made.

"In other words, my only way out of here is to pretend to be in love with you, is that it?" he said when she'd finished.

"Is that so bad?"

"You know better than that." He was irritated. "But I don't like lies. I'm sick of lies and subterfuge. All I want to do is get Liz back and go home."

"Then I'm afraid you'll have to lie just one more time, Domino," she said, "because it's the only way we can get you out of here, and Tío Emilio says that de las Torres is just mad enough over losing the *Maravilla* to you that he might doctor the report from the States even if he did go, just so you'd hang."

"So much for honest Spaniards."

"You did take his ship."

"I know . . . I know." They were standing in the middle of the cell talking, and now Bain walked over, glancing out to see where the guard was, just to make sure he hadn't been listening; then he came over, looking down into Elena's eyes again. "Your uncle's sure this'll work?" he asked.

"He was at the governor's already this morning. Please,

Domino, there's no reason it won't work. He got me an audience with the governor for this afternoon, and we can have you out of here before dark."

He stared at her, studying the soft curve of her face and remembering how many times he'd lain on the lounge outside on the terrace at Barlovento, not knowing who she was and studied her with the same intensity he was studying her with now, as she moved about, nursing him back to health. He'd been attracted to her then, but hadn't realized at the time that her dark hair and tawny skin had reminded him of his wife, Lizette, the one woman in the world he'd never been able to get out of his system, no matter how hard he tried. Even pretending to be in love with Elena was going to make him feel as if he were betraying Liz. Something he knew he could never do. Yet, if he didn't . . .

"All right, I'll go along with the lies, Elena. I don't have much choice, do I?"

"You don't have to make it sound so terrible."

"Well, I don't like it," he answered testily. "And it has nothing to do with you, you know that, it's just that . . . that . . ."

"I know," she said, her voice on the verge of breaking. "It's just that you have a wife whom you love very much. I've heard it all before."

"I'm sorry."

"No, I'm sorry. But we'll talk about it later," she said, and he frowned at the way she said it, but she went on. "Now, remember, if they ask you, we were in St. Augustine together. You remember the rest?"

"I remember."

"Bueno." She tried to smile. "Hopefully, I'll see you later tonight, if all goes well. Now, I'd better call the guard," and she started toward the cell door.

"Elena?"

She turned, her gaze resting on him hesitantly as she lifted the hood back up to cover her hair.

"Gracias," he said, half-whispering, and she sighed, then turned, calling the guard.

The rest of the afternoon and early evening crept by slowly for Bain, and he was so on edge that he jumped at the slightest sound in the corridor, thinking maybe this was it, only to turn back from his cell door in disgust as the guard would walk by to one of the other cells.

Finally—he had no idea what time it was, except that he knew it had to be evening since they'd already brought around their watered soup and biscuits—he heard voices in the hall, and once more his hopes rose.

This time he wasn't disappointed when the guard stopped at his cell and began to unlock the door.

"Come on along, *amigo*," the guard said matter-of-factly. "Looks like you're not to be with us much longer," and Bain stood up from his bed of straw, brushed off his clothes, and joined the guard in the corridor, sighing with relief as the door shut behind him.

Half an hour later, after having to stand in front of the guard and his superior while the papers telling of his release were being read, and answering a bunch of stupid questions, he was ushered to a side entrance where a closed coach and driver waited with its running lights on since it was almost dark.

"Come, hurry," Elena said, her head at the window of the coach, and the driver opened the door for him.

Bain climbed in hurriedly, the driver closed the door, then returned to his seat, picked up the reins, and the coach started down the rutted dusty road from the prison.

"Where's Captain Edelman?" Bain asked as he settled back on the seat.

"He's at the ship probably. There was no use in his coming, really, since you'll no doubt be staying with us."

"I see."

"No you don't see," she answered. "You're supposed to be here to see me and it's only natural you stay with us, as our guest. If you stayed on the ship they'd think something was wrong."

"I guess you're right," he answered hesitantly. "But I don't like it."

"Why? Afraid you might start to forget your precious wife?"

"Never," he said stubbornly. "I came here to find her, Elena, or did you forget?"

"How could I?" She grabbed the side of the carriage as they hit a large bump, and kept herself from getting jostled about too much. "Believe me, Bain Kolter, I remember all too well why you're here," she answered.

He laughed softly. "Aha! So it's not 'Domino' anymore."

"Now you're being cruel."

"Cruel? To you? I think you know me better than that."

"That's just the trouble," she said, her voice tremulous. "I do know you, and it hurts."

"I told you I was sorry. What more can I do?"

"Never mind," she replied. "Just remember, once we get to the house, that you're supposed to be in love with me, because even the servants have no idea what we're up to."

"Then they don't know about Sancho?"

"No. No one knows besides us, except Tía Isabella, your wife, and now the men who brought you here, I presume."

"Only Eric and Waggs. The rest of them only know we're trying to find Lizette. They have no idea of your uncle's connection to the kidnapping."

"Good, then let's hope they don't find out," she answered.

Bain leaned forward and glanced out the window. The road had twisted down the side of the hill as they moved farther inland, and now he could see the bay.

"We're going to have to ride around it," she said when she realized why he was staring. "It's a long ride, I know, but those are the inconveniences of living in Havana."

It was late by the time they found themselves walking up the steps of the house with the heavy oak door and lion's head for a knocker, but Don Emilio was waiting for them in the parlor and his eyes studied Bain curiously as he reached out to shake hands.

"Maybe you'd better not, Señor Pérez," Bain suggested, and showed his hands to his host. "At least not until I've washed the prison dirt off." He reached up, scratching his beard again. "And I'm afraid I'm going to need something to rid myself of a few visitors too."

Don Emilio smiled. "Then by all means, we can talk later," he said, and pulled one of the bell cords. "I'll have my servants set up a tub in your room and you can clean up. Your Capitán Edelman brought some of your clothes, and if you'll leave the boots outside the door they'll be clean by the time you're ready for them."

"Gracias," Bain said, thanking him, then made his apologies a few minutes later and followed one of the servants upstairs, where he was ushered into one of the guest rooms.

Don Emilio's home was a work of art, with gilded, carved balustrades, frescoed ceilings and walls, and mosaic designs decorating the floors. Rich brocades, velvets, and silks complemented its elegance in colors from the deep burgundy in the parlor and hallways to the deep blue-green color of the room Bain was brought to and he walked over to a set of French doors that opened onto a small portico with a wrought-iron railing around it that was directly above elaborate gardens at the side of the house.

The servants hadn't brought the tub up yet, and he had a few minutes to himself so he stood at the French doors, breathing in the warm summer air, the scent of flowers from below sweet and delicate, and he thought over the past few hours.

He had wanted to find Elena, yes, but not like this. All he wanted was to ask her if she knew where Sancho spent his time when he wasn't raiding ships, yet whenever he'd even mentioned anything about Sancho, or Liz for that matter, either that morning while he was still in prison or on the way here in the carriage, she always seemed to change the subject. Why?

And Don Emilio. His first instinct was that he liked the man. There was a gentle, yet firm air of confidence about him that was pleasing. Only one thing he couldn't understand. As heartless as Sancho was, it was surprising his uncle wasn't paying him blackmail to keep his mouth shut about their relationship. Yet, if he were, it was certain that Don Emilio wouldn't be able to live like this. Sancho would have bled him dry years ago.

Bain moved back into the room at a knock on the door, then stood by watching as the servants put down a tub and filled it. His gaze moved about the room, stopping on a picture of a woman on the wall at the foot of the bed. Her hair was dark, she was sitting in a meadow picking flowers, and he was reminded of Liz. An ache began to fill him. My God, how much he missed her. She'd always been there to come home to, her arms so warm, her love so inviting. And the twins. He could almost see Braxton's smiling face, the gray eyes twinkling as he teased his sister. Then tears filled Bain's eyes as he remembered his adorable Blythe lying helpless in that big bed at the Château, her pale hair damp with sweat, and his jaw clenched angrily. Damn Sancho de Córdoba, he cried silently to himself, and when the servants had finished, then closed the door behind them, he cursed aloud as he began to strip the filthy clothes from his body.

It was almost an hour later when he stepped into the parlor once more to shake Don Emilio's hand, and this time the handshake was firm, the introductions by Elena not really necessary. Mario was there also this time. A much taller Mario than when Bain had last seen him, and the anger that had driven Bain all the while he'd bathed, he'd managed to subdue, at least for now. There'd be time for anger later when he had Sancho by the throat.

"Forgive me for not coming to your rescue earlier, Señor Kolter," Don Emilio apologized a few minutes later while they sat with Bain in the huge dining hall so he could have something to eat, since the food at the prison had hardly been palatable. "But you see, I had no idea who you were. All I knew was that a man named Bain Kolter had been arrested and accused of piracy. It wasn't until your friends came that I was able to associate the gentleman Elena had been referring to as Domino with you."

"I guess I can understand that," Bain answered, then washed down the food he'd been chewing with a sip of wine. "Only tell me, living here like you do, how have you managed to keep your relationship to Sancho from so many people? Surely it must be hard, especially now with Elena and Mario here?"

"Shhh . . . please, *por favor, señor*, we will discuss these matters later, in the library, where there's not the chance of being overheard," Don Emilio cautioned, his voice low, and at that moment one of the servants appeared in the doorway carrying a silver tea service. "I'm sure you understand?"

Bain nodded, then watched Don Emilio while the servant was pouring tea. It was quite apparent that Don Emilio Pérez was nervous, and not really too pleased over the day's events, so Bain let them change the subject while he finished filling his stomach and they talked about everything except Sancho de Córdoba.

Later, in the library, Bain faced Don Emilio, his eyes intent on the man as he tried to answer the question Bain had put to him earlier.

"Let's just say there are two reasons," Emilio Pérez said as he stood in front of an open window a few feet from where Bain sat on the sofa next to Elena. "You see, strange as it may seem, Sancho does have a . . . shall we say . . . sentimental quirk when it comes to family. Your throat he would slit in a second, *señor*. Without even giving it a thought. Mine would be a different matter. To kill me, he'd have to be betrayed first, and even then, he would be hesitant."

"You're serious?"

"Quite serious. Elena says you have met him. Did you not see it?" Don Emilio put his hand into a pocket of the dark brown elaborately embroidered suit he was wearing that was in contrast to the pale gold walls around him and pulled out a pocket watch. "To Sancho, family is sacred."

"Sacred?"

"Not in the sense that Sancho has a conscience, *señor.*" He smiled, straightening, and checked the time on his watch, then slipped it back in his pocket. "But you must remember. My nephew was not always a pirate. At one time he cut quite a figure at the king's court."

Bain frowned. "Then why?"

"Why? Who knows? The death of his mother? They were very close. A duel fought over the honor of a *señorita* who did not deserve it, and the death of a man who did? The need to strike out at something, anything, that would satisfy the gnawing emptiness left in his soul? Who knows why a man does what he does except the man himself. *Sí, señor,* in spite of what Sancho is to the rest of the world, to him we are family. Myself, his Tía Isabella, and even his cousins back in Spain. To kill one of us would be like putting the knife to his own throat."

Bain stared at Don Emilio for some time, then looked at Elena. "That's why you knew he'd do as you asked that night back at Barlovento?" he asked.

She shrugged. "He's my brother," she answered simply. "He's ruthless and cruel, *sí,* but we are the same blood. We are family."

"And I presume that means you won't betray him."

Her eyes darkened. "What do you mean?"

"I mean that even if you did know where he was, you wouldn't tell me, would you?"

"But we don't," she answered. "So it doesn't matter whether we would or not. The point is that no one knows where he goes when he's not here. He could be anywhere."

"As he said when he left," Don Emilio offered, "he would be wherever the wind takes him."

Bain stood up. "That's perfect. Then I'm no better off coming here than I was. I should have just searched every island from here through the Indies."

"But you are here, *señor,*" Don Emilio said thoughtfully, "so we'll have to make do. Besides, even if you had continued your search through the islands, it's doubtful you'd have found him. He's an elusive scoundrel. But for now, it's late, and I for one am going to try to get a good night's sleep in spite of the heat." He started toward the door. "*Buenas noches, señor,* Elena." He looked over at Mario, who'd been sitting in a chair a few feet away staring at Bain but not joining into the conversation. "Come along, Mario," he said, his voice leaving little room for argument. "I think you should turn in too. I believe your sister and Señor Kolter still have much to discuss. Besides," he went on after Mario joined him and they started out the door, "we'll be going to the University of San Carlos to get you registered tomorrow and I want you wide-awake," and they left, closing the door firmly behind them. The room grew quiet.

Bain stood for a long time staring at the closed door, then turned as Elena stood up. It was the first he'd really paid attention to her since he'd come back downstairs. Her hair was still in the same chignon, only now diamonds glittered from her earlobes and graced the tawny flesh at her throat, and the deep green dress she wore with its tucked bodice and frilled skirt, the sleeves lacy and delicate, made her appear fragile, yet he knew it to be deceiving.

"Don't you think it's rather hot in here?" she asked as she strolled toward him. "Tío Emilio has a lovely garden at the side of the house—we could talk out there."

"We can talk just as well here," Bain said. "Besides, closed doors are better for what I have to say." His eyes caught hers and held. "And first of all, I want to know what your brother's done to Liz."

"He hasn't done anything to her."

"But this afternoon . . ."

"I said she was all right."

"Then he hasn't hurt her?"

"Not that I could see. She looked fine to me."

"You're sure?"

"No, I'm not sure," she said. "How could I be sure? I wasn't in his cabin with them all night. All I can tell you is that when I boarded the *Piranha* in St. Augustine, your Liz seemed perfectly fine."

"What do you mean, you weren't in the cabin with them all night?"

"Oh, come now, Bain, do I have to draw you a diagram?"

"Are you trying to tell me she was sleeping with him?"

"Well, I'm sure he wouldn't let her sleep on the floor."

"Maybe he slept on the floor."

"Sancho?" She laughed. "My brother wouldn't sleep on the floor for anyone, including your wife."

"You're a liar!" Bain's gray eyes darkened as he stared at her. He was wearing only a white full-sleeved shirt and buff trousers tucked into his Wellington boots that had been shined, and the cords in his neck bulged now beneath the open collar of his shirt. "If my wife was sleeping with your brother it's because she was forced to," he argued heatedly. "He must have raped her."

"That I don't know," Elena said, forcing a calm to her voice she didn't feel. Her insides were trembling. "All I know is that she spent every night in his cabin and she didn't seem to be complaining in the least bit."

Tears welled up in Bain's eyes as he turned and walked to the window, staring out. Not Liz, he told himself, angrily. Not willingly. Not with a man like Sancho de Córdoba. Oh God, if only he'd been home. His fist clenched in frustration. Blythe, now this. He gulped back the tears and turned once more to Elena.

"Where did he go, Elena?" he asked, his voice deep with emotion. "For God's sake, where did he go?"

"I don't know." She shook her head. "I'm telling you the truth, Bain, I have no idea, but he is coming back."

"He's coming back? When?"

"I don't know that either."

He grabbed her shoulders, forcing her to look at him. "Don't lie to me, please, Elena, I have to know, don't you understand? She's my life, I need her, my daughter needs her. I didn't tell you about my daughter, did I, Elena?" he said bitterly as he searched her face. "The night your brother kidnapped Liz, he chased her carriage and it crashed." There were tears in his eyes again as he went on. "My daughter's crippled because of that crash, Elena, because of your brother. She's three and a half years old and she'll never walk again, and she needs her mother, too. Please, Elena, when is he coming back?"

Elena felt a lump in her throat at the sight of the pain in Bain's eyes, and she swallowed hard. "He didn't say," she murmured breathlessly. "He gave Tío Emilio some money when he left, and said he'd be back in a few months, when he thought we might need more."

Bain's hands eased on her shoulders, then dropped from them and he shook his head in disbelief. "That's all he said? No definite time? Nothing else?"

"I'm sorry, Bain," she said, and in spite of the fact that he had rejected her, her love went out to him and she reached out gingerly, touching his arm. She expected him to pull away, but instead he just stood there staring at her. Her fingers tightened and she saw a flicker of understanding in his eyes. "I wish I could help you ease the pain," she whispered lovingly, and her hand moved to his chest as she stepped closer. "Oh, God, Bain, I wish I could be to you what she is, just for a while."

Suddenly his arms went about her and he held her close. She wasn't Liz, but she was someone to hang onto, if only for a little while. Just long enough to still the surging frustration inside him. He held her close for a long time, then finally drew away, looking down into her face.

"Unless I hear otherwise, when he comes back, I'll be here," he whispered gently. "That is, if you and your uncle will let me stay."

She searched his face. "He won't come here to Havana, Bain," she answered. "When he does come, it'll be to the cattle ranch."

"Then I'll wait for him there. But make no mistake, I will wait for him, Elena, because I have to find Liz."

"And if she doesn't want to be found?"

"Then I have to know that too." His face grew hard, his jaw tense, eyes on the verge of tears. "But I know you're wrong, Elena. Deep down inside I know you're wrong, Liz would never do that to me, ever, not willingly."

"Then wait for Sancho by all means, Bain," she said softly. "Only remember one thing: as far as everyone else on this island is concerned, you're still supposed to be in love with me, and you're going to have to make them believe it. It's either that or go back to the dungeon, or worse, if they learn the real truth."

"I know." He straightened and reached out, taking her hand. "I wish I could be the way you want me to be, Elena," he said compassionately. "I wish I could give you the love you deserve and let you be the woman you should be, but there's no way I can ever turn my back on Liz."

"Don't be so sure, Domino," she answered boldly. "You're

a man, not a god, and a man can forgive just so much, even you."

He gazed into her dark eyes, hoping they'd reveal to him whether she was baiting him for her own selfish reasons or if she was really trying to be just a friend, but there was no answer in them, only a depth of emotion he didn't want to even try to analyze.

"You're right, of course," he answered hesitantly. "A man can forgive just so much, but until I know exactly what I have to forgive, I don't have a right to even doubt it, do I? If your brother's forcing Liz to sleep with him, I can forgive that, Elena, but if she's a willing partner, that's another matter. Only I won't know until I see Liz again, will I? So until then, I'll go along with this silly masquerade and you can pretend all you want that what's between us is real, that's up to you. But remember, if you do, if you try to give my words and actions meanings other than what they are, a means to an end, I'm afraid you're going to pay the consequences, and pay dearly."

"Well, I guess you made that quite clear, didn't you?"

"Just so we understand each other."

"We do. Now," she said, her hatred for Lizette driven even deeper by his words, "as Tío Emilio said, it's late, and I have a feeling tomorrow's going to be a busy day, and I suggest we retire, shall we?" and she took his arm.

Bain studied her curiously. Except for the way her eyes glistened, she seemed very much in control of her emotions, and he began to think that perhaps he'd judged her wrong. Only as they left the library, and he ushered her out, closing the fancily carved door behind them, he was sure he saw the corner of her mouth tremble slightly, and later as he settled down in the elegant bed, letting his thoughts go back over the bargain he'd struck for his freedom, he almost had a feeling he might have been safer if he'd stayed right where he'd been, in prison.

Chapter 8

BRIGHT BLUE SKIES scattered with huge white clouds hung on the horizon as the *Piranha*'s crew began furling her sails, the anchor already resting at the bottom of the clear blue-green water that washed lazily in and out over the white sandy beach Lizette was staring at. She had no idea where they were, what they were going to do, or how long they'd be here. All Sancho had told her was that it was a place where they could get lost. And looking at it now, taking in the mixture of flowering trees and shrubbery in brilliant colors from scarlet to gold, against a green background, with palm trees trying to shade it all as it simmered under the heat of the summer sun, she was sure he was telling the truth, and a terrible dread settled deep inside her.

She stood at the rail alone for a long time, watching them lowering the longboats, and her thoughts went back to the night she'd tried to escape. The night they'd left Cuba. Actually it had been in the wee hours of the morning, and by the time they'd gotten back on board, she'd reached the ship's cabin, cleaned herself up and dried off, the sun was starting to tint the horizon with its golden glow, and when she'd looked out the cabin window the island of Cuba had already been lost to sight.

She'd washed as best she could then, and was wearing only her chemise and petticoats, ready to slip into her rumpled lavender dress again, when the cabin door opened and Sancho strolled in. She could tell he was still upset as his eyes raked over her.

"I hope you weren't planning to sleep," he said boldly.

She flushed. "We were up all night."

"That was my fault?"

"Most of it, yes."

He stripped off his jacket and tossed it on the chair as she reached for her dress.

"Leave it!" he snapped angrily.

She stared at him curiously, clutching the dress to her bosom.

"I said, leave it," he said, more slowly this time, and he walked toward her. Reaching out, he snatched the dress from her hands, and it would have ripped if she hadn't let go. His eyes caught hers and there was something in them. "I told you that when we left Cuba I would show you what it is to belong to Sancho de Córdoba," he whispered huskily, and he pulled her against him slowly, gently, and deliberately.

"You . . . you said you don't rape ladies!" she cried breathlessly.

His smile was lazy, insolent. "I don't intend to rape you, or did you forget?" He took a deep breath as he gazed into her green eyes, letting them fire the very depths of his soul. "I said I was going to make love to you," he murmured provocatively, and the hair at the nape of Lizette's neck prickled as it stood on end, while a fear like she'd never known before wrenched at her insides and began to tear her apart.

"Please . . ." she begged helplessly. "Don't . . . don't do this to me. Haven't you done enough?" Tears welled up in her eyes. "You've taken my children, my husband, my life . . . now you'd take this too?"

He drew her closer, and his hand moved into her hair, tilting her head up so he could reach her mouth.

"I only want what I know you can give," he said fervently, and his mouth came down on hers hungrily, the same way it had last night when she lay on the ground beneath him, and in spite of everything, Lizette felt an all-too-familiar stirring deep down inside.

She tried to ignore it, shut it out, but he wouldn't let her as his lips eased on her mouth, sipping at it wantonly, driving home the fact that she was still a woman with feelings she wished she didn't have. She didn't want this, didn't want to feel what he was making her feel, and she hated him for it because she knew she didn't love him. That it was only a natural human response to the tender, seductive way he was treating her, and the tears that had rimmed her eyes rolled down her cheeks.

He tasted their saltiness with his tongue and drew back his

head, but only inches, his lips still so close to hers she could feel his breath.

"Why do you cry?" he asked, frowning. "I do not hurt you."

"Oh, but you do," she murmured, her voice tremulous, breathing erratic. "I don't want this."

"But your body does."

"No . . ."

"Yes," and his lips touched hers again, then played about the corners of her mouth sensuously before moving to her throat. Then, as he nibbled at her earlobe, "You see, you do want it," he whispered against her ear, and he felt her tremble. However, he wasn't prepared for how stubborn Lizette could be, and she turned her head away, shutting her eyes, trying to force her body to pay no heed to what he was saying or doing.

"I'll scream," she blurted furiously.

He laughed a low chuckle, his hand moving her head once more to face him, forcing her so she couldn't look away.

"You will not scream," he whispered softly, "because you are really not afraid of me, you are afraid of yourself, Lizette Kolter," he said. "You are afraid to admit that your body can react to me as it does to that man you call a husband."

His eyes searched hers again, delving into their depths, and suddenly she realized that he was partially right. She wasn't afraid of him. Not the way she had been at first. For some strange reason, she seemed to know that in spite of the fact that with others he was cruel, actually heartless, he wouldn't hurt her. Not really, not physically. She sighed.

"I'm going to have a baby, Sancho," she said, and saw his eyes darken. He became motionless. "Did you hear?" she asked.

He was staring at her hard, but still hadn't moved a muscle. "I heard," he answered hesitantly. "When?"

"In six or seven months. I'm not quite sure."

He was quiet for a long time as he continued to stare at her, still holding her close. "Does Bain Kolter know?" he finally asked.

"I was going to tell him when he got back from Pittsburgh."

"I see." He was still staring at her hard; then slowly his eyes began to soften and he frowned as if puzzling over something. Suddenly he had straightened, his arm still around her, his eyes still on hers, and she had seen the smoldering desire hidden beneath their surface.

"I will wait," he had said after a few minutes, surprising her. "I will wait, Señora Kolter, until after Bain Kolter's seed is through with your body. Then you will learn to love me. Do you understand?"

She hadn't understood. Not then, not now, but she'd been grateful that at least it had brought her a reprieve. For some reason, she had no idea why, this vicious man, who'd slice anyone in two without thought, and cared little what others might think of him, had suddenly changed his mind on hearing she was pregnant. And now, as she stood at the rail waiting for her turn to climb into the longboat and join the others on this isolated island, she could only hope that he wouldn't change his mind again when they got ashore.

She turned at a sound behind her, to see Sancho heading her way. He'd been keeping his beard and hair trimmed lately, taking baths regularly, and had dragged some newer clothes from the hold, a few things they'd confiscated from some of their raids, and she had to admit he was much more presentable. Actually rather handsome in a ruggedly masculine way. If it weren't for the scar at his temple and the hard, cold look in his eyes most of the time.

"You like my little island?" he asked.

"Where are we?"

"Oh, east of somewhere and west of somewhere else. Who cares?"

"You just won't tell me, will you?"

"It would not help."

"So you say."

"So I know." He smiled. "There are hundreds of islands out here, *mi querida*, what is one more—its name would mean nothing to you."

She turned back, looking across the lagoon toward the island again. They'd been sailing for well over two weeks, yet she still had no idea which way they'd been moving. Now she wished she'd paid more attention to her brother Cole when he'd wanted to teach her how to survive in the woods, and what the different stars meant so she could find her direction no matter where she was. But no, she'd been too busy having fun. All she knew was that the sun rose in the east and set in the west, and if the day was cloudy she was lost again.

"It looks like you've been here before," she said as she realized some people were coming out to meet the longboats that had already reached shore.

He nodded. "My home away from home." He pointed off toward a cluster of trees a short distance inland. "There are huts over there," he offered, ducking a little so his head was next to hers to see if she could see them. "The natives take care of them while we are away, and we try to bring them something in payment. Look, see there!"

She followed to where he was pointing and was surprised to see what looked like a number of thatch-roofed wooden huts among the trees; then more people began joining the others, and later, by the time the longboat came back to pick them up, to deposit them on the beach, there were close to a hundred natives, men, women, and children, waiting to greet them.

Lizette was still wearing her lavender dress, and although her hair was clean, face shining, she felt very conspicuous and rather embarrassed when she saw that the women were practically naked, except for either a small grass skirt or a piece of rough cloth wrapped around their hips, and all the men wore were tiny loincloths made of leaves and grasses woven together. They were very dark-skinned too, like the slaves back at Tonnerre and the Château. At least most of them were.

"Did they come with the island?" she asked Sancho as their longboat neared the beach.

"The island is small, only about ten miles long, maybe less, and this is the only cove," he answered as they arrived on shore, and he reached in the boat, picking her up so she wouldn't get her feet wet. A gesture that surprised not only her, but some of his men as well. "The natives were here when we arrived the first time," he went on as he carried her through the gentle surf toward the beach. "And since they did not seem to be much of a threat, we made friends with them. I think maybe their ancestors came from one of the bigger islands. Who knows?" He set her down on the sand, and she took a step back toward him for protection as she realized the natives were all staring at her. "Do not worry, they speak some English," he said, then smiled as he began to greet them, introducing her as his special prisoner, which brought a strange look to the face of one of the women.

She was taller than Lizette, her hair short and thick like

matted wool, her mouth overly generous, the nose just a little too wide to be pretty, but she had a lovely lithe body that intimidated Lizette. Especially since Lizette's pregnancy was already beginning to show, and her breasts had swelled, pushing against the front of her dress.

Sancho introduced the woman as Kalea, daughter of the man who seemed to be the tribe's leader. Kalea looked to be perhaps in her twenties, maybe older, and although she sauntered off with one of the native men, her eyes came back a number of times to rest on Sancho before moving once more to Lizette with that same strange look of disdain. A look Lizette tried to ignore.

By nightfall they were all settled into the huts, stores from the ship replenishing what was already here, and after a supper of roast pig and fresh vegetables furnished by the natives, something the crew from the *Piranha* hadn't seen for some time, the natives disappeared to their part of the island a short distance away, with most of Sancho's men joining them, and Lizette decided she was going to take a walk down to the edge of the lagoon.

It was late. The sun had been down for hours and yet the sand was still hot as it filtered into her kid shoes, making it hard to walk. Sitting down on the ground, she slipped them off, then stood back up, carrying them as she continued to head for the edge of the water, and walked slowly along the beach, savoring the warm night.

She had left Sancho back by the campfire talking to Jigger and was surprised a short while later to hear him calling her name. She had been standing on the white sand at the edge of the water, letting it lap at her toes as she stared off toward the silent ship anchored in the cove, the lines of its masts barely visible in the moonlight, and now she turned, waiting.

"Are you all right, *mi querida?*" he asked when he caught up to her.

For the first time since she'd laid eyes on him, Sancho actually looked relaxed and carefree, the hard suspicious look gone from his eyes, his features softened in the warm moonlit night, and Lizette frowned.

"Why do you always do that?" she asked. "I told you before," and she shook her head, "I can't understand your language, so why don't you just speak English, please?"

"But if I do that, you might not like what I say." He

smiled as he stared at her, suddenly remembering the moment she'd told him she was expecting Bain Kolter's baby, and the strange way those words had torn him apart. He had wanted her so badly only seconds before, and then suddenly he couldn't touch her, not after what she'd told him. Instead he'd wanted to protect her, and now his voice lowered as he looked down into her eyes. "This way I can say what I want without seeing the fire in your eyes," he said softly.

"What does it mean?"

"What?" he asked, pretending innocence.

"What you call me all the time."

"You mean '*mi querida*'?" His eyes chuckled. " 'My love,' 'my sweetheart.' "

"You have no right!"

"Why?" He frowned. "Because he knew you first? That does not mean I cannot love you."

Her mouth fell, and he reached out, touching her chin, closing it, then pulled her into his arms.

"I have never said this before, Lizette," he said in his accented English, his eyes drinking in the warmth from her lovely green eyes. "I have never wanted to, but from the moment I looked into your eyes I knew something was wrong inside of me. Something I could not understand. Now I know why." His voice was filled with emotions new to him. "I have raped women, and killed them, Lizette Kolter, but never have I loved a woman until now." He kissed her lightly on the mouth, then gazed once more into her eyes. "At first I wanted to kill you for doing this to me, but even then I could not." He searched her face intently, as if looking for some sign that she might feel the same, but saw only confusion in her eyes. "I am sorry now that I do this to you," he went on passionately. "I should have waited to kill your husband instead, but I cannot undo what I have done."

"You can take me home."

"No—that I can never do. Not now, not ever."

"Why?"

"If I take you back now, I would have to kill your husband and you would hate me."

"You think I don't hate you now?"

"Ah, but no," he argued. "You do not hate me. At first you did, yes. Then you were afraid of me. But now—now we are friends, and soon, very soon now, we will be more than friends. You will see."

"You're crazy."

"And you are . . . how you say . . . naive." He released her and took a step backward, then drew his cutlass, holding the hilt of it toward her. "Here, take it," he said, but she only stared at it. He put it in her hand, pressing her fingers around the handle so she had to hold it; then he stepped back again, facing her. "Now, *mi querida*," he pleaded softly, "if you hate me so much, drive it through me, here," and his fist drove into his lean belly. "Go ahead, you will never have another chance. Kill me, Lizette Kolter, if you hate me that much!"

Lizette couldn't pull her eyes from his face as she held the sword in one hand, her shoes in the other. The sword was heavy, and she tossed her shoes aside so she could grasp the sword with both hands. He was telling her to kill him, only now suddenly as she stared into his eyes and lifted the sword, pointing it toward him, she knew why: Sancho de Córdoba knew Lizette Kolter better than she knew herself. It would be hard for her to kill anyone, even in self-defense, let alone plunge the cutlass into someone who, in spite of his failings toward others, and regardless of the fact that he was supposed to be her enemy, had treated her the way he had. Even his moments of anger with her, and the unwavering demand for obedience to the commands he gave her, were often tempered with amusement, making them easier to accept. He was right. At first she had hated him, and even now hated what he had done to her life, yet the thought of killing him . . .

There were tears in her eyes as she threw the cutlass in the sand and turned to run, only he was too quick and leapt over the sword, catching her arm, turning her back, pulling her against him, holding her close.

"You see, I know what it takes to kill without hating," he murmured softly against her hair. "It takes the devil in your heart, and you, *mi querida*, could never kill a friend."

"I don't want you for a friend!" she cried angrily.

"I know that too, nor do I want you as a friend. But for now it will do."

She sniffed back the tears and began to extricate herself from his arms, wiping the tears from her eyes as she looked up at him.

"I wish you'd left me back in Port Royal!" she yelled at him. "I wish I'd drowned back in Cuba!"

"No, you do not. Not really," he assured her. "As far as your home goes, you miss it, I know." His eyes narrowed momentarily. "But I will not take you back. As for wishing you were dead . . . ?" Once more his eyes softened. "The new life inside you would never let you take your life."

She frowned, brushing the hair from her tanned face, her head lifting stubbornly. "Why did you change your mind?" she suddenly asked, watching him closely.

"What do you mean?"

"The night I told you about the baby—what made you change your mind about raping me?"

"I told you—"

"Yes, I know. You don't call it rape, I won't argue the point." She sniffed again, the tears gone from her eyes now. "But you haven't answered. Why?"

His dark eyes suddenly had a faraway look in them as he drew them from her face and gazed out over the lagoon.

"You want Sancho de Córdoba to bare his soul for you?" He turned to her again, and for a minute she thought he was going to flatly refuse. Instead, "What will you give Sancho in return?" he asked.

"I won't fight your friendship anymore," she answered hesitantly. "But nothing more, only friends."

"We shall see."

She waited. "Well?" she asked again.

He bent down, picked his cutlass up from the sand, and wiped it off very carefully on his pant leg, thrust it back into the sheath at his side, then took a deep breath.

"I lied to you," he said simply. "I have loved before. I do love now. My family, Elena, Mario—I loved my mother, and once, only once, I loved from the heart. Not as I love you, I know that now. But to me then she was the earth, the moon, the stars rolled into one. For such a one, to me it was like . . . how you say . . . heaven. At first I was not sure of her, for she was high-born, the daughter of nobility, but in time she returned my feelings. At least I think this. Then one day I lost my head and made love to her, only to my surprise she was willing. We were alone far in the country and I sang inside because she gave herself to me. Then I learned the truth. Before we returned to the village, on the way home in the carriage, she became ill and we stopped at a farm for help. By now she was bleeding heavily and the farmer's wife told me she was losing my baby." He struck his breast, his eyes blazing at the remembrance. "My baby! She was two, maybe three months, or more—I don't know, because never had I touched her before."

He stopped for a minute, his gaze once more moving out across the water toward the *Piranha*.

"When I asked her, she told me she did not love me. That her consent to marry me was to give a name to the child she carried. The *bastardo* of the man who was to have married us. She was in love with the village priest, not me!" He turned to Lizette again, the moonlight playing on her hair, and suddenly he wished he could go back and change things. Only he couldn't, so instead he went on. "She laughed at me, Lizette Kolter. I loved her and she laughed at me. Do you know what that can do to a young man's heart? I did not mean to hit her, but I was young, I was hurting, and she laughed at me."

"You killed her?" Lizette asked apprehensively.

"No." He straightened angrily. "But I have killed others since for being like her. Every time a woman laughed at me and made me feel less a man, I made her pay for what Marlena should have paid for."

"The priest?"

"He was dead when I left my father's village, and there was a price on my head because of it."

"So you became a pirate."

"I took what I wanted as it was taken from me."

"I see."

"*Do* you see?" He reached out, touching her face, his hand brushing down it affectionately. "I doubt you really do." He straightened. "I said I would never love a woman again, Lizette Kolter, and I have not, until now. I did not want it and I do not like it, for it makes me feel what I do not want to feel. But it is there even though I do not wish it to be. Now, why did I change my mind?" He sighed, his eyes capturing hers in the moonlight. "If I were to make love to you, and your child would be lost, *mi querida*, not only would you not forgive me, but it would be like before, and that must never be again. There will be time for loving you later."

"What of Bain? You still plan to kill him?"

"If he comes for you, yes. If not? It will please me for him to know you are no longer his, but mine. Perhaps that will be revenge enough."

"He didn't betray you."

"You can swear it is true by all that's holy?"

"No, but I know Bain. I couldn't love a man who'd betray a friend."

"Enough! We will speak no more of it." He stretched, breathing in the fresh tropical air, the warm breeze cool on his face. "It is late, the day has been long." He took a few steps from where they were standing, bent down, and lifted her kid shoes from the sand, holding them out to her. "Come, Señora Kolter, let us see where we will sleep for the night," and after she took the shoes from him, he held her other hand, leading her back up from the white sandy beach to where the huts were nestled beneath the trees.

Jigger was nowhere in sight now, nor was the rest of the crew, and Lizette assumed they had joined the others at the native village. She and Sancho were really alone, only she was sure there was nothing to worry about. He led her to the hut he'd said earlier was his, and showed her that she had her own bed to sleep on in a corner of the hut some distance from where he'd sleep.

"You will be comfortable here," he said. "As you see, we have no beds as such, only palm fronds and grasses to soften the ground, with a blanket on top."

There was one lantern lit in the hut and he walked to his own bed and sat down, then took off his boots, while Lizette stood for a long time staring down at the makeshift bed where she was to sleep. Her shoes were still in her hand, and suddenly she felt so lonely and empty inside.

Sancho glanced over, watching her warily. "Now what is it?" he asked, frowning.

She shook her head. "I don't want to be here!" she yelled, half-choking on a sob. "I don't want to sleep in your stinking hut or stay on your horrible island! I want my children, and my family, and I want to go home!"

He was on his feet in an instant, his long stride carrying him to her quickly, and his words as he stood behind her, bending close to her ear, were soft and caressing.

"Please, please do not cry, *señora*," he whispered tenderly, trying to soothe her, but she shook her head, the emptiness inside her overwhelming. "I will take care of you," he went on, "I will see that you do not cry anymore." He took the shoes from her hand and tossed them aside, then turned her to face him, pulling her into his arms, holding her close. "Nothing will hurt you ever again, *mi querida*," he whispered fervently, "I promise," but she knew he didn't understand, and never would, because he was the one who was hurting her the most, only he was blind to it.

Then suddenly he lifted her into his arms, cradling her against him, and Lizette sniffed back the sobs that were trying to cut loose as she stared at him in surprise.

"No, please, Sancho, no, I can't!" she cried tearfully, only he had already started back toward his bed. He brushed her protest aside.

"You do not have to, not tonight," he said as he reached the other side of the hut and laid her down on his bed, then straightened and blew out the light. The hut was plunged into darkness, and now she felt him beside her.

"For tonight I only want to take away the loneliness, *mi querida*," he whispered as he moved closer. "The rest will come later."

Lizette stiffened and held her breath, not knowing what to expect, waiting for him to perhaps change his mind and try to make love to her anyway. But he didn't. Instead his arm went around her and he pulled her close. She tensed even more.

"Relax, *señora*," he murmured against her hair. "I will not hurt you. Just close your eyes, feel me beside you, and the loneliness will go away. You will see."

Lizette heard his words, yet was afraid to heed them. Then slowly as she lay there, the warmth of his nearness beginning to penetrate her body, the fear of him that had always been deep inside her began slowly to vanish, and tired and weary from the days at sea as well as the turmoil her heart was in, Lizette told herself reluctantly that for now, for just this once, it wouldn't hurt to have someone to hang on to and give her strength. And as she repeated the same thought over and over to herself, trying to convince herself that there was nothing wrong in letting him comfort her, just for tonight, the tension began to ease from her body, and although the sadness was still there, she didn't feel quite so alone, and was finally able to sleep.

The next morning when she awoke, Lizette was alone in the hut. It was well past sunup and she could hear the men outside moving around, talking to each other, some arguing, some laughing. She lay on the lumpy bed staring at the ceiling of the weather-beaten boards that held up the grass and palm fronds it was thatched with, and thought back over the night before with mixed emotions.

Oh God! How she missed Bain. Being held in Sancho's arms last night had made her realize just how much. She'd even awakened once during the night and for a few minutes had thought they were really Bain's arms about her and that this whole thing had been just a bad dream. Then she'd felt the uneven ground beneath the makeshift bed they were on, and smelled the familiar scent of the sea that she'd begun to associate with Sancho, and realized it had been only wishful thinking on her part.

She closed her eyes again now, remembering, as she so often did, how the twins always came in the bedroom in the mornings to wake her and Bain; then she began to wonder how Blythe was, and if she was really all right, as Sancho insisted. She'd looked so still that night, lying on the wet ground.

Ah well, there was no going back, that was certain, and she opened her eyes, sighed, then sat up, stretching as she listened to the birds outside in the trees. God, but they made such an awful racket, and it was going to be hot today too. The sun was already heating up the morning. But she couldn't give up. She just couldn't, and once more she thought of all the stories told about Grandma Dicia and everything she'd lived through.

Suddenly her teeth clenched. She should have run Sancho through last night, dammit! Grandma would have. Then her shoulders slumped in resignation. But then, she wasn't her grandmother. She couldn't even pretend to be anyone except herself, and she stood up, leaving the hut, wondering what the day would bring and swearing that if she ever got another chance to kill Sancho like she had had last night, she'd take it. Yet, deep down in her heart somewhere, as she stepped out into the morning sun, she knew that it probably wasn't really true.

For the next few days the small island hummed with activity as all the men relaxed, enjoying themselves after the long voyage. They also took care of a few minor ship repairs as well as taking advantage of the fresh food and women from the native villages. But for Lizette the days were boring.

Following Sancho's orders, she stayed away from the men as much as possible. Only at times it was rather difficult since things were so primitive, and her one and only lavender dress was not only getting threadbare in places, with a rip in the sleeve, and another in the skirt, but it was getting awfully tight in the waist too, as were the petticoats and underthings. Lizette began to wonder what she was going to wear when they didn't fit anymore at all. And there was really little for her to do on the island, just as it had been on board ship. The men took care of the cooking and getting the food ready, as did the natives, and most of the crew seemed to have an aversion to clean clothes, so there was little washing to be done except her own. She kept alternating from the dress to the men's clothes and back again, wearing the dress most of the time, since it was getting hard to keep the sailor's pants up at her waist.

She did offer to wash Sancho's clothes for him, however, since he had changed from the old military jacket and was wearing fancier things. Only she found out one of the native women was taking care of them for him. So actually she had a great deal of idle time on her hands, and her only pleasure was some books Sancho brought from his cabin on the *Piranha*. So during the day, when she didn't have to try to squint reading by the light from the whale-oil lamps, she'd find a quiet place to read, usually under an old jacaranda tree not far from the sandy beach. At least that's what Sancho said the tree was. It was lovely really, with huge bell-shaped flowers, its leaves soft and feathery like those of a fern. The only problem was most of the books he gave her were in Spanish.

So the days were boring, the nights still lonely, because after that first night, Lizette promised herself she'd never let anything like that happen again. She still had a guilty feeling deep down inside, even though all Sancho had done was hold her.

It was near the end of their first week on the island, and Lizette was under her usual flowering tree with a book of poetry that happened to be in English. She'd been nursing it along, reading only a few poems a day to make it last. Her feet were bare, as they usually were lately because of the sand getting in her shoes all the time, and she was sitting, very unladylike because of the heat, with her dress pulled above her knees and tucked in on each side.

Sancho stood a few feet away watching her, his eyes studying her intently for a while; then he finally called to her so she wouldn't be startled.

"I thought I would find you here," he said when he reached her. She looked at him curiously, pulling the dress farther down over her legs. "Mind if I join you?" he asked.

He had a book tucked under his arm, and she shrugged, nodding. "It's your island."

He grinned and sat down in the sand some feet away from her, then stretched out on his stomach, spreading the book out in front of him. He was still in the shade from the tree, but occasionally a bit of sun would reach through the branches above them and catch in his thick dark hair. He glanced over at her, smiled, then started to read.

He'd done this before and she'd often watched him furtively, wondering just how the brains of such a complicated man worked. She'd asked Jigger one time how old Sancho was, but he'd had no idea. Lizette guessed him to be somewhere in his early thirties, perhaps a bit younger. As she stared at him now, a weird feeling crept over her as she remembered him telling her, the night he told her he loved her, that he'd raped and killed women, and it seemed impossible to think that a man like that could be as gentle with her as he was. And he was, she couldn't deny it, and she felt guilty about that too. But then it was better than what would have happened if he hadn't decided he was in love with her. She shuddered at the thought, then remembered when Grandma Dicia told her about the way the Indians could savagely torture men and women, yet were gentle and kind to those they loved. Suddenly she flushed as he cocked his head, looking over at her, and she realized he'd felt her staring at him.

"You like to watch me?" he asked.

Her blush deepened. "Don't be ridiculous."

"Then why do you do it?"

"I wasn't."

"You were." He closed his book and turned to one side, leaning on one arm as he watched her. "I am glad you interrupted me anyway," he said, and his face grew serious, the hint of a smile gone from the corners of his mouth. "I must talk with you," he said, and sat up straight, moving his legs until he sat cross-legged in the sand. "We will be gone for a few days," he went on, watching her reaction closely. "And you must stay here."

Lizette stared at him, frowning, her eyes searching his face. "What do you mean, gone?"

"Just as I say. The men have rested, the ship is in order, and there is still wealth to be had."

Her frown deepened as the impact of his words settled on her. She hadn't thought . . . They were here, they had gone after no ships during their journey here, and somehow she hadn't given it a thought that they were still pirates. How stupid! And now a new fear gripped her.

"You're going to leave me here on this island alone?" she asked hesitantly.

"Not alone. The natives are here."

"The natives? They don't even talk to me."

"Because I tell them not to."

"Why? Because you're afraid the chief's daughter will tell me she was your mistress?"

"My what?"

"Don't hedge. You know what I mean. I'm sure there's a word for it in Spanish too."

"Aha!" His eyes sparked vibrantly. "You are jealous."

"I am not!" she insisted. "But I've seen the way she looks at me, and she thinks I've taken her place. What if she tries to kill me?"

"She won't, because she knows I would slit her throat from ear to ear."

"Sancho!"

"You think I would not?" He laughed aloud. "You have much to learn of me, *mi querida*."

Lizette hugged the poetry book to her breast as she stared at his hard, chiseled features and firm mouth almost lost in the heavy beard and mustache that he was now keeping so neatly trimmed.

"Besides," he continued more seriously, "she was not my mistress, as you call it, not ever, although she would have liked to be. But I take no black woman to my bed, as a whore or otherwise."

"Oh."

"Yes, oh," he mimicked her. "For my men, it is their business. For me it is something I prefer not to do. How should I say . . ." He thought for a moment. "For me, it is right inside that I do not do this, and I account only to me. *Comprende?*"

"*Comprende?*"

"*Sí*, do you understand?"

"I . . . I think so. I don't know."

"Whatever, you are mistaken, Lizette Kolter. I have no mistress, here or anywhere else. Not yet." His eyes held hers for a moment until she realized what he meant and swallowed self-consciously. "Now," he continued, "as I was telling you—I have already talked to Kalea and she will stay with you so you will not be alone."

"But I can't stay here!" she protested helplessly.

"You have to." He wasn't in a mood to be argued out of it. "We've dallied too long and my men are restless," he went on. "And I cannot take you with me. A ship is no place for a woman during a raid. Especially one who has no heart for killing."

Lizette drew her eyes from his and gazed out across the lagoon to where the *Piranha* drifted lazily in the afternoon sun; then she looked back at Sancho.

"How long will you be gone?"

"Two days—a week perhaps. It all depends on how soon we can find ships to make the fight worthwhile."

"And if they take you instead?"

"They won't."

"I see. Now you're God and control your own fate, is that it?"

He took a deep breath, his mouth twisting arrogantly. "I know I will not die on a ship's deck, nor in the waters," he answered as if he knew the words he spoke were the absolute truth. "Nor will I hang from a gibbet, Lizette Kolter. No, *mi querida,* Sancho de Córdoba will not die that way. He will die in a fancy bed with votive candles to light his last days. I have seen it many times in my dreams, and it will no doubt be when I am too old to fight anymore."

"You believe that?" she asked incredulously. "Because of a dream?"

"Because I know it to be so," he answered stubbornly. "So do not worry. I will be back."

"I wasn't worried. At least not for the reason you think," she replied, putting him straight. "I just don't like the idea of spending the rest of my life on this godforsaken island while you and your men lie at the bottom of the sea and no one knows where to find me," she explained quickly. "Let's face it," and she gestured toward the mouth of the lagoon, its hills blocking a view of the open sea, "you told me you found the place by accident, and I'm certainly sure no one

else will, and the prospect of spending the rest of my days
here isn't very pleasant."

He uncrossed his legs and moved closer to her, his book
momentarily forgotten in the sand.

"I told you, *querida*, I will be back," he whispered huskily, and the weathered tan crinkled the crow's-feet around
his eyes, making them soften. "I will miss you. I will let my
heart cry for you just so long, then I will be back. Only I ask
one thing of you," he went on, his voice low and seductive.
"For me you will do this, and you will do it willingly, *mi
querida*." He reached up and touched her face, brushing a
damp curl back from her forehead, his callused hands caressing her cheek, then cupping her face. "Tonight, when I
blow out the lantern, you will let me take the loneliness
away again as before."

She opened her mouth to protest, but his hand moved, his
fingers touching her lips, silencing them. "This you will do
for me, Lizette Kolter, because I ask it," he said decisively.
"For we sail on the morning tide." Then he leaned forward,
his mouth covering hers, and Lizette had no defense against
the tender kiss.

When he was through, he drew back, his eyes alive, pleased,
and he sighed.

"For you I will come back," he murmured passionately.
"Now, you will walk with me and I will show you the things
you must know while I am gone." He stood up, reached out
his hand and pulled her to her feet, then took the poetry
book from her hands and tossed it in the sand beside the
book he'd been reading, and a few minutes later, when
Jigger came down to the edge of the water to ask the captain
a question, Sancho and Lizette were just disappearing at the
top of the hill that rimmed the mouth of the cove.

That evening after the sun disappeared beyond the horizon and the campfires lit the beach, their fiery glow casting
flickering shadows as the embers settled into a steady heat,
Lizette stood in the doorway of the hut she shared with
Sancho and looked around outside, watching the men. There
was no rum tonight for those who usually drank themselves
into a stupor, and only a few had gone to the village with
native women to take advantage of the little time left them,
but even they'd be back long before morning. Instead, pistols were newly cleaned, with powder ready, sword and dagger were honed, and everything was ready for an early

departure. The men were exceptionally quiet tonight and Lizette wondered what could possibly be going through their heads.

There were few of the crew that she really knew. Most of them she knew just by sight; others had names attached to them, as did Jigger, Mosely, Kidder, the helmsman Drego, a tall lean mulatto with fire in his eyes and a solemn face that rarely saw a smile, and Billie By-God, the cook. Billie was a weird man with an equally weird name. Part Chinese perhaps, or Asian. No one really knew. Some said he was the son of a missionary's daughter and an Oriental warlord, but he wielded his pots and pans with a mixture of Confucian sayings and biblical proverbs. She knew Billie a little better than some of the others because he handed out the food, but even so, he was mostly just a name and a face.

She was just about ready to start looking for a place to sit down, far enough away from the men to please Sancho, and glad that it would please her too, because the less she talked to them, the better, when she saw Sancho step off the path that led to the native village with Kalea walking gracefully beside him. The light from the campfires fell on them, and as usual Lizette's face flushed at the sight of the native woman's bare breasts.

"*Bueno,* I will not have to look for you," Sancho said when they'd reached her, and he gestured Kalea a little closer. "The two of you have met, so there should be no problem there, but I think it good perhaps you talk tonight so that when morning comes you will not be strangers. That is good, *sí?*"

"If you say so," Lizette answered uncomfortably, then looked at the other woman. Kalea was staring at her boldly.

"I will let the two of you talk, then," Sancho went on, looking from one to the other and sensing the hostility between them. He sighed. "Besides, there are things I must do before morning. I will be back." He turned and walked away before either one could protest.

The silence between the two women was awkward for a moment; then finally Lizette spoke up.

"Would you like to sit down?" she asked.

Kalea's expression never changed. "If you wish."

"Well, it's better than just standing here."

"Then we do."

Lizette stepped away from the doorway first and Kalea

followed, matching Lizette's stride as Lizette headed for a bench someone had left far enough from the fire not to feel the heat, yet close enough to still be a part of the camp.

"This should do," Lizette said, and sat down, but Kalea was still on her feet. "You're not going to sit?"

Kalea's back was stiff, eyes still bristling with animosity. "Why you not like me?" she asked abruptly.

Lizette was taken aback. "I . . . not like you?" she asked, bewildered. "I thought you didn't like me."

"I do not, but I have reason. You do not have reason."

"You don't either," Lizette said testily. "You think I'm sleeping with him, don't you?"

"You are his woman."

"I am not!"

Kalea frowned. "You are to have his baby."

"I'm having my husband's baby, and Sancho's not my husband."

Kalea eyed her skeptically, her dark eyes hesitant. "It is not his?"

"Did he say it was?"

"No. He say nothing. But I see," and the black woman glanced at Lizette's thick waistline.

"Well, you see wrong, or rather, you've jumped to the wrong conclusion."

"Conclusion?" Kalea looked puzzled.

"Yes," Lizette explained, realizing that although the native woman did speak English, it was even worse than Sancho's. "What has Sancho told you about me?" she asked. "I mean, besides telling all of you that I was a special prisoner that first day we came."

Kalea took a deep breath, still wary of Lizette. "He say it best we not speak to you so you won't try to escape."

"Escape?" Lizette looked about curiously. "How could I possibly escape from this isolated place?"

"We have . . ." Kalea paused a moment as if trying to think of the word she wanted to use. "Dugouts, Sancho call them."

"You have boats?"

"To fish with, yes."

A spark of hope shot through Lizette. So that's why he didn't want her to get too friendly with the natives or go to their village. The bastard!

"He told you not to tell me about the boats?"

"He say you might learn of boats if we talk. He no want you leave."

"But you just told me. What if I leave while he's gone?"

"You will not. If you leave, we die."

Lizette stared at her incredulously. Kalea's dark skin looked bronze in the dim firelight, and the bright red flower she'd put in her thick hair earlier in the day was wilted, petals drooping. She was wearing a piece of stained pink cloth wrapped around her hips that looked silky rather than rough like the handwoven cloth she'd had on that first day. Lizette was certain it had been given to her by the pirates on one of their earlier visits. Booty from one of their captured ships, no doubt, and its light hue contrasted with the bronze look of her skin. Lizette avoided looking at Kalea's breasts as best she could, trying to ignore the fact that they were even there. She frowned.

"He threatened to kill you?" she asked, surprised.

"He say if you are gone when he return, he will roast us over fire. You no steal boat. We make sure."

Lizette shook her head. "He wouldn't do that."

"He has done before."

The hair on Lizette's neck prickled. "You don't mean that, not really."

"Kalea not lie," she said as if Lizette had insulted her.

"You mean, he really roasted someone over a fire?"

"He do."

"My God, who?"

"One of his men try to kill him, be captain—Sancho kill him slow."

Lizette's hand covered her mouth and her stomach twisted nauseously. "When?" she asked, unable to believe it.

"Long time." Kalea stared at her hand, trying to count on her fingers. "Too many time . . . you call year?" she tried to explain. "Two . . . no, three," she said, holding up three fingers.

"You saw this?"

"Not watch." Kalea shook her head in distress. "Never watch," she gasped fearfully. "No one village watch."

"If none of you watched, then how do you know it happened?"

The native woman's dark eyes widened. "His body there in morning and fire out. Chief Kaleharo help bury him."

"The chief's your father?"

"Yes, and chief not lie."

Lizette stared at the woman for a long time, finding it hard to believe, yet remembering the name Bain had given to Sancho, Sancho the Bloody. She shivered.

"You are cold?" Kalea asked.

"No." Lizette shook her head. "I was thinking over what you just told me."

"Oh." Kalea finally moved to the bench and sat down. "You mean what you say?" Kalea asked Lizette after a few minutes. "You do not belong to Sancho?"

Lizette glanced at the black woman, remembering Sancho's words the day before, and suddenly she felt sorry for Kalea because it was obvious the woman was in love with him. Kalea didn't even seem to care what he was, who he was, or what he'd done. Only Lizette knew how Sancho felt, and as she watched the other woman, she got to thinking that maybe it would be better if Kalea knew the truth so she wouldn't keep on hoping. Yet, how did you tell someone to give up? Especially where the heart was concerned. Lizette sighed. Well, maybe she could let Kalea down easily.

"He wants me to belong to him, Kalea," she finally answered, hoping the other woman would understand. "And he's told me that after my baby comes, I will belong to him. But I don't want that. I belong to my husband, and always will. All of this is Sancho's idea because he says he loves me, it's not mine."

"Then you do belong to him," Kalea said, as if it were a natural conclusion, and there was sadness in her eyes as she stared off toward the campfire. Then suddenly she turned toward Lizette and the sadness changed to what looked like hatred. "I will help you like Sancho say," Kalea said, her voice low and strained. "I will see you are here when he return, because of his threat, but I will still hate you always, Lizette Kolter." She stood up, her eyes holding Lizette's in one last challenge; then she walked away toward the edge of the water and stared out at the vague outline of the ship that was to carry Sancho away in the morning.

Later that evening, as time wore on, Lizette sat on the bench watching the activity in the camp, her thoughts going back over what she knew of Sancho and the way he treated her, in comparison with what she knew of others' experiences with the man, and nothing fitted. She knew, however, that there had to be truth to what others thought of him because his men were even afraid of him. And hadn't she herself seen him have one of them hanged? But what Kalea accused him of . . .

She watched him now, some distance away where he sat on a tree stump, using it as a chair with an old log table in front of him, the lantern from the hut on the table as he went over a list of the supplies they'd put on board *La Piranha* earlier in the day. After a while, seemingly satisfied with what he found, he turned the list over to Jigger, stood up, and suddenly Lizette shuddered as she saw him stretch, then head to where she was sitting, their conversation earlier in the day when they sat reading under the jacaranda tree uppermost in her mind.

"It's late," he said when he reached her, and she straightened but made no attempt to get up.

"Where's Kalea?" she asked.

"Kalea will sleep somewhere else," he answered, and held out his hand for her to take.

"I'm not tired yet," she said stubbornly.

He was just as obstinate and she saw his jaw clench. "I did not ask if you were tired." His hand still beckoned her. "Now, you will come."

She took a deep breath, ready to resist again.

"You will come or I will carry you," he insisted, and she knew he meant it.

She glanced toward the fire, where a few of the men were still talking, then reached up, reluctantly taking his hand.

"That's better," he said as he tucked her arm through his elbow and ushered her toward the hut.

"The lantern?" she questioned.

It was still on the table and Jigger was sitting where Sancho had been, writing on something.

"We won't need it," Sancho said. "After all, we're only going to sleep."

"I know that," she answered, annoyed at his unvoiced insinuation that she expected more.

"Then don't worry about it."

They reached the hut, and he waited for her to go in first. *"Querida?"*

She hesitated, then walked inside, feeling him close behind her, and she moved to the window, then turned, but all she could see was his vague outline over near where they were to sleep.

"The bed is over here," he said, his voice seeming to echo in the darkness.

She didn't answer, but only stood staring, then saw him start toward her.

"Please," she begged softly. "I don't want to do this."

He was directly in front of her now and she wanted so badly to hit him and run, yet knew it would be useless.

"You will do this one thing I ask, *querida*," he said huskily. "Now, come," and he stepped next to her, putting his arm around her, and she had no recourse but to move with him to the other side of the thatched hut. When they reached the bedding, he forced her to the ground, making her stretch out; then he lay beside her and reached out to pull her into his arms.

Lizette stiffened.

"I told you before, I will not hurt you," he assured her.

She was lying on her back and his hand covered the rising mound of her pregnancy, and she shuddered.

"What is it?" he asked, sensing that there was something other than her normal aversion to his attentions. Even earlier he'd noticed a withdrawal of her usual attempt at being civil. "What is wrong, Lizette?" he asked again.

She swallowed nervously, then took a deep breath, all too aware of the tension that was suddenly filling him.

"Is it really true?" she finally asked, her voice barely audible. "Did you roast a man alive, Sancho?"

His hand had been caressing her swollen belly and now it stopped abruptly, his fingers easing slightly, and she knew the question had startled him. But it was the only way she'd ever find out.

"Kalea told you?" he asked.

"Yes." She inhaled sharply. "Did you?"

His lips were close to her ear. "Rum and whiskey have always been able to a dull a man's senses," he answered.

She frowned. "But I've never seen you drink anything stronger than a bit of wine on occasion."

"Now you know why."

"What happened?"

"I would like to forget it."

"I can't."

His hand caressed her stomach again, then rested at the side of her waist, pulling her closer, and he sighed. "Once more I bare my soul to you, *querida*," he murmured gently.

"Is that it? All right, you shall know." He paused, then went on. "We had returned here from a successful voyage. However, one man, his name was François Le Deux, and he was a greedy Frenchman—he was not happy with his share of the spoils and decided it would be better if he were *capitán*. We had all been drinking, and I was just as drunk as the others. All except François, that is. He had decided to stay sober, then tried to take advantage when he figured I was most vulnerable. And he would have too but for Chief Kaleharo. I guess I was having a rip-roaring time and was unaware that Le Deux was aiming a pistol at my back. The chief deflected it, but it grazed my shoulder. Le Deux then turned on Kaleharo and we had to pull him off the chief." His voice lowered hesitantly. "I remember very little after that, *mi querida*," he went on. "Sometimes at night I see vague apparitions in my dreams and I wake up in a cold sweat. So I know I did this thing, but only moments can I remember, and even those I try to forget. So I do not drink with my men anymore. Nor with anyone else, except only an occasional glass of Madeira or good wine, but no more than that, so this thing can never happen again."

"But you threatened the natives if I wasn't here when you got back."

"*Sí.*"

"Then that's all it is, an empty threat?"

"*Sí.* But you see, you know that, *mi querida*, and I know that, only they do not know that."

"That's cruel."

"No." His voice hardened. "That is necessity, Señora Kolter. They think I will do it so they do as I say. My men also. If I were not called Sancho the Bloody I could never control my ship or my men."

Lizette thought over his last words as she stared at the darkened ceiling. "Then you're a fraud, aren't you, Sancho de Córdoba?" she said, and felt his fingers tighten at her waist, his breath warm against her ear.

"Not completely, Señora Kolter," he whispered softly. "It's just that sometimes my upbringing gets in the way of my profession, but believe me, I am far from being a saint, although at the moment I wish I were because it's getting harder and harder to hold you like this and keep the promise I made to you."

He heard the quick intake of Lizette's breath.

"Don't worry, Lizette, I will not break that promise," he offered willingly. "But there is one thing I will take from you, *mi querida.*"

Sancho's lips left her ear and he rose up on one elbow, looking down at her.

"What's that?" she asked with uncertainty.

"This," and his head lowered slowly, until his lips reached hers and he kissed her long and hard, the kiss softening to a warm caress, before finally relinquishing her mouth so she could catch her breath. *"Buenas noches, mi querida,"* he sighed contentedly, then lay back down beside her, pulling her close against him once more.

"Good night, Sancho de Córdoba," Lizette answered falteringly after a long silence, and his only response was to pull her close in his arms and breathe a deep sigh.

Chapter 9

LIZETTE AND KALEA stood on the white sandy beach, watching the *Piranha*'s sails beginning to unfurl, then saw the wind, blowing into the lagoon from the north, start to fill them as the ship lurched reluctantly for a few minutes before finally easing into a steady glide. The sun was just lighting the sky to the east, and a few stars still hung on the horizon, barely visible in the brightening sky as the ship picked up speed with each new sail that billowed out, and within only a few minutes the *Piranha* was disappearing between the hill and the mouth of the cove.

"Well, that's that," Lizette sighed when even the wake the ship left behind wasn't visible in the water anymore, and she turned to Kalea. "Now what do we do?"

Kalea looked at her bewildered, then frowned as Lizette's eyes lit up.

"I know one thing," Lizette said as she gazed out once more at the blue-green water of the lagoon, watching it lick gently at the white sand. "I haven't felt clean for weeks." She turned once more to Kalea. "Do the men from your village come over here very often?" she asked.

"Sometimes they come, but not this time," she answered. "Sancho tell them to stay away until he get back unless there is danger."

"Good." Lizette began unbuttoning the front of her dress. "I'm going to take a bath in the lagoon," she informed Kalea enthusiastically. "I've had nothing but sponge baths since this whole thing started, and I feel like the dirt's ground right in." She began stripping as she talked, then hesitated once the petticoats were off. They didn't fit right anymore anyway. And the only reason they had fit at all so far was because she'd lost some weight the past few weeks.

It was the same with her drawers and camisole. Give her a few more weeks and she'd have to go naked if something wasn't done.

She looked over at Kalea. "That cloth you have wrapped around you—do you have any more?" she asked anxiously.

Kalea stared back at her, puzzled. "I have some at the village, yes."

"Please, could you go get them?" Lizette said quickly.

Kalea frowned. "What will you do?"

"You'll see. Just get them for me, will you?"

Kalea started for the path that led to the village and Lizette called out to her, "I'll take a bath while you're gone."

Kalea disappeared down the path and Lizette ran back up to the hut, grabbed a bar of soap and the old towel she'd used for her sponge baths, and went back to the water, where she stripped completely, then waded in.

The water was still cool from the night air and felt marvelously luxurious against her skin. When it was past her hips, she dived in, swam around for a few minutes just enjoying the feel of it, then touched the bottom with her toes again and stood up, beginning to soap her hair.

The feel of the water caressing her skin suddenly brought back a flood of memories, and as she worked the soap into her hair, trying to get the musty wood smell of the *Piranha* out of it, she thought back to the first day Bain had made love to her. She'd been only fifteen then and he was twenty-three, and it was a day she'd never forgotten, even after all these years, and it had been her hair that had inadvertently brought them together. The thought of Bain and the children, and what might be happening to them, brought tears to her eyes and she let them fall freely for a few minutes, then forced them back. It did little good to feel sorry for herself. She'd discovered that a long time ago when Bain had ridden out of her life, that first time.

Well, she wasn't going to let anything get the best of her now, and after working her curly head of dark hair into a high lather, she ducked beneath the water, holding her breath, and rinsed it before emerging again to shake off the excess water. Then she began lathering her body, admiring the tan on her arms from the long sea voyage and hours in the sun since her arrival on the island. The rest of her looked pale and out of place in comparison.

Her bath over, and rinsed thoroughly, she waded back to the beach, grabbed her dress, moved back into the water, washed it, left the water, and hung it on a rope the crew had strung between two trees, then did the same with everything else she had had on.

At first she felt self-conscious running around in the nude, but after a few minutes, with the security of knowing no one could see her, she admitted it felt good, especially when the sun began to warm the earth and heat the breezes that blew into the cove.

By the time Kalea arrived back from the village with a bundle slung over her back, Lizette's clothes were all drying on the line and she was sitting on the bench where she and Kalea had been the night before, fluffing her hair with her fingers in the morning air, drying it.

"I didn't expect you to bring all of them," Lizette exclaimed when she saw the size of the bundle Kalea was carrying.

"Sancho say to do like you say, so I do," she answered, and Lizette flushed.

"Well, let's get to them, then."

Lizette opened the bundle that was a piece of square dark cloth with the corners tied together, and out of it fell a conglomeration of different remnants of material, all about the same length as the one Kalea was wearing, which was the same pink one she'd had on last night. The colors were faded, some were stained, but they'd have to do.

"Are there any you don't like?" she asked Kalea.

The native woman eyed her curiously, wondering what she could be up to. "There are some I like more than others."

"Pick out your favorites," Lizette said, and Kalea hesitated momentarily, then began sorting through the cloths carefully.

When she was through there were four pieces left. Two different shades of faded blue, one yellow that looked a dirty gray, and a washed-out green.

"May I have these?" Lizette asked, fingering the material to make sure it was still in good shape in spite of being faded.

Kalea scratched her head, puzzled. "What will you do with them?"

"Make a dress."

"A dress?"

"Like on the line," and Lizette gestured to where her lavender dress was hanging. "Only I'm going to need thread and scissors."

She frowned, concentrating, then remembered seeing a small chest in Sancho's hut. If it wasn't locked it was worth a try. She stood up and started for the hut, then stopped, stared at Kalea for a minute, retraced her steps, and took the washed-out green wraparound and fastened it on herself the way Kalea wore hers, only high to cover the slight bulge of her stomach. Her breasts were still bare, but at least she felt a little more decent, and again she headed for the hut, returning a few minutes later with a rusty pair of scissors and some heavy thread. For the rest of the morning, after finding a suitable stone and sharpening the scissors somewhat, and with the help of a small knife she had also retrieved from one of the other huts, Lizette worked on making a dress she could wear that would fit her no matter how big her stomach got. It had to be the middle of August already, or maybe later, Lizette thought as she worked. She'd lost all track of time. But if it was the middle of August, that meant she was at least three and a half months along, and having been pregnant once already with the twins, she was showing much sooner this time.

As the sun moved higher in the sky and the morning breeze died down, leaving the air hot and sticky, they moved the bench to beneath the jacaranda tree, and while Lizette continued making her dress, Kalea worked at finding something for them to eat.

There was some natural fruit on the island, and after stopping for a noon snack of dried biscuits left by the pirate crew and an unusual-tasting fish stew Kalea concocted from some leftovers, they washed it down with coconut milk and finished with a banana Lizette hoped she'd keep on her stomach. Although the morning sickness was gone, there were still times when her stomach rebelled. Especially at strange food.

By early afternoon Lizette stood up proudly, slipped the dress over her head, and modeled it for Kalea. The two pieces of blue material she'd sewn together to form the front and back; then she'd gathered them around the top, making it just big enough to fit around her beneath her arms. This done, she'd ripped the skirt of her petticoat into wide bands and made straps to fit over her shoulders to hold it up, as well as binding the top where it had been gathered so it had a neat edge. Then she'd taken the ruffle from the bottom of her petticoat and added it to the bottom of the blue material, so the skirt came down to just below her knees. It fit perfectly. There was no waistline, and it gave her plenty of room to expand.

"Only I wish it was all one color," she said as she stared down at it.

Kalea had been watching this white woman all morning, and in spite of her jealousy, she was having a hard time hating her. Lizette Kolter wasn't proud or haughty as one would expect the woman of an important man like Sancho to be. And Lizette didn't even yell at her when she did things wrong. Even the village women yelled when she did things wrong. Why not Lizette Kolter? Instead Lizette only laughed, and said it could happen to anyone.

Kalea saw the disappointed look on Lizette's face. "We will make it all one color," she said quickly. "Come," and she headed toward the path that led to the village.

Lizette hesitated.

"Come," Kalea urged. "Only a short way."

Kalea moved again toward the path, and this time Lizette followed. After some four or five minutes of walking, Kalea stepped off the path and made her way to a number of old logs near a damp area where the ground was hot and steamy, the air strong with the scent of decaying wood.

"Here," Kalea said, and moved to the base of a tree where the limbs practically grew along the ground amid a jumble of decaying logs, and she began to break off what looked like weird spongy growths on the wood. She held a handful out to Lizette, who took them from her gingerly.

"What do we do with these?" Lizette asked.

Kalea smiled, pleased with herself. "We take them to the camp," she answered. "Then I show you."

Kalea kept picking until Lizette had her skirt filled; then, holding it up so they wouldn't fall out, and Kalea carrying more in her hands, they returned to the camp, where Kalea had Lizette set them in a dark place in the hut, out of the sun so they wouldn't dry out; then they built the cooking fire back up and put a large kettle of water on to heat.

While the water was heating they raided Billie By-God's hut, going through his cupboards carefully until Kalea found a bottle of cider vinegar. When the water was hot, Kalea poured most of the vinegar in and added the spongy growths they'd brought from the woods, breaking them up as best she could as she dropped them in.

Lizette stood by watching, and was surprised, after a few minutes, to see the water start to change color, turning a dark yellowish brown. When the color seemed deep enough, Kalea had Lizette slip off the strange dress she'd made and she added it to the dark, boiling liquid.

Lizette's clothes she'd washed earlier were dry now, so she put them back on, holding her breath in uncomfortably as she fastened them around the waist, knowing that within a week or so they probably wouldn't even fit this well; then she came back to the fire to help Kalea, who was using a stick to turn the dress over and over in the dark, smelly water.

Sweat was rolling down the black woman's face in the heat, but she didn't seem to mind.

"The color will not last too long with washing," she explained while Lizette stood watching. "And there may be light and dark spots, but it will mostly be the same," and she continued for what seemed like an hour, turning the dress and stirring the pot. Then finally, using the stick she'd been stirring with, she lifted the dress from the hot dye bath and carried it down to the water's edge, where she waded in and rinsed it until it was cool enough to handle with her hands. This done, she draped it over the clothesline; then Lizette helped her empty the kettle, and the rest of the afternoon was spent scouring the kettle with sand and soap to make sure it was clean again.

By the time they both sat down to an evening meal of corn cakes baked in pans on the hot embers of the fire, using more of Billie By-God's supplies as well as his pots and pans, with a rice soup to which Kalea had added some native herbs, both women were tired yet pleased.

The makeshift dress had dried, and as Kalea said, the color wasn't exactly uniform, with light and dark blotches here and there, but it was all one color. An old yellowish brown.

"Why did you help me?" Lizette asked Kalea when they were cleaning up their mess from supper, so they could put the things back into Billie's hut.

"You didn't want me to?" the other woman asked.

"No . . . it's not that," Lizette answered. "I'm glad you did. It's just that you said you hate me, and I didn't think you'd help."

"I did not think I would help either," Kalea answered truthfully. "But you are not like I thought you to be."

"What did you think I'd be like?"

They were heading toward Billie's hut now, juggling the pans and foodstuffs in their arms, and Kalea stopped staring at Lizette, who had also stopped, waiting for her. The sun had dipped over the hill already, out of sight, but its rays still lingered, settling in Lizette's hair, highlighting it like the iridescent feathers of a bird, and her green eyes shone clear and bright as they stared back at Kalea.

"You are much like me, I think," Kalea answered. "You do not like others to serve you all the time, and you do not think you are better than Kalea."

Lizette shook her head. "I'm not. I'm another color—that is, my skin is—yes, but I'm not different from anyone else. In fact my father's part American Indian, Kalea. You should see my brother Cole. He looks just like my father said my grandfather looked at his age, and my grandfather on my father's side of the family was chief of one of the Tuscarora Indian tribes. Have you ever heard of American Indians?"

"I have heard. One of Sancho's men was what you call Indian."

"What happened to him?"

"He was killed during one of the raids."

"I see."

They continued talking as they went into the hut and put the things away, then went back to the fire, making sure it would last awhile.

"What do we do now?" Lizette asked when they were finally through. She walked over and sat on the bench that was still where it had been the night before.

Kalea stretched, her lithe body silhouetted against the darkening night sky, then dropped down cross-legged in the warm sand.

"I think we should make a . . . what you call . . . pact . . . treaty . . . article of terms," she said, trying to find the right word. "Would Sancho say that?"

"You mean decide to become friends?"

"Not friends," Kalea said, still unwilling to give in completely. "But we could bargain. I could teach you, and you could maybe tell me things."

Lizette looked pensive. "Like what?"

Kalea's dark eyes sifted over Lizette from head to toe. "What it is like to be what Sancho call a lady," she answered.

Lizette's frown was mixed with amusement. "Well, one thing, Kalea," she said, flushing, "ladies don't go around with their breasts uncovered," and her eyes shifted to Kalea's bare breasts, then back to her face.

The native woman looked puzzled. "Why?" she asked.

Now it was Lizette's turn to be at a loss. How was she going to explain modesty and morals to someone who obviously didn't even believe in God. At least not the God Lizette believed in. She'd heard the men referring to some of the natives' rituals to honor the spirits, and it was undeniable that the village women slept with the crew from the *Piranha*, although she had no idea whether any of them were married, or if the ones who slept with the pirates were all single. Regardless, either way, they had a strange set of customs that didn't conform very closely with civilized society.

Lizette straightened, then turned sideways on the bench, pulled her bare feet up, wrapping the skirt of the lavender dress about her knees, and hugged them.

"It's sort of hard to explain," she began hesitantly, then proceeded to try to teach civilized society's morals as best she could to a young woman she learned had never been off this small island, and that evening, by the time both of them settled down to sleep in Sancho's hut, a new understanding between the two had started to grow and Lizette made Kalea a promise that when the lavender dress no longer fit her, it would belong to Kalea from that day on.

For the next few weeks the two women were inseparable. Their days were spent with Kalea teaching Lizette all of the little things the native women knew and had grown up doing. Like stripping palm fronds, drying them, and weaving them into baskets, as well as using the fibers of other plants for making rope fishing nets and thread from which they wove rough cloth on handmade looms. And during those weeks Lizette also got her first glimpse of the village where Kalea grew up. It was along the ocean shore on the south side of the island, the huts made completely from grass instead of just being thatched like those of the pirate crew, and they had designated areas for growing many of the vegetables used, as well as having pens for goats, chickens, and pigs that Kalea told her Sancho's crew had brought to them from the civilized world, since none were native to the island.

Lizette discovered that the natives were really friendly, especially the children. And it was evident that many of them had been fathered by Sancho's crew. She could almost pinpoint how many years the pirates had used the small island as a haven from the rest of the world by the age of the oldest child of mixed blood, a girl who looked to be about seven or eight years old with blondish-brown hair and blue eyes.

Kalea's father, Chief Kaleharo, had three wives. Kalea's mother had been his second wife, only she had died when Kalea was very young and her father had replaced her with another who had given him four sons. Tall strapping young men who would have made excellent warriors if there'd been anyone to fight. But all they had to fight here was the sea, and the constant battle for survival. She had three older sisters and two older brothers from his first wife, all of them with families of their own, and his third wife, a much younger woman, had given him four children so far. Two girls and two boys. The youngest, a girl of only about three, reminded Lizette all too well of her own children, and she was glad she didn't have to be around them every day.

Because of Sancho's orders, they spent little time at the village, and during that time Kalea stayed close enough to Lizette to be her shadow. However, Lizette did manage to see the boats one afternoon as the men came in from a day of fishing in the clear water off the reefs that lay beneath the surf on this side of the island. The boats were similar to canoes, but with wooden poles and logs mounted on each side. Contraptions that Kalea told her Sancho called outrigging, to keep them from tipping in the rough waters beyond the reefs. Some were even equipped with small sails, and Lizette eyed them with mixed emotions.

She was certain there'd be no problem in keeping one afloat, and the thought was enticing, until she began to wonder what she'd do if she did manage to steal one and get away, then found out there were no islands close by. And if no ship came along, she could spend days on the open sea, which wasn't a very pleasant thought, especially in her condition. However, if they were to sight a ship someday . . .

She had been interrupted in her perusal of the situation

that afternoon by Kalea, who had noticed her interest in the
dugouts, and for the rest of their days together it became a
contention between them, with Kalea reminding Lizette of
Sancho's threat and Lizette trying to convince Kalea that he
wouldn't really go through with it, even if she were to get
away. Consequently, Kalea stayed even closer than ever.

As summer wore on, with a light rain to cleanse the air
almost every morning, and so many things for Lizette to
learn, it was early one afternoon well into September when
the long lonely wail from a conch shell filled the air, and one
of Kalea's brothers ran into camp to tell them that the
Piranha had been sighted on the horizon, heading toward
the island. In reality three weeks had gone by, and now
Lizette stood back near the hut wearing the strange dress
she'd concocted for herself, with Kalea beside her in the
lavender dress, both waiting for the ship to enter the cove,
while the rest of the natives began to gather on the beach to
greet them.

Lizette was nervous. Kalea had promised not to tell Sancho that Lizette had tried to convince her to let her take
one of the boats early one evening when they'd been up on
the hill looking for cassava roots and had spotted a ship
some distance out on the horizon. But Lizette was afraid she
might tell him anyway. They had argued quite heatedly that
night, and Lizette had almost been tempted to try to take off
on her own anyway after Kalea was asleep. The only thing
that had held her back had been her fear of dying in the hot
sun before another ship might find her, since the first ship
had quickly disappeared from sight. Kalea had explained
that the ship wouldn't have come in anyway because at
Sancho's request her brothers had set up ceremonial poles at
different places along the beach and on various hills of the
island, making any ships passing by reluctant to stop. The
ceremonial poles had colorful banners streaming from them
so they'd be easy to spot, with human skulls, bleached white
from the sun, fastened on top. But she'd never explained to
Lizette just what the significance was.

Now Lizette watched apprehensively as the *Piranha*'s sails
began to slacken more and more, the men filling the rigging.
Then, as it reached a spot some hundred yards or so from
shore, the anchor was dropped, sails furled, and the longboats lowered over the side.

Lizette glanced sideways at Kalea and she could tell Kalea

was nervous too. First she'd straighten the skirt of the lavender dress self-consciously, then pat her hair, her eyes steady on the ship, then following the longboats as they started toward shore.

Lizette turned from Kalea and shaded her eyes with one hand, then frowned. Sancho wasn't in either of the longboats. At least she couldn't see him. Could it be? Her heart began to pound. If Sancho had been killed in one of their raids . . . His presence had been the only thing standing between her and the crew. Especially men like Kidder and some of the others whose eyes had watched her lecherously.

Anxiously she rose onto her tiptoes, then breathed a sigh of relief as she finally spotted him in the stern of the first longboat that reached the beach. However, something was wrong, and she watched curiously as Jigger and the others pulled the longboat ashore; then Jigger hurried back and she saw that he had to help Sancho get to his feet.

Her eyes studied Sancho's big frame apprehensively as she watched Drego, the helmsman, join Jigger, and both men lifted their captain, practically carrying him from the longboat. Even the natives' boisterous greetings had quieted now as Sancho, his feet on the white sands, finally tried to stand on his own two feet. His face was strained, eyes worried, but with his first mate on one side and the helmsman on the other, he was finally able to navigate, and slowly, laboriously, he made his way toward the hut where Lizette and Kalea stood waiting, the natives moving back, opening a path for him.

Lizette couldn't move as Sancho came toward them, and it was Kalea who rushed to his side excitedly, her eyes on his left leg that was wrapped in bloody bandages.

"Lay him on bed inside," she urged fretfully. "I will make potions, clean wound."

Lizette stared at Sancho, realizing he was paying no attention at all to Kalea's concern or the distress of any of the other natives who were beginning to follow the three men toward the hut. Instead his eyes were on Lizette, never wavering, and although she could see pain in them, something else was there too. A stubborn pride, and when he finally reached her where he stood next to the doorway, he stopped momentarily and his eyes held hers.

"I told you I would be back, *señora*," he said, his voice husky with emotion. "And I have kept my promise. Now you will join me." With the help of Jigger and Drego, he managed to enter the hut, limp painfully to her bed, where they helped him to lower himself and get propped against the wall with some pillows behind him, using her bed so it'd be easier for someone to reach his leg.

Lizette had slipped into the hut silently behind him, and now she stood just inside the door watching as Drego and Jigger finished making Sancho comfortable; then he ordered everyone out including a few natives who had followed them inside, curious to see how badly he was hurt. When everyone was gone except Lizette, he motioned for her to come closer.

"What happened?" she asked as she stood staring down at him.

He patted the floor beside the bed of palm fronds. "You will sit while we talk, *mi querida*," he said.

Lizette took a deep breath, then dropped to the ground, her legs tucked sideways under her. He reached out and grabbed her dress.

"What's this?" he asked.

She shook her head. "I asked you first. What happened?" she repeated.

His eyes sparked irritably. "*Madre de Dios!* You are as stubborn as I am," he commented, then sighed. "I underestimated the prowess of my opponent, that's all," he answered.

"And your opponent?"

"He was a good meal for the sharks."

Lizette shuddered.

"You would prefer I was the shark's dinner?" he asked. "Hah!"

"I didn't say that."

"And you better not think it. Now"—he gestured toward her—"what of the dress?"

She glanced down at his leg, then reached out, starting to untie the bandages.

"Leave it," he said. "Kalea will get it. Now, I ask you again. The dress?"

"I had to have something to wear." She pointed to the small chest on the other side of the hut. "I found scissors and thread in there, and Kalea gave me some of her wraparound skirts."

"You should have waited for me."

"For you? You don't know how to make a dress. Besides, I had to have something."

He laughed. "That is 'something,' all right. Something ridiculous."

"Well, thank you," she answered curtly. "But I didn't ask for your approval, nor do I need it."

"You will take it off," he said, surprising her, and Lizette backed away, frowning.

He laughed again, a low chuckle as Kalea came into the hut carrying a pan of water and some clean cloths to start working on his leg.

"Kalea, before you start, go see if Jigger and the men have returned yet from the ship with the things I ordered to be brought ashore," he said. "If they have, tell him to bring the trunk I told him about to me here."

Kalea set the basin down, then nodded and left.

Once more Lizette started to unbandage his leg.

"I said Kalea will do it."

"Don't be ridiculous." The knot she was picking at let loose and she began to unwind the dirty strip of cloth. "It won't hurt to help her."

"I told you to get those clothes off."

"And I don't intend to. At least not until I have something else to put on, and Kalea's wearing my dress."

"So I noticed. Why?"

"Because it doesn't fit anymore."

The bandage fell away, and she got her first look at the deep gash that had gone to the bone, then taken some flesh with it when the blade was withdrawn. It was a sickening mess of bloody tissue that was starting to putrefy.

"It's going to have to be cauterized," she said, but he grabbed her wrist.

"No. Kalea knows what to do. She has herbs and medicine." His fingers loosened on her wrist and he grabbed her hand. "Lizette?"

She drew her eyes from the wound, but was reluctant to look at him.

"Lizette?"

"What?"

"Look at me."

She'd been staring at the wall behind him, and his fingers tightened on her hand.

"I said look at me."

She turned her head slightly, her eyes resting on his face. He looked tired and weary, the dark tan on his face deepening the crow's-feet at the corners of his eyes, his beard and hair in need of another trimming.

"I missed you, *mi querida,*" he whispered softly.

She lowered her eyes and her face flushed as she started to turn away.

"No!" he demanded arrogantly; then his voice softened. "You will not turn from me." His voice warmed as he studied her, noting how the tan she was acquiring made her eyes seem even more brilliant, their green depths like fiery emeralds. "I have waited for this moment since the day we left," he went on. "You will greet me properly, Señora Kolter, the way I said *adiós* to you."

Lizette remembered very well the kiss he'd bestowed on her that before morning they'd left the hut, when the others couldn't see, and now the flush on her face deepened as her eyes lifted haughtily.

"If you think I'm going to kiss you—"

He smiled broadly, marveling at the fight still in her eyes. No wonder he loved her.

"What will you do if I force you to kiss me?" he asked, amused, and with little effort, and still holding her hand, he pulled her toward him so she was off balance. His arm went about her and he held her close against him, her mouth barely inches from his. "You were saying?" he asked.

"I wish they'd killed you!" she gasped through clenched teeth.

Her insult fell on deaf ears. "I'm waiting, Lizette," he murmured softly, and she knew there was no way she could fight him. He'd have his way regardless.

Reluctantly she moved her mouth closer to his, hoping to make the kiss brief and light, but the moment their lips touched she knew she'd lost when his arm tightened around her and his mouth moved against hers hungrily, while deep down inside she felt those same familiar stirrings she'd been hoping to forget.

Seconds later his mouth eased on hers and he released her at the sound of a commotion just outside the hut, and as she settled back away from him, her face flushed, heart pounding erratically, his eyes caressing hers steadily, Jigger backed awkwardly into the hut carrying one end of a huge trunk, with Mosely carrying the other end.

"Where you want it put, Cap'n?" he asked, stopping for instructions, and Sancho had them put it next to the small chest, a few feet from the door, then asked them to go find out what had happened to Kalea.

Lizette started to get up after the men left, and Sancho once more grabbed her wrist.

"You are not to leave," he said firmly. Then smiled. "You are to go over and open the trunk."

She stared at him curiously.

"Go . . . go on," he insisted, releasing her wrist. "The contents belong to you."

"Me?"

"*Si.* When I see them, I say: These shall be for my Lizette. Now, you go look," and he pushed her lightly, so she'd get up.

She started toward the huge trunk, and just as she reached it, Kalea hurried in. The native girl was panting, and her arms were full of a number of bottles with corks in them.

"I ran all the way," she gasped breathlessly. "Billie By-God was out of some things." She dropped to her knees beside Sancho and began tearing more of his pant leg away from the wound, put the basin beneath his leg, then began to wash it. Her eyes flicked back to where Lizette was for a brief second, then she continued.

Sancho's eyes sifted over Lizette's old lavender dress Kalea had on and he smiled as he called over to Lizette. "See if perhaps there may be something you could give to Kalea too, eh, *querida?*" he offered as Lizette lifted the lid of the trunk. Only she didn't answer. She was too stunned, staring at what was inside.

There was dress after dress. Dozens of them in velvets and silks as well as cotton, satin, and gauze, and they were of every color and hue, with a layer of petticoats and camisoles near the bottom. But the most remarkable part was that they had evidently belonged to someone much larger than Lizette and would fit her even now through the waist, with little altering in the future.

She lifted up one of the dresses. It was a deep red burgundy that reminded her of Sancho's sister Elena, and she threw it back down, then took out a bright green silk so delicate it felt as light as a feather, with tiny pink roses embroidered on the skirt, and pink satin ribbons decorating the bodice. All she didn't need now was a reminder of

Elena, and she held the green dress up against her to see how it might look. Suddenly she turned to Sancho.

"Where did you get them?" she asked.

His eyes flashed, and she saw his jaw tense as Kalea continued working on his leg. "It is not important," he answered.

"Oh, yes it is. It's plunder from one of your raids, isn't it?"

"Does that matter?"

"It does to me." She tossed the dress back in the trunk. "What happened to the woman they belonged to?" she went on, her eyes intent on him as she studied his face for an answer. "She's dead, isn't she?"

"She was a nasty bitch!"

"And you killed her!"

"If I did?"

"I won't wear the clothes."

"Stubborn jackass," he muttered half under his breath. "You will wear them and be damned!" he shouted at her, then cut loose in Spanish with what she assumed were more curse words, and she stiffened.

"That isn't going to make me change my mind," she contended.

His eyes hardened. "You will wear them."

She glared back at him. "I won't!"

"We shall see." He winced as Kalea began pouring one of her medications onto the open wound, and Lizette silently prayed that it would hurt him even more. She started toward the door. "Where are you going?" he asked.

She stopped, weighing her answer. "Outside," she said, suddenly realizing that with his leg like it was, he couldn't very well get up and force her to stay. "I'll be back in later." She heard him mumble something behind her in Spanish again as she left the hut to see what the others were doing.

She didn't go far, however, because in spite of her adverse feelings toward Sancho, she still felt safer, when the rest of the crew was around, if Sancho weren't too far away. She moved from in front of the door to the hut so she wouldn't be seen from inside, then stood watching all the activity. The natives were milling about taking everything in, while the crew of the *Piranha* were hauling in new supplies, gloating over their ill-gotten gains, and already starting to pass around the rum.

"Don't wander too far, dearie," Jigger said, startling Lizette, and she whirled around. He was standing behind her, a small keg of molasses resting on his shoulder. "The cap'n ain't in no shape to see you stays all right for a few days, missus," he went on. "So's you'd better not take chances."

Lizette sighed. Jigger was probably the only real friend Sancho had among the crew. "Thank you, Jigger," she said, then frowned. "Jigger, can we talk?" she asked abruptly.

He swung the keg of molasses down from his shoulder and scowled, his eyes studying her curiously from his pockmarked face. "What's 'at?" he asked.

She licked her lips nervously. "Well," she began, "that trunk in there, the one with the clothes in it. What happened to the lady who owned it?"

"Dead," he answered matter-of-factly

She stared at him, her face troubled. "Then Sancho killed her!"

"Guess that's one way of puttin' it," Jigger answered.

"What do you mean?"

"She was half-dead already when we clumb aboard. Guess she got hit when we was shellin' the ship. Her husband was alive enough, though. The Count of somethin'-or-other, he was. He's the one ran his sword through the cap'n's leg when he weren't lookin'."

"I see. Then Sancho didn't actually kill her!"

"Well, he did and he didn't."

"I don't understand."

He propped a leg up on the keg and leaned an elbow on his knee, bending forward. "You see, she was layin' on the cabin floor with all the wreckage around her 'cause the shot tore right through the cabin wall, and part of her guts was splattered on the floor. Well, the cap'n didn't know her husband was hidin' behind what was left of the door and when he come through, the bastard swung with a sword and caught him right b'low the knee, layin' the dang thing right to the bone. And all the while that so-called lady was layin' there half-crazed, callin' the cap'n everything she could think of. I know—I was right behind him. So when he was through with her man, he put her out of her misery too, only he shouldn't have done her the favor and just shoulda let her go on sufferin' till the sharks got her. It was afterward he spotted the trunk and made sure it didn't go down with the ship."

"Then the woman wouldn't have lived anyway?"

"Even if she hadn't been wounded, she wouldn't have lived too long, dearie," he confessed matter-of-factly. " 'Cause when the crew got through with her she wouldn't have wanted to keep on livin'."

Lizette took a deep breath. "There were other women on board?" she asked.

"Afraid not," he answered, then gazed out at the men. "Why'd you think they're all so anxious to get back?" and he lifted his leg, hefted the keg back to his shoulder again, and addressed her once more. "Anything else you wanna know?" he asked.

She shook her head. "No, that's all, thank you, Jigger," and she watched as he headed for Billie By-God's hut with the keg of molasses.

It was almost an hour later when Kalea left Sancho's hut and found Lizette sitting on the bench she'd had Jigger drag up until it was only a few feet from the door. She'd been sitting all afternoon watching the men carrying in supplies and watching them get drunker as the day went on. Usually Sancho wouldn't let them drink until the ship was unloaded, but with him indisposed they were taking advantage.

"He want to see you," Kalea told Lizette as she sat down beside her.

Lizette frowned. "Did he say what for?"

"No. But he in bad mood."

"Did he say anything about you wearing my lavender dress?"

"He say I look better with skirt on."

"He would," Lizette answered disgustedly. "And I know why." She stood up slowly, then reluctantly moved toward the hut, staring down at her bare feet as she walked.

She'd never liked going barefoot actually, but here it seemed the best thing to do. She glanced down at the weird dress she'd made. It wasn't very good, but it was something to cover her. She looked back up just in time to keep from bumping right into Kidder, who had deliberately moved to where he'd intercept her.

"Goin' someplace?" he asked, smiling.

She held her ground. "You know exactly where I'm going."

His smile was more of a sneer and his breath smelled of rum. "He can't do you no good tonight, honey," he said, ogling her lecherously. "He ain't gonna do you no good for a long time, you'll see."

"That's my business," she answered angrily. "Now, let me pass."

"Oh, I see. Just 'cause you're gonna have his kid, now I suppose he's somethin' special, is that it?" he jeered. "Wonder what your husband's gonna think about that."

"What he does or doesn't think is none of your business, Kidder. Now, let me pass," she demanded.

"You heard the lady, move off!" Sancho yelled from behind Kidder, and as Kidder whirled around, Lizette caught sight of Sancho in the doorway, his leg bandaged, leaning against the doorjamb, a pistol pointed at Kidder's chest.

Kidder stood for a minute weighing his chances, then thought better of the situation and stepped aside. "Sorry, Cap'n," he apologized reluctantly. "Didn't know I'd be steppin' on your toes," and he took one last look at Lizette before heading toward a group of native women some distance away.

Lizette watched him go, then turned her attention to Sancho and moved quickly toward the door of the hut.

"You stupid fool," she admonished, reaching him and pushing him back inside. "What if he'd killed you?"

"He wouldn't dare try." Sancho holstered his pistol, then put his arm over her shoulder, letting her help him back to her bed.

She propped the pillows behind him, making sure he was comfortable. The pillows as well as the blankets were obviously more booty from earlier excursions, the Mediterranean look to them making her wonder whether the ship they'd come from had been Spanish, or perhaps from Italy or Portugal. They were worn now, and anything but clean; however, it was all they had, since geese and ducks weren't native to the island and there was no way to get the down for feather pillows.

"Comfortable?" she asked.

"What do you care?" he grumbled half under his breath, and now it was her turn to look amused.

She sat back on her heels, staring at him. "I hope you realize you've made another enemy," she offered.

He snorted irritably. "He is not the first, believe me. Over half of the crew hates my guts." He sighed. "I am alive, *señora,* because they know I am not afraid to kill. So nothing is new."

Lizette stared at him for a minute; then, "Did you tell your crew the baby I'm carrying is yours?" she asked.

His eyes glinted. "And if I did?"

"That's unfair!"

He grabbed her arm, hating himself for having baited her, but she looked so inviting when her eyes were alive with anger that he couldn't help teasing.

"I told them nothing, Lizette," he said, trying to reassure her. "They decide for themselves that the baby is mine."

"Then I suggest you tell them differently," she answered. "Or I will."

"They would not believe you. Besides," he said, "it is better they think this way."

"Better?"

"*Sí.* If they knew the child was not mine, they would perhaps begin thinking you are not mine either, and it would be harder for me to keep you from them."

"I see."

"They believe in sharing what does not specifically belong to their fellow crewmen, *mi querida,* and if they thought I was not sharing something that did not really belong to me, I could end up with a mutiny on my hands."

"Because of me?"

He released her arm and reached up, touching her hair affectionately. "It is a long time since some of them have had a white woman, Señora Kolter," he answered lovingly. "And one as beautiful as you—"

She tried to move away from his hand. "I wish I could understand you," she said, her eyes studying him warily. "You kill the woman who owned those clothes, putting her out of her misery, and yet if she hadn't been hurt you'd have let your crew have her without even caring."

"You think I do not care?"

"You've never stopped them, and I imagine you've joined them."

"I have never stopped them, no," he answered emphatically. "Until you came on board my ship, yes, that is the truth, and I will never stop them, because they are what they are, but I have never joined them. The women I take, I take alone. I am not an animal to rut in front of others."

"But you said . . . I thought you all shared."

"You do not understand. What is mine belongs to me unless I say otherwise, and any woman I claim as mine is mine until I no longer want her. That is my privilege as *capitán*."

"I see."

"No, you do not. I may be the son of a devil, *señora,*" he said bitterly. "I never claimed otherwise, but I am not solely without feeling. If I were, I would never have fallen in love with you."

She flushed, her eyes lowering. "Please don't," she whispered, her voice breaking. "I don't want you to love me."

"We do not always get what we want from this life, *mi querida,*" he said huskily. "You should know that by now."

Evening shadows were beginning to filter into the hut, and wavering spots of orange light from the fires that were being kindled outside began to penetrate the shadows, flickering weirdly on the dirt floor and weather-beaten walls.

"I told Kalea," Lizette offered hesitantly.

He frowned. "Told her what?"

"That it's Bain's baby."

"Oh." He frowned. "Then we will tell her not to say otherwise." He cocked his head, trying to see her face more clearly in the growing darkness. "What is it? Now what puzzles you?" he asked.

Lizette breathed deeply, then smoothed the skirt of her handmade dress. "I've been wondering. Kalea told me . . . and . . . Why did you have the natives put up those poles with skulls on them?" she finally asked, and was surprised to see him grin.

"You really do not know?" he asked.

"I wouldn't have asked if I knew. And Kalea didn't know either."

He leaned back more comfortably against the pillows. "There are strange customs in this side of the world, Lizette Kolter," he answered, evidently pleased with himself. "And one of those is the eating of human flesh. Unfortunately, there are still some tribes who practice it. However, any sea *capitán* worth his salt knows that a skull atop a decorated ceremonial pole is an indication that an island is inhabited by cannibals, and no ship's *capitán* who is smart will venture there." His eyes narrowed slightly as he grew more serious again. "It is my way of saying that this island also belongs to me. *Comprende?*"

"But they aren't cannibals."

He smiled. "I know."

She didn't answer, only sat staring at him and wondering just what kind of man Sancho de Córdoba would be today if he hadn't been betrayed by a woman so many years ago.

"Now what is wrong?" he asked, frowning again.

She shook her head. "Nothing—I was just thinking."

"*Bueno,*" he answered, and gestured toward the doorway. "Then go call Kalea, tell her to bring the lantern and some food. I am hungry—starved. But mind you, do not leave the hut. If she is not near the doorway, send someone for her. I do not think I would be up to another rescue trip on this leg tonight." He winked at Lizette as she rose to her feet and headed toward the door of the hut, her thoughts still in a turmoil over this strange man whose world she'd been thrust into.

Chapter 10

SANCHO WAS ALREADY doing much better the first day after their arrival back on the island, although Lizette knew the leg had been paining him a great deal during the night. He had stayed in her bed, and she had slept in his, and more than once she had heard him moan, then curse softly in the darkness. But with morning, the healing process was starting, and he was in a somewhat better mood. Especially when Lizette walked over to the trunk Jigger and Mosely had brought in the night before, lifted the lid, and began sorting through the dresses.

They had just finished a breakfast of cassava bread, scrambled eggs donated by the natives and cooked by Kalea, boiled salt pork, and guava juice, and Sancho was still wiping his mouth off on the sleeve of his dirty shirt. He set his tin plate down as he watched her, then stroked his beard and mustache, making a mental note to have Jigger trim them again.

"You have changed your mind?" he asked, and she turned around slowly.

It hadn't been what she'd expected to hear him say. She'd thought for sure he'd taunt her and be sarcastic. She straightened, holding the green dress up again to see if it would fit, while avoiding his eyes.

"I got to thinking," she said as she looked down at the fancy dress, then faintly got the courage to face him. "I don't think what you did was right, and I never will condone it. But I can't very well use the pillows and blankets on the beds, and eat all the food as well as take advantage of the other things on what you call your island, and then try to act holier than thou by not wearing them. I'd be a hypocrite, because there's nothing here that wasn't bought with some-one's blood."

The lines in his face softened. "So you will put on the dress?" he asked.

"Yes, I'll put on the dress," she answered complaisantly, and Sancho knew that for now he had won. "Only I need a bath first."

"A bath?"

She laid the dress over her arm, went to the door, and called to Kalea, who was off near the fire helping Billie By-God clean things up from breakfast; then she turned back toward Sancho.

"Yes, a bath," she said, answering him with determina-tion. "Kalea and I have been bathing in the lagoon every day since you've been gone. But since we can't bathe there anymore, there's a place over the hill on the northern shore of the island that we discovered. It's nice and sandy, and it's only about half an hour's walk."

He rose up, concerned. "You're not going alone?"

"Heavens, no." She held the dress in front of her, her hands clasped together. "I wouldn't think of it. Not with your crew of cutthroats out there. Kalea's going with me, and her brothers agreed, right after we found the place, that when the *Piranha* came back, one of them would go with us every day to make sure we'd be all right."

"And if they're out fishing?"

"Then Chief Kaleharo himself will be with us."

He relaxed back against the pillows. "Take Mosely with you too," he said, his eyes deepening thoughtfully. "He's not like the others."

"Thank you," she said softly, then turned as Kalea came up behind her.

So the next few days went along without incident. Kalea used the healing powers taught to her by the village women to take care of Sancho's wound, and day by day Lizette could see a change in it as Kalea explained to her everything that she was doing, as well as letting her help. Sancho was against Lizette's helping at first, but she was just as stubborn as he was, and after a few days he quit complaining. By the end of the first week, Lizette was practically taking care of him all by herself.

Lizette, however, still stayed close to Sancho all the time, even though he was spending most of his time outside now, propped against the side of the hut or sitting on one of the benches watching the men. The only time she was really any distance from him at all was in the mornings when she and Kalea, with Mosely in tow, would disappear to take their daily bath—a ritual no one knew of except Sancho, Jigger, and Mosely, but a curious journey into the woods that had begun to pique the curiosity of more than one member of Sancho's crew, including Kidder.

They had been back a little over a week already, and now Kidder stood near Billie By-God's hut one morning finishing his breakfast while he watched Lizette, Kalea, and Mosely heading for a path the other side of the jacaranda tree where the cap'n's fancy lady spent so much of her time reading those books. A frown creased his forehead. This was the third day he'd noticed them leaving like that, in the same direction, and always in the morning. Hmmm . . . strange, he thought, especially since she never left the cap'n's sight for more'n a few minutes at a time during the day. And she was usually carrying an extra dress with her in the mornings when she left, too; then, when they'd show up again a couple of hours later, she'd be wearin' the dress she'd been carryin'. The frown deepened and he set his empty plate down, took the last biscuit off it, then straightened, starting to saunter toward the jacaranda tree.

It wouldn't do to follow the same path, in case someone was watching, so instead, before reaching the tree, he strolled over, pretending to feed the biscuit to some monkeys in the underbrush, then slipped away, heading in their direction so he could eventually follow the way they were heading, while up ahead, on the newly worn path, Kalea, Lizette, and Mosely were greeting Kalea's oldest brother, Nagubi, who'd share guard duty with Mosely today.

The weather was warm, the air fresh, and Lizette always looked forward to the morning's walk. Not only was it good exercise in her condition, but she'd learned a great deal about Mosely on the way. He'd turned pirate by circumstance, not choice, and although he wasn't too well-educated, he was a proud man.

"Whenever I can, I sends money home to the missus," he'd said one day on their way back from the beach. "But it ain't often anyone goes to London that I knows, and it ain't often I gets money to send. But she still gets letters whenever I can send 'em, even though they ain't writ too well."

Lizette had never intruded into his reasons for leaving his wife and family, but it was evident it had to be something terrible to keep him away from the people he seemed to care about so much.

As they usually did when they reached the beach each morning, the men would make sure everything was clear, then backtrack on the path and sit at a vantage point which was usually a big old rock, and palaver while keeping an eye out for intruders, and that's where they were sitting this morning, talking, their eyes alert, when Kidder spotted them. They probably would have seen him too if he hadn't heard their voices first. But he hesitated on the trail, then slipped off it, letting the foliage of the trees along the path hide him from view until he reached a point where he could see them clearly, but they still couldn't see him.

Satisfied that they wouldn't spot him, and realizing that the women were no longer with them, he made his way northward through the underbrush, circling the two men until he reached the top of a hill at the edge of a wooded area. Then, keeping hidden behind some bushes, he gazed off toward where the ocean broke against the sandy shore, and his breath caught in his throat.

There they were, big as life. The native woman Kalea and the cap'n's fancy lady, and both were stark naked, swimming in the surf. He watched for a long time, letting the sight of them arouse him, then groaned as Lizette Kolter stretched in the morning sun, her pregnancy more apparent now than ever. Even at that, she was something to see. She'd actually been fat when she'd first boarded the *Piranha*. At least she was fatter than the women he usually liked, but now, except for her stomach, her body was golden in the sun, the breasts high and full, hips firmly rounded, legs slender and well-shaped. No wonder Sancho kept her to himself.

He stayed crouched for a long time at the top of the hill that overlooked the beach, peering between breaks in the foliage, trying to think of some way to take advantage of the situation, then licked his lips in anticipation. There was only one way, and that was to make sure Kalea wouldn't be with the cap'n's lady when she took her swim the next time, and with his mind working deviously as he sorted out the various ways he could accomplish what he planned to do, he slipped back into the tropical foliage and began making his way back toward camp, while Lizette and Kalea continued bathing, unaware someone had been watching them.

The next morning, as usual, after a hot night that made Lizette wake up drenched with perspiration, she called for Kalea, then frowned when the other woman finally appeared. Kalea's eyes were bloodshot, her lips trembling, and she was holding her stomach.

"I cannot go this morning," she moaned unhappily, and Lizette saw that her legs were shaking.

"Here, come in," she urged Kalea anxiously. "Good heavens, you look terrible," and Lizette led her to Sancho's bed, where she'd been sleeping every night.

Sancho glanced over from where he was resting on Lizette's bed, and he frowned. "What is it?" he asked, concerned.

Lizette shook her head. "I have no idea. It must have been something she had for breakfast. She seemed all right earlier when she first got up." Lizette helped Kalea to stretch out on the bed of palm fronds, then tucked a pillow beneath the other woman's head.

Kalea was still wearing the lavender dress, and Lizette straightened out the skirt and stroked Kalea's forehead, then pulled a light blanket up over her.

"You just rest here," she insisted. "Sancho can keep an eye on you."

Kalea's eyes faltered. "You must not go alone," she begged.

Lizette shook her head. "But I won't be alone. Mosely'll be with me, and Nagubi."

"Maybe you should stay," Sancho suggested.

Lizette gave him an exasperated look. "Nonsense. I won't swim, I'll just wash, and nothing's going to happen, don't worry."

She touched Kalea's cheek. It was cold and clammy rather than hot. Lizette had become fond of Kalea, and it hurt to see her so uncomfortable. "I won't be long," she assured her affectionately. "But it was so hot last night that I really do need to bathe. Try to sleep while I'm gone, and maybe you'll feel better by the time I get back."

She straightened, looking down at the other woman, and Kalea closed her eyes hesitantly, then Lizette grabbed the dress she was planning to change into from the trunk where she kept her things. It was the green dress with the flowers on it. Her favorite.

"I'll hurry back," she called over her shoulder as she

headed for the door; then, once outside, she joined Mosely, who had sauntered over to the hut when he saw Kalea arrive.

"Where's yer partner?" he asked, frowning, and Lizette explained what was going on while they headed toward the path beyond the jacaranda tree, neither of them aware that up ahead of them on the trail, Kidder was waiting for an unsuspecting Nagubi, and a short time later, Lizette and Mosely were surprised when Nagubi wasn't waiting for them at the usual place. Nor were any of Kalea's other brothers.

"Maybe we should turn back," Mosely suggested, but Lizette was determined. She felt so hot and sticky.

"Not today, of all days," she insisted stubbornly. "I'm sure it was just a misunderstanding. Nagubi no doubt thought it was someone else's turn to come this morning. We'll be all right. Come on."

Mosely studied her thoughtfully for a minute as the morning sun filtered down through the palm trees overhead, highlighting the bronze on her face and brightening the emerald streaks in her eyes. "You ain't afraid to go alone with me?" he asked.

She smiled warmly as she held the dress bunched in front of her and stared at him. "Not anymore," she answered, her eyes assessing him. "But then, I didn't really know you before, did I? Now, come on," she exclaimed, and started forward on the path again. "Let's get to the beach and back so I can find out just what's ailing Kalea." And as Mosely joined her, both of them continuing on down the path that led over the hill, neither of them had the least suspicion that Nagubi's body was lying concealed in a bloody heap only a few yards from the path, or that there was anything wrong.

Up ahead, near the beach, it seemed like hours went by before Kidder finally heard their voices, then saw Lizette and Mosely making their way along the trail toward him. He was about twenty feet from the rock where he had seen Mosely and Nagubi sitting talking the day before, only he was flat on the ground now, next to a half-decayed log that was under some bushes.

His noise twitched slightly as he tried to ease his head away from the musty smell of the rotting wood, only he didn't dare move too much for fear of being seen, and he was keeping his eyes glued to Lizette and Mosely. He held his breath as they continued past him and the rock, then stopped at the edge of the small incline where it met the sand so Mosely could make sure it was safe for her, and Kidder watched as his fellow crewman's eyes scanned the sea beyond the beach, looking for any sails that might be on the horizon. He looked carefully up and down the beach for some time; then, apparently satisfied that nothing was amiss, Mosely said something to the Kolter woman that Kidder couldn't make out, and he saw her nod and start down the incline, while Mosely turned, heading back for the rock.

Kidder couldn't wait too long, he knew. Not if he was going to catch her in the water, so he decided to count to twenty from the time Mosely reached the rock. He watched the other man expectantly as Mosely strolled to the boulder; then Kidder began to count. As he neared twenty, he tensed, every muscle tingling impatiently; then slowly he began to move from the fallen log to a nearby tree, where he finally stood up. Once on his feet, he stepped from behind the tree, pretending he was just strolling through the woods.

Mosely, who had been sitting on the rock daydreaming about his conversation earlier with Lizette Kolter and the fact that she trusted him, was so engrossed in his thoughts that he didn't even hear Kidder at first. All he could think of was that for the first time in years he felt like a human being again instead of scum, and he sighed. It was so long ago that he had left England with a price on his head and an uncertain future to look forward to. And the whole damn thing hadn't even been his fault. But how could you fight something you had no way of disproving? His mind was miles away on the streets of London with all those he'd left behind, when suddenly he heard a twig snap and the rustle of underbrush, and he straightened, alert now, the past set aside again, to be perused another day, and his eyes fell on Kidder, who was making his way through the woods at the side of the path.

"What the hell you doin' here, Kidder?" he asked roughly as he slid from the rock to his feet. He was about the same height as the other man, but huskier, with massive hands that clenched nervously.

Kidder smiled, trying to be casual. "Well, I could ask the same thing," he said, pretending ignorance. He was wearing his pistol, but it was holstered, as was his cutlass, and Mosely relaxed a bit, but not wholly. "One of the natives told me he saw some migrating ducks over this way last evening so I thought maybe I'd take a look. We could use a change of menu." Kidder continued strolling slowly toward Mosely. "But I haven't seen a thing so far, 'ceptin' you."

"And there ain't no ducks either," Mosely added quickly. "If there had been, I woulda seen 'em."

"That a fact?" Kidder asked lazily as he reached the other man; then suddenly, before Mosely even had a chance to react, Kidder, who'd been palming a small dagger in his right hand, sank it deep in the other man's belly.

Mosely's eyes widened in shock and he grabbed for Kidder, the pain already knotting his stomach and weakening his knees. "You bastard!" he blurted, gasping uncontrollably, and as his massive hands began to close on the front of Kidder's shirt in one last attempt to stop him, Kidder twisted the dagger viciously and pulled it back out, slicing through Mosely's stomach and clothes, before plunging it in again, this time at Mosely's throat, cutting off the bellow that had started to well up from it, the only sound leaving the stricken man now being a garbled moan as he fell back onto the rock, then slid down it, landing at Kidder's feet.

Kidder sneered as he stared down at Mosely. He'd never liked the man anyway. Him and his strange ways. Never joinin' the men when there were women to be had in a raid, and preferrin' to pay for what he got when he had the chance. Why, he even had one special woman here on the island he treated more like a man'd treat a wife than his whore. And he was always tryin' to find a way to get his share of the loot turned into gold coin, and lookin' for somebody to take it back to England for him instead of spendin' it. He didn't belong, that's for sure.

Kidder bent over, wiping the blade of his dagger in the grass, then slipped it back into its sheath at the back of his pants beneath the jacket he was wearing, while down on the beach, Lizette was thoroughly engrossed in her bath, trying to finish as quickly as she could so she could get back to camp and check on Kalea.

Her hair was richly lathered, but at the moment she was staring back toward the edge of the woods where she knew Mosely was waiting, and a frown creased her forehead. She'd swear she heard a weird noise, almost like a muffled scream or yell. Then just as abruptly as the noise had brought her to attention, she relaxed as a pair of monkeys swung into view from a mangrove tree, chattering and squealing at each other.

Satisfied that there was no reason for alarm, she watched the monkeys cavorting playfully for a few minutes, then ducked down beneath the surf again, rinsing her hair this time. She was used to seeing the monkeys, especially at camp. They were always sneaking food, and some had even been partially tamed by the *Piranha*'s crew as well as the natives.

With the soap rinsed out of her hair, she surfaced and took a deep breath of air, then headed back toward where she'd hung her clothes on a large piece of driftwood. Wiping the water from her face with her hands, and wringing it from her hair by twisting the back into a knot, she left the water, the warm morning air caressing her skin gently, while sand stuck to her feet.

She was almost to the piece of driftwood when she caught a movement out of the corner of her eye, and suddenly froze at the sight of Kidder heading toward her across the sand. He was completely naked, his clothes and weapons left behind him in a pile at the bottom of the incline, and the sun glinted off a dagger in his hand. His eyes were fixed on Lizette and she held her breath anxiously for a second, trying to decide what to do. He was between her and the woods, and although the beach was long, he was coming fast.

She took a step backward, then another, and another, and kept right on going now, backing down again into the water. It would be harder for him to reach her here. Waves broke at her back as the water deepened, and still he kept coming.

"You won't get away that way, honey!" he yelled, cupping his hand around his mouth.

She wasn't so sure. She felt the water at her back now, the surf breaking against it with a gentle roll.

"Mosely!" she screamed at the top of her lungs. "Mosely!"

Kidder grinned. "He can't hear ya, honey," he answered flippantly. "He just got his throat slit!"

Lizette swallowed nervously. The man was insane. If he had killed Mosely, that meant he intended to kill her too when he was through with her. She watched warily as he slowed, then stopped and stood at the water's edge, staring at her.

"You might as well come out," he said, sneering, his broken tooth making him look even worse.

Her jaw tensed. "Never!"

"Then I guess I'll have to come in."

He took a step forward into the surf, only Lizette wasn't about to wait. With one quick plunge, she was beneath the surface, and her strokes as she swam underwater were broad and quick as she tried to get as far away from him as possible.

Kidder's eyes searched the water, but all he could see was the foaming surf, while beneath the surface, Lizette's lungs felt like they were about to burst. She had to get air, and soon. She had gone quite a way beneath the water, and now her legs scissored, her hands tilting upward, and suddenly she was gulping air into her lungs again. Wiping the water from her face quickly, she glanced back. Kidder had spotted her already and was running along the edge of the water toward her. She exhaled angrily, then looked up ahead. The beach ended just a few yards beyond where she was standing and the land curved, jutting out, the shoreline becoming rocky and uneven before straightening again, with high cliffs that once more curved, this time inward, where they rounded to form the outside of the cove where the *Piranha* was anchored. There was no way she could swim any further without risking the chance of ending up with no way to reach shore again at all. She had to go back.

Kidder was almost to her now, and hoping to confuse him, she pretended to dive in, heading toward the cliffs, but instead turned beneath the surface and began swimming back the way she had come. It was hard work fighting against the undercurrents, and again her lungs started to hurt. She eased the air from them a little at a time. Finally she could go no further, and once more surfaced, glancing quickly behind her as soon as she gulped a big breath of air.

Kidder hadn't been fooled. He knew Lizette wasn't stupid, and the fact that she could swim as well as she did told him she'd never try for the cliffs. So when her head broke the surface this time, he was only a few feet away, and although she tried to get away again, he ran into the surf quickly and reached out, just managing to grab her wrist.

"Let go!" she yelled frantically, only his fingers tightened. "I said let go!"

He pulled her toward him and she cringed as she was

thrown off balance, the strength of the rolling surf carrying her the rest of the way to him.

"That's better." He laughed viciously and began dragging her toward the sand, only she wasn't about to go, not with him.

Her free arm swung in a wide arc, connecting with his face, and his eyes blazed furiously as he tried to pull her back against him, only she was too quick. Her knee jerked forward. It missed its target, but in dodging the kick, Kidder was thrown off balance just enough so she was able to wrench free, and without hesitating to see if she'd done any damage, she moved with the surf, letting it half-carry her as she headed toward the beach on her own this time, with Kidder behind her now.

"I said you'll never get away!" he hollered breathlessly as he fought the surf, but she wasn't even listening. All she could think of was the long expanse of sand stretched out between the water and the woods where she might be able to hide.

Her feet dug into the sand and she began to run now, no longer hampered by the water, only he was still behind her, out of the water too now, and gaining every second. Her heart was pounding, her breath erratic, and she was praying as hard as she could. Suddenly she felt his hand in her hair, her legs faltered, and she let out a shriek as her feet flew up and she went down hard in the sand, Kidder on top of her.

"You want yours slit too?" Kidder asked, his face only inches from hers, and she tensed, feeling the dagger at her own throat now.

"Go ahead," she challenged. "You're going to anyway."

"Not until I have some fun."

Her eyes narrowed as she stared up at him. "You'll never get away with it."

"Why not? Who's to tell? Mosely's dead, Nagubi's dead, and you'll be dead too."

"But you'll have the scars to prove it!" she shot back viciously, and in spite of the blade at her throat, her hand filled quickly with sand and she flung it right at his face while at the same time trying to roll free.

He was too strong, though, and either spotting her hand ahead of time or sensing what she was going to do, he closed his eyes just long enough to keep the sand from getting in them, and all it did was infuriate him more as he opened them again, shaking, blowing, and sputtering excess sand from his face and mouth.

"You'll regret that," he mumbled furiously as the dagger pressed harder against her throat, and Lizette inhaled, her breathing short and jagged. "Now, lay your arms above your head and spread your legs," he ordered arrogantly.

She didn't move.

"I said, spread them."

"To hell with you," she snarled. "You take me, you take me dead!"

Lizette was staring directly into Kidder's crazed eyes, her own eyes rimmed with tears, when suddenly, without warning, a club, stick, she couldn't really see what it was, came streaking out of nowhere and connected with the side of Kidder's head. His mouth flew open, eyes widening like saucers, and his hand clenched hard on the dagger, taking it with him as he flew sideways, then landed facefirst in the sand.

Lizette lay frozen for a second, the shock of seeing the man's head split like a melon shocking her. For a few seconds she had no idea what was happening. Then, swallowing hard, she let her gaze move from Kidder's broken, naked body to the man who had yielded the weapon that had killed him, and she frowned.

"Sancho?" she gasped, and she began to move, starting to sit up to cover her own nakedness with her arms.

The long hunk of tree limb fell from Sancho's hand and he knelt down beside her, then reached behind him to Jigger, who was running toward them from the water with Lizette's clean dress in his hand, while Drego knelt beside Kidder.

"How did you know? I don't understand," she mumbled breathlessly.

Jigger reached them, and Sancho grabbed the dress, giving it to her. "Here, put this on first," he said gently. "Then we talk," and he helped her slip the green flowered dress over her head, then stood up, helping her to her feet so he could fasten the back for her.

Her legs were trembling and she was crying now, silent tears of relief. What would she have done if they hadn't come along? She'd be dead now, that's what, because she wouldn't have given in. She watched Jigger move to join Drego, and they examined Kidder while Sancho buttoned the last button.

"Is he dead?" she asked.

"I thought so at first." Jigger bent down, rolling him over in the sand. " 'Fraid he ain't, Cap'n," he answered, glancing over at Sancho, and Lizette looked up into Sancho's face.

"Too bad," Sancho said, his eyes intent on Kidder. "I was hoping I could save us a hanging."

Kidder moaned agonizingly, and Lizette felt her stomach lurch as he tried to lift his head and she got a good look. His ear was raw flesh, and blood mixed with sand was smeared in his shoulder-length hair, while bruises and scraped skin ran down the right side of his face. He was a mess.

"You think you two can handle him, Jigger?" Sancho asked.

Jigger straightened importantly. "In his shape? Won't be nothin' to it. We'll just tie him to that tree branch you used like we'd tie any other kinda animal, and haul him back to camp safari style."

"He said he killed Mosely," Lizette offered weakly as she stared at Kidder.

Sancho nodded. "We found him, and Nagubi too."

"But why?" she cried helplessly. "Why would any man think that . . . that what he wanted from me was so important he had to kill for it? Why? I'm only a woman, just like any other. He isn't in love with me, it'd be no different . . . there was no reason for it."

Sancho took a deep breath, and his gaze moved to Lizette's face, studying her somberly. "You may be married, and a mother, Lizette Kolter," he answered. "But you do not understand men. To him, you were a prize, the *capitán*'s woman, and because of that, in his mind, with you it would have been like conquering a mountain or winning a battle, and that in itself would have made it different."

"That's crazy."

"No. It is a fact of life." He started ushering her toward the piece of driftwood where her soiled dress lay, while Jigger and Drego worked, trussing Kidder like a hunting trophy and fastening him to the tree limb. "You see, most of what a man feels is in his head, *mi querida*," Sancho went on. "I discover that years ago when I lose my head and kill the priest. However, some men have never learned this, so they think because their head say it, this they must do. They never learn that they can tell their head no, I will not do this, and so they end up like our friend there," and he glanced back toward Kidder while Lizette picked up her dirty dress from the piece of driftwood, then gazed off across the water toward the far horizon.

"How did you know to come?" she asked.

"Kalea."

"Kalea?" She was surprised.

"*Sí,* when we talk after you leave, she say that Kidder brought her some papaya juice to drink with her breakfast. Something he has never done before. Then I remember what happened the other night and the way he looked at you, and I have a talk with Drego and Jigger. Besides"—he straightened, flexing his muscles—"my leg needed the exercise, and I figured it was worth coming even if what I suspected was wrong. Now I am glad I came."

"He was planning to kill me afterward," she said, her lip still trembling slightly.

Sancho nodded. "*Sí,* I know, but now he shall hang, and no one will dare touch you again. Come," and they left the edge of the water, heading for the path that led back to camp, while Drego and Jigger gathered up Kidder's clothes and weapons, then hefted the half-conscious crewman up, trussed to the long heavy limb, and followed behind, with Kidder moaning all the way.

Later that morning, after a quick explanation to the men, the body of Hiram Mosely was brought back to camp and buried in a short, terse ceremony while the body of Nagubi was taken back to the native village, the drums and incantations of mourning filling most of the day. Then, as the sun began to lower on the horizon, Kidder, still naked and bleeding, his arms and legs numb from hanging trussed on the limb where they'd left him hanging all day, and cursing like a wild man, was hanged from a mangrove tree a short distance from camp, his body left dangling till long after dark as a warning to anyone else who might have been harboring the same idea.

Lizette hadn't watched the hanging. She couldn't. It wasn't that she thought he didn't deserve it, because she felt a flood of relief when she knew it was over and he couldn't harm her anymore. But she always had had a squeamish stomach for things like this. So while the rest of the *Piranha*'s crew and the natives gathered around watching Kidder's execution, Lizette stayed back at the hut with Kalea, who still wasn't fully over the effects of the poisonous herbs Kidder had added to the papaya juice he'd given her that morning.

"It will be a long time before any of my men take it into their heads to cross me again," Sancho said later that evening as he and Lizette sat on the bench beneath the jacaranda tree and gazed back toward the campfire where the men were gathered contemplating the day's events.

"I hope you're right," she answered, her eyes moving from one man to another, their faces unreadable in the flickering firelight. "But I'm afraid some of your crew are rather disgruntled about what happened."

"Only because they were wishing for him to get away with it. You think it is easy to lead men like this? Why do you think I sleep with one eye open?"

She looked at him curiously. "Then why don't you quit?"

"Why should I? What is there in it for me except a rope? There is no place for a man like me to hide, *señora*. Even here. Eventually I suppose this too will come to an end."

"You could change your name, go somewhere and start over where no one knew you."

"You would come with me?"

She flushed. "You know I can't do that, I don't love you."

"Not even a little?" He reached out, cupping her chin, forcing her to look into his face. "I think you care for me, Lizette Kolter, more than you want to. We have become friends, *si?*"

"Friends perhaps, if that's what you want to call it, but that's all, Sancho. Only friends."

He leaned forward and kissed her without warning, then drew his head back. "For now that will do, *querida*," he whispered huskily. "But later"—his hand dropped to her stomach and he held it there—"when this is over, we shall see."

Lizette stared at him, unable to answer, the intimacy of the moment bringing strange stirrings deep inside her, and she realized she was beginning to depend on Sancho too much for her own good, just as she had relied on Stuart. And suddenly, determined not to let her feelings begin to stray in a direction she didn't want them to, she vowed silently that regardless of what happened from here on, she was going to have to keep her emotions completely under control at all times.

The next few days were strained between Sancho and his men, but by the end of the following week, when the full moon began to rise again, Sancho was limping only slightly, the affair with Kidder seemed to have been forgotten, and he decided it was time the *Piranha* weighed anchor again. So two days later, with the mists of morning hanging low on the blue waters of the lagoon, he kissed Lizette good-bye and she stood on the beach with Kalea, watching the sails on the ship unfurling, and for some reason, this time as she stood there watching them go, she dreaded the thought of all the lonely days ahead with only the natives to keep her company.

Maybe it was her growing pregnancy that made her feel this way, she had no idea, but whatever it was, a sense of loss swept over her as she watched the ship begin to move, then make its way into the narrow channel that separated the lagoon from the open sea, and she suddenly felt very much alone.

"Well, here we are again," she said as she sighed, turning to Kalea, and the native woman's eyes warmed.

"This time, Lizette Kolter, we understand each other though, do we not?" Kalea said, and Lizette smiled.

"I guess you could say that, couldn't you?" She flung her head back, tossing her long dark hair over her shoulder. "So what shall we do first?" she asked, and both women looked at the water, warm and inviting, and by the time the tip of the last sail disappeared from along the top of the hill that hid the small bay from outsiders, they were already headed toward the water for their usual morning dip, with the realization that they wouldn't have to make the trip over the hill again in the mornings the whole while the *Piranha* was gone, which turned out to be two weeks, four days, and six hours, according to the improvised calendar Lizette had hanging on the wall of Sancho's hut, and the old clock he'd let her have off the ship before it sailed.

The days had moved slowly while he was gone, and Lizette had to admit she missed him more than she thought she would.

It wasn't that Kalea wasn't good company; it was just that she knew nothing of the outside world, and although Lizette could tell her about it, there was no way they could actually share the knowing as Lizette could with Sancho.

Still, having Kalea was better than being alone, and with only

Kalea, unlike when the *Piranha*'s crew was here, Lizette hadn't had to worry about where she went or what she did, at least most of the time.

She did stay away from the native village as much as possible, however, because Sancho had warned Kalea again about keeping her away from the boats, and Kalea had still been certain he'd hold to the threat he'd made. Besides that, Kalea's father had been upset over the death of Nagubi, partially blaming the white woman's presence, as he put it, for his son's death. So the farther Lizette stayed from the rest of the natives, the better, although there were times when she was really tempted to try her luck in the strange dugouts and the open sea. Rather, she would have been if she could have spotted a ship or had any idea at all just how far this island was from any other land. But as she kept telling herself, she was a confirmed coward. It wasn't really the thought of dying that bothered her, though, but the way she'd die. No, the risk was too great; she'd bide her time awhile longer and keep hoping.

So the days went by while Lizette wandered the island working to survive by fishing and gathering food with Kalea by her side, while she longed for home and family and prayed in her heart that someday she'd see them all again, although there were times it seemed futile to even hope. Billie By-God's hut came in handy again too for pots, pans, and other essentials they needed, while the assortment of clothes Sancho had brought back with him last time gave her a number of different dresses to wear, only she wasn't sure just how much longer they would fit her.

She still had the strange-looking dress she'd made for herself the first time he was gone, however, and was sitting in the hut now staring at it the day they came home. She'd been wondering if perhaps she was going to have to wear it after all before her pregnancy was finally over, when she straightened, listening intently, and heard the wailing call from a conch shell as it suddenly began to fill the air, echoing down from the hill surrounding the isolated cove, telling everyone of their return. She tensed, her hands clenching the dress, and wondered. What if he was hurt again, or worse yet, dead? After what had happened with Kidder, she wouldn't have a chance.

She swallowed apprehensively, set the dress back into the trunk with the other clothes, slowly lowered the lid, then stood up and looked down at the dress she was wearing. It had once been a lovely shade of deep purple but now was faded, the matching velvet ribbons that hugged the high empire waist no longer soft and smooth, and some of the lace on the slashed puff sleeves had been mended with coarse black thread from Sancho's chest, where she'd gotten the thread for the dress she'd made. She smoothed the skirt, then tucked her hair back behind her ears before stepping outside, where she stood quietly watching as the ship cleared the channel and slipped into the cove, its sails already slackened, men filling the rigging to furl them.

The beach was no longer deserted, but filling quickly with men, women, and children, and Lizette stepped back a little farther into the shadows from the thatched roof on the hut, especially when she saw Chief Kaleharo and some of his family at the head of the procession that was waiting near the water's edge for the longboats to be lowered.

"You are not going to greet him?" Kalea asked from beside her, and Lizette turned, startled.

"I didn't hear you."

"I know, but I ask, you will not say a welcome to Sancho?"

"When I am ready," Lizette answered quietly, her voice barely audible above the noise the natives were making.

Then she saw him, as the longboats were being lowered. He was standing in the first one, hanging on to the ropes as it eased into the water, and he was all right. He wasn't even hurt. As the rest of the men clambered in and the longboat headed toward shore, she continued to watch from the shadows, looking over the heads of the natives, and studied his tall frame curiously to make sure she hadn't been mistaken. Both relief and anger filled her. She'd be protected from the other men now, yes, and she was glad because they were brutal and unfeeling, but who was to protect her from Sancho?

Her gaze stayed on the *Piranha*'s captain as the longboat was beached; then, to her surprise, instead of leaving it as the other men were doing, Sancho stood for a long time gazing out over the crowd, and she began to wonder. Suddenly his gaze moved in her direction, and she saw him straighten as he caught sight of her, and without even taking time to greet the others who were clamoring around him, he stepped from the longboat and made his way up from the beach, letting them clear a path for him as he came, until finally he stood before her.

"I get no welcome home?" he asked above the din when he reached her.

She looked toward the men and women still pushing and shoving on each side of him. "They welcomed you home," she replied.

He took a deep breath. "That is not what I wish," he said, and reached out, grabbing her shoulders, pulling her into his arms. "This is what I wish," he said huskily, and his mouth covered hers in a long, drawn-out kiss before she even had a chance to protest; then he drew his head back, looking into her eyes.

"You had no right," she whispered breathlessly.

He smiled. "I have every right, *querida,* for now," he answered. "Besides, I missed you."

"Let me go."

"If you wish." He released her and she straightened her dress, flushing, while he turned toward the natives now, finally greeting them; then he turned back to her. It was early afternoon, the sun still high in the sky. "Come, I wish to show you," he said, and grabbed her hand, pulling her with him as he started toward the other longboats that were just reaching shore, and for the rest of the afternoon she stood by and watched amazed at the boxes of goods that were unloaded. Everything from fancy material and food-stuffs to gunpowder, as well as a chest full of gold bars and another fancily carved chest full of jewelry of all kinds.

"And this box is for you," he said proudly as Jigger helped him heft a large box from the longboat and they headed toward the hut. "Come."

Lizette followed hesitantly. It was one of the last boxes unloaded, and she couldn't imagine what was in it.

The camp had quieted some now that their arrival was over and Billie By-God was already preparing supper when Sancho and Jigger set the box down inside the hut; then Jigger went out again, leaving them alone.

"Well?" she asked curiously as she stared at the box. "What's in it?"

"You watch." Without hesitating he went to his private chest and brought back a hammer, then started breaking the box apart, and Lizette stared in awe as the outsides of the crate fell away.

It was a cradle. An elegantly carved mahogany cradle. Not just on rockers, but suspended in a frame so it was more like a swing. Sancho lifted it from what was left of the box and set it on the earthen floor of the hut, then stood with his hands on his hips surveying it.

"It is what you need, *sí?*" he asked, his eyes flashing vibrantly.

Lizette continued to stare at it, only she didn't answer.

"Now what is wrong?"

"N-nothing. I . . ." She turned away quickly so he wouldn't see the tears, but he grabbed her arm, stopping her.

"Wait! Why do you cry?"

"You don't know?" she asked bitterly. "You really don't know?"

"For Bain Kolter?" he asked angrily.

"For Bain, my children, and the one I carry. Oh, Sancho, I want to go home!"

He stared at her and she swore she saw pain in his eyes. "You cannot go home, Lizette Kolter," he said slowly, methodically. "You will be mine for always, and you will love me, you will see."

She closed her eyes. He'd never understand. A sigh escaped her lips and she opened her eyes again, once more looking at the cradle. It was beautiful, the carving so delicate.

"The baby it was for?" she asked apprehensively.

"Do not worry, I have no . . . what you call . . . fight— battle—I do not kill children."

"Your men?"

"The cradle was on its way to New Orleans—to the home of a Frenchman who will not miss it, I am sure. They can make another. Now, I ask you, it is what you need?"

"Yes, it's what I'll need," she answered, and walked over, touching it, remembering all too well when she rocked Braxton and Blythe in their cradles, and a pain shot through her chest, settling in the region of her heart, and she knew it would be there always.

Later that evening after the fires had died some, and evening shadows crept into the camp, settling beneath the mangrove trees and silhouetting the palms against the darkening sky, Sancho once more asked her to join him.

He was still limping, but only slightly, and she moved along beside him, the warm sand grinding between her bare

toes as he headed toward the jacaranda tree. Suddenly he
stopped well beneath its branches and turned to her, wishing
her face wasn't quite so shadowed because he loved to look
into her eyes.

"I have something else for you, *mi querida*," he said
fervently.

She frowned. "Oh?"

"Please, you will listen to me, *sí?*"

"I'll listen, yes," she answered.

His smile was melancholy and a little wistful as he reached
into the inside of his shirt to a small leather bag hanging
from a chain around his neck, and took something out.

"I am not sure even I know how to do this, *señora*," he
began hesitantly, "but I must, for my heart tells me I must."

"Your heart, not your head?" she asked.

"It tells me too, and this time I listen." He took her hand,
raised it to his lips, and kissed it, then pressed something
into her palm, closing her fingers around it. Whatever it was
felt hard and cold. She drew her hand away, opened it, and
stared, but whatever it was was lost in the shadows.

"Here, come," he urged, and they stepped out from beneath the tree to where flickering light from the camp threw
her into relief.

"Oh, Sancho," she cried when she saw what it was. "I
can't take this!"

It was a beautiful emerald, huge and ostentatious, with
diamonds on each side, set in a gold ring.

"It is for you," he insisted. "You must keep it."

"I can't."

"Why?"

"You know why." She held it out for him to take back,
but instead his hand covered hers, closing her fingers over
the ring that was still in her palm.

"You will keep it, *mi querida*," he said emphatically.
"And you will wear it, for I will not take it back. And when
you look at it you will know I love you."

She started to protest, but he drew her close, holding her
hand with the ring in it against his broad chest, while his
other arm held her waist firmly.

"*Por favor,* please, for now you will do as I ask, Lizette
Kolter?" he pleaded fervently, and something in his eyes, a
passionate longing she couldn't ignore, made her hesitate.
He took advantage of the hesitation, kissing her softly.

"That wasn't fair," she said as he drew his lips from hers.

"I know," he answered, then smiled. "But you will keep it?"

She stared at him for some time, then sighed, nodding reluctantly. "For now I'll keep it," she acquiesced, and suddenly his arms engulfed her and she was swept off her feet as he whirled her around, then kissed her again, laughing happily while deep down inside Lizette felt like a part of her had already started giving up hope of ever seeing home again.

For the next few days, life on the island went back to its old routine, only now Sancho himself stood guard for Lizette when she and Kalea took their morning swim on the other side of the island, and Jigger often joined him to keep him company while he waited.

They'd been back not quite a week now. It was early morning and Jigger and Sancho were sitting on the rock where Kidder had killed Mosely, waiting for Lizette and Kalea to finish their swim and join them. Jigger glanced over at Sancho, his eyes intense.

"I don't know if you've noticed or not, Cap'n," he said rather cautiously, since he wasn't used to pointing out his friend's mistakes to him, "but the men are gettin' awfully restless."

Sancho's eyes narrowed irritably. "So?"

"So they don't like it."

"What don't they like?"

"Well, now." Jigger's mouth twitched nervously. "You gotta admit, Cap'n, that ordinarily we'd have hit four or five ships while we were out, instead of just the couple we got these past two times, then we'd have headed for a good time at one of the ports and sold most of the cargo before comin' back here to hole up, only we didn't do that either. So the men been figurin' you're lettin' the Kolter woman interfere in their fun too much, that's what."

"Señora Kolter is my business, and if I want to be with her, that's my business too," he answered.

Jigger shook his head. "Not when the men suffer for it, it ain't just your business," he answered, his pockmarked face reddening from the strain of trying to hold his temper with a man he knew was dangerous to cross. "Except for your lady, Cap'n, the men hain't seen white women for months now and they don't like it one bit. I heard 'em grumbling. Why do you think they weren't all that happy over Kidder's hangin'? They figure he had as much right to her as you."

"Your feelings too, *amigo?*" Sancho asked.

"Hell no." Jigger tried to explain: "It's just that they figure you've got your woman, why shouldn't you be content, but what about them? They been riskin' their lives the same's you, only they ain't getting their share like always. Least not since the Kolter woman come aboard." His eyes hardened. "You keep goin', Cap'n, and you ain't gonna have no crew," he informed him. "And it won't be nobody's fault but your own."

Sancho stared at Jigger for a long time, contemplating his first mate's words, while he thought back over the past few months; then he straightened, taking a deep breath.

"How long since we left Cuba?" he suddenly asked.

Jigger shrugged. "Two, three months, maybe, why?"

"Then I guess you are right, *amigo,*" he said, suddenly making up his mind. "There are others I have been neglecting too, I see." He stood up as the women's voices floated toward them, and he knew they were coming back up from the beach. "Say nothing to the women as yet, *mi amigo,*" he said quickly. "But when we get back to camp you will tell the men to start loading the ship so we sail again in the morning."

"You headin' for Cuba?" Jigger asked.

"*Sí.*" Sancho glanced toward the path and watched Lizette and Kalea reach the top of the incline and start toward them. "And ports along the way," he went on hurriedly. "The men want white women, they shall get them; and in the meantime, while they are doing it they will also spread the news that the wife of Señor Bain Kolter now belongs to *La Piranha's capitán,* Sancho de Córdoba. *Comprende?*"

Jigger watched the expression in Sancho's eyes as they fell on Bain Kolter's wife, and he cringed inside. The men were right, their captain was no longer keeping Lizette Kolter with him solely to avenge Barlovento. He was keeping her for himself because he'd fallen in love with her. Something they'd never expected ever to see.

"Now go—go ahead of us," Sancho urged. "And tell the men, get them started. I will walk the women back to camp," and he stood for a moment watching Jigger hurry away along the winding trail, brushing the tropical foliage aside ahead of him; then Sancho turned to greet the women.

It was early evening, shortly after dark. Sancho had seemed rather edgy most of the day so Lizette had been avoiding him as best she could. Now suddenly he walked over, joining her where she sat on the bench near the jacaranda tree, and there was no way she could refuse his offer to take a walk. It was more like a command.

Smoothing the skirt of the strange-looking dress she'd made for herself the first time he'd been gone, she tucked her hair back behind her ears and stood up. She liked this dress, really. Maybe because it was so roomy and cool, and she could breathe in it without feeling stuffed. Besides, she'd washed all the others and they were still wet, hanging on the line.

She let Sancho usher her off toward the path that led to the beach where they swam every morning, then gazed back toward camp. No one seemed to be paying much attention to them at all. It was the first time they'd wandered off alone like this after dark, but it was easy to see the path since the moon was waxing again, and in its first quarter.

"You said you wanted to talk?" she asked when they were well away from the others. She glanced over at him. He looked so serious. "Well?" she asked again when he didn't answer.

Sancho took a deep breath, smelling the earthy scents around him. It was October already, but unlike lands that changed with the seasons, nothing here ever changed. He could still smell the fragrant scent of the flowering trees mingling with the salt air.

"How would you like to go away for a while?" he answered, surprising her, and she stopped on the path, her heart beating wildly.

"Where?"

"Do not get excited, *querida*. I am not taking you home," he said. "But I promised Elena and Mario to see them, and it is time."

"You're taking me with you?"

"*Sí*, why not?"

They were walking again and he looked over at her. She looked so different from the person he'd forced to come with him, and yet the fire was still in her eyes, the same depth of passion he'd glimpsed so often still there.

"I wish for the whole world to know you are mine, *querida*," he said after a few minutes. "And what better way than to take you with me, for we go not only to Cuba but also to many ports along the way, where they will say, 'Aha, Sancho de Córdoba has finally found himself a woman.' "

"You'd do that to me?" she asked, stopping once more on the trail. "I thought you said you loved me?"

"I do."

"Then don't do this, please," she begged.

They had reached the end of the path now, where it wound down the incline to the beach, and she stopped at the edge, looking up at him.

"If you do this, Sancho, people will think I stay willingly and we both know it's a lie."

"For you, not for me," he answered, and he reached out, touching her face, as he felt the warm breeze from the sea trying to penetrate his beard; then suddenly, as his eyes left hers and he gazed off beyond where they were standing, to the midnight-blue horizon where stars hung in the sky and the moon glittered on the water, he froze.

"What is it?" she asked, sensing something wrong, and Sancho's voice was barely a whisper.

"A ship," he murmured, half under his breath. "*Madre de Dios, mi querida,* there's a ship not two hundred yards offshore." His head moved cautiously and she held her breath; then he inhaled sharply. "And there is a longboat on the beach. Come, we get out of here!" he cried fiercely, and started to turn to go back the way they'd come, but before they had a chance, they heard crashing in the underbrush, and Lizette stared wide-eyed as a bunch of men, guns drawn, broke from the surrounding woods and came toward them on the run.

Sancho tried to grab her hand as he made a break down the hill, only he missed, and instead Lizette lost her balance, slipping over the edge of the incline after him, stumbling erratically to keep her balance.

"Run!" he shouted over his shoulder as they hit the beach, only it wasn't as easy for Lizette as it was for him. He reached back to help her.

"Go . . . go on!" she yelled at him. "Go for help!" But he stood his ground.

"I will not leave you."

He helped her to her feet, then quickly knocked down two

of the men who reached them, and they both began to run along the beach, only Lizette started falling behind again.

"Keep going!" she called when she saw him slowing, and for a second she thought he was going to stop, but one glance behind her at the men who were bearing down on them and he knew he wouldn't have a chance against them. Not alone. So after watching Lizette agonizingly as she fell back, faltering in the loose sand, moonlight turning her running figure into the vague form of a phantom behind him, he ducked into a cluster of mangrove trees at the edge of the sand and began making his way back toward the cove, while behind him, panting breathlessly, Lizette slowed her stride, then stopped, breathing heavily as their pursuers caught up to her.

Chapter 11

LIEUTENANT MARSHALL PHILLIPS cursed at the sand in his shoes as he tried to keep up with his men. Age and too many weeks at sea were starting to catch up with him. He hadn't wanted to come ashore, but one didn't argue with commanding officers, so he stopped now, panting heavily for a minute as he realized his men had gathered ahead of him and were holding on to something or someone.

"What do you have?" he called anxiously as he began to plod awkwardly along through the sand again with his sword drawn.

The moon, bright only moments before, suddenly slipped behind a low cloud, and he cursed again. "Damn stupid thing," he mumbled softly, then sighed as he finally reached his men and the moon reappeared again so he could get a good look at what was going on.

Lizette stared hard at the man in front of her, her eyes studying him curiously. He was in his early forties, with about twenty extra pounds set all in his middle, and he was panting heavily, his face red from exertion. Large hazel eyes stared back at her from beneath bushy brows, while chin whiskers stuck out precariously from his square jaws, and he was wearing a uniform.

"Well, well, I say, what do we have here?" he asked in a crisp English accent as he held the tip of his sword beneath Lizette's chin so she had to hold her head higher to keep it from cutting into her flesh.

"You're British?" she asked, frowning, and saw his eyes narrow.

"American?" he shot back.

"Yes, American," she answered unsteadily, and suddenly tears welled up in her eyes as more and more men began emerging from the trees along the beach to join them, and she realized they had to be British sailors.

"I didn't know," she gasped breathlessly. "Or I wouldn't have run."

"You wouldn't have run?" He lowered his sword, then sheathed it. "Why not, pray tell? That was the infamous Sancho de Córdoba you were with a moment ago, wasn't it?"

She looked surprised. "How did you know?"

"The same way any other seaman who's sailed the Caribbean knows him," he said, exhaling disgustedly. "Through experience." He frowned. "You're his mistress?" he asked.

"His captive!" she answered. "I'm Lizette Kolter. My husband's an American businessman, Bain Kolter, and Sancho de Córdoba kidnapped me months ago in a vendetta against him."

The lieutenant smirked. "You expect me to believe that?"

"It's the truth."

"Well, we shall see, shan't we?" He gestured to the two men holding her. "Get her into the longboat," he ordered hurriedly, and pointed to a few of the other men. "The rest of you go with them. Get her out to the ship and tell the captain we're going overland." He motioned behind them with his head toward where Sancho and Lizette had been standing at the edge of the hill. "That path they came down evidently leads to the other side of the island, where the rest of them are probably holed up. We'll meet Captain Vincent over there, squeezing de Córdoba and his men in between."

Lizette opened her mouth to say something, but he wouldn't let her.

"And I don't need any lies from you, either, young woman," he snapped irritably, his eyes hard, unyielding. "We've got enough of a job on our hands tonight without letting you interfere. Now," he ordered the men who were still holding her. "Take her to the ship and let the captain handle her." He turned to the rest of his men, who had to number well over fifty by now. "As for the rest of us, come on, men, we're wasting time here," and he headed back toward the incline and the path that led to the bay where Sancho and the men were camped, while the sailors holding Lizette dragged her to the longboat, with some of the others following, and they headed for the vague outline of the ship

Sancho had spotted, as it bobbed gently on the water, shrouded in moonlight

Meanwhile, deep in the woods, Sancho had managed to elude some three or four more sailors while coldcocking another before finally breaking free, and now he was moving through the underbrush at a dead run, glad he knew the island as well as he did. It took less than ten minutes for him to reach the path again, and after hesitating only long enough for one quick glance behind to make sure no one was close at his heels, he lit out again, reaching the camp in less than fifteen minutes, a distance that usually took half an hour at a brisk walk.

As he reached the jacaranda tree, he stood for a minute taking a mental note where everyone was, hoping to avoid a panic, then realized a lot of the men must have gone to the native village. He spotted Jigger, ran up to him, and within seconds the whole camp was in a flurry as men began swarming everywhere, from huts, the woods, and within minutes the longboats were full as the first round of men headed for the *Piranha,* taking only their weapons with them.

"We will have to clear the channel before their ship reaches this side of the island," Sancho was telling Jigger as he gathered his things up from a chair in his hut and put on the old uniform jacket he was used to wearing on board ship.

"What of the woman?" Jigger asked.

"There is no way we can get her back, at least not now." Sancho flinched. "All we can do now is hope to save our own skins."

Jigger frowned. "You're sure they're British, Cap'n?"

"Positive." Sancho felt the edge on his cutlass, making sure it was sharp enough, then slid it into its sheath. "And it looked like a third-rater, too," he informed him hurriedly. "That means at least sixty guns and close to five hundred men. We won't have a chance unless we can reach the open sea."

He moved to the door and called to Drego, who was running toward him from the path that led to the village.

"Anymore left back there?" he yelled as he stepped outside.

Drego shook his head. "I'm the last, Cap'n."

Sancho's jaw tensed.

"*Bueno!*" He motioned for Jigger to follow and the three of them headed for one of the longboats that had come back to shore to pick up the last of the crew.

Sancho saw the sails on the *Piranha* already unfurling like a ghost in the moonlit lagoon as he ran as fast as he could. Then suddenly a shot rang out from near the jacaranda tree.

"Jesucristo!" he mumbled angrily as he reached the boat, then grabbed its side. "Push!" he yelled, then jumped in as the boat slid into the lagoon, the men quickly grabbing oars, and with bullets flying all around them from the edge of the camp, the longboat, her oars moving in and out of the water rhythmically, picked up speed, and reached the *Piranha* just as the last sails fluttered down, catching the night breeze. All hands climbed on board, the anchor was weighed, setting her free, and while Sancho took over the helm from Drego, to make sure things went right, back in the camp, Lieutenant Marshall Phillips stepped from the woods, gun in hand, sweat pouring down his face, and watched in frustration. They'd been so close. So very close. Well, now it was up to the *Pinnacle* and Captain Vincent.

Phillips moved down now, standing at the edge of the water, and watched the ship disappear behind the hill into what he assumed was a hidden channel that led to the sea; then he turned back to inspect the camp. The fires were still burning, food and rum half consumed, things the pirates had evidently been holding at the time they'd been alerted, dropped in the sand, as if completely forgotten in the rush for freedom. He strolled over to one hut that seemed larger than all the others, then called out to his men.

"Search the place and see what you can find!" he ordered, and while his men turned the place upside down hoping to find chests full of loot from the pirates' various raids, he eagerly searched Sancho's hut, to find only a small chest with tools in it, a large trunk with a few women's underthings in the bottom, two beds laid out over palm fronds, with fancy pillows and blankets covering them, a whale-oil lamp, still lit and casting shadows on what looked like a handmade calendar on the wall beside a clock that would look more at home on a mantel, one straight-backed chair, and, to his surprise, a decoratively carved baby's cradle made of highly polished mahogany, set against the far wall between the beds.

Strange, he thought as he stared at it, then remembered something else he'd spotted earlier from the woods, and stepping outside, he made his way through the men, ignoring their haphazard searching until he reached two trees with a rope strung between them, and he stared at the women's dresses hung over the line.

"And she said she wasn't his whore," he mumbled softly to himself. "Well, by Jove, it sure as hell looks like she was," and he turned abruptly as one of his men called. "What is it, Foster?"

"We didn't find a thing, sir," Ensign Foster reported nervously. It was his first tour of duty and he was always afraid of making mistakes. "There's not a chest, trunk, nothing. At least not with anything valuable in it. Only some pots, pans, and a few staples." He straightened, trying to look important, the dark freckles across his face prominent in the firelight. "What do you suppose they did with it, sir?" he asked anxiously. "They sure didn't have time to put anything but themselves aboard ship."

Lieutenant Phillips' gaze moved from his men who were still searching, although not as vigorously anymore, to the hut he'd just left, and he frowned.

"Maybe the lady we took prisoner can shed some light on what happened to it," he answered, then straightened formidably. "In the meantime, I suggest we follow that path yonder, the other side of the camp. I have a feeling there's more people on this island besides those cutthroats," and he rounded the rest of the men up and headed toward the native village, while aboard the HMS *Pinnacle*, Lizette was talking with Captain William Vincent.

They stood near the rail on the quarterdeck of the two-masted ship as it rounded the end of the island, the night air cool on their faces. The captain, after listening to Lizette's explanation as to who she was, had explained to her that they'd been searching a number of the nearby islands the past few nights looking for pirates, figuring that they were bound to flush some of them out by moving in after dark. Now, suddenly he pointed off in the distance as a ship sailed into view from behind a mass of high cliffs, her masts vaguely silhouetted in the moonlight.

"Is that where the channel is?" he asked, pointing to it.

She nodded. "Yes, sir, and that's the *Piranha* now, tacking into the wind. She's a fast ship, sir, and she'll no doubt be out of sight before we can reach her."

Lizette was right. The *Piranha* was fast. Not as fast as Bain's sleek ships, no, but faster than the royal ships of the line, especially a third-rater, and she carried three masts to the *Pinnacle*'s two. Still, Captain Vincent hated to admit defeat.

"Reduce sail to downwind!" he yelled over his shoulder, then turned to the helmsman, his voice booming again. "Rudder to starboard!"

Lizette felt the ship heave in the water, pulling away from the island as the men in the rigging pulled the sails into the wind. They were changing their course to follow the *Piranha* and she watched apprehensively. There was no way they could catch the other ship, she was sure, and they didn't, although they followed her close to half an hour before giving up and turning back toward the island, so that by the time they returned, the moon was high overhead, just touching the trees and outlining the cliffs. The *Pinnacle*'s captain, remembering the spot where the *Piranha* had first appeared, sailed carefully into the once-hidden channel that led to the lagoon, then dropped anchor in the cove.

Lieutenant Phillips and his men were on the beach waiting impatiently for them, with some of the natives lurking close by, when the longboat carrying the captain and Lizette was finally rowed ashore, and he was quite put out as he lumbered toward the longboat to meet them. The captain helped Lizette out and she gazed about curiously, spotting Kalea near the edge of the woods, with some of the other women and children standing around. She could see very few of the men, only Chief Kaleharo and two of his sons, as well as about fifteen others. The rest of the men she imagined were out there somewhere hiding in the dark, with weapons ready just in case. However, it was apparent the British didn't seem to be blaming the natives for their friendship with the pirates. In fact, the sailors were paying very little attention to them.

She walked away from the longboat, staying beside the British captain, purposely ignoring Kalea so she wouldn't get her in trouble, and they stopped partway up the beach in front of the lieutenant, who saluted.

"Lieutenant Phillips reporting all secure, sir," he said.

Vincent returned his salute, and the captain looked about eagerly. Vincent was a lean man, somewhere in his late forties, with broad shoulders, slim hips, and long legs. However, his face was extremely round. An unusual contrast to his small eyes, sharp nose, and thin-lipped mouth.

"The natives?" he asked curiously as his gaze fell on

Kalea and some of the others standing in the shadows of some tall palm trees.

Phillips frowned. "They don't know too much," he answered. "And they don't speak much English. From what I can find out, they had very little choice except to be friendly when de Córdoba and his men came along. I shouldn't think you'd have to worry about them."

"Mrs. Kolter?" the captain asked, addressing Lizette. "Is he right about the natives?"

Lizette nodded. "Yes, sir," she answered. "They had no more choice than I did."

"You called her Mrs. Kolter, Captain?" Phillips said, addressing his commanding officer. "Then you believe her story about being captured?"

"Any reason I shouldn't?"

The lieutenant's eyes hardened as he took a better look at Lizette in the light from the campfires his men had refueled with more wood.

"A few," he answered, then suggested that his commanding officer follow him. So while Lizette stood near the longboat, with the captain's men guarding her closely, Lieutenant Phillips took Captain Vincent on a slow tour through the camp, showing him all the trappings of what Lizette had done to make the island seem like home, including the cradle.

Captain Vincent stared at the cradle, his thoughts running over everything he'd just seen.

"Now, do you still think she's really an American woman who was kidnapped?" Phillips asked dubiously. "Or is she really Córdoba's mistress?"

Vincent pondered the question and Phillips went on.

"And another thing, Captain, there wasn't a thing in camp, no chests, no money, nothing. Now, I know that man we saw with her was de Córdoba. I bloody well should, since he's the one caused me to lose my first command, and I know that was the *Piranha* we saw sailing from the lagoon here, so what's happened to the booty from all the ships they've taken? You know jolly well they've taken a lot of ships the past few months, yet they haven't shown up at any of their old haunts in all that time. So where's the loot?"

"The lady said de Córdoba had loaded it all aboard ship earlier in the day," Vincent explained, remembering his interrogation of the woman who called herself Mrs. Kolter.

"She said that he was planning to set sail first thing in the morning."

"Or is it hidden somewhere on the island?"

The captain smirked. "You care to stay and search, Lieutenant?"

Phillips flushed, and Vincent sneered, watching him. "That's what I thought." He turned, leaving Sancho's hut with Phillips reluctantly following, and they headed back toward Lizette. "So gather your men together, Lieutenant," Vincent ordered as he strolled across the sand toward the longboat. "We've missed him again, but I'll guarantee you one thing, de Córdoba won't be coming back here to stay for a long time to come. Tell your men to torch the place. Then if and when de Córdoba does decide to return, he won't find anything except ashes."

Lizette stood near the longboat watching with mixed emotions as the sailors grabbed burning sticks from the fires and began throwing them onto the thatched roofs of the huts.

"Captain, please," she begged when he reached her and she saw the flames begin to ignite the dry palm fronds on the huts. "The cradle! Let me take the cradle, and my dresses off the line."

He looked at her curiously. "The cradle?"

"Whether you noticed or not, I'm pregnant, sir."

He glanced down at the flowing dress she had on, then shrugged and sent two of his men to pull the cradle from the burning hut and grab a few of her dresses from the line.

"And bring my kid shoes too!" she yelled as the men headed back up from the beach. "I'll need them."

Captain Vincent looked down at her swollen stomach again, then up into her face. "Kolter's or de Córdoba's?" he asked.

Her eyes hardened. "My husband's," she snapped back, then watched the men coming down toward the boat with the cradle, the dresses shoved inside it with her shoes on top. "So what now?" she asked, still bristling from his remark.

He straightened and ordered the men into one of the longboats with her things, then helped her back into one of the other boats they'd used to come ashore in, and one by one the longboats with the crew of the HMS *Pinnacle* in them headed toward the warship anchored a short distance away.

"So now we sail for England, dear lady," he answered as they moved along in the water.

"But I want to go home," Lizette countered angrily. "I have to go home!"

The captain looked at her in disdain. "Then you'll have to go by way of England, Mrs. Kolter," he answered emphatically. "Because when we board that ship out there in the lagoon, we'll be headed for the docks of London with no stops along the way." Lizette sat in the longboat staring back at the island in disbelief as flames danced toward the trees, then, caught in the wind that was coming out of the north, feeding the fires that began to consume everything in camp, including the jacaranda tree.

Suddenly a strange feeling crept over her as she watched the jacaranda tree start to burn, its blossoms withering in the heat. She was going home, and she wanted to go home so badly it hurt inside. Yet she was also sad because she was leaving so many memories back on that lonely little island. Memories that were going to be hard to erase. She glanced down at the emerald ring still on her finger and her mouth pursed. She was going to miss Sancho de Córdoba, damn him. It wasn't that she loved him, heaven forbid. He was an arrogant bastard, to say the least. But you couldn't spend almost every waking moment with a person months on end and not feel something. Not even a man like Sancho. She smiled wistfully, remembering the way he'd always teased her, and the ridiculous way he had of insisting that she really cared, and she wondered what sort of man he would have been if he hadn't been betrayed so many years ago. Her gaze moved from the jacaranda tree to the hut where she had stayed with him, and tears welled up in her eyes as she watched the burning roof cave in while flames covered the outside walls, and for some reason she was glad the *Piranha* had eluded capture, even though she knew that someday, somewhere in the future, its luck wouldn't hold out and it would be Sancho's turn to hang from the yardarm. She shivered.

"Are you cold, Mrs. Kolter?" the captain asked.

She nodded. "Yes, Captain, a little," she answered, and he ordered one of the men to give her his jacket. She wrapped it close around her, and continued to stare back at the island.

Even after they'd boarded the ship, she stood at the rail on the quarterdeck for a long time and watched as they weighed anchor. Her last sight of the camp as the sails unfurled and the *Pinnacle* started moving out of the small inland harbor was that of a mess of burning rubble and palm trees silhouetted against the night sky, and her heart gave a little lurch. She was leaving, really leaving, and as the British ship sailed through the narrow channel toward the open sea, the low wailing call from a conch shell could be heard on the night air, drifting down from the hills around the cove, and it was as if the island were telling her good-bye. Tears ran down her cheeks. She was on her way to England, then home, and although she was crying, she was glad.

Warm, sunny breezes swept across the grasslands of Cuba, bringing the scent of the sea with them as Bain rode Amigo along the dusty road above the inland bay where he knew the *Piranha* would show up someday, while beside him, on one of her uncle's sleek Arabian mares, Elena de Córdoba kept him company. He'd been here for months already, and still no sign of the pirate or his ship.

Bain slowed Amigo to a leisurely walk. "I'm beginning to think you've made this whole thing up just to keep me here," he said in Spanish, frowning as he glanced over at her.

She smiled. "It's a nice thought," she said seductively as she continued the conversation in the same language. "But really, Bain, I think I could think of better ways than that to keep you here."

He stared hard at her. He had to admit she looked exceptionally pretty today in her rust-colored riding habit, the feathered hat she was wearing complimenting the thick braid that was twisted into a chignon at the nape of her neck. However, looking into her dark eyes did nothing to him; in fact the only attraction she had for him was her dark hair and tawny skin that reminded him so much of Liz. Otherwise she was nothing at all like his wife, especially in her temperament. Lizette was Lizette, she had no subterfuges, no put-on airs. To meet Lizette was to know her, but there was something guarded about Elena, as if the woman the world knew had no connection to the woman she really was. For some men it was no doubt intriguing, but for Bain it was a reason to be wary.

He'd been here for more than two months already, dividing his time between Don Emilio's ranch, where they had been riding most of the morning, and the city of Havana, some forty miles to the west, where he'd been to enough balls and fiestas posing as Elena's fiancé that he was certain by now that the whole island of Cuba knew who he was. Still, he kept the *Sparrow* in Havana as much as possible in case she was needed, allowing Eric to take her out only on an occasional cruise along the coastline, hoping perhaps she'd run into the *Piranha*.

But he was getting restless. If de Córdoba didn't show up soon, he was going to head for Washington and try to coerce Sam Hewitt into sending Kearney and his men into the Caribbean in search of him. As it was, maybe he'd hunt for Kearney himself and try to talk him into something. After all, word had filtered out to them from Havana just a few days before about Kearney's *Enterprise* running into four of Charlie Gibbs's ships some weeks back off the southern tip of Cuba where the pirates had set onto three well-loaded merchant ships, and Kearney's ships had not only managed to capture the four pirate rigs, but forty of Gibbs's men as well. And Gibbs was one of the bloodiest pirates in the Caribbean. Right in the same league with Sancho. If Kearney had been that close just a few weeks ago, he might still be around, although Bain had heard the *Enterprise* and its fleet were mostly cruising the gulf.

"What are you thinking about now?" Elena asked as they rode side by side, heading their horses inland again along the road, heading back toward the hacienda.

Bain flicked some dust off the sleeve of his light blue frock coat, then straightened his hat with one hand while keeping the reins steady with the other. "I've been seriously thinking about seeing if I could locate Lieutenant Commander Kearney and the *Enterprise*," he answered thoughtfully. "You know, there just might be a chance he'd know where Sancho's most likely to be hiding."

"I told you," she insisted. "He'll show up. He promised. Besides, it was Kearney and his ships who destroyed Barlovento and killed my father."

"Because of Sancho."

"That's no reason to kill a man and destroy his home."

"Your father could have surrendered."

"And spent the rest of his life in prison?" She gazed past him, watching a group of steers grazing some distance away. "He'd have died in prison, just as those steers would die in a pen," she said, then looked back at him. "You're not serious about Kearney, are you?" she asked warily. "I couldn't bear the thought that you might have dealings with him. It would only make Sancho more sure than ever that his vendetta's justified."

Bain sighed. "I'll give your brother a little while longer, Elena, but only a little while, and that's all, because I want to try to settle this reasonably if I can. But if he isn't here by the end of the month, I'll find out where Kearney is for sure and to hell with your brother."

The wind whipped dust whorls up in the road as they moved along, and Bain stared at the cloudless sky. It was hard to think that it was past the middle of October already. Back home they'd be getting ready for the winter months. Although the winters in South Carolina were never really very cold, they did have an occasional snowfall and there were days when the temperature dropped somewhat lower than usual, but here, Emilio had told him, the change was so slight as to be unnoticeable.

Elena glanced over at Bain, studying him as they rode. The man was either a saint or a eunuch, she thought silently to herself. Yet neither description fitted when she remembered what his wife was like. Then what was he? It wasn't as if she hadn't played her cards right, because she had. He'd had so many opportunities to make love to her since he'd arrived that it was ridiculous, and there were times she even felt shameless over the way she was throwing herself at him. Still, nothing worked. Well, maybe after tonight things would be different, she thought eagerly. She had everything planned so well, there was no way he'd be able to refuse the temptation. She smiled, pleased with herself.

"You did say you were going to join us tonight, didn't you?" she asked as she patted her horse on the neck, then eased her hold on the reins, slowing her mount slightly.

Bain nodded. "Since you insist," he answered. "But it seems to me we had enough parties in Havana."

"Not like this. It's a masquerade ball, and there'll be so many more people here who never show up in Havana."

"I just hope your brother shows up."

"Mario or Sancho?"

"You know which one," he answered. "And I meant what I said, Elena. I don't like playing let's pretend, especially at all these balls and soirees. So make this the last one."

"You're impossible, Bain Kolter." She was pouting provocatively. "But I'll try to understand."

"You do that." She could tell he was irritated with her again. "Like I've been telling you," he went on, "I'm a married man and I don't intend to jeopardize my marriage any more than I have to, otherwise bringing Liz back would only be a mockery."

Elena's jaw clenched and she gave him a disgusted look. "You win, at least for now," she offered flippantly. "But once Sancho does arrive, we'll see who has the last laugh, Bain Kolter," and with a flick of her riding whip she set her mare at a fast canter, then glanced back to see if he'd try to keep up. He didn't. Not Bain Kolter. There were times when she thought his aloof manner was a deliberate ploy to get even with her because he knew she cared, yet it could also be his way of fighting his own temptation, because she was sure he cared too. Ah well, tonight would tell.

Tío Emilio would no doubt drink too much tonight, the guests would leave late, and no one would even know if she slipped something into Bain's last drink of the evening, then wandered into his bedroom by mistake after the cantharis took effect. Ah yes, tonight he'd show his true colors and she'd prove to him that she could match his precious Liz when it came to making love. She slowed her horse again, waiting for him so they could ride the rest of the way to the hacienda together.

Unlike Don Emilio's regal home in Havana, the cattle ranch was built for comfort and relaxation as well as work. High stucco walls, baked white from the sun, surrounded the main buildings, with wooden gates at the front and back to keep out intruders if need be, and the hacienda itself was at least five hundred feet from the front gate, with a huge courtyard situated right in the middle of the house. It was here in the courtyard, now decorated with fancy lanterns and streamers of flowers, that the festivities were taking place tonight.

Bain leaned against a post that held up one of the balconies overlooking the courtyard and sipped wine from the crystal goblet he was holding while he gazed about watching all the activity around him. The party had been going on for some time already, and even the governor was here. Rather a surprise, too, since Elena had been so sure no one would travel this far from Havana just to have fun.

But it was Don Emilio's sixtieth birthday celebration, and even Bain had to admit he liked the man. Don Emilio was nothing like his niece or nephew. His life was an open book, his personality warm and receptive, his dislike of subterfuge and intrigue quite apparent, making it obvious that he despised having to lie about Bain's true reason for being in Cuba, even though he'd been forced to go along with it.

In a way, Bain felt sorry for the man, and often wondered what would happen to Don Emilio's position here in Cuba if his contemporaries ever found out about his relationship with Sancho. So far no one had, and from the looks of things, no one would. At least not if Don Emilio could help it.

Bain continued to look around for a few minutes longer, then glanced down at his costume, feeling out of place as a court jester, since most of the other guests wore costumes portraying everyone from kings to clergy. And he was certain the dark green tights he wore made his knobby knees more prominent. He had no idea that in reality, rather than detracting from his looks, the outfit he wore only tended to emphasize his muscular physique, while the short black tunic he had on over the tights brought out the deep russet highlights in his hair. A silly hat with bells and tassels was perched on his head, and earlier in the evening he'd had a guitar he couldn't even play slung on his back. He'd gotten rid of the guitar in a hurry, though, since there was no way he could sit with it in place, and besides, everyone kept asking him to play a tune.

His gray eyes studied the crowd from behind a black satin mask, the soft sounds of guitar music from the far end of the courtyard mingling with the light laughter of the crowd. So far everyone seemed to be having a good time, even Elena, he thought, and he smiled to himself, amused as he stared across the room and caught sight of her trying to charm one of the governor's aides.

However, his smile soon faded, turning to a frown as he remembered the feelings that had torn through him when she'd first appeared downstairs earlier in the evening, just before the guests started to arrive. And he was certain she knew just what she was doing, too, because her clothes were quite appropriate to the task. She was going to try to seduce him, he just knew it. He had no idea how soon, when, or exactly where, but it would be sometime tonight because except for the green silk mask covering her face, she was wearing an outfit almost identical to the one she'd been wearing the night they'd said good-bye at Barlovento a little over two years ago. It consisted of a white blouse, long green skirt, bare legs with sandals on her feet, and she'd plaited her hair very simply with one long thick braid hanging down her back.

The blouse even kept falling off one shoulder all evening as it had then, and the contrast to her usual attire of late was striking. Somehow, as before, the peasant clothes made her seem much more innocent yet sensuous, and brought back a flood of memories. Memories that Bain had wanted to forget because he knew they made him more vulnerable, and he was certain she knew it.

It wasn't that he loved her. He'd never loved Elena, not the way he loved Liz, but there were feelings there that he couldn't completely deny. A warmth and affection. And given the right fuel, they were feelings that could easily get out of hand if he let his natural instincts get in the way of his common sense. After all, it had been months since he'd held Liz in his arms and made love to her, and Elena knew it.

He continued to stare at her for a few minutes, watching as Elena excused herself from the gentleman she'd been talking to and headed toward the refreshment table; then he let his gaze move off into the crowd as the faint chimes of a grandfather clock somewhere in the distance struck eleven. They'd be unmasking in an hour, and soon this charade would be over and he could go back to waiting again. In the meantime he made a mental note to avoid Elena as much as he could tonight and not be caught alone in a room with her, while across the courtyard Elena had felt Bain's eyes studying her while she headed toward the refreshments and she was pleased. Although she was sure if he knew what she was up to he'd be madder than hell. It had been so apparent when she'd walked down the stairs earlier in the evening that he recognized the clothes she was wearing and remembered, and that was good. It would make things easier.

She reached the refreshment table and stood for a moment staring at the food, then sidled over slowly toward where the servants were pouring wine for the guests, and her hand moved into the pocket of her skirt, her fingers tightening on a small packet there. Just a small amount. No more than what was in the packet was needed, the woman had told her, and Elena's eyes shone as she ordered the servant to pour her a glass of wine while she remembered the strange encounter with the old woman the day before.

She'd been so melancholy, that's why she'd been riding alone. Ordinarily she'd have never even talked to the old crone, let alone bared her soul to her, but she'd been so unhappy while she sat on the riverbank, and sadness wasn't easy to hide, so that when the old woman came along it seemed only natural they should talk about love and men. Now she was glad she had, and smiled, pleased with herself as the servant handed her the goblet of wine she'd pretended to be getting for her uncle, and she headed toward a quiet corner of the courtyard with it, far beneath the overhead balcony, where she tried to look as inconspicuous as possible while she set it on a stand, then took the small packet from her pocket, ripped it open, and surreptitiously poured the contents into it.

This done, she quickly shoved the empty packet back into her pocket, then picked up the goblet again and stared at it apprehensively. The powder wasn't dissolving. Small particles of it still floated on top, and she pursed her lips, disgusted. After glancing about furtively, she headed back toward the refreshment table, then set the glass down again. Still making sure no one was watching, she picked up a spoon and stirred it hurriedly, hoping no one would see, since it would seem strange to stir a goblet of wine. Satisfied that it was finally all dissolved, she set the spoon back on the table, picked up the goblet and examined it once more, pleased this time that only the clear red wine was visible, even though she knew it was laced with what, according to the old woman, had been used as a love potion for centuries, since before the conquistadors. For a brief second she felt a little guilty about what she was doing. Then brushed the thought aside. After all, what was that old saying, anything's fair in love and war, and this was both.

Now her only problem was, how soon should she give it to Bain? Not just yet, she was sure, so she had to find a place to put it where no one would find it until she was ready. Someplace no one would look. She stood for a minute, her eyes scanning the room, then let her gaze fall on the walk that led to the downstairs bedrooms in the south wing. Her own bedroom was at the far end of the walk. She could take it there, leave it on the stand by the bed, then bring it out later when most of the guests were gone. No one would know the difference.

With her mind made up, and acting quite nonchalant, pretending the goblet was her own, she began to make her way slowly through the crowd, smiling at those who recognized her beneath the green silk mask, and pretending shyness to those who had no idea who she was, and she breathed a sigh of relief when she reached the edge of the courtyard. She was just ready to step onto the flagstone path that led to her bedroom when suddenly she froze, holding her breath as she stared at a tall figure in the brown robes of a monk. The man was coming toward her from the direction of the front gardens, and a frown creased her forehead. The walk, the familiar sway of the shoulders . . . She was sure she recognized them. Her hand tightened on the goblet and she stood waiting as the monk slowed, then stopped before her, his face in the shadows. Yet she knew.

"Sancho?" she questioned hesitantly.

"Shhh," Sancho cautioned, his voice barely a whisper. "Come on, let's talk," and he reached out, taking her arm, ushering her off the path toward the gardens he'd emerged from, while she stared at him incredulously, the goblet in her hand completely forgotten for the moment.

Sancho was hot under the monk's robes that were hiding his regular clothes, and he was sweating profusely, wishing he could chuck the damn things, yet knew to do so would be foolish. There were too many men here tonight who'd recognize him, and he couldn't take the chance. As it was, he'd almost bungled his arrival, and he was glad he'd run into those two vaqueros back on the road who'd told him about the party his uncle was having tonight, or he'd have walked into a mess. As it was, he was going to have to be damn careful. Of course he'd had to go all the way back to the ship and try finding something to put on, and it had wasted precious time, but at least he was here now, and so far no one had spotted him.

"Where's Tío Emilio? I didn't see him in the crowd back there," he said when they were out of earshot of the others. Although some of the guests had spread out from the courtyard, the gardens were fairly deserted.

Elena shrugged. "He was in there a bit ago. But how . . . what are you doing here?"

"I told you I'd be back."

"But why tonight?"

"Why not tonight? What's wrong, Elena?"

"Kolter's here," she answered hesitantly. "He's been here for months, hoping you'd show up."

"Jesucristo!" he exclaimed, and without asking, he grabbed the wine goblet from her hand. "Here. I need that more than you do," but before he could get the goblet to his lips, her hand flew out unexpectedly and caught the side of it, knocking it away, and it smashed against a stone, wine spilling all over the ground.

"Now, what the hell did you do that for?" he asked in surprise.

Elena took a deep breath. "Because you almost drank it."

"So?"

"It was Bain's."

"He's got a monopoly on the wine?"

"No." She flushed, embarrassed. "But there was something in it. It would have . . . well you wouldn't have . . ."

"What was in it?"

"You don't have to know."

"Maybe you should tell him, Elena," Bain interrupted from only a few feet away, and both Elena and Sancho whirled toward the balcony as Bain stepped from the shadows. "Why did I know you'd show up tonight?" he asked as he walked slowly toward Sancho, and Elena held her breath, not knowing what to expect. "It is Sancho, isn't it?" Bain asked as he stopped next to Elena and stared at the tall figure in the monk's robes.

Sancho laughed, low, throaty. "By God, you're a calm one, Kolter, I'll say that for you." He slipped the hood back off his head to reveal his face, the scar at his temple outlined in the pale moonlight, with the faint lights from the courtyard throwing the rest of his face into relief at the same time. "So, we meet again."

Bain straightened arrogantly, unintimidated by him. "Where's my wife, de Córdoba?" he asked.

Sancho's eyes hardened. "You mean my mistress?"

"I mean my wife!"

"Same thing," Sancho shot back, and Bain made a grab for him.

"Please!" Elena yelled, trying to keep her voice down. "The guests, they know nothing, think of Tío Emilio!"

Bain's eyes were blazing as he stared at Sancho, but he

lowered his voice, realizing he didn't want to create a scene either if he could help it.

"Where is she, Sancho?" he asked furiously. "What have you done with her?"

"Me? I haven't done anything with her, *amigo*," he answered smugly. "The last I saw her she was being chased by a bunch of British sailors, only she couldn't run too fast with her stomach in the way like that, and I'm afraid she got caught."

"What are you talking about?"

"I'm talking about Lizette," he answered, knowing he was goading Bain on and enjoying every moment. "Pregnant women can't usually run very fast, Señor Kolter."

Bain couldn't believe what he was hearing. "That's not true, Lizette wasn't pregnant."

"She is now, *señor*." His dark eyes flashed victoriously. "She was mine before they took her, *señor*. For that you can blame me."

"You lying bastard!"

Bain lunged toward Sancho, who instinctively started peeling off the monk's robes, but not quickly enough, and Bain connected a savage blow to Sancho's bearded chin, the thought of trying not to make a scene completely forgotten now. Sancho flew backward, with Bain following, and they began to grapple, neither man making much headway; then Sancho, finally managing to throw off the robe, pushed Bain back and drew his cutlass.

Elena screamed. "No, Sancho, don't, please," she pleaded. "He had nothing to do with Barlovento. Let his wife be enough, not Domino!" but Sancho paid no heed as he planted his feet firmly and stood, sword in hand, waiting.

By now a crowd was forming in the garden, and Bain, realizing it, glanced quickly out the corner of his eye. "A sword," he yelled anxiously, his hand reaching out. "Somebody give me a sword, a rapier, anything!"

In seconds, he too stood with a sword in his hand, and now he waved it toward Sancho, hefting the feel of it. It had been a long time since he'd used one, but he hadn't forgotten.

"All right, Sancho, you want your vendetta, I'll oblige," he sang out confidently. "Only first, before I kill you, where's my wife?"

"Like I say before, *señor*," Sancho answered, grinning viciously. "From what the natives said after the British ship was gone, they've taken her to London, and that's where I'm heading to claim her as soon as I settle with you."

"Never!" Bain shouted. "Never, do you understand? She's mine and she'll always be mine!"

Sancho laughed. "You're a dreamer, *señor,* but go ahead, have your dream, it will be your last," and as he thrust forward, Bain parried with his blade. The clang of steel against steel suddenly filled the air, bringing more people into the garden, including Don Emilio. He stared for a moment in disbelief, watching while Elena took a step toward the two men to stop them.

"No, Elena!" Don Emilio called, quickly grabbing her arm. "Let them get it over with. Let it be done here and now."

"But he'll kill Bain!"

"Or Bain will kill him. Either way, it will be over."

"But I love Bain!"

"And we both love Sancho. But this has gone on long enough, Elena. Better one should die now. If it is Sancho, then your Bain shall live. If it is Bain, then they will no doubt hang Sancho anyway, so let it be," and his eyes were troubled as both he and his niece once more turned their attention to Sancho and Bain, who seemed to be evenly matched as they fought their way in and out among the colorful shrubs and flowers, barely missing each other.

The two of them fought, the guests watching in hushed tones with only an occasional comment; then suddenly Bain saw his chance. Sancho, for all his skill, was overconfident. He was so used to having people cringe helplessly as soon as they heard his name, and confronted unprepared men who barely fought back, that he'd underestimated Bain's prowess.

Picking his spot carefully when he saw the opening, Bain thrust forward. Sancho tried to parry, but Bain sidestepped just far enough so the position was awkward for Sancho, and the pirate missed. In that split second Sancho suddenly knew he'd made a mistake and the hair at the nape of his neck prickled seconds before he felt the cold steel rip through his flesh like a harpoon, tearing into his right side savagely, and his dark eyes widened in disbelief.

"*Madre de Dios!*" he blurted breathlessly, pain shooting through him, and before he had a chance to even try to salvage the moment, his knees buckled, he gasped for air, and the world round him became fuzzy. Then as the voices of the crowd blurred together into a horrid cacophony, everything went black and he hit the ground on his knees, sprawling awkwardly.

Bain stood over Sancho, breathing heavily, and stared down at the man's body, the sword he'd borrowed still in him.

"Is he dead?" he asked breathlessly.

One of the onlookers hurried forward and knelt down, feeling his pulse.

"*Sí*," he answered, and Bain tore his eyes from Sancho's prone body, looking over at Don Emilio and Elena.

"I'm leaving for London," he announced bitterly. "Just as soon as I can get my clothes together."

"And Sancho?" Don Emilio asked.

"Throw him to the sharks," Bain answered angrily. "And his men too, if you want. I imagine the *Piranha*'s still in the bay," and he turned abruptly, starting to walk away, feeling even more ridiculous now in the stupid costume he was wearing than before, even though he had taken off the mask.

His heart was heavy. He hated killing, even men like Sancho. Yet it wasn't just killing Sancho that bothered him now. It was what Sancho had said about Lizette, and anger hardened his features as he headed for the guest room where he'd been staying since he'd come to the ranch. It wasn't true. It couldn't be true. Yet he had to find out.

Behind him, Elena glanced down at her brother, then frowned. What should she do? Tears filled her eyes. Sancho was dead, she could do no more for him, but there was a chance for Bain. For her and her Domino, especially if her brother had told the truth.

"Now, what do you do, Elena!" Don Emilio asked as he watched the troubled look on her face.

She tensed, making her decision quickly. "I'm going with him," she cried helplessly. "I have to, Tío Emilio," and she turned, running toward her room for a few things to take with her, hoping she could catch Bain before he left.

Bain was in the stables saddling Amigo when Elena rushed in carrying a bag, and he stopped what he was doing to stare at her.

"What do you think you're doing?" he asked.

She stood her ground. "I'm going with you."

His gray eyes narrowed. "Why?"

"Because if Sancho was right, and there is nothing left between you and your Liz, I will be there for you."

He took a deep breath. "And if he was lying?"

"Then I will come back to Cuba and you will see me no more." Her eyes softened, pleading. "I deserve that much, Domino, please. I did not lie to you, Sancho came back."

She was right, she hadn't lied. "All right, get your horse and we'll saddle her," he said, and before half of the guests even realized what had happened, Bain, still dressed in the costume of a court jester and riding Amigo, with Elena, on one of her uncle's mares, the peasant skirt showing her bare legs as she rode astride, was heading out the front gate into the star-filled night, on his way to Havana, some forty miles away, where the *Sparrow* would be anchored, waiting to take him to London, and Lizette.

Chapter 12

A LOW HUSH had come over the guests when Sancho's body slumped to the ground, and now, at the sound of the two horses galloping off in the distance, everyone slowly began to mingle again and come to life, starting to see if they could make sense of what was going on.

"What do we do, Don Emilio?" the man who'd lent Bain the sword said as they stood staring down at Sancho's body.

Don Emilio shook his head, trying to keep the tears from his eyes. "I don't know. Send for a priest, I guess."

"But who is he?" asked someone else.

"And what were they fighting about?" came another voice.

Then, "My God, it's Sancho the Bloody!" exclaimed one of the other guests, and Don Emilio frowned.

How was he going to explain this? "Pick up the body," he ordered some of his servants, and without questioning him, they moved forward, grabbed Sancho's arms and legs, and hefted him up.

"Wait, my sword!" The man who'd lent it to Bain reached out very unceremoniously and grabbed the hilt of the sword, pulling it from what they thought was a dead body, only suddenly they heard a low moan, and Sancho's lips moved.

"He's still alive, Don Emilio!" one of the servants shouted as he stared at the man whose arms he was holding, and even Don Emilio was surprised.

"Then quickly, take him to my room," he ordered, and his heart started pounding rapidly.

"But Don Emilio, he's a pirate!"

Don Emilio glared at the man. He was the same man who'd recognized Sancho, but Don Emilio wasn't about to be crossed.

"I don't care if he's the son of the devil himself, he's still a human being, Señor Álvarez," he answered. "And as long as he's under my roof he'll be treated as a human being." He gestured again to his servants. "Take him to my room and have the housekeeper send for a priest."

"You think a pirate will want a priest?" Señor Álvarez asked sarcastically, then sneered. "That's just your trouble, Don Emilio, you have always had too soft a heart." He laughed sarcastically. "It'd do the blackguard good to die in his sins."

"I'd rather let the Lord be the judge of that, *señor,*" Don Emilio answered curtly, then turned to the rest of his guests, excusing himself and apologizing for the fact that, under the circumstances, it would be best if the party broke up.

So as the guests left, Sancho was stripped of his bloody clothes and made comfortable in his uncle's bed while one of the guests, a doctor and an old friend of Don Emilio's, tended him, with Don Emilio standing nearby.

"He won't last until morning," the doctor said as he finished, checking the wound in Sancho's torso, then pulled the sheet up to the middle of his chest.

Don Emilio stared down at Sancho, who hadn't regained consciousness since they'd laid him in the bed. He looked so different like this.

"I've already sent for a priest," he said as he continued staring at his nephew, and the doctor nodded.

"*Bueno, mi amigo.* Now, tell me, are you really his uncle?"

Don Emilio's head jerked up, and he frowned. "His uncle?" he asked in surprise.

Dr. Antonio Rodríguez' eyes studied his old friend calmly, and he shook his head. "Don't worry, *mi amigo,*" he said, rolling down the sleeves of the priest's cassock he'd worn tonight to the costume party. "It would do no good for me to tell the others, not now. But he is in your house, he was talking to Elena, and while I was taking care of the wound he was mumbling something incoherent about Tío Emilio and Lizette and a number of other things equally incriminating." Dr. Rodríguez ran a hand through his gray hair, smoothing it back off his forehead as he continued to study Don Emilio. "I am right, *sí?*" he asked again.

Don Emilio nodded. "*Sí,*" he answered. "My sister has been dead many years, but she had three children. Elena,

Mario, and Sancho. Elena and Mario I took into my home when their father died. Sancho is a renegade, but he is of my blood. He was never welcome here, but that did not stop him from coming."

"And Señor Kolter? What does he have to do with Sancho de Córdoba?"

"There is a vendetta between the two because of something that happened in the past."

"And this Lizette that de Córdoba has been calling for?"

Don Emilio looked at Sancho again, studying him, wondering too why he would call her name. "She is the wife of Señor Kolter," he answered, and Dr. Rodríguez nodded.

"I see." He started to walk away from the bed, then happened to glance down as Sancho's eyes fluttered, then opened, and although they were still glazed with pain, there was something else in them. A fear, a sense of terror, and hurt.

"Please," Sancho whispered, his voice barely audible. "Please, Father, don't leave."

Don Emilio touched the doctor's arm. "He thinks you're a priest."

Dr. Rodríguez was looking directly into Sancho's eyes, and he could see the pain. "Then that's what I will be," he answered, and reached out, taking Sancho's hand.

"Yes, my son."

"No, not your son, never," Sancho mumbled bitterly. "But I am God's son, and yet I die with the devil's blessing."

"What does he mean?" Don Emilio asked, but the doctor cautioned him to be silent.

"Listen."

Sancho's lips moved again. "I am dying, I know," he murmured agonizingly. "It is like I told her." Sancho's gaze moved from the face of the priest before him to the votive candles on the stand beside the bed he was in, and he remembered his dream. "Even the candles," he said softly, and to Don Emilio's surprise there were tears in his nephew's eyes. "You must do this for me," he said, turning slowly to face the doctor again, thinking he was talking to a priest. "I have sinned greatly, I know . . . my life is filled with anger and there is no forgiving, even though I would wish it." He paused, coughing uncomfortably. "God knows I was betrayed, but I could not turn back, and for these things I will suffer, sir, but not for Lizette." His dark eyes warmed gently. "She gave me back my heart to feel, and for this she must not pay."

Don Emilio frowned. "Then it is true, what you told Señor Kolter?" he asked.

"No!" Sancho's breath was ragged, his breathing unsteady. "You must tell him, so she will be happy. The baby is his. I did not touch her." He coughed again. "As God is my witness, it is true, I did not touch her. I loved her too much to hurt her, and she would have loved me too if he had not found her first."

Sancho lifted his hand weakly and tried to make them understand. "She must forgive me, she must understand."

"And Kolter?" Don Emilio asked hesitantly.

Sancho closed his eyes. "Kolter has won, Tío Emilio." He took a deep breath and coughed again. "The vendetta is no more, and I go with it. Jigger was hiding out there watching . . . he will take the ship and the men, so this you must do. You must tell Kolter the truth. She was always his in her heart . . . and, may God forgive me, so is the child his, though I wish it were not so, that it could have been mine."

Again he paused, and this time when his eyes opened, he seemed to be staring at something only he could see, and a peaceful look came to his face.

"For what I could not control, forgive me, Father," he gasped breathlessly, and his face began to pale. "And for the hidden reaches of my heart, understand." Once more tears filled his eyes, and both men stared in awe. "Please, Father." Sancho's voice was hushed and raspy. "*Por favor,*" he begged plaintively, "let me come home," and as they watched, his eyes slowly closed, a smile tilted the corners of his mouth, and he lay still.

For a moment neither Don Emilio nor the doctor moved; then Dr. Rodríguez reached out and felt for his pulse. "He's really gone this time," he said quietly, and Don Emilio straightened, still staring down at the man in his bed.

Sancho had always been so alive, so full of life, gruff and robust, and it didn't seem right that he should be lying here so still.

"You're sure?" he asked.

The doctor nodded. "Very sure," he answered, and Don Emilio sighed.

"So now, what do I do?" he asked, bewildered. "How do I explain all this to everyone?"

"Whatever way you want, old friend," Dr. Rodríguez said. "What was, is your secret, *amigo,* and there is no reason to tell it to the world so far as I'm concerned. As for the rest, I don't even know what he was talking about."

"I do," Don Emilio said as he continued to stare at Sancho's lifeless body. "Only the man it was meant for is on his way to Havana, and how can I possibly catch him before he sails for England!"

"You mean Kolter?"

"*Sí,* Kolter."

"You could send one of your men. It's worth a try."

"You may be right." Don Emilio watched the doctor pull the sheet up over Sancho's face and he blew out the votive candles the housekeeper had lit; then the two men left the room.

It did little good to send anyone to Havana, however, for by the time the servant got there the *Sparrow* had already sailed hours before, and late the next afternoon, during the private ceremony that ended the existence of Sancho de Córdoba on the earth for good, Don Emilio watched his nephew's body being lowered into the grave and asked his forgiveness this time, because now he was the one who would have to let Sancho down, because although he knew Bain and Elena were headed for London, he had no idea where he might reach them, so he was just going to have to wait. "But someday," he promised his nephew as the first shovelfuls of dirt were dropped onto the casket and he put his arm about Mario, who'd come to the ranch for the funeral, "someday I will see that your message gets to him," he murmured softly.

"Did you say something, Tío Emilio?" Mario asked from beside him.

Don Emilio shook his head. "No, nothing, Mario," he answered, for the boy was still upset over the death of his brother and blamed Bain Kolter for everything. "It's just that I wish this whole thing could have been avoided."

"What of his ship?" Mario asked. "And the men. Surely one of them came ashore with him."

"From what Sancho said, Jigger came ashore with him, but there was no sign of the ship later when I sent some of my men out to the bay."

Mario stood for a moment, continuing to watch the men shoveling dirt into his brother's grave, and his jaw set hard. "Perhaps someday I'll find the *Piranha* and she'll have a new captain, Tío Emilio," he said angrily.

Don Emilio frowned. "No, Mario, absolutely not," he insisted. "That you will not do. It would serve no purpose but to dishonor your brother's memory. Even Sancho knew it was over, that Kolter had not lied to him, and the vendetta was over—that's why he wanted me to tell Kolter the truth. No, Mario, you will not follow in the footsteps of your brother. For my sake, the sake of your sainted mother, and for your father's honor you will go back to the university and you will become the man Sancho could have been, but for a quirk of fate. This you will promise me, *sí?*"

Mario looked hard at his uncle, staring at him for some time; then he remembered his brother admonishing him aboard ship, and the promises he'd often made to his father, and he flushed, knowing they were right.

"*Sí,* Tío Emilio," he finally conceded, and glanced back once more to his brother's grave on the hillside overlooking the Cuban countryside, and he sighed. "I guess maybe you're right. There isn't really much future in pirating anymore, is there?" and Don Emilio put his arm about his nephew and they walked back to the carriage, then headed toward the sun-baked walls of the hacienda below in the valley to wait for some word from Elena and Bain so they could deliver Sancho's message.

It was a cold windy day near the end of November when Lizette stood at the rail of HMS *Pinnacle* and watched it slip into its moorings at the London docks. There weren't enough docks built yet for all the ships that sailed up the Thames, and many of them anchored midstream, but the *Pinnacle,* as a military vessel, had its own berth, and Lizette was glad she didn't have to be rowed ashore.

Although it was inappropriate for late autumn, she was still wearing the silly-looking dress she'd made for herself back on the island, only she had the top part of the purple velvet dress on beneath it, and had taken the skirt from the same velvet dress, and with needle and thread borrowed from her rescuers, had fashioned a cloak with a hood so she could keep warm. The result was far from perfect, but her pregnancy was quite evident now, and as she stood at the rail trying to keep the wind from chilling her, the warmer clothes felt good.

"I really must take you to the authorities before you go anywhere else, Mrs. Kolter," the captain said as he joined her.

Lizette frowned. "But I told you before. I know my uncle will help."

"Then, like I said, the office of naval intelligence can get in touch with him." Captain Vincent's gaze sifted over her languorously. She hadn't given them any trouble, he had to admit, but then she hadn't given them any information about Sancho the Bloody either, and he was sure the authorities would want to know what she was obviously holding back, and why.

She tucked a stray curl beneath her hood and they both watched as the ship dropped anchor, the lines were tied, sails furled, and the gangplank lowered. Knowing there was no way she was going to leave the ship by herself, Lizette let the captain usher her down the gangplank and onto the dock; then she waited with him while one of his men hailed a hack.

So this was London, she thought a few minutes later as she gawked out the window of the hackney carriage he'd hired as it made its way down the street. She had been to a lot of different cities with Bain, but never anything like this. They were moving along the river and she watched the ships, some coming in, others setting sail. They were all sizes and makes, from sleek sloops to the big East India merchantmen, and it reminded her a little of Beaufort, only bigger. The waterfront was longer here and terribly crowded, and they stayed on the same street for some time before moving on past what the captain pointed out to her was London Bridge, until they reached Southwark; then the carriage turned right, heading into the heart of the city with its narrow streets and close-fitting shops and factories, dirt and noise everywhere.

After a while the narrow winding streets with their shabby surroundings were left behind, and Lizette soon found herself staring in awe as they passed a huge domed building with frontal columns and spires on each side.

"That's St. Paul's Cathedral," Captain Vincent informed her when he saw her interest in it, and a little later on, when he saw her lean over, looking out again, he added, "We'll be turning off Fleet Street onto the Strand soon."

"And you're taking me where?" she asked as she straightened, looking over at him.

His arms were crossed, face solemn. "To someone who will help, I hope," he answered, and before long their hack was pulling up in front of an impressive building where, a short while later, Lizette, after being escorted from first one office to another, found herself sitting stiff and uncomfortable in a hard, straight-backed chair across from a stern-looking man who'd just been introduced to her as Mr. George Canning, in charge of foreign affairs.

Her gaze roamed the office, taking in the portraits on the wall, all of men in uniform, and the businesslike odor of old wood and paper that filled her nostrils. At least it was better than the salty smell of the open sea she'd endured for so long. The gentleman behind the desk cleared his throat, bringing her attention back to him again, and she realized he was staring at her.

"So, what can I do for you and Mrs. Kolter, Captain Vincent?" Mr. Canning asked after appraising Lizette's shabby clothes and obvious condition.

The captain was rather ill-at-ease. He'd been shuffled from one person to another and no one seemed to know what he was supposed to do.

"I'm hoping you can help me, sir," he stated, hat in hand, eyes troubled. "No one else seems to be able to. You see, my ship was on assignment in the Caribbean. We'd been cruising off some of the islands, going ashore here and there in the hopes that we might flush out some of the cutthroats that have been going after our shipping in the area, when we stumbled onto one of the most vicious pirates in the whole Caribbean, Sancho de Córdoba. Unfortunately, he was able to get away, but we did manage to capture Mrs. Kolter here."

"I told him," Lizette cut in, "de Córdoba kidnapped me from my home in South Carolina months ago, only the captain here thinks I was the man's mistress."

Canning's eyes had continued studying her. She was a strange-looking sort, with her tanned skin, bright green eyes, and dark hair. Almost looked like a native herself. "Aren't you?" he asked, glancing down at the lap she didn't have anymore.

"This is ridiculous!" Lizette shifted her position in the hard chair. She'd lost so much weight recently and wasn't used to sitting on lean bones, and it hurt. "Look," she went on hurriedly, "I tried to tell him, and I'll tell you. I have an uncle here in England who'll vouch for me." She gestured toward the captain. "If he had just let me fend for myself when we got here, it would've saved all this trouble. After all, it shouldn't be that hard to locate the Earl of Locksley."

Canning frowned. "Teak Locksley's your uncle?"

"That's what I tried to tell him," she said, glancing briefly at the captain. "Only he wouldn't believe me."

"I didn't really see any reason to, sir," Vincent offered apologetically. "After all, she was with de Córdoba, and from the looks of the camp, their relationship was evidently more than platonic."

"That's a lie!"

"Can you prove what you just said, Captain?" Canning asked.

Vincent shook his head. "No, sir. But it was apparent she'd been living in the hut he occupied. There was even a cradle in it."

Canning looked pensive, rubbing his chin thoughtfully. "De Córdoba's?" he asked, gesturing toward her stomach.

"My husband's," she informed him irritably, then flushed. "Look, will you please either notify Uncle Teak or take me to him?" she pleaded helplessly, and tears welled up in her eyes. "I've been away for so long. All I want to do is go home!"

Canning drummed his fingers on the table as he stared at her for some time, then finally straightened. "There's only one problem, Mrs. Kolter," he replied. "The earl is out at Locksley Hall and it's at least a two-day ride from the city. What do we do with you in the meantime?"

"Surely there's an inn where I could stay?"

"At whose expense? The government's?"

"I'll pay for it myself."

"With what?"

"I'll borrow it from my uncle."

"And if you're not his niece?"

"Don't be absurd!" Lizette's green eyes were sparking dangerously. "Does my uncle have a town house?" she asked.

Canning nodded. "But you can't go there either. Not without his permission."

Lizette was furious. She'd had just about enough of the British Navy and Britons in general. Her hands clenched on the arms of the chair, and suddenly an idea struck her as her gaze fell on the emerald ring Sancho had given her.

"All right, then," she said as she confronted George Canning boldly. "Let your captain here take me to the nearest jewelers and I guarantee you I'll raise enough money myself to take a coach to Locksley Hall."

"I'm afraid I can't do that either," Canning answered curtly. "It would be in the poorest of taste. Now, believe me, Mrs. Kolter, I actually don't know what to do with you."

"Well, I do," she finally said, and she stood up, whirled around, and before Canning could get out from behind his desk, she was out the door, slamming it solidly behind her.

"Well, stop her, Captain! Stop her!" Canning yelled, but Vincent, also taken by surprise, stumbled his way to the door, and by the time he got it open, she was already disappearing around the corner at the end of the hall.

"You bumbling idiot!" Canning yelled, and Vincent, bristling over the reprimand as well as the way he'd been treated earlier, when all he'd been trying to do was his duty, suddenly stopped his pursuit of her and turned back, eyeing George Canning hostilely.

"I, sir, am not an idiot," he stated authoritatively. "And I refuse to stand here and be called one by you or anyone else. I did my duty and brought the woman here, so now she's all yours. You want her, you go after her, because I'm going back to my ship. But remember, sir, she was with Sancho de Córdoba, one of the worst pirates sailing the Caribbean, and she just might be able to tell you where he's to be found. That is, if you can get her to talk. I couldn't. Now, good day, sir," and he turned rigidly on his heels, a distinct military gesture, donned his captain's hat, straightening it to just the right angle, and sauntered leisurely along in the same direction Lizette had gone, leaving Canning fuming behind him because he knew the Kolter woman could no doubt hide in a city like London forever and there was nothing he could do about it except wait for her to show up somewhere.

Out on the walk in front of the building, Lizette was running as fast as she could toward the carriage that had brought her and the captain here, remembering that the captain had ordered the driver to wait. Reaching it quickly, she gave the driver orders to take her to the nearest and best jewelry store, then climbed in, settling back against the seat. As the carriage moved away from the front of the building, mingling in with the other carriages, she glanced back furtively just in time to see the captain emerge from the front door of the building. Oh no, she thought, and prayed as hard as she could that the driver wouldn't see him, and the captain wouldn't yell or make a fuss, and it seemed like an eternity before the building was finally left behind.

Three-quarters of an hour later, with the carriage waiting out front for her, Lizette, straightening her clothes and trying to look the best she could, walked into an exclusive shop somewhere in London. She had no idea what street she was on, or even the name of the place, because she hadn't bothered to look, but as she closed the door behind her, the tinkling bell heralding her entrance, she knew by looking around that the driver had done as she asked, and brought her to one of the best. Beautiful clocks with mother-of-pearl inlay and carved ivory lined the walls, some with gold on their faces, others with precious stones, and fancy lamps of various kinds were here and there amid cases that held expensive jewelry.

She stood quietly for a few minutes gazing about, then approached a lone man at the back of the shop, who'd been dusting things before she came in. He was staring at her curiously, having heard the bell over the door, and his gaze swept over her rather dubiously as she came toward him. Lizette flushed.

"Something I can help you with, madam?" he asked, noting the distinct bulge showing beneath her strange-looking clothes.

From the look on his face Lizette could tell she wasn't the sort of customer he was used to greeting, only she wasn't about to be intimidated. "There might be, sir," she answered as haughtily as she could, and his eyebrows raised.

"Oh?"

She looked down at the ring on her finger, studying it for a minute, remembering how it came to be there, and almost

changed her mind. However, this was no time to be sentimental, and brushing the memories aside, she slipped it off
and held it out to him.

"I'm afraid I've come on hard times, sir," she explained
dolefully. "If you could see your way clear . . . It's the last
precious thing I have left between me and starvation. Please,
sir?"

The shopkeeper eyed her even more closely now, then
reached out and took the ring from her. He looked down
first at the ring, then at her.

"It is genuine, and it is mine, sir," she explained hurriedly, and smiled, not realizing how dark her white teeth
made her tanned skin look, but the smile was genuine, warm
and pleading. "Please, sir." Tears came to her eyes. "It's all
I have and I'm so hungry."

He stared at her for a few minutes longer, then shrugged
as he moved back behind the counter he'd been dusting and
began studying the ring intently.

"Where did you say you got this?" he asked after a few
minutes.

She hesitated. "I didn't," she answered. "But it was given
to me by a friend."

"I see." He looked the ring over again, then glanced up at
this unusual-looking woman in the weird clothes. "Your
friend has good taste," he said, then rubbed his knuckles on
top of his bald pate before smoothing down the gray fringe
at his ears. "I can give you two hundred pounds for it, but
that's all," he answered.

"Two hundred pounds?"

"You're American?"

"Yes."

"It's a fair price."

"But isn't it worth much more than that?"

"To me, yes, because now I have to try to sell it, but to
you? Without me to know whom to sell it to, it's worth
nothing."

He was right and she knew it. Still, she wasn't even sure
what the rate of exchange was from British pounds to American coin. Ah well, if he was cheating her, after she found
Uncle Teak, she'd bring him back here with her and make
the shopkeeper do the right thing by her. After all, earls no
doubt were rather important people and had to have some
authority.

"All right, I'll take the money," she conceded, and as the man counted it out for her, she put it into a fancy beaded bag she had to buy from him in order to hold it all, while trying to remember if Grandpa Roth or Bain had ever mentioned anything about the difference between English money and American silver and gold dollars, but nothing came to mind. Well, at least now she wasn't completely helpless, and when she left the shop, things looked a little brighter for her.

By late afternoon Lizette, with her feet cold from wearing only the kid shoes without stockings beneath them, and with very little food in her stomach because she was afraid to venture too far from where the hack had dropped her off earlier in the day, telling her it was where the mail coach stopped, found herself on that same mail coach, bundled into a corner and headed out of the city of London toward the coast along the English Channel, where Locksley Hall was located. Besides being cold, she was also uncomfortable, being jostled about with the other three passengers inside the coach, and she had to swallow hard for the first half-hour when her stomach started to rebel for no apparent reason. It could have been the small kidney pie she'd eaten shortly before getting on board, but whatever it was, it was the first time in a long time her stomach had played the rebel, and she prayed it would quit.

She leaned against the side of the coach as they rode along, so she could see out the window, and listened off and on to the coachman talking to the passengers who were sitting on top with him, and the guard who sat over the boot with his blunderbuss across his lap in case they ran into a highwayman. They didn't talk much, but occasionally a few words floated down to her, and it kept her from becoming too bored, as did the beautiful countryside, even though winter was setting in.

Ordinarily the passengers got off during the night and stayed at one of the inns, catching another coach in the morning, but Lizette, knowing so little about the area, had decided she wasn't going to leave the coach until she left it at Locksley Hall, except for an occasional bite to eat and to relieve herself now and then at the various inns where the horses were changed, so that before her journey was over she could expect to spend two nights trying to sleep in the coach, and they were two nights she dreaded.

It was the middle of her second night, and she'd been restless all evening. Probably because she wasn't alone tonight. Last night, except for herself, the coach had been empty, but tonight she was sharing it with a big, husky brute of a man who'd gotten on shortly before dark when they'd stopped for food and to change horses at the last inn. The man was a strange-looking sort with dark red hair, piercing brown eyes, and a square face with features that looked like someone had worked them over with his fist. It was hard to tell by a person's looks just what he was like, however, and as Lizette curled into a corner, trying to get more comfortable, she smiled to herself in the dark. He was probably completely opposite from the way he looked, and would no doubt turn out to be only a church caretaker or handyman, or something equally harmless, with a heart of gold.

Right now, though, in the darkened coach, where she could barely see, his shadowy figure across from her, visible only occasionally in the faint moonlight that filtered in at the window, made her apprehensive. After all, from the way people were acting ever since she'd left the captain back in Mr. Canning's office, you'd think the only women traveling on their own in England were women of questionable reputation, and she guessed that her being in the family way didn't help. Besides, the coach was so bumpy. She'd lost the first baby she ever carried just from riding a horse, and she was surprised the long ride she was on now wasn't giving her more trouble. All she'd had so far were a few muscle cramps and twinges here and there.

Regardless, she settled her head back against the side of the coach and tried to close her eyes, knowing it had to be late already, with the moon so high, and she needed the rest because tomorrow was going to be a tiring day. The driver said they should reach Locksley Hall sometime before noon, and she had no idea how Uncle Teak was going to take all this. After all, they hadn't kept in touch much over the years, what with the mail system being the way it was. There was never any guarantee that a letter would even get through. He and Aunt Ann seemed to be doing all right, though, and she remembered Grandma Dicia telling her that they had two boys. Five-year-old Quinn, named after his grandfather, and Seth, who'd be at least two years old by now. Suddenly she was a little anxious for the long ride to be over. She'd really given little thought to it before, but it would be fun seeing Aunt Ann again, and Uncle Teak, even though his visit to the Château back in the last few days of the war had been rather hectic and full of intrigue.

So, curling her legs up against the seat in an unladylike fashion, she shifted into a different position, making certain the beaded bag she'd bought was settled securely in her lap; then she forced her eyes to stay shut so she could imagine in her mind what it was going to be like seeing them again, while the coach continued on through the dark countryside, jolting across every rock and rut in the dusty road as it lumbered in and out among the shadowy trees that lined it.

It was sometime later. Lizette had no idea how long she'd been asleep, or if she'd been asleep and not just dozing, when suddenly she bolted upright, eyes wide, and stared at the other passenger in confusion. Something was wrong, but what? Then she realized the coach was slowing, and before she had a chance to even try to find out why, the driver pulled the horses to a complete stop, and she looked out the window in time to see a number of masked riders surrounding them, pistols waving in the air.

"Throw down the box!" one of the riders called to the driver.

Lizette's heart sank. Oh, no! Not now, not here, and she slipped back into the shadows inside the coach, hoping they hadn't spotted her. However, the other passenger, without even saying a word, opened the door and stepped out, and she knew she didn't have a chance of being overlooked when she heard him call to one of the riders.

"He don't have it, Tom." His deep voice carried in the clear night air as he went on. "It's under the seat inside, tucked away neat as ye please!"

"Damn ye, Jocko, why didn't ye say so 'fore I wore me lungs out?" the one named Tom called back, and the one he'd called Jocko laughed.

"Well, I told ye now," he answered, and turned back to the inside of the coach, reaching up under the seat he'd been sitting on, and lifted it, to reveal a large compartment with a chest in it. "And she's full of at least five thousand pounds, me buckos, so one of ye help me get her out of here," and he stepped into the coach with his back to Lizette, who was still cowering as far back on the seat as she could, staring incredulously.

There were at least five riders, all wearing masks, and the one called Tom dismounted quickly, joining the passenger from the coach while the rest continued holding guns on the driver and guard, who evidently hadn't even had a chance to use his blunderbuss.

"Well, what do ye have here, Jocko?" the masked rider asked as he entered the coach to help, and caught sight of Lizette, who moved back even further on the seat.

Jocko's smile broadened. "That's a wee bit of icin' on the cake, Tom," he answered. "I'll tell ye about it in a minute, but first help me out with the damn box," and while Lizette watched, the two men reached into the secret hiding place, straining as they lifted the box of money that was obviously being sent to a bank somewhere, or was to be used for some businessman's payroll, and they stepped down from the coach, setting it on the ground; then the two of them straightened, the masked one named Tom gazing back toward the mail-coach door.

"Ye said she was frostin'?" Tom asked eagerly.

Jocko smiled again. "Aye, lad. From what the driver says, she's supposed to be a relative of the Earl of Locksley. Now, if we takes her with us, he just might be willin' to pay a goodly sum to get her back in one piece. What's say?"

"Hold her for ransom, ye mean?"

The other riders all looked at each other, then back to Jocko, who, from what Lizette could see as she peeked out the window, looked like he was actually their leader.

"We done it afore, Tom," he explained roughly. "No reason it won't work again."

"But Locksley . . . he ain't to be fooled with, Jocko. Ye knows yerself that he's got a temper."

"Which ain't gonna do him no good if we got the lady, now, is it?"

"She's a lady?" Tom laughed. "Looks more like she's come from Maude's Place 'stead of the Hall."

"Hold yer tongue, Tom. She ain't dressed much like a lady, I know, but mind ye, that don't always mean nothin'." He motioned to the other riders. "Keep yer pistols on 'em, boys," he urged, pointing toward the driver and guard, then turned back, sticking his head into the coach, looking directly at Lizette. "And ye step out, lady," he ordered.

Lizette frowned, but didn't move.

"I said out with ye!" he repeated.

"Why?"

"Now, surely ye heard me talkin' to me men," he answered sarcastically. 'Lessen yer deef, which I know ye ain't. So get out here so's they can get a better look at ye."

Lizette's jaw clenched in frustration. She was so close, now this. "Look," she said as she moved from her seat and stepped down from the coach onto the dusty road, "I don't have anything." She'd hidden her money beneath her cloak, tying the bag to the strap of her homemade dress where it went over her shoulder, and anger was quickly replacing her frustration. "And I don't want to go with you, either." She glanced about. "Any of you. I've had enough of kidnapping, piracy, and the whole lot, and I'm not going to let it start all over again. I've been held prisoner on an island, run away from the British Navy, and by God I'll fight the whole lot of you if I have to," and she straightened, trying to look tough and mean.

"Hey, she's a feisty one, ain't she!" one of them yelled.

Tom laughed and leaned close, reaching out to pat her stomach. "And she's in the family way too."

She slapped his hand aside and stood her ground. "I said I'm not going!"

"Oh, ye'll go, all right," the one named Jocko contradicted gruffly. "Because if ye don't, that babe ye're carryin'll be payin' for it. Now, which'll it be, me lady? A ride on a horse with Jocko or a buryin' fer ye and the babe?"

Tears filled Lizette's eyes. This wasn't happening. It couldn't be happening. Not now. But it was, and she watched as the one called Tom mounted up.

"Well?" Jocko asked again.

Lizette's chin tilted stubbornly, and tears ran down her cheeks, only she wouldn't let them know she was crying. "Do I have any choice?" she snapped angrily.

They all laughed, and the man named Jocko, who'd been the passenger with her on the coach, walked over to one of the men who was leading an extra horse, and took the reins from him, then came back to help Lizette mount.

"Here, I'll help ye," he offered.

She brushed his hands aside. "I can mount myself," and she put her foot in the stirrup, then hefted herself up. Only the second she hit the saddle, she dug the horse in the ribs, leaned low, and broke through the other riders, heading down the road as fast as she could in the direction the mail coach had been traveling.

Jocko shouted, the others yelled, and Tom, who was in the saddle again, took off after her.

Jocko gestured to two of the other men. "Go give him a hand!" he shouted. "And don't come back till ye got her!" and while the three of them chased after Lizette, Jocko and the rest hurriedly emptied the chest of its money, then tied the driver and guard to some trees. This done, they turned the horses loose, keeping one for Jocko to use, even though he'd have to ride it bareback; then they set out after the other three, hoping they'd catch up.

Lizette knew what she was doing was risky, but didn't care. All she could think of now was that if she didn't get away, she'd be subjected to God knows what at the hands of men who were as ruthless and cunning as Sancho had been, and obviously not half as friendly, and she couldn't stand that. Any chance was worth taking, only it was awkward riding, with her stomach making her front-heavy. But she'd always ridden well, even bareback if she had to. However, the reins were flying free and the only way she had of guiding the horse was by pulling its mane. Well, that she could do too, and she glanced back behind her to see how close the others were.

Luckily the horse she was on was their leader's, and naturally he'd pick the best of the lot. She was glad, because instead of being overtaken, she seemed to be outdistancing them, a feat she wouldn't have thought possible under the circumstances.

If only it weren't so dark, and she wished she knew the lay of the land. But there was a moon, and with her head bent over, her eyes narrowing to keep out the wind, she kept the animal at an even gallop, never letting up for a minute, while behind her Tom and the other two were cursing their luck as they saw her disappear around a bend in the road up ahead.

It hadn't taken Lizette long to realize that this bend in the road was followed quickly by another, and she glanced off to her right, where a split-rail fence separated a pasture where some horses were standing up, some sleeping, others saun-tering about, and she knew she couldn't keep this pace up much longer. With one jerk of her mount's mane she veered off the road, galloping toward the fence, took it in one smooth leap, rode her horse in among the other horses, then fell prone in the saddle, slipping as far as she could to one side, hoping that in the moonlight she and the animal would blend in.

She raised her head cautiously to look over the horse's neck, and saw Tom and the other two fly by first, followed a few minutes later by the rest of them. Good. It had worked. However, afraid they might double back when they discovered she wasn't on the road ahead of them, as soon as the last of them was around the other bend, she straightened, leaned out far enough to get the reins in her hands this time, took off at a gallop again across the moonlit pasture, then slowed a short time later as she headed in the general direction the road was taking, yet kept far enough away from it so no one would spot her.

Lizette had been riding through the pasture for well over an hour already, and now she slowed her mount even more, easing the horse into a walk because of the rough terrain, guiding the animal down a small incline, then across a brook before entering a small wood. A few night birds called, but she had no idea what kind they might be, since she had never been to England. Back home she'd have been able to distinguish them easily, and suddenly the thought of home brought tears to her eyes that burned her cheeks slightly as they rolled down, and she realized her face was chapped some from having cried earlier and not wiped the tears away.

Damn, stupid predicament anyway, she thought as she continued maneuvering her horse between the trees, looking for patches of moonlight in the darkness to help her so she could see where she was. Then her heart sank. As she rode out from among the trees into another open field, off ahead was another split-rail fence. Well, she couldn't stay in the pasture forever, and making sure no one was around, she slapped her horse on the rump and headed straight for the fence, horse and rider taking it again in one fluid motion; then she slowed the animal again, studied the sky for some time, trying to pick out what she thought would be the North Star, and headed in the opposite direction, hoping she'd find a road that would take her the rest of the way to the village of Locksley, thankful she'd been able to elude her pursuers, at least for now.

The night had gone slowly, and by the time the sun broke the horizon, Lizette was tired, cold, and saddle-sore since it had been so long since she'd been on a horse. But she was still free and that in itself was an accomplishment, although she had no idea where she was or what time it might be. All she knew was that it was morning, and a cold one at that. Her fingers were half-frozen, and she was holding them under the cloak for warmth, and her toes felt like ice as she rode her horse out from a small wood into the open, and a ribbon of road finally stretched out before her. She knew the only hope she had was to follow it, so, nudging her horse in the ribs, she headed down it, watching carefully ahead and behind in case she met anyone along the way, which she did a short while later, only she was glad. At first, when she saw the speck behind her, in the distance, headed her way, she was apprehensive, and actually reined her horse off the road into some bushes just in case. But discovering it was only a farmer with a wagonload of geese, she maneuvered her horse back onto the road again and caught up with him.

"Excuse me," she asked as she drew her horse alongside the wagon, "but can you tell me if I'm going in the right direction to reach the village of Locksley?"

"Aye," he answered, then squinted, getting a better look at her, and he frowned. "But are you sure you're goin' in the right direction? You don't look like you'd belong in Locksley, ma'am."

"Well, actually I don't," she answered self-consciously, aware that she was a sorry sight with her bare legs showing astride the horse, the makeshift clothes she was wearing, and her tawny skin darkened from the sun, not to mention her protruding stomach. "In reality I'm trying to locate Locksley Hall and the Earl of Locksley, sir."

"Then you'll take the next road to your right, and the next to your left," he answered matter-of-factly. "It's still a long ride, but you should be there before noon. You'll see the gates with therest on 'em. Can't miss 'em."

Lizette thanked him, then spurred her horse faster, leaving the farmer behind as the morning sun crept higher in the sky, although it did little to warm the air. She'd ridden about two miles when she came to the first road and turned to her right, surprised to see a sign some distance ahead that read "Village of Locksley." Curious, she glanced about as she rode. Well, at least it looked like her uncle was prosperous.

Even though it was winter, the farms, orchards, everything looked in good shape.

She was just past the sign about three hundred yards when suddenly she heard a noise and glanced behind her, and her heart leapt into her throat. It was the outlaws from the mail coach, and they were heading right toward her from across one of the fields. She'd forgotten that they probably knew the country and were no doubt expecting her to come this way. If she just weren't so weary. But she was too close to give in now, and digging her horse in the ribs again, she took off at a gallop, hoping the next road on the left would lead her to Locksley Hall and freedom, and she was praying all the way.

Chapter 13

IT WAS GETTING colder outside, but here in the library at Locksley Hall, Teak felt warm and secure. Locksley Hall had originally been a Norman castle, built like a fortress and perched atop high cliffs on the coastline that overlooked the English Channel. It was a sprawling place with a huge tower in front and smaller towers at the end of the wings that spread out on each side, and in the summer it caught the warm breezes from the Channel. However, in winter it could be so cold the fires had to be fed constantly to keep the chill from going to the bone. Teak Locksley loved it here, though. It was the sort of place that got into a man's blood and made him glad he was alive. Especially on a day like today.

A roaring fire glowed in the fireplace, breakfast had been filling, the children were with the governess, servants busy elsewhere, and he had his wife all to himself. He gazed down into Ann's sloe eyes, marveling at how he used to hate sloe eyes, and smiling inwardly as he remembered how he'd grown to love them. And he'd never been sorry he'd married Ann six years ago, either. She and the children were his whole world now.

Ann Chapman had been his stepsister, his mother and stepfather having adopted her at the age of five. Roth and Loedicia Chapman had been moving cross country through the wilderness on their way back from Fort Locke on the shores of Lake Erie at the time, when they'd stopped at a Delaware Indian village, and Loedicia had fallen in love with the dark-eyed little girl the minute she'd laid eyes on her, and since Ann was an orphan it had been easy for the tribe to let her go. Her mother had been Delaware Indian, her father English, but to Teak, who had been only fifteen at the time and living here, in England, she'd never again be anyone except Lady Locksley, his Ann. All the anger and resentment were behind him now, as was the war, and all that was left for him to do was to love her and try to keep her happy.

"You're not with me, love," he teased as he held her in his arms, studying her face.

Ann sighed. "I'm sorry, Teak." She reached up, stroking the side of his thick head of blond hair, then ran a hand down his firm jawline while she stared up into his brilliant blue eyes. Teak was so tall, with broad shoulders, and at forty-two he was still a handsome lumbering sort of man who oftentimes looked out of place in the fancy dress of his station, although he never complained about it. Everyone said he was the image of his father, a man she wished she could have known, only Quinn Lock, or Locksley as he came to be known after taking over the title Teak had inherited, had been dead and buried at sea long before she came into their lives. "I was thinking," she said, her fingers toying with the lapel of his white silk shirt. "About that letter we got last week." She frowned. "Do you suppose Bain will ever find Lizette?"

"Who knows?" He shook his head. "The world's such a big place, and the Caribbean's even more remote. There are a thousand places a man can hide out there."

"Oh, Teak." She moved closer, resting her head on his shoulder, the warmth of his arms making her feel safe and secure. "If only there was something we could do. I always did like Liz. She was a little headstrong at times, and did crazy things when she was younger, I know, but marriage had really agreed with her. . . . Now this."

He reached up, burying his hand in her long straight amber hair; then his hand fell to the back of the bright blue morning dress she had on, where his fingers stretched out, palms open, and he kneaded the flesh beneath, pulling her even closer against him and marveling at the way it always made him feel. He was just ready to kiss her when suddenly there was a knock on the huge oak door and his arms eased from about her.

"Come in."

"Beggin' your pardon, my lord," Wickham the butler stammered as he stepped into the room. His usual haughty expression was changed to one of dismay, and he looked rather harried. "But there's, excuse me, sir, a person in the front hall says she's your niece, sir, and I don't know quite what to do with her."

Teak frowned. "What do you mean, you don't know what to do with her? Who is she? Where is she?"

"Well, she's just inside the door, sir," he answered. "Rode up on a horse with some men chasin' her and just shoved her way in when I was lettin' the cat out. Don't know where she come from nor why, but the gents what was chasin' her didn't look any too respectable, and when they saw me, well, they just grabbed the horse she'd been ridin' and took off down the drive like the devil was on their tails."

Teak glanced down at Ann, then took her arm. "Take us to her, Wickham," he ordered, and he ushered Ann from the library, heading down the main hall that separated the wings of the big stone mansion, following closely behind the butler.

Ahead in the entrance hall Lizette leaned against the frame of one of the windows that flanked the huge front door and brushed the hair from her eyes. Her hands were shaking, stomach tied in knots, and she was so relieved at reaching her destination that she could hardly move, her knees beginning to weaken. She reached out, her hand trembling, and took a corner of the curtain that covered the window, picking it up so she could look out just to make sure the outlaws weren't coming back, and her eyes narrowed as she squinted to see better, realizing she'd ridden right by a small lake with swans swimming in it that was nestled neatly in the center of the curved drive. And she hadn't even remembered running up the front steps after dismounting, either. All she remembered was riding through the big front gate and hoping someone would be around. Well, she was finally here and there was no sign of the outlaws anymore and she sighed, breathing heavily as she heard footsteps and voices coming from the back of the foyer.

Dropping the edge of the curtain, she leaned back again, her head resting on the edge of the window frame as she saw the silhouettes of two people at the back of the foyer.

"Aunt Ann? Uncle Teak?" she called breathlessly.

Ann wasn't quite sure. "Liz?"

"Lizette?" Teak's eyes widened as he moved toward her. "My God, it *is* Lizette!" and Lizette felt her knees weakening even more.

"Grab her," Ann cried as they both reached her, and each of them took one of her arms, trying to keep her on her feet, but she was too exhausted.

"Let me take her," Teak said, and letting go of her arm, he reached out carefully, lifted her off her feet, and cradled her against him, then glanced over at Wickham, who'd stood aside somewhat, watching them. "Go call Maggie and send one of the boys to the village for the doctor," he told him, then turned to Ann. "We'll take her up to the blue room in the west wing. You can turn the covers back on the bed and take care of her while I get a fire going," and he headed across the marble floor of the foyer toward the fancy carpeted staircase. A few minutes later he was putting Lizette down on a huge mahogany bed, paying little attention to the dirt from her clothes that was smudging the clean sheets.

"Now, I'll get the fire," he said as he backed away, and while he tended to the fireplace, Ann took over with Lizette, loosening the hood under her chin and taking off her cloak; then she began to rub Lizette's hands, trying to get the circulation back in them. They looked so cold, and nothing like the pretty hands they used to be. Now the nails were broken and uneven, calluses on the palms just beginning to soften.

Lizette stared up at Ann, trying to think of something to say, but her insides were trembling so badly, and she was having a hard time finding her voice. She closed her eyes and let the warmth of Ann's hands soothe her as Ann reached down and removed her shoes, then began massaging her feet.

Tears rimmed Lizette's eyes and she opened them again to look at her aunt.

"I . . . I thought I'd never make it. Those men . . ." She gasped breathlessly as the warmth began to penetrate her body and Ann started to pull the sheet up over her, then saw the beaded bag still tied to the strap of her dress and began untying it.

"Who were they?" Ann asked.

"I was on the mail coach . . . they robbed it."

Teak had managed to get the wood to catch in the fireplace, and now he strolled back over to the bed, looking down at his niece. It was still cool in the room and he rubbed his hands together.

"It was no doubt Jocko and his gang," he told her.

Lizette's eyes acknowledged his statement. "That's what they called their leader."

"If Jocko's moved this far south, the authorities are bound to catch him this time," Ann said, and looked up at Teak. "They've just been waiting for something like this." She turned her attention back to Lizette. "He's a notorious highwayman whose gang's been plaguing the roads just north of here for some time now, then hiding in the woods with friends, only I doubt he has any this far south . . . but he's not our worry now, Liz, you are, and I don't understand," she said, concerned. "What are you doing here and how on earth did you get here?" She managed to get the bag untied and set it aside on the nightstand. "The last we heard of you, you'd been kidnapped by some pirate and no one knew where you were."

Lizette sighed, trying to relax as Ann set her shoes and cloak aside at the foot of the bed, then added a blanket to the sheet that covered her, noticing as she did that Lizette was expecting a baby, although Lizette didn't realize her aunt had noticed. Lizette rubbed her feet together, the nerves still tingling as the circulation continued warming them; then she reached up wearily and wiped a few tears from her bright green eyes that were puffy and bloodshot from lack of sleep.

"I was kidnapped," she answered lazily, the warmth starting to make her drowsy. "And we were on an island . . . then there was a British warship . . . when we got to London they wouldn't believe me when I told them . . . Oh God, Uncle Teak, I thought I'd never make it!"

He leaned over, stroking her forehead and trying to soothe her. "Well, you're here now, and there's nothing more to worry about." He smiled graciously. "Just close your eyes, Lizette, and sleep for now. We'll talk about the whole thing later."

Lizette looked first at Teak, then at Ann, then took a deep breath as her eyes closed.

"She's exhausted, poor thing." Ann stood up, putting her hand on Lizette's forehead. "It feels like she's getting a fever, too."

"I wouldn't doubt it, and in her condition a fever's no good."

"You noticed too?"

"How could I not notice?"

"Then for heaven's sake," Ann responded, "tell Maggie to hurry and get up here, and maybe we can do something about keeping it down," and she turned, walking to the fireplace to stir the fire to make the room more comfortable while Teak left hurriedly to find the housekeeper, then waited impatiently for the doctor to arrive.

For the next two days Lizette lay in the huge mahogany bed in the guest room at Locksley Hall and fought fevers and chills that racked her body constantly, while outside, the weather became even colder, with a thin sheet of ice covering the lake in front of Locksley Hall, forcing the swans to seek shelter in the stables and bringing roaring fires to the rooms of the old stone mansion. And while Lizette lay feverish, trying to fight her way back to reality, downstairs Teak sat at his desk in the library and wrote a nice long letter to his mother in America, then rode into town and posted it.

It was early morning, the third day after Lizette's unexpected arrival at Locksley Hall, when her fever finally broke and she came back to reality again. The blue draperies at the windows were partially open, the fire in the fireplace was still glowing from the log Maggie had placed on it when she'd come to check on her in the wee hours of the morning, and now Lizette stirred, groaning, and opened her eyes. For a few seconds she couldn't remember who she was, where she was, or what she was doing here; then suddenly it all came flooding back to her and she looked up at the ceiling and smiled. She was here at Locksley Hall. She'd made it, and she knew now that what she'd thought had been only a dream had been reality.

Instinctively her hands moved to her stomach, and a sigh escaped her lips, the smile on her face softening. It was still there. She hadn't lost the baby, and a tingling sensation shot through her as she trailed her fingers over the hard mound. The poor little thing had been through so much with her, yet hadn't given up. Well, maybe that was a good sign, because she hadn't given up either, and she patted her stomach gratefully, then took a deep breath and tried to move. Every bone in her body hurt.

Finally, after a few minutes of flexing her muscles and squirming about uncomfortably, she managed to push herself up enough so she could see about the room. Even with the fireplace going it wasn't really warm in here. Not the way it was at home. Stone walls and floors seemed to have a way of keeping the cold deep in them even in the glow of the warm fire, and she began to wonder what Uncle Teak saw in the place, and how Aunt Ann could possibly like living here after growing up at the Château. But then, this was just one room; the others were no doubt more modern and comfortable.

She nestled her head back into the pillow again, then reached up and touched her forehead. The fever was gone. That meant she was on the mend, and a few minutes later, after breathing deeply a few times and trying to get back some strength, she got brave, tossed the covers aside, and slowly sat up at the edge of the bed, swinging her feet over the side, where they barely touched the cold floor; then she glanced down at the nightdress she had on. Sometime since her arrival they'd undressed her and put her in a long-sleeved, high-necked gown of soft pink flannel, and she stared at her feet sticking out from beneath it.

Lord, but she'd lost weight. She lifted the nightdress a bit and stared at her legs. They actually looked skinny. She hadn't been this thin for years, and she unbuttoned the wristband of the gown and pushed up the sleeve. Even her arm was bony, and she laughed lightly. No one would even know her if she went home looking like this.

She buttoned the sleeve and her hands moved to her face, feeling the hollows in her cheeks, her fingers smoothing down the length of her jawbone. Wait till Bain saw her. He'd be shocked. Her head tilted back and she breathed in deeply, suddenly realizing that the earthy smell of the cold stone and pungent odor from the wood-burning fireplace were overlaid with the scent of something sweet and fragrant. Cape jasmine? she thought, puzzled, then remembered that Aunt Ann had always been partial to it, and her eyes began to search the room, her gaze suddenly stopping on a small crystal bowl on the stand next to the bed. There were dried, crushed flowers in it, and she knew they were cape jasmine. A touch of home here in England. It had to be her aunt's doing.

Straightening lazily, she stretched, wincing uncomfortably, trying to get the kinks out, and started to get up, then sat back down on the edge of the bed as the door opened and Ann came in.

"Lizette, what on earth . . . ?"

"But I feel all right now," she explained.

Ann shook her head. It was still early morning and she was wearing a green silk dressing gown over a matching nightdress, with quilted slippers on her feet, her long hair pulled back and plaited into one large braid. She hurried to the bed. "I don't care how good you feel. You know you shouldn't be trying to get up. You've been through a horrible time and you need your rest. Now, lie back down," and she stared at her niece stubbornly, waiting for Lizette to obey.

Lizette stared back. She didn't feel like lying down. She'd been lying down long enough, but then she let her toe touch the cold floor and a chill ran through her. Maybe Aunt Ann was right, she thought, and slowly drew her legs back up, shoving them under the covers again, then let Ann fluff the pillows up so she could at least sit up in bed.

Lizette flushed. "How long have I been here?" she asked.

Ann finished straightening the covers over her. "Today's the third day."

"That long? And you've taken care of me all this time?"

"All of us have, including Teak."

"But . . . I don't remember a thing, not really. The last I remember was being chased by those horrible men. The rest all seems like a dream."

"Well, it was real, all right. Only you won't have to worry about those outlaws anymore. The authorities caught them the night after you arrived. I guess they tried their luck one too many times and ran right into a trap. They won't be riding the roads around here anymore, or up north either."

"They were going to hold me for ransom because they'd found out I was related to Uncle Teak, then after I got away, I think they thought they could catch me before I reached Locksley Hall."

"Well, all they got back was their horse, Liz."

"Good."

"I'm just glad you got away." Ann looked relieved. "Only now, young lady," she went on, "you don't want to overdo things your first day, so what say you rest a bit longer while I go tell Maggie to bring you some breakfast and we'll have a nice long talk later."

Lizette agreed, so while Ann opened the draperies, poked up the fire, then left the room, promising to send the house-keeper back up with something for her to eat since she'd had nothing except thin broth and tea for the past two days,

Lizette settled back into the warm bed again, pulling the covers up to her chin, and then dreamed about the trip she'd soon be taking home.

Downstairs, after giving Maggie her instructions about Lizette's breakfast, Ann joined Teak at the dining-room table, where he was staring at the letter they'd received from their mother only a few days before.

"Well, have you decided?" she asked after sitting down and starting to toy with her food. "She's awake now and talking rationally."

"Not yet." He mulled it over a little longer in his mind. "We'll give her a little more time to get her breath," he answered, his blue eyes darkening with his decision. "But then we have to tell her, Ann. She has a right to know."

Ann nodded. "I know," she said, and her face saddened. "Only how do you tell someone something so cruel?"

"Don't worry, we'll think of a way." He patted her hand, then tucked the letter back into the inside pocket of his morning coat. "Now, let's enjoy a quiet breakfast before the boys wake up, love, because once they discover we're out of bed already, you know what'll happen," and they both smiled outwardly at the thought of their two boisterous sons, even though each of them was saddened inwardly at the thought of having to tell Lizette about her daughter, Blythe.

Lizette stayed in bed for the rest of the day, even though she kept saying she felt well enough to be up, and her health improved tremendously, so that by the following afternoon she was strong enough not only for a bath, with her hair getting washed, but to have her nails manicured so they were all even, and Ann had even found a dress for her to wear, one she'd worn during her own pregnancies. Lizette actually felt like a real woman again, for the first time in months, as she modeled it before the full-length mirror in the corner of the guest room.

Earlier in the day she had told Teak and Ann as much as she dared about the events of the past few months, leaving out only her strange relationship with Sancho, and admitting only that he cared for her, even though he knew she didn't return his feelings. However, she purposely hadn't gone into all the rest of it. Not only wasn't it any of their business, but they probably wouldn't understand, because there were times when she herself didn't understand her feelings toward the man. She stood in front of the mirror now, staring at the contrast of her still darkly tanned skin against the pale yellow dress Ann had lent her, and suddenly she wished with all her heart that she'd be able to leave for home before the rest of the week was out, and she brought the subject up later that evening, shortly after dinner, when they were all sitting in the parlor. Only Teak didn't agree.

"But why can't I leave now?" Lizette argued. "A few more days and no one'll even know I've been sick." She was standing near the fireplace in the huge sitting room with its hanging tapestries and heavy furniture, the light from two overhead chandeliers with whale-oil lamps in them helping the wall sconces to cheer the room that was heated by marble-manteled fireplaces on each end, and she walked toward where Teak sat holding his younger son on his lap. Seth was two and a half, with his father's blond hair and his mother's sloe eyes, and she was reminded of her own children. "I can pay you back when we get to Beaufort, Uncle Teak."

"It isn't the money, Lizette," he tried to explain, hoping to be able to convince her. "Believe me, it's not that. It's just that you're in no condition to travel now, that's all. And by the time you do get your strength back, you'll be too far along. Now"—he switched Seth, shifting him into a more comfortable position—"why don't you just wait till the baby comes, then we can all go with you, even the children."

"But I've been away so long. You have no idea what it's like." She glanced at the boy in his arms. "If I don't see Braxton and Blythe soon, I think I'll go crazy, and I miss Bain so. You must understand."

"I do . . . and that's another thing." He reached into the inside pocket of his dark brown frock coat and pulled out the letter, deciding now was as good a time as any to tell her. "There are some things you're going to have to know before you go home anyway," he said, his face solemn. "And I guess maybe you might as well learn about them now."

Lizette stared at the letter apprehensively. "What's that?" she asked.

He held the letter out to her.

"It's a letter from my mother," he explained. "Read it, Liz. There are some things in it you should know."

Lizette smoothed the skirt of the pale yellow dress Ann had lent her, then reached out and took the letter, opening it hesitantly before walking over to the window seat and sitting down on one of the cushions where the light from one of the wall sconces made it easier to see. She began to read.

Suddenly her face paled visibly in spite of the deep suntan, and tears rimmed her eyes.

"Oh, my God! Blythe!" she cried helplessly. "My poor baby!" and she choked, unable to read on.

Ann, who'd been watching her closely from where she was sitting playing with young Quinn, grabbed a handkerchief from the pocket of her red silk dress, got up, and hurried to Lizette's side.

Lizette looked over at her, unable to control the sobs. "Grandma says she'll never walk again," she cried, half-choking. "Oh, Aunt Ann!" and she reached out, took the handkerchief, and blew her nose, then threw her arms about her aunt, hoping to be comforted, but life wasn't that easy.

"There's more to the letter, Liz," Ann said after a while, and Lizette drew back, staring at Ann tearfully, then gulped back more tears, wiping her eyes, and once more she started reading, dabbing at her eyes and nose with the handkerchief as she read.

Ann had moved back to where Quinn was playing with some lead soldiers, only she was still watching Lizette closely as Lizette continued to read. Again Ann could see that something was disturbing her niece, and she knew she and Teak had guessed right.

While Lizette was delirious, she'd been ranting, raving, and mumbling about one thing and another, and Ann and Teak had tried to piece some of it together. When the name Elena had escaped Lizette's lips, with a bitter agony from deep inside, they were certain that the letter from Dicia would also have even more of a meaning for Lizette, and from the look on Lizette's face now, Ann was more certain than ever that they were right, because Dicia had mentioned receiving a letter from Bain a short time before, telling them that he had found Elena de Córdoba and was staying with her and her uncle, waiting for Sancho to return to Cuba so he could locate Lizette.

Now Ann saw a bleak look fill Lizette's eyes.

"He's in Cuba?" Lizette mumbled to herself, remembering Señor Pérez's ranch, and the bay where she'd almost escaped from Sancho. "Oh, no!" and again tears came. This time for herself.

"Don't worry, Lizette," Teak assured her. "I'm sure from

what you've told us about Bain that by now he's probably given up hope and headed back home."

"Not if Elena has her way," Lizette countered, and sniffed, wiping her nose again, her whole world suddenly seeming too much to bear. "Why?" she cried, crushing the letter instinctively in her fist, then realizing it wasn't hers to destroy and straightening it. "Why did all this have to happen? Just because one man thought he was betrayed. And poor Blythe." Tears of anger and resentment rolled down her cheeks. "It just isn't fair. Blythe didn't deserve this."

"Nor did you," Teak offered. "That's why I said I thought it'd be best if you just stayed here for a while. I wrote a letter to Mother yesterday, and by the time word reaches Bain in Cuba that you're all right, the baby should be here and he can meet you back in Beaufort."

"But the baby's due in February. That's three whole months away."

"And three important months, Liz," Ann reminded her. "You've been lucky so far, but from now on—"

Ann was interrupted by Wickham, who stood in the doorway clearing his throat.

"Er . . . excuse me, Countess, my lord . . ."

Teak was irritated by the interruption. "Yes, Wickham?"

"Beggin' your pardon, my lord, but there's a gentleman at the door, sir. Says he has to talk to you and that it's important. A Mr. George Canning."

"George?" Teak glanced at Lizette, then back to Wickham. "Bring him in, Wickham, I'll talk to him here."

Wickham flushed, his graying hair looking even whiter against his red face. "I'm afraid Mr. Canning has requested that he talk to you alone, my lord," he informed Teak, and Teak's brows knitted together thoughtfully as he set Seth on the carpeted floor, where he hurried to his mother; then Teak stood up.

"I'll be back shortly," he said, excusing himself, and Lizette frowned, worried, as she remembered where she'd heard Mr. Canning's name before.

Teak pulled the sleeves of his frock coat down, then smoothed the sides of his wavy blond hair as he followed Wickham from the room and on through the stately hall, then headed toward the foyer alone while Wickham left him to go to the kitchen.

"Well, George," Teak said, reaching a hand out to greet

his old friend. "What brings you all the way out here to Locksley?"

George reciprocated his handshake and smiled. "Good to see you, Teak. It's been a long time."

"Like I said," Teak replied, releasing George's hand. "What brings you to Locksley Hall?"

"You don't know?"

"I might."

"I put the Bow Street Runners on her, Teak," George answered, his smile fading. "They traced her through the driver of the hack that took her to the jewelry store where she sold that expensive emerald ring, then to the mail coach. And it certainly didn't take long after talking with the driver of the mail coach to figure out that she'd end up here."

"I see."

"I have to talk to her, Teak."

"It all depends."

"On what?"

"Whether you're just going to talk or start interrogating."

"Come now, old man, you know very well I've got a job to do."

"And my niece is part of it?"

"She was living with de Córdoba, wasn't she? That makes her part of it."

"She wasn't living with him. He'd been holding her prisoner."

"That's what she says."

"That's what happened."

"Then a few questions shouldn't hurt, now, should they, old chap?"

Teak stared hard at Canning. He'd worked for the man during the war and knew he could be ruthless if crossed.

"She's been sick, George," he cautioned. "You can talk to her, but not alone."

Canning shrugged, straightening the front of his fancy blue frock coat with its velvet lapels; then he smoothed the hair back from his ears, his eyes steady on Teak.

"Your presence won't bother me a bit, my lord," he answered confidently.

"Then shall we?" Teak gestured toward the back of the house, then moved off in that direction with George at his elbow.

Lizette was sitting in the chair Teak had vacated a few

minutes before and she was holding Seth on what lap she had left, watching him tug at the gold velvet ribbons that trimmed the bodice of her dress, when Teak returned with George Canning, and she pulled the little boy close, holding him tighter than usual at the sight of the man, using the rounded warmth of the child to give her moral support.

"You know George," Teak said to Ann, who looked up from where she was still sitting on the floor with Quinn, toy soldiers spread between the folds of her crimson dress as if they were on a battlefield, and Ann nodded.

"George? What brings you all the way out here this time of night?" she asked.

"Work, Countess," he answered, then glanced over to Lizette. "Good evening, Mrs. Kolter."

Lizette tensed. "Mr. Canning."

George studied her appreciatively, his eyebrows raising. "I must say, my dear lady," he said as he leaned back, a thumb thrust into his watch pocket as he gazed at her, "Teak says you've been ill, but you look extremely well to me, and far different from the woman who was in my office only a few days ago. The air out here in the country must agree with you. Especially after what the driver of the mail coach told us happened. And you must be an excellent horsewoman too, from what he says."

Lizette caught the patronizing tone in his voice. "I've ridden all my life," she answered. "In fact, I have my own mount at home."

He smiled. "Aha, I thought as much. You did quite well, outriding Jocko and his gang."

"Maybe because I was on Jocko's horse."

"Possibly."

"However, you didn't come here to talk about Jocko, did you, sir?" she said, and he took a deep breath.

"You don't mince words, do you, Mrs. Kolter?"

"I know when I'm being patronized, if that's what you mean, sir," she answered. "You tried it in your office and it didn't work then either, if you'll remember. Now, just what do you want of me?"

"He said he'd like to ask you a few questions, Liz," Teak cut in, then looked briefly at Canning before turning back to Lizette, who was trying to keep Seth from climbing off her lap. "I told him you'd been sick, so if you don't want to talk to him now . . ."

Lizette helped Seth stand on her knees, with his arms around her neck, and she hugged the boy affectionately, her emerald eyes sparking as she looked directly at George.

"Ask away," she said calmly. "I have nothing to hide," yet her hands felt clammy and her heart was pounding erratically.

George Canning straightened, trying to remember what the strange-looking woman who'd sat across from him in his office had looked like, because there wasn't a bit of resemblance between her and the woman he was confronting tonight. If this woman was the true Lizette Kolter, then he wished he'd had the foresight to hold on to the other Lizette Kolter, because she had looked much more cooperative.

"To start with," he began after clearing his throat, "how long were you with de Córdoba?"

"He kidnapped me on the Fourth of July, only I'm afraid I have no idea what the date was when Captain Vincent showed up. It was somewhere around the middle of October, I guess."

"So that would be about three and a half months, am I right?"

Lizette shrugged. "Give or take a few days, yes, I guess so."

"And during that time, where were you?"

"On his ship and on an island."

"Where was the island?"

"I haven't the slightest idea. Didn't you ask Captain Vincent?"

"We know where you were when you were rescued, if you prefer to call it that, Mrs. Kolter, but surely that wasn't the only island de Córdoba hid out on."

"It was, as far as I know." She set Seth on her lap again and let him play with her fingers, finding comfort in the child's nearness. "If he went any place else, I don't know about it."

"But Liz—" Teak began.

Lizette looked over at him and her eyes held a warning. "As I told you, Uncle Teak," she said, her words a little too precise, "the only time he and his men left the island was to raid ships." She addressed George Canning again. "Other than that, Mr. Canning, I have no knowledge of where they might have gone."

Canning saw Teak frown, his expression puzzled, but he didn't press the issue. Instead, he continued with Lizette.

"Then you have no idea where the man and his ship would be now?"

"None whatsoever."

"But you'd like to know?"

"No . . . I'd like to forget I ever met him."

"Only that's quite impossible, isn't it?"

"What do you mean?"

"Come, come, Mrs. Kolter," George said, tsking outrageously. "Maybe your uncle is willing to shut his eyes to the obvious, but the rest of the world isn't blind, you know. Just how long do you think you'll be able to palm off the child you're carrying as your husband's? Especially when it's already filtering through the back streets as to who the father really is."

"That's a lie!"

"Is it? Then maybe I have something with me that'll put truth to my words." He turned to Teak. "If you'll excuse me, my lord," and there was a note of sarcasm in his voice, "I have something outside in my carriage . . . if you'd get someone to help me bring it in."

Teak straightened hesitantly, then walked over and pulled the bell cord, instructing Wickham, when he came in, to help Mr. Canning.

As soon as George and Wickham were out of sight, Teak turned to Lizette, his eyes sparking angrily.

"Why did you lie to him, Liz?" he asked, and she frowned. "Lie?"

"Yes, lie. You know very well that the letter your grandmother sent said Bain wrote and told her de Córdoba had dropped his sister and brother off in Cuba, and yet you never even mentioned it."

"And I don't intend to." She hugged Seth even tighter. "Don't you see, Uncle Teak," she went on, trying to explain quickly before Canning returned, "it wouldn't do any good to tell them about Don Emilio. It would ruin the man's life, and he has no more control over being Sancho's uncle than you have over being mine."

"You're sure that's the only reason?"

"What other reason would there be?"

Their eyes held and neither backed down until a noise at the door heralded George Canning's return, and he backed into the room carrying something quite large that had a heavy quilted cover tied over it, with Wickham handling the other end. Whatever it was, Teak had them set it down in the middle of the parlor, then confronted George.

"All right, old boy, what's this supposed to be?" he asked.

Canning smiled. "You'll see," he said, and began untying it, then let the quilt fall away. "Look," and they all stared as the quilt hit the floor to reveal a lovely carved mahogany cradle, the one Lizette had asked the captain's men to bring for her. She'd forgotten it back on the ship.

"So what does this have to do with Liz?" Teak asked.

George's smile grew smug. "It's hers, Teak," he answered. "Captain Vincent said that when they rescued her, she begged him to let her bring it along, only she left it on board his ship when she ran off."

"Which should prove something," Lizette snapped. "Or hadn't you thought of that?"

"On the contrary, my dear," George disagreed. "It only proves that you had no way of retrieving it off the *Pinnacle*. It was given to you by de Córdoba, am I right?"

"And if it was?"

"Well, now, I've never yet heard of a bloodthirsty cutthroat like de Córdoba with a heart big enough to buy a cradle for another man's progeny."

"He didn't buy it."

"I see." Canning's eyes widened. "You mean he stole it?"

"Have you ever heard of a pirate buying anything, Mr. Canning?" she asked.

"You mean . . . ?"

"It was loot from one of his raids."

"And you accepted it?" George glanced over at Teak. "Does that answer your question, my lord?" he asked confidently.

Lizette didn't like the scowl on Teak's forehead as he turned to her. "Is this true, Liz?" he asked.

"Good heavens, Uncle Teak," she answered testily, "what was I supposed to do? Everything he had, the food, clothes, I mean everything was there as the result of his piracy. Was I to starve to death and run naked just so I could say my conscience was clear? Well, I wasn't about to starve to death. I wanted to live as much as anyone else would have, and I'd have been a hypocrite to eat the food and pretend that it wasn't bought with the same blood. So I accepted what he gave me, including the cradle, because it was the only way."

"He gave you the ring too?" George asked abruptly.

Again Teak was taken by surprise. "What ring?"

"The emerald ring I told you she sold in order to get money so she could come here," George answered. "He did give it to you, didn't he?" he asked her again.

"The ring was mine to sell, Mr. Canning."

"The ring was one bought and made right here in London for the Duchess of Kent's granddaughter, who lives in Barbados, Mrs. Kolter," he informed her arrogantly. "It was being sent there on a ship that we know now was scuttled by de Córdoba and his men."

"I was supposed to know that?"

"Then he did give it to you?" Teak asked.

Lizette turned to her uncle, then looked at Ann. Surely she'd understand. "I had no choice but to take it," she answered. "No one argued with Sancho de Córdoba about anything." She looked again at Teak. "And I mean no one," she emphasized. "Only I'm glad I did accept it, Uncle Teak, because without it I wouldn't have made it here."

George eyed her curiously. "Why'd he give it to you?" he suddenly asked.

She looked at him in surprise. "Well, now, I never asked him," she answered flippantly, knowing full well why he'd given it to her. "But I presume he wanted me to have it."

"In other words, he's in love with you?"

"Who knows?" She cocked her head, watching George for a minute, then let Seth slide to his feet on the floor since he'd started to squirm again. "Am I on trial, Mr. Canning?" she asked curiously.

Canning flushed. "Not exactly, Mrs. Kolter. But you see, the British government has been trying to put an end to men like Sancho de Córdoba for some time now, and if we thought perhaps the man was in love with you, and that you knew where he might be found, or that maybe you were his mistress and could be used as bait to lure him into the open . . . You do understand?"

"Oh, I understand, all right," she said, straightening as she leaned back in the chair, her chin held high. "Only I wasn't his mistress, Mr. Canning, and even if I had been, it certainly wouldn't have been by choice."

"But you did sleep with him?"

"You're going too far now, George!" Teak interrupted. "It's one thing to come out here and ask a few questions, but what you're implying . . ." His eyes were hard as he stared at his old friend.

"Then let her tell me it's not true."

Lizette clasped the arms of the chair and stared at him, her eyes dangerously insolent. "Do you mean, did I sleep in the same bed with him, or was I intimate with him, Mr. Canning?" she asked defiantly. "Because, you see, they are two separate things, sir. Contrary to what most people believe, it is possible to sleep in the same bed with another person without being intimate."

George's eyebrows raised. "Oh?"

"And if by intimate you mean, did we have marital relations, the answer is no, sir, I did not, as you put it, sleep with Sancho de Córdoba."

"Then why has word filtered into the ports and bawdy houses that you were his mistress?"

"I have no idea, unless it's just a matter of bragging, sir. You see, Sancho told me a number of times that his vendetta against Bain would be all the sweeter if he could make Bain believe that I stayed with him willingly, and he was planning to tell the lie to anyone who'd listen, so I imagine he's sailing into all the ports he's used to frequenting and doing just that."

"Because of a vendetta against your husband?"

"Well, it wasn't against me."

"And the cradle?"

"Who knows?" she snapped. "Maybe he likes children."

"Mrs. Kolter!"

"Well, how should I know why he thought I'd like the cradle?" she shot back. "All I know is he thought I'd need it because he certainly wasn't expecting the British Navy to rescue me."

"I see." Canning studied her again for a few minutes. She was a lovely woman even with the dark tan. "But you won't tell me where the man is, right?"

"I don't know where he is, and that's the truth."

George Canning pondered her answer, then cleared his throat. "You know," he said thoughtfully after a few minutes, "I have a strange feeling that there's more to all this than meets the eye, Mrs. Kolter, and I also have a feeling that you could tell me what I want to know, too, if you really wanted to, now couldn't you?"

"This is ridiculous." Lizette's hand moved to her stomach

and rested on the firm hard mound. "Mr. Canning, I was expecting this child before I was kidnapped," she explained readily. "And I happen to be very much in love with my husband. Now, as far as Sancho de Córdoba is concerned, I was a means to an end for him, that's all. Where he went, and what he did when he left the island where he kept me prisoner, I have no idea, but the man did treat me decently. I have no idea why, but he did, and I'm grateful for that because I know things could have been worse. But he was still a pirate, I was his prisoner, and wherever the man is, I hope he pays for what he did, not only to me and my husband, but my daughter as well."

"Your daughter?" George asked, surprised.

"Her daughter was crippled during the crash of the carriage the night she was kidnapped," Teak explained.

George shifted his feet uncomfortably. "I didn't know," he said. "I'm sorry, Mrs. Kolter."

"Are you really?" Lizette's green eyes snapped testily and she reached up, brushing an unruly dark curl from her forehead. "I doubt it, sir. But then, I wouldn't expect you to be, because you haven't believed a word I've said, have you?"

He smiled, the smile crooked, more like a sneer. "You're very perceptive, Mrs. Kolter," he answered, straightening as he looked about the room, then back to Lizette. "I wish I could believe you, but your story just doesn't ring true, at least not all of it. You see, a man like de Córdoba doesn't treat a woman decently, as you put it, unless he has a bloody good reason, because he's a vicious blackguard with a reputation built on fact, not fantasy. No, Lizette Kolter, I don't believe you, only there's no way I can prove otherwise, at least not right now. So, for what it's worth, I suggest you stay in England for a while, just in case."

"In case of what, George?" Teak asked.

"In case we decide to have another talk with her," he answered, then straightened arrogantly. "After all, Teak, even you have to admit that what she's told me is bizarre, to say the least, and I'm not sure I'll be able to get anyone back in London to believe it. Now," he went on, and sighed, "ordinarily I'd ask you for a night's lodging, old friend, but I've already made arrangements with Lord Densby just to the north. Ran into his carriage on the road earlier and accepted his invitation to stay."

"Then I guess we won't keep you, George," Teak answered, glad he wasn't going to be forced to offer the man his hospitality.

After bidding him good-bye, Lizette and Ann watched quietly while Teak ushered Mr. Canning from the room.

Ann was still sitting on the floor with Quinn, and Seth had joined them, plunking down in her lap. Lizette glanced over at her aunt.

"You believe me, don't you, Aunt Ann?" she asked.

Ann's eyes were intense as she studied Lizette. "I believe that what happened, happened the way you said, yes, Liz," she said. "But you have to admit what George said about Sancho de Córdoba does make a person wonder. And you could have helped by telling him about Cuba and de Córdoba's sister and brother, now couldn't you?"

Lizette flushed, then stood up and walked to the window seat, staring out at the cold winter landscape. Could she have helped? If she had told him about Elena and Mario, it would definitely have led them right to Don Emilio, and she didn't want that. But she could probably have told them about the bay Sancho used when they went to Cuba without telling them about Don Emilio, and they could possibly have intercepted Sancho near there, or gotten permission from the Spanish authorities on the island to set a trap for him, only even that might have led them to Sancho's uncle. That wasn't the only reason she hadn't helped, though, and she knew it. As much as she hated what Sancho had done to her life, there was no way she could deny the fact that he wasn't just a bloodthirsty pirate like everyone said. She'd learned to know him like no one else ever could, and had seen the man behind the facade he'd shown to the world, and now suddenly she had to admit he'd grown on her, and she had a hard time trying to visualize him hanging for his crimes. The thought was even frightening. Still, she couldn't let Aunt Ann and Uncle Teak know how she really felt. Actually, she couldn't even rationalize her feelings to herself.

"Even if I had told him about the bay in Cuba, it wouldn't have helped," she answered after a few minutes. "Anything I could have told him would have led right back to Don Emilio, and I couldn't do that to an innocent man."

She was still looking out the window and didn't hear her uncle return until he spoke.

"Besides, they might catch de Córdoba, right, Liz?" he said from the doorway.

She whirled around, realizing he sounded upset. "What do you mean by that?"

He stepped the rest of the way into the room, his tall blond figure intimidating. "George was right, wasn't he?"

"Right?"

"I'm not stupid, Liz, and neither is your aunt," he went on heatedly. "An emerald ring, the crib," and he gestured to the crib still sitting in the middle of the parlor. "Like George said, a man like de Córdoba doesn't play family man unless there's a reason."

Lizette's eyes narrowed. "The baby's Bain's!"

"But the woman belonged to de Córdoba, right?"

"The woman never belonged to anyone," she yelled furiously, and tears sprang to her eyes. "Except Bain. I'll always belong to Bain."

"And de Córdoba?"

"To hell with de Córdoba," she cried. "I wish I'd never heard of the man," and she stared hard at them for a few seconds, tears glistening in her eyes; then her hand covered her stomach and she rushed from the room, heading for the front stairs.

Ann and Teak watched her go; then Ann got to her feet, a hand resting on the top of her younger son's head while he clutched at her skirt, wanting to be lifted.

"Well, and just what do you make of that, Lord Locksley?" she asked Teak.

He frowned. "I wish I knew, Lady Locksley," he murmured softly. "I wish to hell I knew," and he took a deep breath, walked over, picked up young Seth and held him close, then gazed down into his wife's dark eyes. "I have a terrible feeling, though, my love, that Lizette doesn't know the answer either," he said, and she winced at the worried look in his brilliant blue eyes.

Chapter 14

THE WIND WAS BRISK, air sharp and cold as the *Sparrow*, running later than they'd expected because of storms, generally foul weather, and a layover in Barbados to repair some sail and rigging, plowed through the foaming waters of the English Channel, nearing the Strait of Dover. It was one whole week past the new year of 1822 already, and Bain stood on the quarterdeck bundled up in a heavy coat, hat pulled down to his ears to ward off the icy spray. It had been warm even for November when they'd sailed out of Havana, but the farther north, the colder it got, and he'd wished more than once that he'd brought warmer clothes with him, or at least bought an oiled slicker in Barbados. Even his toes were cold inside the Wellington boots, and his nose felt numb. He rubbed it, then glanced across the deck toward the helm, where Eric was talking to the helmsman. At least Eric had his slicks to wear so he could keep his clothes dry. Bain's were still on the *Raven*, where they'd been since early summer when the *Raven* and her crew had dropped him off in Pennsylvania on his way to the ironworks.

He rubbed his hands together, then thrust them in his pockets and turned at a noise behind him.

"Ah, *buenos días*," he said as he watched Elena shut the door that led to the cabins belowdecks, then saw the involuntary shiver she made as she pulled the cloak she was wearing tighter around her against the bitter winter wind.

Her eyes studied him for a minute; then she looked off toward the horizon, seeing nothing but gray-blue water and knowing it'd be the same on both sides.

"It's a *horrible* day," she answered in Spanish, and his eyes darkened as gray as the clouds overhead as he answered her back in the same language.

"You didn't have to come, you know. It was your choice."

"Let's not go through that whole thing again." She walked over to the rail and looked down at the water and Bain continued studying her curiously.

Elena was an enigma. There were moments when she seemed so naively innocent, and yet at other times her subtle attempts at seduction could be classified as nothing less than experienced, and he'd wondered a number of times whether it was pure instinct on her part, or whether she'd had a lover or two since the last time they'd met, although she'd never mentioned anyone. He watched her now as she stood at the rail, her hair plaited in a single braid and wound against the back of her head, where it was secured with diamond-studded hairpins made of whalebone. She looked snug enough, yet her nose and cheeks were red from the cold.

She pulled the hood of her cloak up over her head, and a strange warmth shot through him as he remembered their first night aboard ship together. As it was, they'd ridden the forty miles to Havana in record time, only the *Sparrow* was far from ready to sail and it took at least an hour to round up everyone and make sure there were enough supplies on board.

So it was close to morning when the anchor was weighed, the sails unfurled, and she slipped from the harbor, heading for England. Elena had taken time to get more clothes from her uncle's house in Havana while he was rounding up the crew, and by the time they'd reached the open sea she'd changed from the costume she'd been wearing to a lovely silk nightgown and wrapper, the delicate peach color complimenting her dark hair and eyes.

He too had changed from his costume, only he'd been wearing the usual attire he always wore aboard ship. Boots, pants, and white shirt open at the throat, and he'd been standing near the capstan, watching the *Sparrow* ply her way toward the open sea, when she'd stepped up beside him, the warm breezes catching in her long hair that was loose now and hanging to her waist.

"I'm surprised we made such good time," she'd said, her voice dropping huskily, and he'd looked over at her, really seeing her for the first time since they'd come on board. It was still dark out, and moonlight was playing in her hair, reminding him of Liz, and an ache filled his whole being.

"I shouldn't have let you come. You know that, don't you?" he said.

She sighed. "Guilty conscience? Come on, Bain, you don't have anything to feel guilty about. At least not yet."

"But you wish I did, right?"

"Why not?"

"What happened to the young woman I used to know, Elena?" he asked.

Her gaze rested directly on his eyes. "She's been alone too long, Domino," she whispered softly. "Love does strange things to people. You should know that."

His eyes searched her face, then rested on the soft tawny flesh of her skin visible above the wrapper that didn't quite cover the top of the nightgown that concealed her small breasts, and it was hard not to remember the feelings he knew could be conjured up at the sight of their fullness. Her body was nothing like Lizette's luscious curves, but he couldn't deny that she was a woman, nor could his body, and the longer he was without Liz, the harder it was to deny himself. Especially when the temptation was practically thrown in his face. He breathed deeply.

"I can't give you what you want, Elena, you know that," he said, then tensed as she moved closer, her body touching his lightly.

"It isn't that you can't, Bain," she replied, and her eyes filled with longing. "It's that you won't, and you know it, and I think you're a fool. You heard Sancho, and yet you stay celibate while you know she didn't."

"She was forced."

"Forced? By Sancho? You don't know my brother very well, Domino." Her hand rested on his chest, her dark eyes pleading. "His men may rape women, but not Sancho, believe me. If he made love to her it was because she wanted him to, not because she was forced."

"That's not true, and you know it."

"Ah, but it is true. That was the way Sancho was. He was cruel, I know, and could be vicious at times, but even his men will tell you that he never forced women, he seduced them. No, Domino, if he made love to your Lizette, it was because she let him."

"You expect me to believe that?"

"Remember, *mi querido*, my brother wasn't always a pirate. At one time he was quite a cavalier and he knew how to treat women, even your Lizette." Her eyes softened. "How could she possibly blame you for wanting something she didn't deny for herself, and for the same reason, because she's human."

Bain was facing her and she leaned closer, her perfume filling his nostrils, the warmth of her body all too familiar, and he felt himself responding. My God, how long had it been? he thought, and a shiver ran through him.

"You see," she whispered sensuously. "You are human after all, Domino." Her hand moved up and she caressed his cheek. "Don't fight it, *mi querido,* please, don't fight it anymore." Her face tilted upward, lips only inches from his, and he swallowed hard, perspiration breaking out on the back of his neck.

She moved against him and a deep yearning shot through him, and before he realized what he was doing, his lips covered hers hungrily and his arms engulfed her, pulling her even closer. The kiss was deep, searching, its effect devastating as his whole body came to life, and he groaned helplessly. Then slowly, as if dredged from the depths of his soul, the memory of Lizette's soft body in his arms, so different from Elena's, began to war with his natural instincts and his head gradually began to clear, the passionate emotions that had been driving him only seconds before replaced by a feeling of dread at what was happening to him. Elena was right, he was human, and that was the trouble. Suddenly he remembered something and drew his lips from hers, gazing down into her languorous eyes.

"You never did say," he said breathlessly. "What was in that drink you knocked from your brother's hand back at the house?"

She sighed, and with his face shadowed, the moonlight behind him, she didn't realize the passionate moment was passing. "Cantharis," she murmured softly, then realized her mistake when she felt him stiffen.

"Spanish fly?" His arms eased from about her and he pushed her back, staring hard into her dark eyes, the moon full on her face. "You'd do that to me?"

"It's only a love potion."

"A love potion? Elena, it's a dirty trick to play on anyone." He looked disgusted. "And you thought I'd make love to you?"

"I wanted you to. *Por favor,* please, *mi querido . . .*" She hesitated, her eyelids lowering self-consciously. "I did not think it would hurt you . . . I only thought it would make you love me like the old woman said."

"What old woman?"

"The one who gave me the potion." She lifted her gaze again, searching his face. "*Por favor,* Domino, I am not experienced in the ways of love, I only know my heart tells me that it yearns for you."

"And you'd try any means to get me, right?"

"*Sí . . . no . . .* you must understand." She reached out, her fingers caressing his cheek. "It is painful to love and not have that love returned, Domino," she said, her voice hushed. "Especially when I know you would, if not for her, so forgive me if I have played the fool where you are concerned, Bain Kolter. But I do love you as much as she, if not more."

He stared down into her dark eyes and once more the innocence was there and it was hard to deny her.

"I'll make you a promise, Elena de Córdoba," he offered huskily. "One I hope I will never have to keep, but if the day ever comes when I feel that Lizette is no longer mine to love, I'll not deny you. Is it a bargain?"

Elena's heart leapt at his words, and yet she saw sadness in his eyes. "I will be here for you," she said, her voice breaking with emotion.

"In the meantime, give me room to breathe, Elena, *por favor,*" he said, his hands trying to ignore the feel of her velvety skin beneath them as he held her arms, setting her from him. "You don't want me this way. You know you don't, and all the coaxing in the world won't ever get me to change my mind. All it'd do is make us enemies, and I know you don't want that either, do you?"

So she'd agreed to abide by his wishes, only there were still those rare moments when she'd look at him, her eyes pleading, the yearning in them too strong to even mask, and intimate moments shared together that couldn't be erased from his memory, and through most of the trip he'd felt like a cad. Even now, as he stood quietly watching her standing at the rail looking so lonely, he couldn't help but feel sorry for her. Only it wasn't just his concern for her that bothered him, it was the fact that she had become special to him these past few weeks in a way he hadn't wanted her to.

Not special the way Liz was special, but they'd had their moments of fun along with the frustrations, and it was going to be harder saying good-bye than it had been the first time. He lifted his coat collar against the wind and spray, then sighed, wondering where the best place to start inquiring about Lizette would be, since London was such a big place. He knew her uncle lived somewhere nearby, but had no idea where. All he knew was the man's name, Teak Locksley, the Earl of Locksley.

By late afternoon they'd already sailed through the Strait of Dover into the North Sea and were well up the Thames River, nearing the London docks, only there were no berths empty, and Eric hailed Bain as they sailed in as close to shore as possible, trying to avoid the other ships at anchor.

"We'll have to drop her in midstream and row ashore," he said more as a question than a statement, and Bain nodded, his eyes scanning the harbor, taking in all the other ships, thick in the water.

"Only pick a good spot, if you can," he said. "We're going to have to put up at an inn now until morning unless we spend another night on board, and I don't really relish that. I'll be anxious to get started in the morning."

"Then I suggest we drop anchor here," Eric said. "It's not the best part of London, but it's where most of us stay when we're here. I know the landlords, and they're not apt to ask questions."

"Discretion, eh, old friend?" Bain replied.

Eric nodded. "It'd be a good idea under the circumstances. At least until we find out just which way the wind blows. After all, your wife was with de Córdoba, and we have no idea what the British might make of it."

Bain sighed. "I know, I've thought of that." He looked out across the water toward the streets that lined the docks, then gave Eric his orders. "Drop anchor here, then, and get out the longboats," he said after a few minutes. "And tell Elena we're going ashore."

Eric nodded, yelled orders to the men, then headed belowdecks, where Elena was gathering some clothes together to take with her, and within half an hour the longboats, with part of the crew from the *Sparrow* aboard, including Elena, Bain, Eric, and Waggs, were tying up at one of the landings along the river, where they ascended to street level by way of stairs built into the short landing pier.

Bain helped Elena up the steps, with Eric and Waggs close at their heels, then Eric hesitated while the rest of the crew tied up the longboats and joined them, bringing along the bags Bain, Eric, and Elena had packed, and Bain and Elena stood to one side while Eric gave the crew orders to spread out, be careful, and see what they could learn before meeting him at the Rooster's Head near Wapping in about three hours' time.

"That should give them enough time to discover if anyone knows anything," he said, and he sauntered over to Bain and Elena, after picking up their baggage and handing her traveling case to Waggs. "Well, are you ready, Bain?" he asked.

Bain took Elena's arm. "You know the way, friend," he said. "It's been a number of years since I've set foot in London, and I imagine it's changed a great deal since then."

Elena glanced over at Bain as they started making their way through the afternoon crowds. "You have been to London?" she asked in her stilted English.

"Once," he answered, his gaze darting from shop to shop while trying to take in everything at once. "Only it was years ago, before the war."

"He lets us handle this part of the business for him," Eric offered, and Elena looked over at Bain's *capitán*, aware once more, as she had been since the start of their journey, of the hostility he seemed to have toward her.

"You conduct his business here?" she asked.

"I do."

"And he's a shrewd horse trader too," Bain cut in seriously.

She frowned, picking the skirt of her turquoise dress and the edge of her cloak up so they wouldn't drag through some scummy debris as they turned a corner.

"What is this, 'horse trader,' you say?" she asked. "I have never heard it said."

"It means he knows how to wangle a good price for us, both coming and going," he explained in Spanish, and she smiled.

"Ah, *sí*," then once more she continued in English. "That is good for Señor Kolter, sir, and I thought you were only a ship's *capitán*, Señor Edelman."

Bain's eyebrows raised. "Only? You do him an injustice, Elena, and it isn't 'Señor Edelman,' either. I think by now you could call him Eric, don't you?"

They were nearing a building that had a sign in front with the head of a rooster on it, and she glanced at Eric as he stepped up, opening the door for her, and once more, as she had off and on during their sea voyage, she noticed how blue his eyes were. And they were so intense. He was really rather good-looking, she supposed, only no one could compare with Bain, not even his *capitán,* and she let Bain follow her in, then took his arm and all four walked to where the innkeeper was drying some mugs. Within minutes they were being escorted to some rooms upstairs at the back of the inn.

The innkeeper said there were only two rooms left, so Elena would take one, the three men the other, and now Elena and Bain headed for the room at the end of the hall after retrieving Elena's traveling bag from Waggs.

"This room should be a little better, for you," Bain said as he swung the door open for her. And it was. Bigger anyway, if not any better furnished. They were used to the river trade here at the Rooster's Head and each room had at least four rope beds, two chairs, and a dresser crammed into what should have been a single room. "Anyway, you'll have it all to yourself," Bain continued as he set her baggage down, then started to work at lighting the fire in the fireplace.

Elena sat on one of the beds, her nose wrinkling disdainfully, her cloak still hugged around her for warmth while he worked at the fireplace.

"What do we do now?" she asked in Spanish again, since there were only the two of them.

He blew on the straw and paper, trying to get the flints to take so the logs would catch, then glanced back at her. "I'll try to find Lizette."

"I know that," she remonstrated. "But how?"

"*Quién sabe?* I guess the first thing I'll have to do is locate her uncle."

"You said he is an earl?"

"*Sí.*" He finally saw flame burst forth and blew on it once more for good measure, then straightened as tongues of fire began to lick at one of the logs. "His title is the Earl of Locksley. At least I'm presuming she'd look him up once she reached here. That is, if the authorities let her."

"And how will you find that out?"

"By asking questions, I presume." He walked over and stood looking down at her. "Only you're going to have to stay here, I'm afraid, agreed?"

Her lips pursed stubbornly. "But I want to go with you."

"I've brought you this far, but the rest of the way I go alone."

A scowl deepened the disappointment in her eyes. "And if you find her, you will not return?"

"If I find her, we'll both return."

"To shame me?"

"To say good-bye and make arrangements for your return to Cuba." He reached out, she took his hand, and he pulled her to her feet, his eyes searching her face. "I'd never shame you, Elena," he said, his voice deep with feeling. "Nor would she."

"She hates me."

"Hates you? She barely knows you."

"Yet I saw hate in her eyes when we met. You told her of me, didn't you?"

"There was nothing to tell."

"Wasn't there?" Again her smile was silky, seductive, yet her eyes played the innocent. "For you, perhaps not. For me, what we shared then, and what we share now, is very much."

He let her words sink in; then his eyes narrowed. "I never asked you, Elena, what did you tell Liz when you were with her on board ship? I mean about us," he said.

She sighed. "The truth."

"As you see it, or as I saw it?"

"As it happened."

"Including what happened while we were waiting for Sancho?"

"I shouldn't have, should I?" she said, feigning the innocence she was so good at.

Bain stared at her, a sinking feeling settling inside him. How stupid he was. He should have realized there was no such thing as naiveté when the heart was involved, and he could just imagine what Lizette had thought. Still, she should know him well enough by now to know he'd never willingly jeopardize their love because of another woman. Yet he couldn't really blame Elena. As she pointed out, it was hard to love and not have that loved returned, and jealousy was a strong emotion. It could make a person do almost anything.

"All right, I can't undo what you've done," he said, his heart suddenly heavy. "But for God's sake, Elena, from here on in, don't interfere, *por favor*. If things don't work out between her and me, I don't want it to be because of you, *comprende?*"

She lowered her gaze from his face, and he saw tears at the corners of her eyes.

"I warned you before we left Cuba," he reminded her.

She nodded. "I know, but that doesn't make it any easier." She pushed him away and strolled to the only window in the dingy room and looked down into the narrow alleyway. The afternoon sun was already low on the horizon and the alley was in deep shadows. It would be dark soon. She turned again to look at him, seeing once more not Bain Kolter, businessman and husband, but Domino, a man with only a name and no memory, and she wanted to cry out her love for him, but knew it would be useless. The past two years hadn't changed him physically. He was still as ruggedly handsome, his muscular physique still honed to perfection, yet he wasn't really the same and she knew it. He had loved his wife before, and she had admired him for it, but now Lizette seemed to be more of an obsession with him. As if his life depended on her fidelity.

"It's too late today to go to the authorities, isn't it?" she asked.

He glanced behind her at the dark shadows outside, then checked his pocket watch. She was right. By the time he got to any of the government buildings to ask any questions, everyone would be gone for the day. Besides, he rather wanted to wait to see what the men might have found out. After all, word could sometimes spread fast on the waterfront.

"I guess you're right at that," he said, tossing the key to her room up and catching it, then gesturing toward the door. "So maybe it'd be a good idea, now while the room warms up, to go get Eric and Waggs and try to find something decent to eat. After all, I think we're all tired of dried beans, rice, and the rest of the ship's fare, don't you?"

Eric and Waggs were as anxious to get food in their stomachs as Elena and Bain, and since the Rooster's Head also served its customers, they quickly found a table at the back of the room and ordered roast beef, boiled potatoes, fresh bread, coffee, tea for Elena, and some ale for the men to wash down the plum pudding that went with the meal.

At first the conversation was sparse; then shortly after the food was served, one of the men Eric had sent out came in to join them and brought surprising news. From what he'd heard by eavesdropping and asking questions, word had traveled through the grapevine that Sancho de Córdoba's mistress had been captured in the Caribbean and brought to London on HMS *Pinnacle,* and rumors were circulating now that de Córdoba was dead.

"They say he was killed in a duel somewhere and his men took over the *Piranha.* Seems she was doing pretty good, too, until they ran into the *Enterprise* just north of Cuba, near the gulf, and took a few hits broadside. From what I heard, his first mate, a man named Jigger, and two of the other crew got away in the dark, though, and they were still hanging on to part of the debris from the *Piranha* a few days later when they were fished out by a British freighter on its way back home. They're in Newgate now, scheduled for execution the day after tomorrow."

Bain's appetite had started to leave him halfway through the man's recitation, and he held the knife in his hand, butter still on it, the slice of bread in his left hand only half-spread as he stared at the man. Parody was as reliable as they come, only Bain had a hard time believing it all.

"Where'd you hear this?" he asked, his gray eyes deepening keenly.

Parody motioned with his thick head of sandy hair, his hazel eyes steady on his employer. "There's a place about two streets over where most of the riffraff hangs out, and it didn't take no time at all to pick up the grumblings of the crowds. Seems most of them are glad the *Piranha*'s finally gotten her due." He glanced over at Elena. "Beggin' your pardon, *señorita,*" he apologized, "but there's them that sails, who didn't exactly welcome the sight of your brother's ship, and that goes for most honest seamen."

"There is no need to apologize to me, Señor Parody," Elena replied testily. "What my brother did was his affair, not mine. I was his sister, not his confessor."

Bain glowered at her. "He was only trying to be nice, Elena."

"Then forgive me my ignorance, *señor,*" she said to Parody, who nodded and smiled.

"So what do you do now, Bain?" Eric asked.

Bain didn't answer right away, but sat contemplating for some time, then finally took a deep breath. "I think I'll pay a visit to Newgate Prison," he finally said, and looked at Eric. "You'll go with me?"

"I think I'd better, after what happened in Havana. After all, there's no guarantee you won't bump into someone else who'll remember that you used to be Captain Gallant."

"God forbid. I wouldn't relish languishing in Newgate. El Morro was bad enough." Bain looked over at Waggs, set his silverware and bread down, then wiped his mouth off with the rough napkin he'd had covering his lap. "I'd like you to stay here and escort Señorita de Córdoba back to her room when she's finished eating, if you don't mind. Will you?" he asked.

Waggs agreed, only Elena wasn't too pleased.

"Perhaps I could go with you?" she suggested, but Bain was emphatic.

"Not to Newgate, Elena. Never to Newgate. You saw what El Morro was. Newgate's worse."

She frowned. "Then you will be careful?"

"I'm always careful." He smiled, a forced smile, but a smile, as he stood up. "Ready, Eric?"

Eric, who'd hurriedly finished his food while they'd been talking, stood up, grabbed both their hats from the back of their chairs, and handed Bain's to him.

"Don't forget the lid," he offered. "The street's even colder now with the sun down," and they bid good-bye to Elena, Waggs, and Parody, then left.

"You think she'll be all right with those two?" Eric asked once they were outside and headed toward the nearest street corner, hoping to catch a hack, although not too many frequented this neighborhood.

This time Bain's smile was genuine. "I think perhaps Elena is quite adept at taking care of herself," he answered. "Don't worry, she'll survive them." He glanced over at Eric. "You don't like her, do you?" he asked, surprising his captain.

Eric shrugged. "It's not that I don't like her, it's just . . ."

"Just what?"

"She's a schemer, Bain."

"So what woman isn't?"

Eric laughed. "Touché, my friend. But that's not the way I meant it, and you know it." He flushed. "She's in love with you, Bain, and dammit, I don't see how you're going to explain that fact to Lizette when you see her and still keep the peace."

"Maybe I won't have to," Bain answered, his voice deep with emotion. "That's why I'm going to Newgate."

Eric shook his head, then quickened his pace to hail a lone cab that was heading their way, hoping it was empty.

Eric had been past Newgate Prison a number of times during his stays in London, but never inside; however, he always seemed to get the same feeling of despair whenever he saw the place, and tonight was no exception.

It was dark already, the faint light from the keeper's house barely visible when the hack they were in pulled to the side of the road and let them off in front of the place. Bain paid the driver, then turned his attention to the building. It looked as morbid and uninviting as El Morro had, and he almost felt sorry for Sancho's first mate, Jigger, and frowned, trying to remember what the man looked like. If he wasn't mistaken, Jigger was a good deal shorter than most men, rather rough in looks and speech. Other than that, it had been so long ago since he'd seen him. He looked over at Eric as the hack pulled away.

"Ready?" he asked.

"As ready as I'll ever be."

"Good," Bain answered. "Then let's find out how we go about getting to talk to a condemned prisoner."

It didn't happen to be as difficult as Bain thought it would be, so he quickly discovered. All he had to do was come up with a healthy stipend, which he happened to have on him, and they were soon following the turnkey past the prisoners' chapel, through the open yards where half-frozen prisoners were huddled, hoping the cold fresh air would help heal their lungs from the damage the damp cells inside had done, and on to the back, where the condemned prisoners were kept.

"That's 'im over there, gents," the turnkey said when they reached the cells, and he pointed to the last cell at the far end of the room.

Bain gave the turnkey a few coins, following the keeper's earlier suggestion, requested he return to let them back out in about ten minutes, then he and Eric walked up to the bars of the cell after the turnkey had disappeared into another section of the huge stone building.

At first they couldn't see anyone in the narrow cell; then slowly, as their eyes became accustomed to the dim light from a whale-oil lantern on the far wall, they made out the vague outline of a man sitting on the floor with his back against the wall.

"Jigger?" Bain questioned, and he reached up, holding the bars, trying to see through them.

The voice that came out of the darkness was bitter and hard. "Who wants him?" Jigger asked.

Bain straightened, unsure just how the man would react. "Kolter," he answered. "Bain Kolter."

He heard a distinct intake of breath, then slowly the figure moved, and Jigger stood up. He was half-frozen, his feet felt numb, and he couldn't walk, yet managed to stand

"Kolter?" he echoed, and his voice vibrated ominously. "The bastard who killed Sancho de Córdoba?"

"If that's what you want to call me," Bain answered. "Yes."

Eric touched Bain's arm. "Be careful," he whispered. "He doesn't sound any too friendly."

"Who the hell's that?" Jigger asked.

"Captain Edelman, from my ship the *Sparrow.*"

"So you got a ship left—bully for you, Mr. Kolter. That's more than I got. 'Course I ain't gonna need one anymore, am I, since they'll be hangin' me day after tomorrow."

"I'm sorry about that, Jigger," Bain said, wishing he really meant it, only he couldn't seem to conjure up any sympathy for the man. "But there's nothing I can do about it, even if I wanted to."

"Which you don't?" Jigger shot back.

Bain stared at the man's hunched figure, barely visible in the dark cell.

"Would you expect me to?" he asked. "After what you and Sancho did to me? Come now, I'd be a fool not to hate you for it, wouldn't I?"

"Then what're ya here fer, mate? To gloat?"

"To find some answers," Bain replied, then one hand fingered the bars again. "I've heard rumors, Jigger. Rumors I don't like," he went on, choosing his words carefully. "And since you were there, I figure you'll know whether they're true or not."

"About what?"

Bain looked over at Eric, then back toward where Jigger was still standing, leaning against the cold slime-covered wall.

"About my wife and Sancho," he answered, and his voice was strained.

Jigger could see the silhouettes of Bain Kolter and his captain against the light from the lone lantern that hung in the corridor, and he felt a sense of hatred sweep over him. He smiled wickedly, only they couldn't see it. "You worried about her, mate?" he asked.

Bain inhaled sharply. "Will you answer me truthfully, please?"

"Why not?" Jigger answered. "What good would lies do now? Whatta ya wanna know?"

Bain swallowed hard and Eric leaned close. "You want me to ask him?" Eric offered.

Bain shook his head. "She's my wife." He fingered one of the bars again, then rubbed a hand over his beard. It needed trimming. "I have to know, Jigger," he began softly, hesitantly. "You were there. What went on between Sancho and Lizette?"

"You've asked her?"

"I haven't found her yet."

"But you'll ask her when you find her, right?"

"Yes. Only before I do, I'd like to hear what you have to say."

"Well, I'll tell you now, mate," he answered brashly, "I don't rightly know what all went on between them, since I didn't sleep in the cap'n's cabin on board ship, nor his hut on the island, how's that?"

"You're saying Lizette did?"

"I am."

"He forced her to?"

"That I couldn't say either, mate." His voice had lost the ring it once had to it, and he sounded weary, yet there was a harshness to it that couldn't be ignored. "But I'll tell you one thing. If he did, it was the first time I ever knowed of, and it sure didn't take much force either, because there weren't a mark on her. Not aboard ship nor when we was holed up. Fact is, they was pretty friendly fer a while there." He paused, then went on. "Anythin' else ya wanna know?"

"Sancho said she was pregnant."

"That why you killed him?"

"Was it his?"

"Could be, could be it ain't. She never said."

"And Sancho?"

Jigger shivered, feeling the slimy mass that clung to the wall of the cell dampening the back of the dirty shirt he had on, and he wished he could see Kolter's face, so he'd have some satisfaction for what he was about to say. Then he coughed. The cold had gotten to his lungs, but he guessed it didn't really matter. Not anymore.

"I'll tell ya now," he said, his voice gravelly, yet Bain was sure it held a note of insolence. "As far as me and the men was concerned, she belonged to the cap'n, and so did the kid, and he never denied it, so take it for whatever it's worth to ya."

Eric saw Bain stiffen. "He could be lying, Bain. I wouldn't put it past him."

"Why would I lie?" Jigger asked as he lowered himself toward the dirty floor of the cell again and tried to curl into a ball to keep warm. "I liked the lady. She was really somethin'."

Eric tried to see into the cell better. "You liked Sancho de Córdoba too, didn't you?"

"Aye, that I did, mate," Jigger answered thoughtfully. "He was the best I ever sailed with, but that don't change the way things was." He coughed again, then cleared his throat and spit into the wet straw that covered the floor. "Now, 'lessen you gents can get me outta this hellhole with a future ahead of me to look forward to, I ain't much fer entertainin' visitors and makin' small talk. She was his mistress, Kolter, plain as the nose on your face. I knew it, the men knew it, and if you don't believe it, that's yer problem, pure and simple."

Bain frowned, his gray eyes filled with dread. "You're sure?"

"No, I ain't sure. Hell, like I said, I didn't sleep with 'em. All I know is what I saw, and from what I saw, there weren't one man with us that didn't think the same."

"Come on, Bain, let's go," Eric said, and took Bain's arm, hoping to dissuade him.

Bain let Eric start to lead him away, then he turned back. "Thank you, Jigger," he said, as if it were an afterthought, then realized the turnkey had come back to show them out.

"Anytime, gents," Jigger called after them, then laughed contemptuously before going into a fit of coughing that lasted until Eric and Bain were out of sight.

Both men pulled their coats about them some minutes later as they left the keeper's quarters, and Eric looked over at Bain.

"I'll try to hail another hack," he said.

Bain shook his head. "Let's walk a bit first. I think I need some air."

They walked silently for about three blocks; then Bain stopped suddenly and stared straight ahead. "What would you do, Eric?" he asked, surprising his captain, and Eric frowned.

"You mean about Lizette?"

"I know you haven't been around her a lot to know what she's like, but . . ."

"Don't you trust her, Bain?" Eric asked.

"That's just it, dammit." He took a deep breath, then exhaled. He'd never told anyone about Lizette and Stuart, not even his family, but now the gnawing remembrance was haunting him like a festering sore and had been ever since this whole thing began. He wanted to trust her, but it was so hard.

"I don't know," he said simply.

Eric stared at him for some time; then they started walking again, slowly this time, both contemplating.

"Then why don't you wait until you've talked to her first before condemning her?" Eric finally said, shoving his hands in his pockets from the cold.

It was beginning to snow some, and the flakes looked delicate against the streetlamps.

"I guess you're right," Bain answered, his thoughts clouded by doubts. "But you see, Lizette's so vibrant, so alive."

"And she loves you."

"I know that."

"Then why the doubts, Bain? Just because Sancho wanted to get even with you for what he thought you'd done doesn't mean that what he said was true. Give her a chance to explain first. Besides, have you thought . . . what if she's already left England? After all, she must have been rescued over two months ago. If we hadn't lost all that time in Barbados . . ."

"You're right, I hadn't thought," he said, frowning. "She could be on her way back home by now. But if she is carrying a baby, she just might decide not to do any more traveling until it's born, and we don't know how far along she might be."

The wind was starting to kick up. "You want me to find us a ride now?" Eric asked, and Bain nodded. They were still a long way from the Rooster's Head and for some reason he suddenly felt tired.

Much to their surprise, when they finally reached the inn and entered, Elena and Waggs were still sitting at the table where they'd left them. Both men glanced at each other, then strolled over.

Bain looked at Elena. "I thought you were tired."

She smiled. "I am, but you have the key to my room, remember?"

"This place ain't fancy enough to have two keys," Waggs added.

Bain's hand went to his watch pocket, and he looked at all of them sheepishly as he pulled out the key.

"My oversight," he said, flushing from embarrassment, then held his hand out to Elena. "Well, come on, then. Since I've got the key, I might as well walk you up." He glanced at Waggs and Eric. "Our room locked?" he asked.

"Was last time I checked," Waggs answered. "You callin' it a night, sir?"

"Might as well, I have a feeling tomorrow's going to be a rough day. You coming?" he asked Eric.

Eric shook his head. "Think I'll have another ale." He reached in his pocket and pulled out the key to their room, tossing it to Bain, who caught it, even though the throw was unexpected. "You might as well take that." He looked at Waggs. "Join me?"

Waggs grinned. "Ever know me to turn down a drink, Cap'n?"

Bain winked at him. "Just make sure you don't try to outdrink each other," he said. "I might need some help tomorrow. Elena?"

She stood up, took his arm, and they headed for the stairs at the side of the room while Eric watched, a frown marring his features.

"What's the matter, Cap'n?" Waggs asked, his eyes on Eric.

Eric's frown deepened. "I'm not sure, Waggs, only I just don't trust that Spanish lady," he said. "Especially when she had a brother like Sancho de Córdoba."

"She's after Kolter, right?"

"And I don't think she cares how she goes about getting him."

Waggs too was frowning now as he drew his eyes from

Eric and watched Elena and Bain disappear from view up the stairs.

"Did you find out what you wanted to know?" Elena asked Bain as they walked to her door, reverting once more to Spanish.

"*Sí,*" he said. "At least, I think so. I don't know." He unlocked the door for her, then pushed it open.

She stepped inside. The room had warmed considerably with the logs in the fireplace still burning, and her cloak came off quickly. She tossed it onto the bed, then turned to face Bain, who was holding the key to her room out toward her.

"Your key, *señorita.*"

Her eyes found his and she felt a tingling thrill run through her. "Why don't you keep it?" she asked huskily.

He stared at her, not answering, and she walked toward him, stopping directly in front of him.

"Or maybe you'd like some coaxing," and she started to reach up, to pull his head down, her lips soft, inviting.

"Don't, Elena, not now," he murmured softly. "Not after what I heard tonight."

"Jigger told you about Sancho and Lizette."

"He told me."

"Yet you still don't believe."

"I can't, not until I've talked to her."

She backed away, her eyes bristling irritably. "Then talk to her," she said painfully. "And I will say I told you so when you come back and walk through this door to take me."

His hand moved out, touching her chin, tilting it up so he looked down into her face. She was angry at him for refusing her invitation again, yet he knew the anger dwelt only on the surface. Beneath the facade of anger was a yearning that he easily recognized.

"And if I don't come to take you?"

"You will."

His hand dropped from her chin and he took her right hand in his and put the key to her door in it.

"Then make sure you're here to open the door for me," he said intimately. "I'd hate to have to break it down."

"I would not mind," she answered, then suddenly stood on tiptoe, pulled his head down until her lips found his, and kissed him full on the mouth. "I hope you do find her tomorrow," she said breathlessly as she stepped back again, staring at him hungrily. "Because I don't know how much longer I can wait."

Bain stared hard at her for a few minutes, then turned and walked away without even saying good night, because he didn't trust himself anymore. You could say no just so long, and he didn't want to give in. Not yet, not until he'd talked to Liz. As he shut the door behind him and headed back down the hall toward the room he shared with Eric and Waggs, he suddenly felt a sense of loss because he knew that even if things didn't work out between him and Liz, Elena would be a poor substitute. And she'd be only that, a substitute, because no one could ever take Lizette's place in his heart.

By late the next morning Bain had not only learned that Lizette was still in England, but he had had Amigo brought ashore on a flat barge, bundled himself up against the weather, and was on his way out the King's Highway heading south from London toward Locksley Hall.

Chapter 15

LIZETTE WAS feeling miserable. She didn't have quite a month to go, according to her calculations, and although she certainly wasn't as big as she had been with the twins, she was carrying this baby straight out in front, and more than once had to catch herself from falling because of it. And she'd put a little of her weight back on too. Other than the usual burdens of pregnancy, though, she really had no reason to complain, because physically she was doing quite well. Her misery came from her decision that Uncle Teak was right. That she should stay until after the baby was born, and it had sent her general state of being into a sort of limbo.

She'd spent Christmas Day playing with Seth and Quinn, trying to keep her thoughts from Blythe and Braxton, only it didn't always work, and by the time the new year rolled around she was so lonesome for them that she sat down and wrote each of them a letter, slipping them into one she'd written to her mother and father. She'd also written to Grandma Dicia and Grandpa Roth. However, neither letter had been anything more than informative at this point. She'd keep the details until she could tell them in person. And even then there were things she'd never tell anyone. Maybe not even Bain. After all, how could she explain to Bain about some of the intimate things she'd shared with Sancho?

Even though she didn't love Sancho, she couldn't deny that she did have some feelings for him, strange as they were, and as she sat at the window seat in the parlor early one afternoon watching the snowflakes that had started the night before begin clinging to the grass and shrubs, she suddenly felt so alone. Just like she had the night Sancho had picked her up and carried her to his bed.

She had tried to explain to Aunt Ann and Uncle Teak about the cradle and the ring, had even tried to make them understand why telling the authorities about Elena, Mario, and Don Emilio wouldn't help, and she was sure she'd convinced them. At least they told her they understood, and they'd still been treating her the same way they had since she'd first arrived, but there were moments when she'd caught them watching her and had the uncomfortable feeling they were still trying to sort things out in their minds.

Well, there was no way she could force them to accept what had happened. Besides, she didn't have to account to anyone for her actions except Bain, and she was sure he'd understand. At least she hoped he would, and she had at least two months to decide just how she was going to go about telling him everything.

Reaching up, she redid one of the fancy combs that held back her dark curly hair, then picked up some knitting from the sewing basket beside her. Aunt Ann had lent her some needles, then given her yarn to use, and she had halfway finished a bunting to put the baby in for the trip home. She'd made other clothes too, at her aunt's insistence, and Ann had even helped.

She worked to the end of the row she was on, then glanced out the window again just in time to see a rider disappearing up the drive toward the front of the house. It looked like Uncle Teak was going to have company. Probably a belated birthday caller who'd missed the dinner party they'd had the other night celebrating his forty-third birthday. She hoped it wasn't Mr. Canning. He'd been out here again shortly before Christmas, and nothing had really been settled, so he'd threatened to come back.

Craning her neck as far as she could, she tried to see if she could still see the rider, but he was already out of sight, so she went back to her knitting, while out front Bain reined Amigo up to the ornate hitching post, dismounted and fastened the reins to the ring in the lion's head, then stood taking in his surroundings.

So this was Locksley Hall. He'd heard the story of Lizette's real grandfather's battle to claim the title so many times, and as he stood for a minute staring at the stone towers soaring high into the sky, snow blowing against them, and smelled the salt air from the Channel a short distance away, he could almost imagine how lovely it would be in the summer, and he could understand why Lizette's uncle liked it here.

He'd never met the earl, however, and he turned toward the heavy oak door that was at the top of the few stone steps in front of the place and looked at it with trepidation. Somewhere in that huge mansion of stone was Liz, and his stomach was full of butterflies. He'd waited so long to be with her again, and yet so much had happened.

Straightening solidly, he turned the collar of his coat back down so he looked more presentable, frowned as the cold snowflakes hit his neck, then started up the steps.

Teak was in the library when Wickham came, and he glanced up from the desk where he sat working.

"What is it, Wickham?"

"Beggin' your pardon, my lord, but there's a gentleman at the door says he's Mr. Bain Kolter. Should I show him in?"

"Bain here?" Teak's eyes widened as he stood up. "Yes, certainly, bring him in here, Wickham," he said, and slowly closed the ledger on the desk while he watched the butler leave.

Bain here? he thought, silently this time, and walked from behind the desk to wait. Bain must have gone home to South Carolina, discovered Liz was here, and headed over right away. Teak straightened, watching the door apprehensively. After all, he'd never met the man, although from what Liz had told him about Bain over the past few weeks, he felt sure he could probably pick him out in a crowd.

The door suddenly opened.

"Mr. Bain Kolter, my lord," Wickham announced haughtily, and Teak stared hard at the man who stepped into the room.

He was at least six feet tall, his short russet beard and mustache damp from the snow that had been clinging to them only moments ago, and he hadn't as yet removed the greatcoat he was bundled into, although the hat he'd been wearing was in one hand, leaving the other free. He stepped forward, holding his free hand out, his gray eyes studying Teak.

"I'm afraid I've never been schooled in the proper way to greet an earl, sir," he said uneasily. "Will a handshake do?"

"It'll do fine," Teak answered, and was pleased at the firm grip his niece's husband extended. "Here, let me take your coat," Teak offered, and Bain flushed.

"I guess I was in a hurry." He wriggled from the heavy greatcoat, revealing a lighter frock coat in a shade of deep green that brought out the red highlights in his dark walnut hair.

Teak took Bain's coat and hat, set them on a chair, and there was an awkward moment of silence as neither man spoke; then finally Bain couldn't contain himself any longer.

"Where is she, sir?" he asked.

Teak pondered his question for a minute; then, "You look cold," he said. "Maybe you'd better warm up with a drink first."

Bain's eyes darkened suspiciously. "All I want is to see my wife."

"And you shall. I only thought it might help you relax some. Contrary to how you probably think you feel, I'd say you are no doubt carrying a few extra knots in your stomach about now. Am I right?"

"Even if I were, drink wouldn't help, sir. She's all right, isn't she?"

"You read the letter I wrote to my mother?"

Bain shook his head. "I didn't read anything."

"You mean you haven't been home?"

"Home? No, why?"

Teak frowned. "Then how did you know Lizette was in England?"

"De Córdoba."

"You saw de Córdoba?"

"I did."

Teak was taken by surprise. "And you talked to him?" he asked.

"Before running him through, yes," Bain answered. "He told me she was on her way to England, and he told me she was pregnant, and I killed him. Now, where's Liz?"

Teak took a deep breath as he stared into Bain's face, surprised to hear him state so casually that he'd killed a man. Even a pirate. Yet there was something he liked about Bain, a firmness, a rugged honesty, but would he be willing to forgive? He wondered.

"She's in the parlor, I'll take you to her," he said, and Bain sighed.

"Thank you, sir."

Teak gestured toward the door, and they left the library. Locksley Hall was huge, and Bain couldn't get over a feeling of being dwarfed by its massiveness. Even now as they walked down what he assumed was the main corridor, he felt overwhelmed by it, and when Teak gestured him into the sitting room, for a minute he was so busy looking around at the tapestries and relics from the past that he didn't see Lizette, who was still sitting on the window seat knitting.

She turned toward the doorway at the sound of footsteps, and suddenly her face paled at the familiar stance of the man who was standing next to her uncle. The knitting dropped from her hands, her feet touched the floor, and at that moment Bain caught sight of her too.

For a brief second Bain felt like he was dreaming as he stared toward the window seat at the lovely but very pregnant woman who was reaching toward him. Her blue-black hair was curling riotously about her head, and the soft flowing pink dress she had on brought out a deep, near-bluish tint to her emerald eyes, which were wide with wonder.

How long he stared, he had no idea; then slowly his feet began to move forward, and with a groan wrenched from deep inside him, he reached her, pulled her into his arms, and held her tight, afraid to let go.

"Oh, God," he murmured breathlessly against her hair. "I thought I'd never see you again," and he drew his head back, looked deep into her yearning eyes, and Teak turned away, leaving the room, as Bain's mouth came down on Lizette's in a long, luxurious kiss that held all the magic for both of them that had always been there.

Lizette clung to him desperately, loving the familiar feel of him beneath her hands; then, when he finally drew back, she stared up at him, her breath caught in her throat.

"I was just thinking of you," she finally managed to say, a hand reaching up to touch his face, and he reached for her hand, holding it tightly, and kissed the fingertips while he searched her face, his eyes scanning the familiar lines he knew only too well. He thought she'd be much thinner from all she'd been through, but then realized she'd been here for well over a month already.

"It really is you, isn't it?" he whispered.

She nodded, her eyes filling with tears; then she smiled, and the warmth in that one smile dug its way deep into his heart as it always did.

He kissed her again, softly this time, with a deeper longing, then finally straightened. There was so much that had to be said. His arms eased from her as he realized her stomach was in the way, and he didn't want to hurt her.

"You're all right?" he asked.

"I am now." She saw him glance down at her stomach and flushed. "Who told you?" she asked. "Uncle Teak?"

"No." A coldness suddenly crept into his eyes and she felt him drawing away from her. Not physically, but emotionally. "Sancho told me," he answered, and saw the puzzled look on her face. "I was waiting for him to return to his uncle's place in Cuba, and he finally showed up."

"He told you I was pregnant?"

His eyes darkened. "He told me everything, Liz."

"What do you mean, everything?"

"You should know. You were with him." His eyes snapped irritably. "What was it, Liz, Stuart all over again?" he asked.

"That's not fair!" The wonder of their brief moment of joy at seeing each other again was quickly fading, and she pushed him away, his accusation tearing into her. "He told you the baby was his, didn't he?" she said, and knew by the look on his face she'd guessed right. "That bastard! And you believed him?"

"Well, you weren't pregnant when I left."

"Wasn't I?"

"Not that I know of."

"I was going to tell you when you got home."

He frowned, his eyes guarded. "Why didn't you tell me before I left?"

"Because I didn't know then."

He stared at her, his thoughts running over all the things he'd heard these past few weeks. All the rumors, and Jigger's statement that verified Sancho's confession.

"I wish I could believe you, Liz," he said, his face grim. "But there's been so much."

"Like what?"

"You can't deny Stuart, so how do I know it wasn't the same with Sancho?"

"I told you nothing happened between me and Stuart. Not this last time, anyway."

"Liz, I married you to give Stuart's baby a name, remember?"

"I thought it was because you loved me."

"I did . . . I mean, I do—that's why I could forgive you."

"How nice of you."

"That's not how I meant it."

"Isn't it? Yes, I turned to Stuart once because you weren't there when I needed you, and I would have turned to him again when I thought you were dead, except for Julia. But it's always been you, Bain, and you know it. Always."

"Then why can't you ever wait for me?"

"I did!"

"Did you?" He glanced down at her stomach again. "If you'd been raped, I could understand, Liz, but every cutthroat from here to the Caribbean swears you were his mistress. Even Jigger confirmed it."

"Jigger? What does he know?"

"He was there too, you know."

"So was I, and I say it's a lie!"

"Why would he lie?"

"He'd do anything for Sancho."

"Even when he's staring death in the face?"

"What do you mean?"

"Then you didn't know he was in Newgate Prison in London?"

"I . . . I had no idea. No one said a word."

"They were to hang him this morning."

Her face paled. "And Sancho?"

"He's already dead."

She stared at him dumbfounded, a vision of Sancho de Córdoba's strapping body dangling from the executioner's scaffold popping into her head, and tears filled her eyes.

"They executed him?"

"On the contrary, I killed him."

She stared at him in disbelief. "You? Why?" Her fist rested on her stomach. "Because you thought he did this?"

"Because he'd have killed me if I hadn't."

"No." She shook her head. "Once yes, but not now."

"Why is now different?"

She inhaled sharply, her voice lowering. "Because he said he wouldn't, that's why."

"I see. You asked him not to, so just like that he wouldn't, is that it?"

"That's not it . . . it wasn't like that."

"Then how was it, Liz?" His gray eyes were steady on her, trying to read her thoughts, but he couldn't. "How is it that Mr. Canning back in London told me Sancho gave you an expensive ring you sold so you'd have money to come out here, and why did the men who raided Sancho's island that night tell me you were in Sancho's arms when they first spotted you? I talked to them, and they'd have no reason to lie. And why would de Córdoba give you a cradle for a baby he didn't father? Men like de Córdoba don't do things like that."

"I don't know!"

"He taunted me with it, Liz. He said you gave yourself willingly."

"It's not true."

"You slept together?"

"In the same hut, yes, but not together."

"Never together?"

She straightened, her hand still on her stomach, the baby's nearness giving her strength, and her fingers pressed it firmly. "A few times he held me in his arms and it was comforting, yes, because I was alone, Bain. But that's all he did. Held me."

"You expect me to believe that?" Bain sneered. "I suppose he never kissed you either."

She felt her stomach constrict. "I didn't say that."

"Didn't, or can't?"

"All right, can't," she shot back. "I didn't want him to, but he's bigger than I am, remember?"

"Oh, I remember de Córdoba. I remember the man very well, Lizette. Maybe that's the trouble. I remember him too well. They may have called him Sancho the Bloody, but he was a handsome devil and you started crying when you thought he'd been hanged. Why?"

"Because he was who he was, I guess . . . how should I know?" She drew her gaze from his angry eyes and turned to the window for a moment before turning back to him. "Remember, he wasn't just a name to me, Bain," she said, facing him again. "I was with him for three months. To me he became a human being, a person."

"And you cared for him, didn't you?"

"Yes, I cared," she answered. "I didn't love him, no, but I cared."

"Sometimes I wonder if you really know what love is, Liz," he said, the timbre in his voice deepening. "You bend so easily with the wind. First Stuart, now this. . . ." His eyes sparked angrily. "Dammit, why, Liz?" he pleaded. "Why couldn't you just hate him like any other woman would?"

"Because he wouldn't let me!" she cried, and threw her hands up helplessly. "But you wouldn't understand that, would you? He wasn't what the world thought he was. He was, but he wasn't!"

"He was a vicious pirate who kidnapped my wife and got her pregnant."

"I told you, the baby's yours."

"Prove it!"

She flinched. "My word's not good enough?"

"Not this time, because even the world says different."

"Because he wanted it that way, don't you understand? He wanted the world to believe it to get back at you." She stared at him, hoping and praying and waiting to see some warmth in his eyes again. There was none. "Besides, he figured if his men thought I belonged to him, they'd leave me alone."

"Then he had to love you, didn't he?"

"All right!" Tears of frustration rolled down her cheeks. "So he loved me. At least he said he did, so condemn me for it. But I couldn't stop him from loving me, could I?"

"No, I guess you couldn't," he answered, bitterness in his voice. "Just like you couldn't stop Stuart from loving you either, could you?"

"Oh, Bain!"

He shook his head, his insides twisting violently. "I can't do it, Liz. I just can't," he said roughly. "Not again. I married you to give Stuart's baby a name, you know that, but at least we were the only ones who knew it, but I won't be made a laughingstock now and take you back just to give de Córdoba's bastard a name when all the world knows the truth. I love you, yes, I've always loved you, but I'm not that big a fool."

A sob broke from deep inside Liz, and she gulped back tears, trying not to lose control completely as she stared at the man she'd loved so very much for so long. He didn't believe her, and there didn't seem to be any way to convince him otherwise. Sancho had done his work well, and she cursed him silently.

"Then I guess there's nothing more to be said, is there?" she replied tearfully.

"If he'd forced you, then maybe I could understand," he said hesitantly. "But he didn't, did he?"

"No, he didn't," she answered truthfully. "Sancho never

raped ladies," she went on, echoing de Córdoba's words. "And he said I was a lady."

Their eyes met, and for a brief moment she hoped; then he straightened stubbornly, staring at her, wanting to believe her, yet remembering all too well the past and the doubts it dredged up again, as well as the talk being bandied about now, along with Sancho's taunting words. Words that Jigger had put truth to.

"I'm sorry, Liz," he said, hating himself for the hurt in her eyes, yet feeling too betrayed to forgive again. "But I can't ignore the facts. Even Elena said her brother never forced women, and now you just confirmed it."

"So you think that means I let him make love to me?" Tears welled up in her eyes again, and she felt defeated. "Oh, Bain! All right, go ahead then, believe what you want," she said. "You will anyway, just like you did when you shot Stuart. Only just remember, I told you the truth then, and I'm telling you the truth now. Sancho de Córdoba never touched me."

He was still staring at her, wanting the doubts to go away, yet knowing they'd never quit tormenting him. "I wish I could believe you," he said huskily. "Oh God, Liz, do you think I want this?"

Her eyes narrowed furiously. "I think Elena wants it," she answered, and saw him flush. "Then you did bring her with you, didn't you?" she said, knowing she'd hit on the truth. "Where is she, Bain, back in London waiting for you, or tucked away in some nearby inn?"

"What are you getting at?"

"Don't be an ass, Bain, I'm not that gullible either," she said. "You've been with Elena practically the whole time while I've been gone, haven't you? Don't worry, I read Grandma's letter about your being in Cuba."

"I was waiting for you."

"Waiting for me? Ha! Don't make excuses, Bain. I've met Elena, remember?" This time the anger was in her eyes. "She told me all about Barlovento, and how you made love to her while you were there."

"She told you I made love to her?"

"She did."

"I didn't touch her."

"Not even a kiss?"

His face turned crimson.

"Aha! I knew it." Lizette was furious. "And you're accusing me!"

"I don't have to accuse you, the world's done it for me."

"Fine!" she yelled. "Then go back to your little dark-eyed bitch, because that's what she is, Bain, a bitch. Oh yes, she made sure I knew all about you and her just as soon as she had the chance, but you see, I was loyal, and I didn't believe her, Bain. At least not at first—but now . . . tell me, is she as good in bed as her brother was, Bain, or do you think I could teach her a few things?"

Bain's eyes flashed, the cords on his neck tightening, and he stared at her hard. "So, I was right after all, wasn't I?" he said savagely. "He did make love to you. For all your denials, the truth finally comes out."

"Well, that's what you wanted, isn't it?" she raged recklessly. "My confession of guilt so you could ease your conscience? Well, now you've got it, Bain Kolter, for what it's worth." Tears were close to the surface again, but she held them back. "So now you don't have to feel guilty for Elena de Córdoba, do you, any more than I have to feel guilty about Sancho. And don't you worry, my dear husband, I won't ever ask you to accept this child as yours. I'd rather die first."

Bain couldn't believe he was hearing right. She was actually admitting what she'd been denying so vehemently. He studied her face, flushed beneath the tan that was starting to fade, and his eyes saw only what he'd expected to see, hostility and anger. The same hostility he'd seen once before when she told him she hated him that morning three years before when he'd dueled with and shot Stuart. The same defiance she'd asked him to forgive and forget later when she'd come after him to make amends, and suddenly he wanted to hate her for what she was doing to him. To lash out at her for betraying their love.

"Good," he cried through clenched teeth. "Because I wouldn't accept it as mine anyway, not in a million years!"

"Then go," she yelled heatedly. "Get out of here! Go to your Spanish whore and let me be. I don't need you, I don't need anyone anymore, I never did!" She picked up her skirt and brushed past him, hurrying toward the front hall and the stairs, hoping she could reach them before he saw the tears that were flooding down her cheeks now.

Bain stood motionless, watching her go, then reached out

as if to go after her, only something inside him warred with his instincts, and instead his hand slowly dropped and he watched her small figure disappear into the vast corridor of the huge stone mansion; then the room grew silent. He stared, his breathing heavy, the pounding of his heart echoing in his ears, the last words she had flung at him hanging in midair like a phantom, reminding him that she was gone, and suddenly anger began to stir in him again. Anger and disbelief. She'd lied to him and tried to make him think the child was his. Damn her!

His gaze left the doorway, and he turned, shifting it to the window seat. He reached over, picking up the bunting Lizette had been knitting, and stared at it, letting the full fury of her betrayal sweep over him.

"Damn you, Liz!" he murmured under his breath. "Damn you for doing this to me," and he threw the knitting across the room, not caring where it landed, then headed back toward the library to retrieve his coat and hat.

Teak was at his desk again and he glanced up as the door opened and Bain strode in.

Instinctively Teak knew something was wrong. "Bain?" he questioned hesitantly.

Lizette's husband stalked to where his greatcoat lay across the chair, snatched it up, and began shrugging into it. His eyes were dark and stormy, his face like granite as he buttoned the coat, then reached for his hat.

"I'm sorry, my lord. I guess that's the proper address—am I right, sir?" Bain said as he looked over at him. "But I guess I just don't have a wife anymore, do I?"

Teak inhaled, shocked at the unexpected words. "I . . . I don't understand. The two of you—"

"The two of us?" Bain laughed. "There is no more 'two of us,' my lord," he said abruptly. "And you knew it all along, didn't you?"

"I . . . ?"

"Oh, come now, sir. There's no need to lie or pretend anymore, the truth's out," Bain went on. "That's why you were so reticent to take me to her when I arrived, isn't it? You knew all along the baby wasn't mine."

"But she said—"

"Did she? Then ask her again, sir, and maybe this time she'll tell you the truth like she told me. Now, good day," and he jammed his hat on his head, left the library, and hurried out the front door without even looking back, and if he had looked back, he'd have seen a very perplexed earl standing in the foyer, staring after him, trying to make some sense out of what was happening.

Teak moved to the window beside the huge oak door, its slamming still echoing in the foyer, and he watched Bain Kolter untie his horse's reins from the hitching post, mount him, turn the collar of his coat up against the wind, and start down the drive; then Teak turned and headed down the corridor, looking for Lizette, but she wasn't in the sitting room. He found her a few minutes later in her bedroom staring out the window watching the lone figure of her husband disappearing into the stormy afternoon, snowflakes swirling about him, shrouding him like some strange illusion that wasn't really there, and his heart went out to her.

She hadn't responded to his knock, but he'd come in anyway, somehow sensing that her thoughts were miles away. He stared at her now. She looked so lost and alone, and he hoped he could help. Stepping up behind her, he followed her gaze out the window.

"What happened, Liz?" he asked.

She trembled, her eyes still misty, making it hard to see, yet she knew the blurred speck in the distance was Bain riding out of her life.

"He didn't believe me, Uncle Teak," she answered, her voice shaky. "I told him the truth and he didn't believe me. He didn't want to believe me."

"Nonsense." Teak's blue eyes studied the back of her head. So many times she reminded him of his mother when she was younger. "He came for you, didn't he?" he said. "Why wouldn't he want to believe you?"

"Why?" She sniffed and he knew she was crying. "He has Elena de Córdoba, that's why," she answered. "He doesn't have to believe me."

"You don't mean that."

She could no longer see Bain, and turned from the window, facing her uncle. "He's gone, isn't he?"

Teak frowned. "Bain said you told him the child wasn't his."

"It was what he wanted to hear."

"It was the truth?"

"No."

"Then why?"

"I told you—he doesn't want me anymore. He has Elena. He even brought her to England with him."

"That doesn't mean he doesn't want you."

"Doesn't it?" Her eyes still glistened with tears. "He didn't come to take me home, Uncle Teak," she explained tearfully. "He came to make sure the rumors about my being Sancho's mistress were true, that's all. Oh God, I thought he loved me, Uncle Teak. But he didn't even care enough to believe me. It was as if he wanted the lies to be true, and I know it's because Elena's become his mistress. I had to be guilty of the same thing, don't you see—that way he can justify his own betrayal."

"Lizette, you can't know that."

"Can't I? Then why wouldn't he believe me? Why was he so quick to accuse? His mind was already made up before he got here. All he really wanted was to have it confirmed."

"I can't believe that." He reached out, his fingers touching her chin, tilting her head so he could look into her eyes. "You still love him, don't you?"

"More than anything in the world."

"Then why don't I go after him and bring him back, Liz? Maybe I can make him understand."

"No." She reached up, holding his hand and thanking God that Teak Locksley was no longer the angry, vindictive man he used to be. "It wouldn't do any good," she said, glad to be with him now, for he was a strong, warm man and gave her strength. "If he wouldn't believe me, he won't believe you." She squeezed his hand. "No, Uncle Teak, I have to face it, he just doesn't love me anymore." Teak, knowing what she needed most now was security, folded her into his arms and held her close, his gaze shifting to the window again to stare down the drive in the hopes that Bain Kolter would decide to change his mind and come back for her, yet knowing he was probably asking for a miracle.

Bain's hands were somewhat warmer in the gloves he'd bought the afternoon before after leaving Locksley Hall, but his toes were still cold in the Wellington boots and his cheeks above the clipped beard felt numb. He clenched the reins tighter, his free hand moving up to press some warmth into his face as he rode along; then he tried to huddle into a more compact position to get warmer. Except for the cold that he couldn't ignore, he'd paid little attention to his surroundings ever since leaving Locksley Hall the day before, his mind still on the conversation he'd had with Lizette, and no matter how many times he went over it, he still had a hard time accepting what had happened.

Even last night when he'd stopped at an inn, it had been the same. He'd dozed occasionally, yes, but with every waking moment, as he stared into the flickering shadows from the fireplace in the room he'd rented for the night, the agony of what he was going through was there before him like a firebrand searing into his heart and bringing a physical ache to his chest.

And yet more than once he'd almost turned back as he rode down the drive and away from those stately Norman towers. But every time the thought began to nag at him to just forget the whole damn thing and take her in his arms, he'd remember what she'd said, and the words would goad him on, making him spur his horse even harder, anger and frustration driving him until he knew he couldn't go back. Not now, not ever. He'd forgiven her once too often, and God help him, he couldn't do it again. Not this time. Not with the whole world looking on.

It was late in the day and he was nearing London already, the tops of buildings clear on the horizon, the stench of the city beginning to mingle with the clean crisp air that swirled the still lightly falling snow ahead of him on the partially frozen muddy road, and yet he was still oblivious to it all. Lizette had been his whole world ever since that first day he'd laid eyes on her when she was just barely fifteen, a saucy tempestuous girl with emerald eyes that talked to him as none had ever done before, and a smile that tore into his very soul and made him love her in spite of himself.

And he did love her, even now, with all that had gone before and now this. He still loved her.

"Damn you, Liz," he cursed softly to himself as he reined his horse around a carriage, moving past it at a brisk canter. "Why did you let this happen?" and once more he felt the outrage of her betrayal, gnawing doubts again beginning to prick at his already weakened faith in her, and he wondered if maybe he'd been too quick to forgive back then too. After all, he had only her word that she and Stuart hadn't become lovers again. What if she'd been lying then as she'd first tried to lie her way out of this now? Had he been a fool all these years? He probably would have believed her now too if she hadn't been pregnant. After all, Julia had been so sure. What a stupid fool he'd been. Liz wasn't his. Not the way he wanted her to be. She didn't need him. Not the way he needed her. For her it seemed anyone would do. For him love wasn't love without Liz.

Or was it? He'd doted on her so long, telling himself that no one could ever take her place, that only she could still the ache inside him, and now suddenly as he rode along, deeper into the city, its raucous noise beginning to penetrate his thoughts, he began to wonder. Had he been wrong all these years? Was love really what made it so good with Liz, or had he been fooling himself all along into only thinking it was better? Maybe he didn't really need her after all. Maybe life could be just as full without her. After all, the world was full of women, just as it was full of men, and she'd proved to him that any man would do, hadn't she?

His jaw tightened and he shook his head to clear away the thoughts that had been holding him prisoner on the long ride in from Locksley, then looked around, finally taking his bearings and studying the streets and buildings he was passing to make sure he was heading in the right direction. The sun had been absent from the sky all day, and now even the light was fading quickly, so it would be dark by the time he reached the Rooster's Head. He slowed his horse, remembering something he'd forgotten. Elena was at the Rooster's Head, and she was waiting for him.

He swallowed hard, aware of the feelings of guilt that were already beginning to nibble at his conscience along with the feelings of expectation that he'd felt at the thought of Elena, and he clenched his teeth, trying to fight them. He had no reason to feel guilty, dammit. He'd tried. He'd gone after Liz, hadn't he? And he'd wanted to believe her. It wasn't his fault she'd given herself to Sancho, it was her fault. All her fault, and he had no reason to feel guilty. She didn't need him; well, then, he didn't need her either, and he'd prove it. He'd prove it could be just as good without her, and she could go to hell. Sancho's bastard! What kind of fool did she think he was anyway?

He squinted, a short while later, suddenly realizing that he'd reached the Rooster's Head, yet barely remembered the last few miles he'd ridden, with anger at himself and the fool he'd played all these years driving him on.

He reached the inn and dismounted, walking around the

corner to the livery, and handed Amigo's reins to the man in charge, then headed back toward the front door of the place. It was a little more crowded than it had been four days ago when he'd left, and his gaze sifted over the room, spotting Eric and Waggs at a table in the corner. He walked over, hat in hand, brushing the snow off it, and began unbuttoning his coat.

"Where are the rest of the men?" he asked, and Eric, who hadn't seen him come in, jerked his head, startled, then frowned at the hard cold look in his friend's eyes.

"You just get back?" he asked, glancing behind him to see if anyone was with him.

"Don't worry, I'm alone," Bain snapped, then asked him again, "Where are the men?"

"All over, around. I guess I can round them up if you need them."

"Good." Bain inhaled deeply as he straightened. "We'll sail in the morning," he went on, ignoring the puzzled look on Eric's face. "See to it the ship's ready. It's a long way to Cuba."

"You taking the lady home?"

"Maybe," Bain answered. "And then maybe I'd just like to go there. Any objections?"

Eric's eyes darkened as he studied Bain. The man was ready to explode. "No, no objections," he said, then glanced at Waggs before turning back to look at Bain. "I'm just surprised you're leaving so soon, that's all. I thought maybe you'd be staying awhile."

"Unfortunately, there's nothing for me to stay for, Captain Edelman," Bain answered. "Now, if you'll excuse me, I'm tired. Do you have the key to the room?"

"It's open," Eric offered. "We figured there wasn't much anyone could steal."

"Then I'll go on up." Bain reached in his coat pocket and pulled out some coins, tossing them to Waggs. "Here, Waggs," he said as he started to turn away. "Amigo's in the livery. See they get paid and make sure he's aboard in the morning before we sail, all right?"

"Right, sir," Waggs echoed, and without another word, Bain kept walking and disappeared up the stairs.

Waggs looked at Eric, who was frowning, and Waggs was sure he knew why.

"I guess it didn't go too well, huh?" he asked, watching the captain closely, and Eric sighed.

"I'm afraid we're in for one hell of a trip, my friend," Eric answered, shaking his head warily. "I've known Bain Kolter for a long time, but I don't think I remember ever seeing him in a mood like that. Yes, sireee, I think we're in for a bad one," and he took a big long gulp of the drink in front of him, then ordered another.

Bain had ascended the stairs slowly, and now he moved down the hall like a snail, his steps faltering while his thoughts played havoc with his conscience. At first when the idea crossed his mind he'd done like he'd always done and rejected it without question, but then slowly, as the feeling of betrayal took root more deeply, the idea became even stronger, until now it was no longer just an idea, but something he knew he had to do to prove to himself that he was still a man. That he didn't need Liz to feel, to know the fulfillment a woman's body could bring him, and the nearer he came to the door to Elena's room, the more certain he was that she could be the one to rescue him from the prison Liz had been keeping him in for so long. A prison of his own making, true, but no less a prison than any other, capable of sucking the lifeblood out of a man and leaving only the shell.

He stopped, staring at the door to Elena's room for a long time, still unable to completely shake off the knowledge that what he was about to do was wrong, and his stomach tightened, sending waves of apprehension through him. Only he wasn't about to listen, not anymore, and without giving himself time to change his mind, he reached up to knock, then inhaled, startled as he heard the key turning in the lock. The door opened and Elena stood facing him.

"I was at the window and saw you take your horse to the livery," she said in Spanish.

All Bain could do was stare. She was wearing a wrapper of pink silk that hugged her body so closely he could tell it was the only thing next to her skin, and her hair was plaited into one huge braid down her back, the wispy hairs at the side of her face held back with fancy combs. In the flickering light from the lamp in her room, she reminded him of Liz as she'd looked the last time he'd seen her, at Locksley Hall, and the memory was painful.

Now he knew more than ever that he had to get over Liz. That he had to prove he didn't need her, and yet it had been so long since he'd made love to any woman other than Liz. He couldn't even remember who it might have been or what it had been like. All he knew was that with Liz it had been a taste of heaven.

He took a deep breath, his gaze settling on Elena's face, and forced himself to think only of here and now and the woman before him. His voice was low as he stepped into the room, closed the door behind him, and looked down into her eyes. "I told you if I came back alone, I wouldn't deny you," he said huskily, and saw her quick intake of breath.

"Oh, Domino!"

Her lips parted, one hand moving up to rest on the lapel of his greatcoat. "I knew you would come to me, *querido,*" she said softly, and he sighed.

"You're sure?" he asked.

She nodded. "I am sure," and he peeled off his greatcoat, threw it and his hat on one of the beds, following it closely with his frock coat, then began unbuttoning his shirt.

"Here, let me help," she begged, and her hands caressed his chest as she worked with the buttons, opening each one slowly, deliberately, and kissing the flesh beneath it.

Each time her lips touched him, Bain flinched, the sensation unnerving as he felt it clear to his toes, and he leaned forward, his lips brushing her cheek, and he nibbled at her ear.

Her fingers tightened on his shirt button and she closed her eyes, savoring his nearness and basking in the warmth from his lips against her ear, and she groaned.

"Don't stop, *por favor, mi* Domino," she murmured breathlessly. "Give to me now what you have promised would be mine," and stubbornly ignoring the conscience that had always held him back before, Bain reached down, picked her up, and walked to one of the beds with her, setting her down gently, his hands fumbling with the front of her wrapper until it fell away; then his hands ran down her body feverishly, searching for the soft pliable mounds of flesh they were so used to, only instead he was caressing tight skin over hard bone, her ribs rigid beneath his fingers, her breast lost in his sinewy hand, the nipple hard, yet so small his tongue barely found it.

Bain tried to pretend it didn't matter, that it was still the same as he buried his face between the two small mounds, his tongue touching her skin lightly, and again she moaned.

At least she was enjoying it. This was ridiculous, he thought, and even more determined than ever, he closed his eyes, moving his hands down her body again as his mouth covered hers, and he kissed her with an urgency born out of fear. Fear that he'd discover he was wrong as his hand slid over her hipbone, then dipped into its concave hollow.

His lips left hers, and he straightened quickly, then got to his feet and unfastened his breeches, determined now to keep going. She was a lovely woman, and he was a man, and that's all that was needed, wasn't it? His pants hit the floor, and he stepped from them eagerly, then kicked off his boots, followed closely by his underwear, and he lay down on his stomach beside her, looking into her dark eyes. They were warm and languid, her face flushed with longing, and he bent over, kissing her, his eyes closed again, letting the warmth of her lips soothe him and arouse him, and a thrill shot through him as he felt himself hardening, a wild throbbing sensation flooding him from head to toe.

"Yes, yes," he murmured against her mouth in English, only she didn't seem to notice as she moved closer to him, responding to his need, and his body covered hers, his knee parting her thighs to give him room. With one quick thrust he was inside her, the sharp pain of entry ceasing as quickly as it began, and with his mouth still clinging to hers, he started moving gently, like a tender caress thrusting in and out, until suddenly she nearly bit him, then he drew his lips away and heard her cry out.

For her it was over, but now for him it was just beginning, and once more he closed his eyes, reaching down this time to lift her fragile hips to meet him, and with a persistence brought on by the pent-up fury that filled him because of Lizette's betrayal, he plunged into Elena savagely, trying to complete the thing he'd sworn to do. To prove he was still a man, and he climaxed forcefully, burying himself deep in the woman he'd chosen to help him succeed.

Only he didn't succeed, and seconds after it was over, he knew he'd lost and Lizette had won when he fell down beside Elena, cradling her head on his shoulder, and realized that all the while he was supposed to be making love to Elena, he was really making love to Liz, and that even pretending fell far short of what it should have been and would have been with his wife.

He lay on his back now, the warmth that usually swept

through him missing. He felt nothing but a faint pulsing through his body. There was no languorous tingling, no spontaneous joy, no fulfillment. Only a nagging desire for something that seemed to have eluded him. Something he couldn't seem to grab hold of, and tears surfaced at the corners of his eyes, only Elena didn't see them.

Yes, he could still perform. He was still a man, but he knew now that without Liz things would never ever be the same again, and with that realization, as he reached out, pulling the covers over the two of them, preparing to spend the night, not for himself, but for Elena, he knew that in spite of the fact that without Liz life had lost its meaning, he'd still be sailing in the morning because he just couldn't forgive and forget this time, and he cursed Sancho de Córdoba for ruining his life.

Chapter 16

DARK CLOUDS ROLLED across the lowering sky, bringing with them the threat of more snow, or perhaps even rain this time, since the air had warmed some the past few days. Lizette stood at the window of her bedroom at Locksley Hall and watched them gathering, then let her gaze wander past the lakefront to where the gates stood open.

It had been at least two months since Bain had ridden through those gates and out of her life, and so much had happened since then. Lizette turned from the window and walked to where the cradle Sancho had given her stood beside the bed and looked down into it, staring at the face of the baby that had triggered so much of her heartbreak; yet she couldn't hate her. How could anyone hate something so precious?

Genée Kolter had been born earlier than they thought, less than a week after Bain left, and for a while they weren't even sure she'd survive. But like her mother, she seemed to have a lust for living, and before long she was nursing happily at her mother's breast and growing stronger every day. Now, as Lizette stared down at her new young daughter, she couldn't help smiling. She looked so much like her father. Her dark hair had a deep chestnut cast to it, and even though her eyes were blue now, Lizette was sure they'd end up as gray as Bain's. And she had come into the world so easily. Nothing like the twins, who'd kept her in labor for hours before their arrival. True to the enthusiastic way she seemed to be accepting life already, Genée had given her mother no warning except a few twinges in her back, then one big long pain, and within only a few minutes' time she was here in all her glory, crying outrageously, as if the ordeal, short as it was, had taken too long.

What was it Aunt Ann had said? "Fifteen minutes to have

a baby? It's absurd." Even Maggie, the housekeeper, said if she hadn't seen it she wouldn't have believed it. But it was true. Genée Kolter had come into the world the way her mother had carried her for the past nine months, indifferent to convention and what was supposed to be, and now, as Lizette studied her sleeping face, then reached out and touched the side of her soft velvety cheek, she was so glad that even though the world thought otherwise, she knew the truth in her heart and the child was Bain's.

Her hand moved from the baby's cheek and she touched the top of the cradle, her fingers tracing one of the carvings, and she frowned. How many times she thanked God that she'd already been pregnant and known it when Sancho kidnapped her, and the thought of what might have happened if she hadn't been made her tremble. It was bad enough that the world thought the worst of her, but at least she had the satisfaction of knowing they were wrong.

She stared at the cradle, remembering the day Sancho gave it to her, and wishing she could forget, but it wasn't that easy. Now Sancho was dead. The thought was a strange one because she just couldn't imagine him gone. He was so alive, so vibrant and magnetic, and she closed her eyes for a moment, wondering if his dream of death had become a reality. After all, Bain hadn't told her how Sancho'd died, only that he had killed him. Uncle Teak was the one who had said Bain told him he'd run the man through, and she remembered when Sancho had challenged her to run him through with his own cutlass, and she couldn't. At least Bain wasn't the coward she was, and she opened her eyes again, wiping the tears from them at the thought of Bain and how much she missed him.

They were leaving for home today, she and Genée, and she glanced at the clock on the mantel. The carriage would be coming around to the front soon. How long she had waited for this day, only now that it was here, she was afraid. Not for herself. Aunt Ann, Uncle Teak, and the boys were going with her, just as he'd promised, but it was Genée she was apprehensive about. She was still breast feeding and that wouldn't be a problem, but she'd wondered for so long now whether her family back home would be able to understand everything the way Aunt Ann and Uncle Teak did, or would they side with Bain and refuse to believe Genée was his? The thought had disturbed her often over the past few weeks, and even though she could see Bain in the baby, she wondered: Would others see it too? If not, she'd be exposing her daughter to a life of pain and heartache. Her fist clenched stubbornly. They had to know she was Bain's. They just had to.

There was a sudden knock on her door, and she turned. "Come in."

It was Ann, resplendent in a midnight-blue traveling suit with a short fur cape, the hat on her head trailing a matching scarf she could tie under her chin if the weather got worse.

"Are you ready?" she asked, moving into the room and stopping to look down at the baby.

"I am, but she's still asleep," Lizette answered. "All I have to get is my hat and cape," and she strolled to the bed, picked up a fancy pleated bonnet of heavy gold brocade lined with silk that matched the green-gold suit she had on, then slipped into the quilted cape that matched the hat and touched the floor, leaving only slits for her arms to come through so she could hold the baby. Her aunt and uncle had insisted on having some clothes made for her for the trip home, and her luggage with all the new clothes in it was downstairs already with everyone else's, tied onto a wagon that was to follow the carriage. After all, the trip was to be a long one and required more than just the few pieces of baggage they'd need if they were going to be away only a fortnight.

"Teak's waiting with the boys in the foyer," Ann said as she watched Lizette closely. "And the carriage is on its way out front."

"Then I guess this is it, isn't it?" Lizette said, and looked about the room. "I don't think there's anything I've forgotten." Turning back to the bed again, she straightened the bunting she'd finally finished knitting, then took the baby gently from the cradle, laid her inside, and fastened it.

Genée started to open one eye at first, then seemed to change her mind, and satisfied this spot was as comfortable as any, closed it again, quite oblivious of the fact she was going home. When the bunting was all fastened up, Lizette lifted her just enough so she could tuck a warm blanket around her for good measure, then picked her up and looked at Ann.

"Now we're ready," she said.

Ann glanced at the cradle.

"We can still take it with us if you want to."

Lizette shook her head. "No, I don't want it, Aunt Ann. I have enough reminders of Sancho de Córdoba's ugly vendetta without taking that with me. Let's go," and without looking back at the room she'd called home for the last few months, and the cradle that had rocked Genée to sleep so often since her birth, Lizette headed for the door, waited for Ann to open it for her, then went out, heading downstairs, where her uncle, his two young sons, their governess, and the carriage awaited to take her to London, to the ship Teak had booked passage on for them that would take her back to Beaufort and home.

The sea was still choppy after last night's storm as the *Sparrow* bobbed helplessly on the water, her rigging full of men making repairs. Eric had been bustling about all morning making sure everything was done right, and now he took a breather, walking over to the rail, leaning back against it as he took a quick survey of the ship. Along with a few minor repairs, they'd darn near lost a good section of the mainsail during the storm, and he'd ordered Waggs to get a crew working on it as soon as he could, so he was pleased to see they were taking care of it. Only it was going to be harder fixing the spar the sail was fastened to, since they'd lost most of the lead line when the end broke off. However, the *Sparrow* had a good carpenter, and if all went well, they'd be on their way in a day or two.

His gaze moved from the rigging to the quarterdeck and he straightened as he spotted Bain, shirt open to the waist, leaning over the side, staring off toward the horizon to the west. Actually they probably wouldn't even have been in a storm last night if it hadn't been for Bain, but he'd had them change course four times already since leaving England. The first time, they were barely out of the English Channel when he'd told Eric to set a course for Lisbon instead of Cuba. Then, when they were only about thirty miles off the Portuguese coastline, he suddenly decided he wanted to go to France instead, and the *Sparrow* had heaved to in the water, changing her course, heading back up the coast again. Only, much to Eric's surprise, they spent just one day at the harbor in Le Havre before Bain got restless again, this time telling him to chart a course for Tangier.

However, they'd never reached Tangier either. Just north-west of Gibraltar, he'd suddenly ordered Eric to set his course again for Cuba, and so far it didn't look like he was going to change his mind again. Eric had already informed Bain that they were going to have to stop off in Barbados or somewhere to put on more supplies, since he hadn't expected to be at sea for such a long stretch. They had replenished a few things at Le Havre, but they were still running dangerously low on a number of things, and last night's storm wasn't helping matters any.

Eric studied Bain for some time, watching him surreptitiously. The man was like a caged animal until you talked to him, then he was as testy as a cobra, and so far he'd refused to say one word about what had happened in London. Everything Eric knew about Bain's sojourn there had been gleaned from Elena, only it wasn't much. Just that Bain had returned without his wife.

His thoughts on Elena now, Eric was surprised to see her step from the gangway and stand stock-still, looking around for a minute before heading toward him, and he had to admit she looked quite pretty today, and especially under the circumstances. She'd had to do with the same clothes for ages now, washing them herself and trying to keep them looking nice, only he had a suspicion she was getting weary of the ordeal. The *Sparrow* didn't have a young cabin boy to handle all the dirty work, and even Bain couldn't have talked the seasoned veterans who sailed on the *Sparrow* to wash out women's wear. They'd rather take a flogging instead, so the whole load had fallen on her.

Eric and Elena had been talking more and more as the days went on, and as he watched her now, coming toward him, he realized he'd begun to enjoy her company. Maybe it was just the fact that she was a woman. Whatever the reason, he was pleased she'd decided to act a little more friendly, because on the way to London from Cuba, she'd hardly noticed he was on board.

"*Hola,*" he greeted when she reached him.

She smiled, amused, the pale blue cotton dress she was wearing making her skin look even more bronzed than he'd remembered from the last time she'd been on deck, which was two days ago, before the storm.

"You said only English, *capitán,*" she reminded him.

He returned her smile. "Ah yes, so I did."

She glanced up at the rigging where the men were working

and shielded her eyes from the sun that felt hot enough to fry an egg.

"We have drifted far this morning?" she asked.

He gauged the position of the sun, then remembered the setting on the quadrant earlier in the day.

"Far enough," he answered.

"You know where we are?"

"Approximately."

"And?"

"Let's just say it's still a long way to Cuba. Why? Anxious to get home?"

She blushed.

"It isn't going well, is it?" he said, and her blush deepened.

"I do not wish to talk of it, *capitán*."

"I think you'd better," he answered. "You've been wandering about too long with a downcast face."

"But it is not right I should talk of these things with you, *señor*. You are a man."

"And being a man, don't you think I just might be able to help?"

She studied him for a few minutes, as if she were trying to decide whether he was really sincere or not, and watched the sun dance off his hair, turning it to pale gold; then she took a deep breath. "Perhaps you could," she finally said, and her voice became low, hushed. "It is . . . what you say . . . a fiasco," she whispered softly.

His eyes darkened. "You know why, don't you?"

"*Sí*, I think I know why, but I am not sure." Her mouth drooped unhappily. "He cannot forget Lizette, *sí?*" she asked, and there were tears in her eyes. "I have played the fool, have I not, *capitán?*" and he saw her lower lip tremble. "I tell him he is obsessed with her, but he has not the obsession, it is love he has, is it not? It is I who was obsessed with him perhaps, and now . . ."

"Now it's not what you thought it would be, right?"

"You have been in love?" she asked.

"Dozens of times."

She eyed him dubiously. "That is not love, *capitán*," she informed him. "That is . . . what you say . . . infatuation."

"I see."

"No you do not. There is a difference."

"And you know the difference?"

"I think I do now." Her dark eyes were steady on his, her

face troubled. "We, you and I, have talked much these past few weeks," she said, brushing a dark hair back from her damp forehead. "Now I need a friend. You will be one, *sí?*"

He saw the sadness in her eyes. "I will be one," he said, then asked, "When did it change for you?"

She flushed crimson, her eyelids faltering self-consciously.

"I can't help you if I don't know what the trouble is, Elena."

She bit her lip. "I thought it would be different," she finally said, embarrassed. "Everyone always made such a fuss about making the love . . . and the way I feel inside. I thought it should fill my heart and warm me, but it did not, from the moment it happened."

Eric stared at her curiously for a minute, then frowned. "It always hurts a little for a woman the first time, Elena," he explained.

"But then it should be good?"

This time Eric turned three different shades of red. "Yes, it should be good," he answered, remembering Daisy back in London, who'd be waiting for him again the next time he sailed into port.

"Then why was it not?" she asked, confused. "Why do I not feel loved? For a moment there was . . . what you say . . ." Her eyes said what she couldn't put into words. "Then there was nothing, *capitán*. Nothing but the doing." Her eyes were misty again. "Where is the tenderness in him like there once was when I first knew him? He is like a stranger. It is as if he is playing a part just to please me, and yet it does not."

"Poor Elena."

"You laugh at me?"

"No, never." He reached out, cupping her face in his hand. "But you've grown up, Elena," he went on, making sure he could look deeply into her dark eyes and noting, as he'd often done since Bain had first brought her aboard ship, how delicate and lovely she was. So vibrantly sensuous. "You've discovered that love has to be returned, and when it isn't the heart suffers, right?"

"But I love him!"

"Do you? Then why do you still call him Domino?" His hand dropped from her chin. "He's Bain Kolter, Elena. Father and husband. He doesn't belong out here anymore. He belongs in a stone house back in Beaufort and he knows it, although he's too stubborn to admit it yet, but I think you're beginning to realize it too. And he'd be there yet if it weren't for your brother, wouldn't he?"

He saw the indecision in her eyes.

"You didn't love Bain Kolter, Elena, and you don't now," he went on, trying to make her understand. "You were attracted to Bain, yes, and you no doubt thought it was love at first, but I think perhaps you loved what you thought Domino was, rather than the man himself. That's why you still want him to be Domino, your mysteriously exciting stranger, and he can't be."

"But he can . . . he was, until London."

"No, he was Bain Kolter before London too, Elena," he said, surprising himself that somehow he knew he was right. "But you were looking at him with your heart instead of your head. Since London you've been looking at him with your head as well as your heart, and you don't recognize him anymore, do you? Look at him now," he told her, and they both glanced across the ship's deck to where Bain still stood staring off into the distance, where there was nothing to see except water and sky. "Whom do you see there, Elena?" he asked. "Domino or Bain Kolter?"

Elena's gaze rested on the back of Bain's head, the sun trapping its red highlights, the gentle breeze that was rocking the ship and filtering through the damaged sails ruffling his hair slightly, and she watched him straighten, stretching as if to catch the breeze, and she knew his eyes were closed now, with the full heat of the sun on his face. Then Bain relaxed again, opening his eyes, face once more turned toward the horizon, and she knew there'd be the same faraway look in his eyes she'd seen so many times already, and her heart sank.

"He looks like my Domino, but he is Bain Kolter, isn't he?" she answered.

Eric drew his eyes from his employer and gazed down at the woman he knew Bain had been sharing his bed with since that night back in London, and he nodded. "And Bain Kolter can never change, even though he tries to pretend he has. So what do you do now?"

"He has done it already."

"Oh?"

She was no longer watching Bain, but was also avoiding Eric's blue eyes that always had a way of making her feel uncomfortable, and her cheeks turned pink with embarrassment as she too gazed off toward the far horizon.

"He no longer pretends with me even," she answered, and her words were almost lost to him, they were uttered so softly. "It has been over a week."

"Are you glad?"

"I am puzzled."

"How's that?"

"He is still kind, he treats me well, and yet he uses the excuse . . . he is tired, he does not feel well." She looked at him again. "If he does not want me, why does he not just say so?"

"Because any man, no matter who he is, hates to admit he made a mistake, and Bain Kolter did make a mistake, didn't he, Elena? And I think you knew it was a mistake, only you didn't care. In fact, I don't doubt that you even helped him make it, didn't you?"

"I thought you were my friend."

"I am."

"But you just accused me!"

"Accused you? No, Elena, I told you the truth. Isn't that what friends are for?"

She tensed, her eyes wary. "You say I cause him to be like he is, when it is she who causes it. It was she who betrayed him with Sancho. I did nothing."

Eric was still leaning back against the ship's railing, and now he straightened, glancing up at the men in the rigging, pretending to see how things were going, only his thoughts were not on sails and spars or anything else on board ship, except Elena. After a few minutes he relaxed again, turning his attention back to her.

"Don't lie, Elena, not to me anyway," he said, his voice lowering so he wouldn't be overheard by anyone who might be standing nearby. "I watched you from the moment we got to Havana, and all the way over on the trip to England, and I knew right from the start what you were doing. I even warned Bain, but he wouldn't listen. You made it much too easy for him to believe the worst of his wife, and you know you did. You turned him against a woman who's been his whole life for years now, and yet you say you did nothing?"

"I did not make her pregnant!"

"And your brother did? You're sure?"

"How else could it be?"

"She could have been pregnant already."

"Then why would Domino not know this?"

"Are you pregnant now, Elena?" he asked.

She frowned, puzzled. "What do you mean?"

"Just what I asked. Are you expecting a baby?"

"No, not that I know of."

"Then if I were to make love to you tonight, and next week you'd discover you were carrying a child, whose child would it be, Elena?"

"That is not fair!"

"It's just as fair as what you did to Bain. You made him doubt his wife every chance you had, when you could very easily have helped him to believe in her."

"And if I had?"

"You wouldn't be wondering why he's no longer your precious Domino."

Her eyes narrowed. "You are cruel, *Capitán* Edelman. I tell you my feelings, and you throw them back in my face." She started to walk away.

"Elena?"

She turned back, facing him, her dark eyes hard, unyielding.

"I'd still like to be friends."

"When hell freezes over!" she shot back, and continued walking toward the bow of the ship, while Eric watched her, a scowl wrinkling his forehead.

Bain had turned from his perusal of the horizon a few minutes before and had glanced across the deck, catching sight of Elena and Eric talking, and now he frowned as he watched Elena, looking quite angry, walk away. He wondered what they'd been talking about. Eric never had liked Elena, ever since she'd come aboard, at least Bain hadn't thought so, but then he suddenly realized he'd seen them talking together alone quite often over the past few weeks, and his frown deepened. He decided to find out for himself. Strolling over toward where Eric was once more turning his attention to the ship's repairs, Bain called to him, and Eric, who'd started climbing up into the rigging to see how Waggs and the crew were doing, dropped back down.

"Need me for something?" he asked.

"Just curious," Bain answered. "What were you and Elena talking about that made her so upset?"

Eric pretended surprise. "Upset? I didn't notice. Was she upset?"

Bain's jaw tightened and his eyes grew dark, threatening. "You're not being funny, Eric. What's going on?" he asked.

Eric took a deep breath, staring Bain straight in the face. He'd never backed down from him before, and he wasn't about to now, friend or no.

"We were discussing her love life," he answered truthfully. "It seems you haven't been living up to her expectations."

"The hell you say!"

"No, she says," Eric answered. "Good Lord, Bain, when are you going to wake up?" he went on. "You're no more in love with her than she is with you, and you never will be, so why don't you just let go?"

"Why, so you can have her?"

"Don't put ideas in my head."

"They're there already."

"Don't be ridiculous. She's a scheming, conniving little witch, and I wouldn't want her if you gave her to me."

"Then why is she discussing her love life with you?"

"Because she didn't know who else to talk to." He gestured about the ship. "Do you see anyone else who'd listen?"

"I'd listen."

"You're her problem."

"Bullshit!"

"You're still in love with your wife, Bain."

"The hell I am!" Bain felt his stomach tighten at the mention of Lizette, and a strange yearning swept over him. He tried to ignore it. "And don't mention her name again, do you understand?"

Eric inhaled, his eyes still steady on Bain, and he nodded.

"Have it your way, friend," he said curtly. "I'm only the captain around here," and he went back to what he'd been doing before Bain came over, and was soon climbing all over the rigging with the men, while Bain stalked off to sulk.

That night as the *Sparrow* continued to bob about with her sails still not ready, and little wind to fill them even if they had been, Bain made love to Elena for the first time in over a week, only this time, not only was there no pretense at tenderness, but afterward when she lay in his arms, still hoping someday it would change and be better, she could have sworn she heard Bain whisper Lizette's name just before falling off to sleep.

By the next afternoon the sails were ready, the repairs

finished, and as a stiff breeze began to blow, whitecapping the water, the *Sparrow* unfurled her sails, let the wind catch them, then once more headed for Cuba, and life on board ship settled back into its daily routine.

However, as the days went by, Eric sensed that there was a subtle change going on aboard ship. Especially between himself and Elena. She'd been furious with him only a short time before, but now, whenever she was on deck he'd happen to glance her way only to find her staring at him curiously. And it was not the sort of look to expect from a woman who was someone else's mistress. It was a sensuous, provocative look that always shot right through him and made him wonder why he'd alienated her in the first place.

Then finally, one evening close to dusk, when she'd been watching him a little longer than usual, and after he'd glanced her way at least a half-dozen times and caught her at it, he strolled over to where she was sitting on the steps that led to the poop deck over the cabins, and stood staring at her, his eyes curiously alive.

Usually she wore her hair in its one long thick braid down her back, but it was loose now, as it had been all day, and she was fighting, trying to keep it from blowing across her face, while also trying to keep the skirt of her pale yellow dress from exposing the petticoats beneath it. There were some stains on the side of the skirt that hadn't come out during laundering, as well as a few on the tight-fitting bodice, but by now she'd become accustomed to not looking immaculate and she stared back at Eric for a long time, one hand against the side of her head to hold back her dark hair.

"*Por favor,* what is it? What did I do?" she finally asked as his eyes bored into hers.

His gaze settled on her hair, the last of the pink sunset tinting it a strange soft rosy shade that contrasted with her dark eyes and bronzed skin.

"What happened to the braid?" he asked.

Her hand twisted in the hair, then slid down, releasing it, and she held her hand palm out so he could see her fingers. The tips of two were blistered, and he frowned.

"I was trying to show the cook how to make tortillas yesterday," she answered. "And I accidentally touched the hot griddle."

"You like to cook?"

"No, but I thought perhaps it would be a new way for us

to eat the *frijoles,* your beans. One can eat just so much soup and rice before one becomes not able to face it again, *sí?"*

"Sí," he said. "Only I'm just sorry it didn't work, because I'd love to taste your *frijoles* sometime, *señorita."*

"You are making to laugh at me again," she protested, and slid down from the steps, starting to leave.

"No." He grabbed her arm. "Don't go," he said. "I didn't come over here for you to run away."

"I am not running."

"Aren't you?"

He was still holding her arm and his fingers eased on it, then ran down its length, and he caught her hand in his. "I could braid your hair for you," he offered as he stared down at her.

Elena flushed. "You?" Her eyes were steady on his. "What do you know of my hair?"

"A sailor knows how to braid rope. Your hair's no different, only softer." He reached out with his free hand, grabbing a handful of her long dark hair. "It's like silk," he said huskily, and Elena felt a strange tingling begin at the top of her ears and travel to her toes.

"There is no need," she answered, surprised at her response to his nearness. "The day is almost over and I will go belowdecks soon."

"But first I'll braid your hair. The night's hot, you can't sleep with it tangled all over."

She stared up at him, knowing she should say no, yet unable to, and sensing there'd be no more protesting on her part and still holding her hand, he led her away from the steps, to the capstan, where he could perhaps catch some of the last few rays of daylight to see by, and he perched on top of the capstan, turned her so her back was to him, then drew her closer, between his outspread legs, and reached up to do her hair.

He'd been right the first time: it was like silk, soft and filmy. Only when he grabbed the first few strands, pulling them back to keep them in place, he realized that it wasn't going to work. At least not here. For one thing, it was getting darker with each minute, and with the quickening shadows had come a breeze that snatched at the delicate strands every time he managed to get them in place, and tugged them from his hands. It was impossible. Only he'd begun to enjoy the task and didn't want to lose the feelings that were building inside him.

"I can't do it here," he said after a few minutes of fumbling that also made him aware some of the men were eyeing him curiously. "We'll have to go down to my cabin, where it isn't so windy."

She took a deep breath and glanced back at him, scowling.

"Don't look so vicious," he said, trying to be nonchalant. "I'm not going to bite you. I'm only going to braid your hair."

He'd already let go of the silken strands he'd been trying to keep together and reached out, taking her by the shoulders, putting her away so he could stand up; then he gestured toward the door that led belowdecks.

"After you."

She hesitated, but only for a moment, then stepped forward, and he opened the door, following her inside and down the gangway.

Once in his cabin, he quickly lit the lantern over the table, then came back to where she stood staring at him, and he smiled.

"You act as if I'm going to rape you," he said as he took her hand and led her toward the table that was secured to the floor, and he boosted himself onto it to bring him level with the back of her head, as he'd done abovedecks on the capstan, and waited.

"Well, do you want it braided or not?" he asked.

Elena was at a loss for words. Suddenly she was seeing *Capitán* Eric Edelman in a new light, and it was disturbing, and had been disturbing ever since their frank talk some weeks back. When she'd first met him she'd been aware he wasn't what she'd expected the *capitán* of a ship like the *Sparrow* to be, but then few men ever turned out to be what she'd expected. However, she had dismissed her instant feeling of attraction to him as the result of a young woman who'd been too long without handsome suitors, and Domino's unexpected appearance in her life again only a short time later had only served to nurture the thought. But now, how quickly things could change.

"Well?" he asked again. "'Are you just going to stand there and stare?"

Her eyes softened, and the corners of her mouth tilted, amused. "You are a rogue, *Capitán* Edelman," she whispered, flushing, and she turned her back to him, then let him settle her firmly between his legs while he once more began to work on her hair.

His fingers were strong and deft this time, with no wind to catch the silken strands, and in no time at all he'd finished plaiting the thick dark braid, and he sat for a minute with the end in his hand, then sighed.

"You know what we forgot, don't you?" he asked.

She'd been staring straight ahead, and tried to turn her head to look back at him.

"There's nothing to tie the end with," he explained.

She'd been quiet during the whole time he'd been braiding, her thoughts running back and forth over the remark he'd made about raping her, and although she knew he'd only been teasing, the thought had bothered her. Not the idea that he would really rape her, because she was certain Eric Edelman wasn't the type of man to do anything so horrible, but there'd been something about the way he'd said it that had brought a response she hadn't expected, and she looked into his eyes now. They were twinkling at the corners and she warmed to them.

"So, what do we do?" she asked.

"I guess I'll just have to hold it."

"You are being fastidious."

"You mean 'facetious,' don't you?"

"Does it mean you are making fun?"

"In a way, but not in the way you always think." He was still holding the end of the braid. "For some reason, you seem to have a nasty habit of thinking I'm laughing at you instead of with you."

"Perhaps because I do not laugh much anymore."

He ignored the fact that he was still holding the end of her braid together and reached out with his free hand, turning her to face him, while lifting the braid and resting it over her left shoulder. The light from the lamp overhead fell across her face, and Eric inhaled sharply as he caught the depth of longing in her eyes.

"You're too lovely to forget what it is to laugh," he said, and tucked the end of the braid back between the last two fingers on his right hand, leaving the rest of his fingers free, and he reached up, touching her face, while his other hand made its way about her tiny waist, pulling her even closer. "I could make you laugh again," he whispered.

She stared into his eyes, as brilliantly blue as the afternoon sky had been, only now they were dancing with shiny flecks of silver that challanged her boldly.

"I could make it good for you too," he went on, surprising even himself, and before she could answer either way, his lips suddenly touched hers, lightly at first, then moved against them more urgently, as he realized he'd been wanting to do this for a long time.

Elena hadn't been taken by surprise, not really. Her only surprise now was that his kiss was doing to her what it was doing. She felt giddy and light-headed, and now suddenly, as the kiss deepened, she felt herself drift even closer against him, her body on fire, her heart pounding madly.

His mouth eased on hers and he drew back, gazing into her eyes.

"I thought you hated me," she murmured.

He sighed. "Did I say that?"

"No. But you said such terrible things to me."

"I told you the truth. You're a scheming little witch, Elena," he said deliberately. "And you connived to get Bain Kolter just as surely as you've made up your mind to seduce me."

"Why, you . . ."

He pulled her harder against him. "There you go, getting mad again." His eyes danced wickedly. "Now, don't start swearing at me in Spanish. It won't do you any good because I don't know the language that well. Besides," he went on, and the gleam in his eyes became a smoldering caress, "I wanted you to seduce me, and I find the thought marvelously enchanting."

Elena couldn't believe what she was hearing. Then slowly, as if beginning to realize that if nothing else, Eric Edelman was being honest with her, she relaxed slightly and studied his face more intently.

"You are not being fastidious now, *sí?*" she asked.

"You mean 'facetious.' No, I'm not being facetious," he answered. "I want to make love to you, Elena, and show you what it's really all about."

"And Domino?"

"To hell with Bain Kolter," he murmured passionately. "He had his chance. Now it's my turn to show you what love is really like."

"But you don't love me."

"How do you know? Besides, he doesn't either."

Elena trembled. "It will be good?" she asked.

"It'll be very good," he answered softly, and knowing she'd given her answer, Eric forgot all about the end of the braid as he slid from the table, led her to his bed beneath the windows, and began to undress her, while outside the captain's cabin, the final curtain of night descended on the *Sparrow*, obliterating the far horizons from Bain's view as he stood on deck in the bow of the ship and watched the last vestiges of the day play themselves out.

Bain stood for a long time near the jib, feeling the salt spray from the Atlantic as it flew up with every wave they hit, and his jaw tightened irritably. Dammit, why couldn't he find peace? he thought. It was as if the whole world had turned upside down and there was no place to hide from it. He continued to stare into the empty night, going back over everything that had happened since he'd left for Pittsburgh, and even the things that had happened before that. Back to his first meeting with Liz, his fight not to kill Stuart when he'd come home only to discover she'd been having an affair with him. And then everything between. Barlovento, his sudden return from the dead, his duel with Stuart, Elena, Sancho . . . the baby.

She'd no doubt had it by now, he thought, and wondered whom it looked like and whether it was a boy or girl. Why the hell he cared, he had no idea, yet it rankled him. Then, as he went back in his mind, trying to find the answers to why he was so restless, he remembered the last time he'd made love to Elena, if you could call it that, and suddenly he knew what was wrong. He was wrong, and he had to admit it. He hadn't wanted Elena, he'd wanted Lizette.

When he took Elena to bed, it wasn't because he loved her, or even wanted her. It wasn't even to prove himself anymore, not really. It was to get even with Lizette for what he thought she'd done to him. Yet she'd sworn she was telling the truth. Was it possible? Could everyone else have been lying? He'd gone back over everything these past few days, and now slowly he began to realize what had happened. No one had lied really, except Sancho. Everyone was seeing it as it was. Only what they were seeing wasn't what was really happening, but only what Sancho wanted them to see and believe.

Now, tonight, he'd suddenly realized that Liz had been

telling the truth, and he thoroughly castigated himself by admitting that even if she hadn't been, he'd pretend she had anyway, and try to believe it as hard as he could, because he sure as hell couldn't go on like this. She was his life, and without her he was empty inside. He didn't even feel like Bain Kolter anymore. He felt like some stranger adrift in a sea of unhappiness with no way out.

Only there was a way out, and as he breathed in now feeling the night air caressing his face, and heard the slap of the sails overhead as the ship cut the water, he knew his decision had been made, and he turned to look around, wondering where Elena was, or where Eric might be, so he could tell him. Ah well, he'd tell him in the morning. First he had to tell Elena, and he turned, his long stride carrying him the length of the ship and on down belowdecks to the cabin he'd been sharing with her, only she wasn't there. Ah well, he'd tell her in the morning. So, putting the distasteful off a little longer, he gathered all of his clothes together, then left, taking them to one of the empty cabins, where he proceeded to make himself at home. And for the first time in weeks he was able to close his eyes and sleep without having nightmares, while down the passageway from where he lay peacefully sleeping, Elena was nestled close in Eric's arms, happier than she'd been in months. She'd been right. Eric was a rogue, all right, but oh, what a wonderful one. Her body was still glowing from the aftermath of his love-making, and still he hadn't quit. His lips nibbled at her ear, then found their way to her mouth, and he sipped at it again lazily, letting the wonder of it sweep over them both before entering her again, eager for what he knew awaited.

She was more than he'd ever dreamed she'd be, and Eric, who had told himself over and over again since the first time he'd taken a woman that there'd never be any special one for him, was slowly beginning to change his mind, and for the first time since he'd met Elena back in her uncle's sitting room, he suddenly realized why he'd been treating her so badly. He'd no doubt started falling in love with her even then, and now, as he made her live again, bringing her the joy she hadn't found in Bain Kolter's arms, he made up his mind that before tomorrow was over, he was going to do something about it.

"I have to go," Elena whispered a few minutes later, and he frowned.

"I don't want you to."

The lantern was still lit, hanging over the table, casting shadows across the wide bunk they were in, and she studied his face, marveling that she'd never noticed before how handsome he was. Or had she? Strange how fickle the heart was. All along, she'd been thinking she was in love with Bain Kolter, when maybe she wasn't really in love with anyone, or was she? Eric? He certainly made her feel loved, but she had a sneaky suspicion love was more than just this.

She ran her fingers across his lips. "Bain is expecting me, *querido*," she said, then sighed. "You know I do not want to go."

"Then don't."

"I have to."

"Why?"

"You know why."

Eric's eyes held hers and his face grew serious. "I'm going to tell him tomorrow," he said, and felt her stiffen. "I have to, Elena, for all our sakes, and his too. Maybe with you out of his bed he'll decide to head back home."

"Is that why you did this?" she asked. "So he would go back to her?"

"Don't be the fool he is," Eric answered. "I did it because I care, because I wanted to make you smile again." His voice lowered passionately. "Because I wanted you."

"Then let me go tell him," she offered, and started to get up.

"Not tonight," he said, stopping her. "Go, but don't tell him tonight. We'll both tell him in the morning. All right?"

She nodded, then left his bed, and a few minutes later she was heading down the passageway, dressed again, trying to think of what she was going to say to Bain if he decided he wanted to make love to her tonight, because she knew instinctively that she couldn't let him, not now, not ever again. Eric had spoiled her for any other man.

She opened the door to the cabin she shared with Bain and peeked inside, only to frown, then open the door wider, staring at the empty room. She'd have sworn she heard Bain come down the passageway while she was with Eric. Ah well, it was no doubt for the best. This way she could climb in bed and feign sleep when he came down, and she wouldn't have to worry. So, moving quickly, hurrying to finish before he might decide to return, and not noticing that his clothes were no longer in the cabin, she undressed, slipped into a nightgown, and climbed into the wide bunk, closing her eyes, and without realizing it was happening, she dropped off to sleep dreaming of a pair of bright blue eyes that took away the pain she'd felt for the past few weeks.

It was near dawn the next morning. Bain had been dreaming of Lizette, and when he opened his eyes, for a minute he couldn't remember what he was doing here or why. But then, as he stared at the ceiling of the small cabin he'd brought his things to, he remembered, and felt a surge of new life leaping through his veins, and he smiled.

"What fools we mortals be," he whispered softly, then took a deep breath, stretched, and sat up, rubbing his head. God, he felt good for a change. For the first time in months he felt whole again, only he frowned now at the thought of how he was going to explain himself to Elena. After all, it wasn't really her fault he'd made such a mess of things. She'd been convinced Liz was lying, but hers was an honest mistake. She'd only been repeating what she had seen, and who wouldn't think the worst under the circumstances? Hadn't everyone else thought the same thing? But that didn't mean it was true. After all, Lizette thought he'd been sleeping with Elena, and that wasn't true, at least not at first, and suddenly he felt a sickening feeling in the pit of his stomach. What was he going to say to Liz? It was one thing to admit he was wrong and decide to go back, but how was he going to talk her into forgiving him?

He glowered as he sat on the edge of the bunk and stared across the dingy cabin. Ah well, first things first. He'd cross that bridge when he came to it. She had to believe him, that's all. Right now he had to decide how to go about telling Elena, and as he slipped into his clothes, he kept running words over and over in his mind, hoping to come up with something that wouldn't hurt her too much, and yet anything he said to her was going to come as a shock.

A few minutes later he was at the door to the cabin he'd been sharing with her, and he wished he had someone with him for moral support. Opening the door as quietly as he could, he stepped inside and stood for a few minutes staring toward the bunk where Elena lay sound asleep. She must have dozed off last night while she was waiting for him, he thought, and was just about to wake her, when she stirred, then settled back into the pillow again, still sleeping. She looked so peaceful he didn't have the heart to disturb her. Deciding to let her have maybe a few more hours before turning her life upside down again, he tiptoed back to the door, opened it, stepped into the passageway, closed it behind him, and decided to go tell Eric instead.

Only Eric wasn't in his cabin. For a minute Bain had forgotten Eric always rose early. Well, fine, he'd catch him up on deck, he liked seeing the sun come up anyway, and today he was looking forward to it even more than usual.

With a sprightly hum on his lips, Bain headed for the gangway, taking the stairs two at a time, and opened the door to step out, almost bumping into Eric, who was on his way back down again.

"Well, I was looking for you," Bain said briskly. "Have a minute to spare?"

Eric was surprised. Not that Bain wanted to talk to him, but that he sounded almost human again. It was the first time he'd heard that lilt in Bain's voice since they'd left Charleston last year.

"I've got all the time you need," Eric answered. "Besides, I wanted to talk to you too."

Bain's eyes widened curiously. "Oh? Well, it'll have to wait until I have my say first," he said, and straightened, rubbing a hand across his beard and making a mental note to have it trimmed, then tucked his shirt in at the back of his pants where he felt he'd missed it earlier. "Only let's not stand in the doorway," he went on. "Your cabin, or the deck?"

"The deck'll do," Eric answered. "Besides, we're in for a beautiful sunrise, look," and he pointed across the water to the east, where the first few rays of the sun on the horizon were just beginning to sprinkle the water with shards of pink and gold.

"It's a good omen, Eric," Bain said.

They climbed to the poop deck, then stood near the rail at the stern of the ship, watching the sun come up over the horizon.

"What's wrong?" Eric asked as he studied Bain.

Bain took a deep breath, and for a moment searched for the right words. "I'm going home, Eric," he finally answered. "I'm really going home."

"To Lizette."

"To Beaufort, yes."

Eric stared at him for a few minutes longer, then smiled, pleased. "You finally came to your senses, eh?"

"I've been a damn fool." Bain sighed. "Why do we always seem to work so hard at ruining our lives?" he asked.

"Then you believe her?"

Bain turned away, looking out over the horizon. "Whether I do or not doesn't really matter . . . only, yes, I do, and I can't help loving her, Eric. I miss her, and the twins, and now with a new baby . . ."

"Your baby, Bain?"

"Yes, mine. Only . . ."

"Only what?"

Bain looked apprehensive. "How do I tell Elena that it's all over? That I'll be dropping her off at her uncle's in Havana and heading home?"

Eric rubbed a hand over his clean-shaven face and remembered the way Elena purred last night when she brushed her lips over his cheek, telling him how delighted she was that he didn't have a beard. "Maybe she'll understand," he began cautiously. "After all, she took her chances coming with us, didn't she?"

"And I've treated her badly. Dammit, Eric, how did I let myself get in this mess?"

"Like you said, you were a fool."

"You don't have to rub it in."

"Hey, look," Eric said, hoping the words would come out right. "Is Elena the only thing that's bothering you about the whole thing now?" he asked.

"What do you mean?"

"I mean, are you certain you're not really in love with her or anything like that?"

Bain eyed him skeptically. "What are you getting at?"

"Just answer me," Eric insisted, and Bain frowned, but he answered.

"No, I'm not in love with her, I told you that. I think she's nice, but that's as far as it goes. Why?"

"Good," Eric said, and he grinned from ear to ear, then sighed. "Whew, I didn't know how I was going to tell you," he went on, his face flushed, "but you see, last night . . . Well, I'll tell you, I've been watching her ever since we left Havana last year and . . . Well, anyway, Bain, you don't love her, so do you care if maybe when we get back to Havana I sort of stay around there a little longer than usual?

You know how to captain the *Sparrow*, and I'll have to have all the time I can get to talk her uncle into letting me—"

"Now, wait a minute," Bain cut in. "Are you trying to tell me you and Elena . . . ?"

Eric's flush deepened. "You're always telling me I should find a good woman and settle down."

"But Elena?"

Eric straightened to his full height, the sun glinting off his fair hair, his broad shoulders flexing beneath the dark shirt he was wearing this morning, and his bright blue eyes darkened.

"Now, just what's wrong with Elena?" he asked, his jaw tightening defensively.

"Nothing, I guess," Bain answered. "Only don't I recall your saying she was a scheming woman, and warning me to stay away from her? You even said she was a witch."

"So she isn't perfect, but who cares? Look, Bain," he went on, "I think I'm in love with her, it's as simple as that, and I think I'd kill you if you ever touched her again."

"Well, well," Bain said, his eyes steady on Eric. "And all this while you tried to get me to think the two of you couldn't stand each other. And Elena?" he asked, watching Eric closely.

"I made love to her last night, Bain," Eric replied. "And I don't think she'll be wanting to go back to you, ever again."

Bain stared at him for a long time, then sighed with relief. "Then I guess my worries are over, aren't they?" he said, only he frowned. "Now all I have to do is hope Liz can forgive me," and he turned once more, gazing off toward the horizon, wishing they were closer to Cuba so he could get rid of the past that was such a strong reminder of the stupid fool he'd been, and head for home.

Chapter 17

THEIR ARRIVAL IN Charleston had been hectic enough without the long ride to Beaufort to put up with, but now Lizette could thank God it was almost over. Grandpa Roth had a house in Charleston as well as the Château at Port Royal, and he had written to Teak telling him to use the closed carriage there and hire a driver to bring them down, since he and Grandma Dicia wouldn't be able to meet them in Charleston because it was planting time. And he'd even given Teak names of people he could contact to make sure he'd find someone reliable. So they'd hired two men. One was a husky Irishman named Gallagher, who could handle horses as if he were born with reins in his hands, and the other a free black, who could carry a trunk on each shoulder without taking an extra breath, yet had the manners of a gentleman's gentleman, and the unusual name of Greenbriar.

Lizette could hear him now sitting up on the seat beside Gallagher humming a sprightly tune as the coach lumbered along, and she glanced down at the sleeping baby in her arms and smiled. Genée had taken the whole trip far better than the boys. Even now Seth and young Quinn were sitting, one on each side of Teak, arguing over who could see more out of the carriage window, even though Seth was sitting on Miss Shelton's lap. Mollie Shelton, the governess, had been with the Locksleys ever since Quinn was born and it had seemed as natural to bring her along as it was to bring the boys. She was an energetic young woman with a cleft in her chin as deep as the dimples in her cheeks, large topaz-colored eyes that never missed a thing the boys did, and hair more orange than red that was nothing but a mass of ringlets. Lizette was sure she was younger than she claimed to be, which was thirty, but she looked barely twenty. Yet she was old beyond her years.

Lizette watched her now, admonishing Seth to sit still, and she smiled. Mollie had even helped Lizette at times with Genée during the crossing, and Lizette was thankful, although she had missed having Pretty to help.

She glanced out the window, watching the fields go by, then tensed as she spotted a fence she recognized that was the start of the far northern tip of her parents' plantation, Tonnerre. Uncle Teak had ordered the driver to take the long way to Port Royal, which took them farther to the west and bypassed the swamps south of Charleston, since it was the rainy season, and they'd approached the island of Port Royal by way of the Coosaw River, having the coach, horses, and themselves poled across at the ferry. Now, as the horses' hooves beat hard on the dirt road, still damp from a light rain the night before, Lizette's stomach fluttered wildly at the thought that they were almost there.

Teak Locksley settled Quinn firmly on the seat beside him and glanced across at his wife where she sat next to Lizette; then he looked at his niece, watching her eyes trace the top of the split-rail fence as they rode along.

"Recognize anything yet?" he asked.

Lizette nodded. "It's Tonnerre land."

"And the house is about a mile or two farther down, dear," Ann offered.

Teak acknowledged her statement and turned his head, tilting it back so he could reach up and open a panel overhead to talk to the driver. "Pull into the next drive we come to, Gallagher," he ordered. "There should be a house off toward the river," and Gallagher's voice came back quickly in assent.

"But we're going to the Château, Uncle Teak," Lizette reminded him.

Teak smiled. "First you say hello to your parents." He straightened, rescuing his hat from Quinn before it ended up on the floor. "Besides," he said, "I never did get to see Tonnerre when I was here last, and I'm anxious to see where my sister lives."

Lizette smiled a silent thank-you, then felt the baby stir in her arms as if Genée knew something important was about to happen, and a short while later, Lizette's arms tightened about her new young daughter as Gallagher slowed the carriage, then maneuvered the horses off the main road, heading up a long winding drive toward a stately mansion nestled beneath huge oak trees hung heavy with Spanish moss, the bright sunlight escaping their barrier in places just long enough to give life to a colorful panorama of blooming bushes and flowers on a lawn that extended down almost to the river's edge.

Inside the plantation house, Rebel and Beau Dante were just finishing a light lunch of soup, ham, rice, biscuits, and sweet potatoes whipped with honey and served with glazed pecans, a dish Beau was extremely fond of, but one Rebel kept telling him was the reason he'd put on a few pounds during the past few years.

Beau never took her seriously, though, because he was far from being out of shape, and most of the weight he'd gained was pure muscle, because unlike the rest of the plantation owners in the area, he was always right beside his hands, working the fields and running the place himself, along with his overseer, Aaron, a black who'd been with him for years. Now he put his spoon down on the table in the dining room, glanced over at Rebel, who was unable to finish the dish set before her, and was just about to make a comment about her insult to his physique when the children's old nursemaid, Hizzie, bustled in, wringing her hands, eyes wide with excitement.

"It's a carriage, Miz Rebel," she blurted hurriedly as she came through the dining-room door. "I seen it comin' up the drive with my own eyes. And they's a whole passel of trunks on top and tied in the back."

Rebel looked over at Beau and her heart skipped a beat. "Lizette?" she asked.

He smiled. "Who else."

"But they're going to the Château first. At least they're supposed to."

They both stood up, throwing their napkins on the table, and followed after Hizzie, who was already heading for the side door. She reached the door, holding it open for them, letting Rebel and Beau step out first, then followed close behind, and the three of them stood at the edge of the drive waiting anxiously.

Inside the coach, Lizette was nervous, her hands clammy against the soft wool of the blanket the baby was wrapped in, and she leaned over close to the window to catch a glimpse of the house she'd been raised in. Tonnerre and the Château were both like home to her, and her mouth went dry as she saw movement and color near the side door where the drive began to curve toward the slaves' quarters. They'd seen them coming, she just knew it, and as the coach drew nearer, she could see her mother's fair hair, golden in the sun, the red dress she had on like a homing beacon in the bright sunlight. And her father was there too, and Hizzie.

She leaned back in the seat, hugging her daughter tightly, then took a deep breath and glanced over at her uncle.

"Thank you, Uncle Teak," she said softly.

He winked. "It'll do you good," and before she had a chance to even try to hunt for the right things to say to them after such a long time, the carriage had stopped, Greenbriar had climbed from his seat, pulled the steps down into place so he could open the door, Ann had taken the still-sleeping baby from her, and Lizette was holding Greenbriar's hand, stepping from the coach and into her mother's outstretched arms.

Tears ran down both their cheeks even though Rebel was laughing, and even Beau's eyes were moist in the corners as he watched his wife hug their daughter; then he hugged and kissed her himself before taking her by the shoulders and holding her at arm's length to get a good look.

"You look marvelous, Liz," he said happily, and hugged her again, then stepped aside to let Hizzie have her turn.

Again a flood of tears coursed down Lizette's cheeks and she was at a loss for words. Hizzie held her tight, cooing like she always had when Lizette was a little girl, and for a minute Lizette wished she were that little girl again, only there was no going back, and her arms eased around Hizzie. She turned toward the coach, and Ann held the baby out toward her. Lizette walked over, and without having to be told, Greenbriar reached into the carriage, took the small bundle from Ann, and gently laid Genée in Lizette's arms.

"She's still asleep," Lizette informed them as she turned back toward her parents and Hizzie. But just as Lizette pulled back the edge of the blanket so they could get a good look, Genée opened her eyes lazily, blinked a couple of times as if getting accustomed to the light, then stared at all of them wide-eyed, looking them all over with an intensity unusual for such a small baby.

"Well, don't I get a hug too?" Teak called as he took Ann's hand so Greenbriar could help her from the carriage, then followed her out with the boys and Mollie close behind, and for the next few minutes all the slaves who'd been wandering around the grounds at Tonnerre, busy at their various tasks, stopped and stared at the commotion at the house while Rebel greeted her younger brother, who towered at least three inches over her husband's six feet, and her stepsister, who was now a countess, as well as the two small boys, who didn't really seem to know what was going on, but thought whatever it was had to be fun, and were trying to prove it to their governess by being as energetic as they could.

After all the hellos were over, and since it wasn't even one o'clock in the afternoon yet, Rebel insisted they stay long enough for a bite to eat. So while Beau took Teak on a tour of the house he hadn't been able to see during his stay in Port Royal some years before, Rebel had the servants get the table ready again, and a welcome meal was prepared.

After eating and giving Lizette time to nurse the baby, Rebel and Beau changed into traveling clothes, their guests climbed back into their coach, and with Rebel and Beau following in their own carriage, they all headed back down the road again toward the Château, farther down the island.

Loedicia was in the garden at the Château, between the stables and the pier, sitting beneath a shade tree near the riverbank, visiting with Blythe, who was resting in a special chair Roth and Jacob had made for her, when the two carriages from Tonnerre turned in at the drive, and she stared at her great-granddaughter for a minute, frowning. She'd been talking to Blythe, and now she glanced up at the sound of the harness and horses, then stood up slowly, shading her eyes to get a better look.

"Pretty! Pretty, come here!" she yelled, calling down to the black woman, who was at the edge of one of the flower gardens setting out some plants, and Pretty glanced up, then brushed the dirt from her hands onto the apron she was wearing.

"Somethin' wrong, Miz Chapman?" she called back.

Loedicia pointed toward the drive. "Look."

Pretty stretched up as high as she could; then her eyes widened in surprise and she sprang to her feet, still wiping the dirt from her hands, but more vigorously now as she hurried over.

"It's your ma, hon," she told Blythe, who was staring at Pretty curiously; then the young black woman looked at

Loedicia. "You go meet 'em, ma'am," she said. "I'll stay with my baby," and Loedicia, who was used to doing things most ladies shied away from, and giving in to an unladylike urge to let them know she had seen them, began waving one hand back and forth as she lifted the skirt of her periwinkle-blue dress and ran through the garden, barely keeping to the walks until she reached the side lawn; then she stopped, waiting near the mounting block as the carriages slowed and pulled to a stop at the foot of the front steps.

What if it isn't Liz after all? she suddenly thought as she stood staring, then brushed the thought aside. It had to be, because Rebel and Beau were in the other carriage behind.

Willing her feet to move forward again, Loedicia tucked a wayward strand of hair back to join the rest of her gray hairs, and approached the huge coach that she recognized now as being the coach from their place in Charleston, and her steps quickened.

Inside the coach Lizette wasn't as nervous this time as she had been at Tonnerre. Partially because her parents had assured her that Grandma Dicia and Grandpa Roth were looking forward to her return, but also because she had always seemed closer to her grandmother than to her mother and had spent much more time at the Château than at Tonnerre the past few years. And then too, her children were here and she was so eager to see them. Grandma Dicia had written to her, assuring her that both Braxton and Blythe were all prepared and anxiously awaiting the arrival of their new little sister. So when Lizette stepped from the carriage this time, into her grandmother's arms, then held the baby out for Grandma Dicia to see, the tears in her eyes were tears of joy and relief, and they kept right on coming, along with the laughter, as she watched Grandma Dicia greet all the others with the same warm enthusiasm, kissing and hugging them all exuberantly, and marveling at how much Teak looked like his father, her first husband, Quinn.

"And you, young man," Loedicia said, touching the top of young Quinn's head, then bending down to talk to him, her hands resting on her thighs. "Just how old did you say you were?"

"I'll be six on the fifteenth, ma'am," he answered.

"Aha!" She winked at him. "And if I know your Grandpa Roth, you're in for a good time while you're here too.

Now"—she looked around her at Ann and Teak, her violet eyes alive and dancing—"I suggest the rest of you go in," she went on, then looked at Lizette. "I think perhaps it'd be best if Lizette came with me alone first and brought the baby to greet Blythe. You see, there are still times yet when too many people frighten her."

"Where is she?" Lizette asked as the others headed up the steps toward the front door that was already held open by Mattie, the cook. "And where's Braxton?"

"Your grandfather and Braxton are at the cotton mill," Loedicia answered, looking off upriver a short distance to where the top of a huge building could be seen amid trees draped with Spanish moss. "But Blythe is down here with Pretty. Come," and she motioned toward the flower garden with her head, and promised her son and his family that she'd be back in the house with them in a few minutes.

The chair they'd made for Blythe was strong and sturdy, the back fixed so that if she tired it could be lowered or raised, and there was a footrest so her feet wouldn't just be dangling. Pretty had turned the chair around when the carriages arrived, and now Blythe was no longer facing the river, but able to see across the garden. She watched her mother approach, her gray eyes, the same shade as her father's, scrutinizing Lizette closely as she came.

Lizette stopped barely a half-dozen feet from her elder daughter and stood stock-still, staring at her. How much Blythe had changed. Her pale blond hair was still light, perhaps even lighter, almost white, and her face had lost its round baby look, although Lizette could see the slight indentation where the dimples were still in her cheeks, and although Blythe's eyes were still the same shade of gray they used to be, there was a depth to them that hadn't been there before. The carefree-little-girl wonder was gone, replaced by an intensity that was almost frightening to see in a child who had just turned four a few months back.

"Hello, Mama," Blythe said, her voice tremulous, and Lizette broke into tears.

"Oh, my baby, my precious baby," and oblivious of the daughter she was already holding in her arms, she lunged forward, throwing herself at Blythe, one arm around her, hugging and kissing her as if she didn't dare let go.

Finally a tiny voice broke through Lizette's sobbing, and she sniffed, trying to get her tears under control.

"You're squashing my new sister, Mama," Blythe was saying, tears in her own eyes as she patted her mother's back lovingly, and Lizette straightened quickly, aware now that Genée had not only woken up and discovered she was being unceremoniously squeezed, but had begun to protest, grunting and squawking furiously.

As soon as the pressure eased on her, however, she let out one last protest that was loud enough so no one could miss it, then shut her mouth quickly and stared directly into Blythe's face, while Lizette, who'd been half-lying across her young daughter, tried to get into a better position and yet stay close enough so the baby was practically resting on Blythe's legs.

"She has blue eyes, Mama," Blythe observed thoughtfully, and Lizette continued watching Blythe silently, while Blythe studied her sister. "Only she looks like Papa. See, there, the way she looks at me and holds her mouth." Blythe looked at Lizette, who was kneeling now beside her chair. "Did I look like her when I was little?" Blythe asked.

Lizette smiled and glanced up at Pretty so Blythe wouldn't see the tears in her eyes. "Well, did she, Pretty?" she asked.

Lizette's hand was on the back of Blythe's chair, and Pretty covered it with her own, letting Lizette know she understood.

"You was just as precious, honey," Pretty answered, and Lizette watched Blythe's face.

"But did I look like Papa, the way she does?" she asked.

"No, child, I think you looked more like your mama and grandma," the black woman said.

"I'm glad," Blythe replied as she continued to study her sister. "Because she's gonna look awful funny if she grows up lookin' like Papa." She turned abruptly, looking at Lizette. "Grandma said Papa's not coming home, Mama," she went on. "Why not?"

It was the one question Lizette didn't want to answer, yet knew she couldn't avoid.

"I don't really know why, dear," she answered, trying to choose her words carefully. "We had a terrible argument, though, and I guess he just got too mad to say he was sorry."

"Oh." She seemed to ponder the answer for some time as she continued to look at her sister; then finally she reached out and put her hand next to the baby's, letting Genée twine her fingers around her thumb. "Then maybe I'll be able to walk again by the time he gets over his mad, do you think, Mama?" she asked, and Lizette wanted to cry.

"Maybe you will, dear, who knows?" she said, fighting hard to hold back the tears, and they were all suddenly distracted by an exuberant voice ringing loudly and clearly from behind the stables, where a path led up the river a short piece to the cotton mill, and Lizette stood up, one hand still resting on the baby just to make sure she didn't fall off Blythe's lap while she watched her son running pell-mell across the low-cut field, then zigzagging along the walkways in the garden, with his great-grandfather following close at his heels.

"Mama! Mama!" he shrieked.

Loedicia stepped aside, giving him a clear path, and when Lizette knelt down, he hit her with full force, almost knocking her over, and she coughed, trying to catch her breath as her arms went around him.

"It is you . . . it is! I was waitin'," he cried breathlessly. Then, after giving her a slobbery kiss, he straightened as best he could and took a peek at the baby in his sister's lap.

"She looks funny, don't she, Bly?" he said, wrinkling his nose.

Blythe looked at him in disgust. "She looks like Papa."

Braxton grinned, the dimples in his cheeks deeper than Lizette had remembered them. "She don't have no whiskers, silly."

Blythe looked at her mother. "She don't need whiskers, does she, Mama?"

This time Lizette smiled as Grandpa Roth cut in.

"I hope not," Roth said, joining them, and he reached a hand out, helping Lizette to her feet, then gave her a hug and kiss. "It's good having you back, Liz," he said.

She sighed. "And it's good to be home too." Then she saw the baby start to pucker and suggested it might be best if they took her in before she really set up a squall.

So Lizette picked up the baby, Grandpa Roth carefully picked up Blythe, and Grandma Dicia ushered Braxton along in front of her, while Pretty went on ahead to tell one of the houseboys to bring Blythe's chair in, and they all went up to the house.

For the rest of the day there was little work done at the Château as Lizette's Uncle Heath and Aunt Darcy, who'd spent the day in Beaufort, also returned, and in spite of the shock at seeing Blythe being forced to sit and watch while her twin brother enjoyed the freedom she used to have, Lizette was glad to be back. Only later that evening, after her parents had left for Tonnerre and the house quieted down for the night, she stood looking down for a few minutes into the cradle Grandma Dicia said used to be hers, at her younger daughter, who was sleeping so peacefully there with a full stomach, and she buttoned the front of her nightgown, then turned the lamp on the dresser down low and walked to the window of the upstairs guest room she was in that overlooked the Broad River at the back of the house, and she stood staring out. It was crazy to even think this way, she knew, but as she stood there watching the faint lights from a barge as it floated downriver, she wondered unhappily where Bain was tonight, and what he might be doing, and a tear rolled down her cheek.

The next few days were hectic at the Château as everyone settled in. Teak and Ann were planning to stay for at least three weeks, and Lizette wasn't sure just how long she'd be here, although they let her take over the guest room she had used the first night they were there, since Pretty and Blythe were already sleeping in the bedroom Lizette and Bain usually used when they stayed overnight. It was at the far end of the hall, with Teak and Ann right across from her, while the two boys joined Braxton in the bedroom next to them. Grandma Dicia and Grandpa Roth's bedroom was opposite the boys, while Heath and Darcy were at the top of the stairs in the bedroom that had once been Ann's. So everyone had a place, although Lizette didn't like being so far from Blythe.

However, since Pretty had taken over Blythe's care completely after the accident, it was better Lizette wasn't right in the room with her, because Lizette had a tendency to coddle Blythe, and when she did, Blythe always took advantage of it, becoming even more helpless. So the time Lizette did spend with Blythe was spent not as a mother normally would, but more as a friend, entertaining her and bringing Blythe into closer contact with her little sister while taking her cues from Pretty, and letting Pretty continue to be the child's buffer against the unfair world she'd been thrown into.

As the days went by, Lizette was also more than pleased to see that although Braxton wasn't confined the way Blythe was, he hadn't really deserted his twin, but made sure each day that he kept her informed about everything he was doing, in his exciting world of toads, bugs, and other marvelous discoveries, by bringing each item to her for scrutiny, accompanied by a long, drawn-out story about it to tantalize her. And he often brought her flowers too. Not from their grandmother's gardens—Blythe could see them anytime she wanted—but wildflowers, from the fields where he spent most of his time.

Lizette and the others had arrived at the harbor in Charleston the last day in April, and it had taken them almost another week before they'd reached the Château, and now, only a few days after their arrival, Lizette suddenly decided at breakfast this morning that it was time to make a call on her in-laws in Beaufort so they could meet their new granddaughter, even though Bain had denied she was his.

"And I'd like to stop by the house too while I'm there," she said as she set down her napkin. "I imagine it's a mess by now, and something'll have to be done with the place." She glanced to the end of the table where Loedicia was sitting. "Will you go with me, Grandma?" she asked.

"I'd love to," Loedicia answered, then had a suggestion. "But do you suppose maybe we could wait for your mother, Liz? Rebel planned to come down this morning anyway, and it's been a long time since she's seen Madeline. I'm sure she'd like to go with us."

Lizette agreed, and after breakfast she went up to her room, put on a dress of green silk that had been at the Château when she'd been kidnapped and had been moved to this room when she returned, hunted up the bonnet that went with it and set it on the bed in readiness, then studied herself in the mirror. The dress was somewhat big on her. That meant she hadn't gained quite all of her weight back yet, and she was pleased. Only she knew it probably wouldn't be long before she did, and the thought was annoying.

Making sure there was a parasol to go with the bonnet, since the bonnet didn't have a brim big enough to shade her from the sun, she concentrated on getting the baby ready next, having Mattie find a large wash basket to put her in because it was such a long ride, and Lizette knew how uncomfortable it was to have to hold Genée all the way. Then, after putting a long dress of muslin and lace on Genée, she brought her downstairs to wait. When her mother arrived, which was only a short time later, she tucked Genée inside the basket with a small pleated cap covering her dark hair and a soft cashmere shawl around her, joined her mother and Grandma Dicia out front in the carriage that Rebel had ridden down in with old Job driving, and they headed inland toward Beaufort, a good two-hour ride away.

While they were gone, Heath and Teak, who'd never really gotten along that well, but who'd agreed to let the past die a welcome death, joined Grandpa Roth on horseback for a ride around the place so they could show Teak what he'd missed on his first visit, and Darcy, with Ann at her side, helped Mollie and Pretty entertain all the children with a picnic on the lawn.

The day was warm and beautiful as it always was the first part of May, and although the ride to Beaufort was a long one, it seemed like no time at all before the carriage was pulling up in front of the Kolters' fancy brick house. Probably because Lizette was still rather apprehensive about facing them again, even though her mother had assured her on the way in that Madeline and Rand Kolter were convinced that what Bain was doing was insane. They were even anxious to see their new grandchild, according to Rebel, and it wasn't long before Lizette realized her mother was right, when she was greeted warmly by her mother-in-law, although Rand Kolter wasn't at home.

Madeline assured them, however, that he was going to be terribly disappointed at having missed them, and since they'd arrived so close to lunchtime, she insisted they join her out back on the terrace, ordering the servants to set out three more places; then she escorted them on through the house.

The Kolters' backyard was a work of art, with beautiful formal gardens and a winding walk that led to a quiet summerhouse where Lizette and Felicia Kolter used to play when they were children. They had even used the summerhouse when they were older too, telling their parents they were going to picnic in it, while in reality, they'd sneak out of the yard by climbing over the fence beyond it, and they'd go exploring some of the seamier sides of life in Beaufort, such as the cockfights in one of the neighbors' barns.

So now, during lunch while they sat beneath the trees eating, with everyone talking, Lizette would glance back occasionally toward the winding walk, only each time she did, it brought back so many memories. Not only memories of when she was a child, but memories of Bain and Stuart too. But mostly Stuart. Because she and Stuart had been standing in that same summerhouse the day Stuart had first told her how much he loved her. That was why, even though she and Bain had lived only a short distance from the Kolters, they'd seldom visited his parents. So that neither of them would be hurt by the memories.

However, today the memories were there, even though she didn't want them to be, and she was thankful, after lunch was over and the others all decided to sit in the garden and talk, that she could retreat to one of the guest rooms upstairs to feed Genée.

However, by the time she came back downstairs, putting the sleeping baby back in her basket on the wrought-iron bench near her grandmothers, Lizette realized there was no way she was going to escape those memories. She was going to have to face them all, even now, so she asked her mother if she and Grandma Dicia would be able to keep an eye on Genée for her while she went over to the house she and Bain had lived in, and they agreed.

"But wouldn't you like one of us to go with you, dear?" Rebel asked as she looked down at the sleeping baby, then up at her daughter.

Lizette shook her head. "It's better I go alone."

"Well, at least let Job drive you."

Lizette declined that offer too, insisting that she'd rather walk.

"It isn't really all that far," she said, making sure the front of her dress was straightened. "Only a few blocks, really. Besides, I've been away so long, it'll be nice to see all the familiar places again."

Rebel finally relented. Lizette stopped in the foyer for her hat and parasol, then left the house, using the walk that separated the circular drive out front. With her parasol up to keep the sun from her face, she began to stroll slowly down the street, keeping to the walkway at first; then after a while she crossed over toward the center of town and passed stores where she used to shop, occasionally surprising someone who'd recognize her and stare dumbfounded, since few people knew she'd returned.

It was nice for a change to be by herself without having to worry about babies or answering questions, she thought as she strolled along, and it was good to walk familiar streets again too. Because although she'd been born and reared at Tonnerre, she'd spent enough time in Beaufort that it had become a second home to her now. The only problem was that everywhere she went she was reminded of Bain. There was the shop where he always got his hair cut, the cobbler who made the special Wellington boots he wore, as well as the tailor who made sure his clothes were a perfect fit.

Even on the way to Beaufort there had been reminders of him. There was the track at Palmerston Grove where she'd challenged him to a horse race, the Palmers' plantation house he'd helped her sneak into when her cousin Heather was being held prisoner there, and the field with the family graves in it where they'd dug up the casket full of rocks one night to prove Lizette's nephew Case hadn't really died at birth, as her cousin had been told.

Unfortunately there'd been other reminders too on that long ride. Memories she wished she could forget, of the carriage crash near River Oaks, and that horrible rainy night that had started this whole terrible mess.

She sighed, resting the parasol back onto her shoulder, and slowed some as she neared the edge of town where their house stood. Grandpa Roth said he'd been sending Luther down once a week to keep the lawn cut and the bushes trimmed, but still, as she drew nearer now she could see that grass was beginning to creep farther and farther into the driveway, narrowing it, and the flowers that had always bloomed profusely in their special beds were sprinkled generously with a heavy mixture of weeds. Even the windows looked hazy and unkempt, although Grandpa Roth also said he'd sent some of the slaves down now and then with Luther to do dusting and keep things in order.

She stopped and stared for a long time. In spite of everything that had been done to keep it up, the place still looked abandoned. There were no horses grazing in the paddock out back, the clotheslines were empty, and it looked so quiet and still with the windows and doors all shut. Reaching into the small beaded handbag she was carrying, Lizette pulled out the door key her grandparents had found in her handbag and been keeping for her since the night she'd been kidnapped. When Bain left, he'd taken his with him, figuring he wouldn't be gone long. Lizette glanced down at the key, pursed her lips, then took a deep breath and started across the street toward the house.

The minute she pushed the door open she knew that in spite of the fact that the place had been cleaned and dusted regularly, it had been a long time since it had really been aired out. Scowling uncomfortably at the stale odor filling her nostrils, she exhaled, rubbing her nose, and tried to get used to the hot, close smell. It was terrible after the warm fresh air from outside; however, she shut the door behind her and stepped the rest of the way into the entrance hall, then began her tour of the place.

It hadn't changed really; nothing had. Everything was still in its place, just as she'd left it, except upstairs. The children's armoires were empty now, all their clothes having been taken out to the Château, and whoever had gathered them together had left the door to the armoire open in Blythe's room. She walked over, shut it, then turned to the window that faced the street. If she didn't get some fresh air in here . . . She could hardly stand the stale smell, and it was so hot.

After setting her parasol and handbag on the bed, she unlocked the window, opened it as wide as she could, then took a deep breath of fresh air. It smelled so clean and refreshing. Without bothering to pick up her parasol and handbag again, she turned from the window and sauntered back into the hall, stopping just outside the door to the bedroom that had been hers and Bain's. The door had been left ajar and she stared at it for a few minutes, trying to get up the courage, then reached out with her foot and gently pushed it open. Everything seemed to be in place here too; even the pillows on the bed were plumped up beneath the satin coverlet.

Stepping in, she hesitated for a moment, then walked to the window that overlooked the lawn and paddock out back. She should open this one too, she thought, and unlocked it, pushing it up so a cross-draft could blow through the house from front to back. The fresh air did wonders for the place, and she stood for a few minutes enjoying it, then turned and walked to the dresser. The drawer that held Bain's things wasn't pushed in quite all the way, and she paused for a second, then opened it. A few shirts were missing, things scattered around, and she knew he must have left hurriedly. He'd had some of the things with him already from his trip to Pittsburgh, but he hadn't taken his favorite shirt on that trip. It was gone now.

Closing the door again, she opened the window on this

side of the room, then went back to the foot of the bed and stood for a minute just staring at the big four-poster. There were memories here too. Too many. She'd lost her first baby in this room, and the twins had been born here. But most of all . . . A shiver went through her as she tried not to think of the love she and Bain had shared in that old bed.

After a few minutes of feeling sorry for herself, and with tears near the surface, she was just ready to turn around and go back downstairs to open some of the windows there too, when she heard a noise behind her, a light footfall, and knew someone was standing in the doorway. The hair at the nape of her neck prickled, and she turned, then froze, staring at the man who stood watching her.

"Hello, Liz."

For a minute she thought it was Bain, the way the light shone on him, highlighting the russet streaks in his hair and turning the waves to a deep golden bronze. It was the same familiar clipped beard and mustache, the shoulders broad and muscular, same nose. He was eight years older than his brother, but he even scowled like Bain. However, looking into his clear blue eyes, there was no mistaking who it was.

"Stuart?"

He was staring at her intently. "I was riding past and saw the window open . . . the house has been closed up . . ."

"It was so stuffy, I couldn't breathe."

He continued to watch her, noticing how the green bonnet and dress matched her eyes. She'd never looked lovelier and he felt a stirring inside he wished he didn't feel. "I heard you were coming home." He took a deep breath and stepped into the room, looking down at her. Her eyes were glistening with unshed tears. "I also heard what Bain did to you."

Her gaze faltered and she tried to look away, but he reached out, catching her by the chin, tilting her head up so she had to look at him.

"He's a fool," he whispered softly.

Liz didn't know what to do. Stuart's uncanny resemblance to his younger brother had always been her nemesis. They were almost like twins, and there were times when she was so afraid that maybe she loved both of them. Perhaps she did in a way, but Bain had been her first love, and it was to Bain that she knew her heart belonged, and yet why did Stuart always have this strange, unexplained effect on her?"

"I thought you were in Washington," she finally said.

His hand dropped from her chin. "Congress recessed on the eighth. I got home yesterday."

"Oh."

He studied her curiously. "Are you all right, Liz?"

"Why shouldn't I be?" She inhaled, straightening, more aware every minute that being here alone like this with him was dangerous. If only he wasn't so much like Bain. She did notice that there were a few more lines in his face now, but other than that, he hadn't changed a bit. He was still the same man she'd shared so much with at one time.

"Don't try to pretend with me, Liz," he said, and the scowl on his face deepened. "I know you too well, and you're still hurting."

"Then why did you ask?"

"Politeness, I guess." His eyes hardened. "I wanted to kill him when I heard, and if he were here now I think I would." He was bristling with pent-up anger. "Dammit, Liz, he had no right to do this to you."

"You know the whole story?"

"I know he thinks you were a willing captive and that the baby you had is the result."

"What do you think?"

His eyes softened, the black frock coat he had on making them look even bluer. "Does it really matter what I think?"

"It shouldn't, but it does."

His gaze still rested on her face. He'd remembered every line so clearly, the way her thick lashes almost touched her brows when she looked surprised. The funny way her mouth tilted when she was amused. He even remembered the soft velvet feel of her in his arms, so unlike his wife's thin frame.

"I wouldn't care either way, Liz, and you know it," he answered. "But for what it's worth, I'd believe you, not all the rumors."

"Even if you knew I'd once had an affair with your brother?"

"He threw that at you?"

"That, and Washington as well. I think what happened these past few months made him even doubt what happened then too."

"So he left."

"With Elena de Córdoba!"

"Now, that part I didn't hear." He looked at her skeptically. "You're sure? Absolutely sure?"

"I don't need the sky to fall on my head to know it's raining. Of course I'm sure. He left me for another woman. He doesn't care about me anymore. Why should he, when he can have someone like her? I told you once before, Stuart, I'm fat and ugly. Look." She gestured to herself. "I was so nice and thin when they rescued me, and now . . . Why can't I stay thin like her?"

Stuart stared at her, his insides fluttering wildly. She was calling herself fat. My God, what he'd give to hold her again and feel flesh for a change instead of Julia's hard bones. How dare his brother do this to her! He wanted to reach out and touch her face, take her in his arms. He stepped closer.

"Don't, Liz," he pleaded, his voice breaking. "Don't let him do this to you. You don't have to be thin to feel. You know that."

"What good is feeling when there's no one there?"

His gaze was intense. "I'm here," he said.

She trembled. "You?"

"Yes, me. I know I told Bain and Julia I didn't love you, but I can't lie to my heart, Liz." His arm circled her again, pulling her against him. "Don't turn from me, please," he begged, still holding her close. "Let me make you feel again. Let me prove that his leaving had nothing to do with you as a woman." His voice lowered. "Let me love you, Liz," he begged. "Please, let me make up for what he's done."

He was so close, and his arm about her waist felt good. It had been months since she'd felt what it was like to be in a man's arms. Even the attention Sancho had given her, although it went no further than it did, had been enough to ease the pain of being without Bain. For four months now there'd been nothing except those few bittersweet moments she and Bain had shared back at Locksley, and now she felt her body responding to Stuart like someone dying of thirst, who'd just found a bubbling spring.

Her gaze met his, and their eyes locked. Hers were full of tears. "It wouldn't be fair," she whispered softly.

"Fair to whom? You? Bain?" He reached up and untied the ribbons of her bonnet, then lifted it from her head, tossing it onto a chair near the dresser. "Don't tell me it wouldn't be fair to Julia. I rarely touch her anymore."

"But she's your wife."

"It's what she wants, not me." His eyes darkened. "Even

when I do, it's not the same, Liz. It never has been. Not since you."

Her mouth went dry. "It wouldn't be fair to you," she answered. "I'd only be using you, and I can't let you be a substitute for him again."

"Is that what you think I'd be, a substitute?"

"Wouldn't you?"

He cupped her head in his hand, fingers sinking deep into her dark curls, his eyes boring into hers; then he bent down, pulling her head toward him. His mouth covered hers, lightly at first, then deepening, until all Liz could feel was the kiss sweeping through her and flooding her entire body clear to her toes.

A few seconds later, his mouth eased on hers. "Now tell me who I am," he murmured.

She sighed. "Stuart!"

He kissed her again, then maneuvered her to the side of the bed, and she looked at him helplessly.

"I said I'd never hurt you again."

He took hold of her shoulders. "Hurt me?" His arms went around her and he drew her close. "My God, Liz, you bring me life. You always have. How could that hurt me?"

"You're a senator, Stuart. If anyone found out . . ."

"They won't.'"

"We thought that the last time."

"I'll be more careful."

His eyes were warm, the love in them overflowing, and Lizette wished she could forget how it had been with them before, only she couldn't. Her feelings were too alive, and she needed him now more than ever.

"Do we really dare?" she asked, her voice breaking. "Can I live with myself if I do?"

"Can you live with yourself if you don't?"

Lizette trembled, knowing what could be hers. "Just this once!" she whispered fervently. "Do you think maybe just this once . . . would it be so wrong, Stuart?"

"Wrong? For whom, Liz, us? Never!" and as his lips touched hers again, his fingers began to fumble with the buttons on her dress, and she didn't care anymore. Not for Julia or Bain or anyone except herself. It was her turn to feel, to know, to be fulfilled, and all that mattered was the moment.

Stuart undressed her slowly, remembering with each garment that came off, the first time he'd undressed her years ago in the old barn near River Oaks. And yet tonight was so different. They were both older now, and so much had happened in their lives. The magic was still there for him, though, and after tossing her chemise aside where he'd thrown her dress and bonnet, he cupped her breasts, the afternoon sun streaming in at the window, turning their tips a golden brown, and they were full.

"You're nursing?" he asked.

She flushed. "I'd forgotten."

"It doesn't matter." His smile was warm, tender. "They're still beautiful," and he kissed the crease between them, finished undressing her, then looked down at her. "You're lovely," he whispered, and began shedding his frock coat while she stood watching him, unable to move.

It had been so long, and yet she was self-conscious. Something she'd never been with Bain. Bain! Tears flooded her eyes, blurring them, and she couldn't see Stuart anymore.

He tossed his last piece of clothing on the chair with hers, then saw the tears in her eyes.

"For him?" he asked.

She shook her head. "I don't know, for me perhaps, or you. Oh, Stuart, I don't know," she cried helplessly, but he didn't let her search for the answer as he reached out, drawing her against him, the sudden contact of flesh against flesh igniting her once more, and she knew there'd be no turning back.

She needed Stuart, just this once. Only once, she kept telling herself, then she'd be whole again, and as he kissed her, then lowered her slowly onto the coverlet, Lizette didn't care anymore that she'd promised never to let him become a part of her life again, and she gave herself to him freely, loving him the way she'd loved him once before, the way she'd loved his brother Bain, with no restraints, because she needed him.

A short time later Lizette still lay in his arms trying to understand what was happening to her, only she was having a hard time doing it. It was over. That wild heat of passion, the driving need to feel loved and wanted was over, and now she held her breath, suddenly realizing that she'd done the very thing she had vowed never to do again. Slowly, methodically, the guilt began to set in, and she felt ashamed.

He kissed the soft skin below her ear and nuzzled her neck, an arm pulling her closer against him.

"Tell me I'm not dreaming," he said.

She sighed. "I wish you were."

"Oh?"

"Why?" she asked, tears glistening in her eyes again. "Why did I do this, Stuart?" She let him turn her head to face him, and once more his resemblance to Bain made her feel so strange inside. It was almost as if Bain were beside her, and yet she knew it was Stuart. "I said I'd never let you touch me again."

"They were the words of a woman who felt loved. You didn't have to prove anything to yourself when you said them."

"What about Washington? We thought Bain was dead, and yet I still kept my promise."

"You thought he'd died loving you."

"I guess."

She looked away, staring up at the ceiling. His hands began to caress her again, and it felt good. Her body, although still throbbing inside from the pleasure Stuart had already given it, began to tingle again delightfully with every touch he bestowed on her, and she turned to him.

"Kiss me again, Stuart," she begged tearfully. "Kiss me and tell me I'm not a horrible person. Please, take the shame from me," and he not only kissed her, but entered her again, more slowly this time, trying to wash away the guilt he knew she was feeling, with all the love he'd been harboring for her over the years.

Sometime later, when they finally left the stone house behind, each going their separate ways, the bed straightened as it had been before, with the pillows fluffed up, and the windows closed, Lizette was still uncertain of everything. Especially where Stuart was concerned. And although, when they parted, she told him they didn't dare let anything like this happen again, she knew that given the right time and place, she could no longer promise her conscience that it wouldn't.

Chapter 18

LIZETTE HAD WATCHED Stuart ride his horse down the drive and on up the road before locking the door and leaving the house herself, and now, after a brisk walk, since she'd spent more time away than she'd planned, she crossed the street at the other side of town and hurried toward the Kolters' red brick house. She'd noticed very little during her walk back, since her thoughts were still on Stuart and the feelings he'd rekindled in her that were now warring constantly with her conscience.

Dammit anyway, she thought. Why do I always have to be trying to do things right? Why can't I just do what I want and to hell with the world? She straightened her bonnet as she walked along, and smoothed the skirt of her dress, making sure the buttons were all in the right buttonholes so no one would suspect anything, then stopped at the end of the walk, staring at the house, the parasol shading her face, and she knew why. Because she was Lizette Kolter, that's why, and Lizette Kolter had been brought up to know right from wrong.

A frown suddenly settled across her forehead. It had been so wonderful, though, and as she thought back over the way she'd felt while Stuart made love to her, the frown began to vanish, to be replaced by a look of sheer contentment that made her eyes shine and brought color to her cheeks. However, she was unaware of it as she inhaled sharply and began walking toward the front door.

"Good heavens," Rebel exclaimed when Lizette finally joined them in the garden a few minutes later. "You were gone so long, dear, we were afraid you'd decided to start cleaning the place to move in."

Lizette's face reddened uncomfortably. "Afraid not, Mother. Unless Grandma Dicia's tired of having us."

The baby had awakened only a short time before and Loedicia was holding her. "Nonsense," she said. "You and the children are welcome at the Château for as long as you like."

Lizette smiled. "Thank you, Grandma," and she walked over to Loedicia, holding out her hands. "Here, I'll take her."

Loedicia started handing the baby to Lizette.

"You should have come back a bit sooner," Madeline said as she watched her daughter-in-law start taking the baby from Loedicia. "Stuart dropped by on his way out to his place and I think it would have been nice if you could have been here to say hello."

Lizette was clutching the baby now, and her face paled. He hadn't said a word about stopping by his mother's.

"I didn't know he was home," she replied, hoping her voice sounded steadier than her knees were, and she sat down quickly in one of the chairs.

"Neither did we." Madeline didn't seem to notice Lizette's discomfort. "But he said he got home yesterday. And, oh yes, dear," she went on. "He got so much enjoyment out of seeing the baby. Said she looks just like Bain."

"Did he really?" Lizette was trying hard to appear nonchalant, knowing she'd have to go on with the pretense of not having seen him. "Does he know about Bain?" she asked.

Madeline flushed. "I hope you don't mind, dear, but I believe Julia wrote and told him while he was still in Washington."

"It doesn't really matter, I guess," Lizette answered. "By now I presume all of Beaufort knows."

"It is something that's hard to keep secret, Liz," Rebel said, joining the conversation. "After all, you did come home without him."

Lizette's jaw clenched stubbornly. They were right, and she knew it, but that didn't make the hurt any easier to take. She inhaled deeply, then hugged Genée closer, her cheek against the baby's, and she wished she could tell them all that at least one man still loved her. The thought was sheer folly, though, and instead she changed the subject, asking about Felicia and Alex and the new baby Felicia'd had that was about the same age as Genée.

Later that evening, back at the Château, Lizette, after

having finished nursing the baby and putting her to bed a
short time earlier, finally decided to excuse herself too, and
headed up to her room, leaving her grandparents sitting
alone together on the back terrace where the three of them
had been enjoying the balmy evening. It was quite late and
everyone else had been in bed for at least an hour already.

Loedicia watched her granddaughter leave, then looked
over at Roth. He was sitting in his favorite chair with his feet
up on a footstool, light from the foyer inside turning his
white hair into a thick golden mane, only his face was
hidden because of the shadows. She leaned closer, her violet
eyes full of concern.

"Roth, have you noticed anything different about Lizette
lately?" she asked.

He studied her curiously for a few seconds. "Like what?"

She took a deep breath, leaning even closer, and brushed
some stray hairs off her forehead, then reached back, making sure all the pins were still in the back of her hair. Even
gray, the curls were unruly, the same as they had been when
she was young.

"Oh, I don't really know," she answered. "Except it seems
like ever since she got back, she's looked so sad and melancholy. Even when she was laughing, there was always an
emptiness inside her, and a restlessness that was so unlike
the way she used to be. Then suddenly, this afternoon . . ."
She hesitated, trying to pick the right words.

"What happened this afternoon?"

"That's just it," she answered. "Nothing happened this
afternoon. At least nothing I know of, or anyone else for
that matter. But when Lizette came back from going through
their old house . . . Roth, I swear when she joined us again
out on the terrace she had one of the most contented looks
on her face that I've ever seen, and her hair was even
mussed a bit in back and on the sides. As if she'd tried to
redo it."

"So what are you trying to say?"

"I'm not sure." She stood up, walked to the edge of the
terrace, and stared out across the back lawn toward the
river. The night was so quiet, the moon just reaching the top
of the trees, and everything looked so tranquil. She held her
breath for a second. If only life could be so peaceful. She
turned to face Roth again, then strolled over, standing next
to the chair he was in. After a few seconds she sat down

beside his feet on the footstool and dropped her hands into
her lap, spreading the skirt of her deep violet dress over her
knees. "Do you remember back three years ago, to when
Bain shot Stuart, then came back on board the *Interlude* up
in Baltimore?" she asked.

He sighed. "How could I forget?"

"Do you remember what he told us that night?"

"You mean about Lizette and Stuart having been lovers
before he married her?"

"Bain said she'd been pregnant with Stuart's baby when
she became his wife, then lost it later and got pregnant with
the twins."

"Aha, I think I see," he said knowingly. "And Stuart's
back in town, right?"

"Well, it is plausible."

Roth stared at Loedicia. Her eyes were mirroring the
turmoil inside her, and he understood what she was going
through only too well. She'd seen both her children and her
grandchildren go through so much over the years, and now
. . . She looked so beautiful as she watched him too, waiting
for him to say something to still her fears. And how young
she looked tonight. At sixty-seven, the years had been good
to her, and as the light from inside fell across her face, he
studied every line lovingly, remembering distinctly when
each new one was added.

"But you said earlier that he told all of you he came back
yesterday," he finally said, hoping to appease her.

She frowned. "I know, that's just the trouble. And yet . . ."
She gazed at him, trying to see his face more clearly, but
it was too dark. "Something changed Liz's outlook on things
today, Roth," she went on. "And I can't see it being
that house. Why, I thought for sure she'd come back with
her eyes all red from crying. Instead, I swear she looked
happy."

Roth straightened, then leaned over and took her hands,
holding them tightly. She was the woman he loved, had
always loved, and as his fingers caressed hers, their strength
and firmness belying her age, he smiled.

"So what are you planning to do?" he asked.

She squeezed his hands back and frowned, searching his
face until she caught the vague outline of his eyes, and she
stared into them intently.

"I'm going to watch to see what happens, and if I find out something's going on, I'll try to stop it."

"And if you can't?"

She hesitated. "Then at least I'll know I tried." She was determined. "This family has had enough tragedy, darling, we don't need any more."

He leaned forward and kissed her, then drew away. "I guess that's why I really fell in love with you, Dicia," he said, watching the tiny crow's-feet crinkle about her violet eyes. "You never could stay out of the middle of things."

She pulled her hands from his. "Are you insinuating I'm a meddling old fool?"

"Good heavens, no." He laughed. "It's just that you never were the type to sit back and just ignore everything going on around you, and I guess I like you for that. It takes a lot of courage to interfere in other people's lives when you know that nine times out of ten they'll resent you for it, but you've never let that stop you, no matter who it was, or what the consequences were."

"So I'm stubborn," she reflected. "But it's a good stubbornness, Roth, it is. I know it is. I've never interfered maliciously, have I? But if by being stubborn I can keep just one person from hurting himself or anyone else, I feel I have to."

"Well then, I guess you'd better help me tonight, lady," he said playfully, "because tonight I'm the one who's hurting, and I'm hurting real bad."

She smiled, knowing what he meant, and her face flushed profusely. "Then I guess we'd best go upstairs, don't you think, Mr. Chapman?" Her eyes grew soft and languorous, her voice lowering seductively. "After all, it wouldn't be fair for me to let you go on suffering, now, would it?"

Roth stood up, then pulled her to her feet, and his arms went around her. She was so short, and yet he didn't mind bending down at all. In fact he was glad she was small because it was easier to carry her, and with muscles he'd never let get flabby and useless over the years, he reached down, picked her up, and left the terrace with her cradled in his arms, moving into the foyer and on upstairs to their bedroom, where the years rolled back for both of them and they were young again in spirit if not in body, as they made love to each other with a passion undimmed by time or age. And for a while Loedicia forgot to worry about her granddaughter or anyone else as she found contentment in Roth's arms.

The next few days went slowly for Lizette. All she had to sustain her were her memories. Those, and her children. Only even they couldn't make the time go any faster. Aunt Ann and Uncle Teak were planning to sail from Beaufort on the twenty-fifth of May, heading back to England, so Rebel and Beau had decided to have a party in their honor the weekend before they left, which was the eighteenth. Gallagher had already been sent back to Charleston with the coach they'd ridden down in, because it wasn't needed in Port Royal, and Greenbriar, who claimed he'd hired on solely for a means of coming south, had disappeared the day after they arrived, which surprised everyone, including Teak, and no one had seen him since.

By early Saturday evening, May 18, Lizette was restless again. It had been over two weeks since she'd been with Stuart, but that wasn't the reason she was uneasy. It was because he was going to be at the party at Tonnerre tonight, he and Julia both, and Lizette wasn't sure she'd be able to face him in public and not give herself away. All the while she'd been up in her room getting ready she'd been apprehensive, and now as she said good-bye to the children, promising to bring them some sweets from the party, she could feel her insides quivering.

Her flow of milk had begun to slow down a few days after her visit to her in-laws and by the end of that week she'd been forced to ask Grandma Dicia if they could find a wet nurse for Genée. Something she'd been hoping she wouldn't have to do, although she had to admit that the past couple of weeks it had been nice to have her freedom. Like tonight. If she were still nursing, it would be harder for her to leave.

Since none of the slaves at either the Château or Tonnerre had given birth recently, Grandpa Roth and Lizette's father, Beau Dante, had gone on one of their infrequent trips to a nearby slave auction and come back with a shy young slave girl, still in her teens, whose owner had decided to sell her after she'd given birth to the second stillborn baby in the past two years.

"When they ain't no good for breedin', they ain't no use keepin' 'em," his overseer had told Roth before the auction even started. "But if you need a wet nurse . . . ain't that's what ya said? Well, she should do fine."

So soft-spoken, blue-eyed Dodee joined the household at the Château. Her papers stated that she was seventeen and had been born at Palmerston Grove and sold at the age of two along with her mother to one of the other neighboring plantations from where Roth had acquired her. However, no mention was made in the papers that she was the offspring of a white man, and Roth was certain he knew who the man was. Everett Palmer, as well as his sons, had been known to frequent their slave quarters. A practice that Roth and Beau detested.

At the age of seventeen, Dodee was frightened to death at first, not knowing what to expect, but it took her only a few days for her to realize that her days of beatings and being subjected to any number of indecencies were over, and that here, at the Château, she was going to be treated like a human being. Something that had rarely happened to her before, and by the end of her first week, she had already taken an unusual liking to Genée. Her soft blue eyes, such a contrast to her brown skin, dark kinky hair, and slightly Negroid features, would often watch the rest of the family secretly, and she'd wondered so many times already how she'd managed to end up here, because except for the fact that her life was still not her own and she belonged to someone else, she really liked the place.

Lizette had already said her good-byes to Blythe, and she left the boys' room, going back to her own room to give Dodee her last-minute instructions, then took one last look in the mirror to make sure she looked all right. The dress she had on was a little more revealing than what she had planned, but Aunt Darcy and Aunt Ann both said low décolletage was all the rage now, so she smoothed the satin pleats that tapered away from her bustline and ran all the way to the edge of her shoulders, then reached beneath her breasts to make sure the corset she was wearing was tight enough, since the dress she had on didn't have an empire waist. Instead, made of peach-colored satin with an overskirt of sheer gauze the same color, it hooked down the back, making her waistline appear slimmer, she hoped, and had small puff sleeves with gauze ruffles that hung to her elbows, and tiny seed pearls scattered here and there on the over-skirt and bodice. It was a dress Lizette had worn on her twentieth birthday, but it had had a high neckline of gauze and ruffles then. All they had done for tonight was remove

them, and she was wearing a pearl necklace and earrings,
her hair piled to the back of her head and resting lightly
above her forehead. It was the first time she'd dressed so
extravagantly since her return, and she wondered as she
stared into the mirror if Stuart would like it.

The thought made her blush, and she tried to shove it
aside quickly as she heard the unmistakable sounds of the
horses and carriages being readied outside. She patted her
hair in a couple of places, walked over and picked up a short
white velvet cape off the bed, along with her gloves and a
fan, then went to the open window, looking down toward
the drive at the other end of the house. She could just barely
see the horses' heads as they were being backed into their
harness, and she turned to Dodee.

"I'd better get downstairs," she said. "Now, you have
your instructions?"

"Yes, ma'am." Dodee's voice was as timid as everything
else about her. "And if I needs you for anythin' at all, I's to
tell Mattie and she'll see someone fetches you, right?"

Lizette took a deep breath. "Right." She walked over and
looked down at Genée, who was lying in her cradle quite
unconcerned that her mother was going out. Bending over,
Lizette kissed her on the cheek, then squeezed her hand.

"Now, remember," she told Dodee. "If she's asleep before ten, just let her sleep and don't wake her for a feeding."

The young woman nodded, and Lizette left, a little apprehensive about leaving the girl alone for so long with the
baby, but then, she wasn't really here alone. If she did run
into any real trouble, Pretty and Mollie were both in the
house. With her mind eased a little, she joined the rest of
the family, who were all near the front door waiting, and
they left for Tonnerre.

They had to use two carriages tonight, and Lizette rode
with her grandparents, very aware that she'd no doubt be
the only woman tonight without a proper escort. At first the
thought had rankled her, but then stubbornness set in, and
she was determined to enjoy herself in spite of it.

It was a beautiful evening, the breeze off the water filling
the air with the scent of the river as the carriages from the
Château joined the others that were already there, and after
being greeted enthusiastically they were escorted into the
huge ballroom that had been built at Tonnerre years before,
where the guests of honor were treated to what could be

described more as a royal welcoming rather than the bon-voyage party it was meant to be.

Some of the people Ann knew only vaguely, and didn't remember. Some she didn't know at all, and others she remembered only too well, including Martin Engler and his wife, Priscilla. It was strange seeing Martin again, and she watched him curiously, her sloe eyes amused as he talked to Teak, trying to ingratiate himself because of Teak's title. The man always had been blinded by money and position, she thought. Thank God she'd been in a position to refuse his offer to be his mistress years ago. If Teak knew of it, he'd probably throw Martin out, instead of standing talking to him. But that was the past, and it was so unimportant now. What was important, and also hilariously funny to Ann, was here she was, the young woman none of the blue-blooded families had wanted their sons to become serious over because of her Indian blood, and she was a countess. She smiled inwardly to herself more than once during the evening at the thought.

The party had been in progress for almost an hour by the time Stuart and Julia arrived, and Lizette was glad because it meant she wouldn't have to meet them face-to-face until she was ready, and she had no idea when that would be, because she had to summon up more courage.

She'd been standing at the far end of the ballroom when she heard people whispering, and wondered if they had come in. Her heart skipped a beat. She couldn't let them spot her, not just yet, so, moving to the stage where the orchestra was playing, she ascended the steps onto it and hid behind an oversize potted plant, trying to see without being conspicuous, while she glanced off toward the doorway. They were there, all right, with the light from hundreds of candles in the chandeliers overhead making it easy for her to see them. Only she was afraid they'd see her too, and panicking, she left the stage, heading quickly toward the French doors at the side of the ballroom, hoping maybe she could slip out before they'd see her, but she wasn't quite fast enough as she heard her mother-in-law's voice behind her and stopped, then turned to face her.

"There you are, dear," Madeline said as she greeted her. "Didn't you hear? Julia and Stuart have arrived, and I happen to know you haven't seen them yet since you came home." She frowned, concerned as she took Lizette's hand, her own encased in a blue lace glove that matched her dress. "Now, come along. I've already told them you'd be here, and believe me, dear, they've been dying to see you. And they don't think anything bad of you over what happened either, believe me. Now, don't you think it's rather silly the way you've been avoiding them? Because I know that's what you've been doing."

Lizette stared at her, furious that now she'd be forced to see them before she was ready. Only she smiled instead, and tried to laugh off Madeline's statement that she'd been trying to avoid them, while she let her mother-in-law drag her, elbowing their way through the crowd toward the door where Senator Stuart Kolter and his wife were still being greeted by friends and constituents, because after all, no one in his right mind would forgo the opportunity of trying to get on his good side.

Lizette let Madeline lead the way, realizing as they went that her father-in-law wasn't far behind them, and occasionally as she'd glance back, she had the distinct feeling he was watching her a little too intently, and it bothered her because Rand Kolter was the only one, except for Stuart and Bain, who knew about her affair with Stuart before she was married, and, she wondered now if he was remembering it. By the look on his face, something was bothering him, because he was about as pale as the gray frock coat he had on, and even the colorful striped cravat couldn't put color in his cheeks.

Lizette brushed the thought aside quickly, then almost froze at her first sight of Stuart, and it was only by sheer will that she managed to keep her feet moving. He was still talking to Teak and Ann, with a few other people gathered around, the deep turquoise coat he wore clashing with Julia's pale blue dress, and without wanting it to happen, Lizette could feel her face begin flushing, and her heart was pounding. She tried to pull her hand from Madeline's, but her mother-in-law was hanging on like a leech.

"Excuse me," Madeline said, slipping by a couple Lizette barely knew, and Madeline smiled as Teak and the others turned toward her. "Look who I found," she exclaimed, pulling Lizette forward and putting an arm about her waist. "I told her she has to quit hiding herself away, especially from family."

Lizette could feel the heat in her face and she wanted to die, but instead she forced herself to stand as tall and straight as she could, tilted her chin up stubbornly, and looked directly at Stuart.

"She thinks I've been avoiding you and Julia," she said, holding her voice as even and steady as she could. "If I have, it has nothing to do with you, either of you, believe me," and she glanced at Julia, who had suddenly grabbed Stuart's arm and was holding it tightly. A gesture Lizette had spotted right away. "And it has nothing to do with the fact that some people think I should feel ashamed over what happened, because I don't. It's just that you look so much like Bain, Stuart," she went on as she looked over at Stuart again, "and right now I'd rather not be reminded of Bain."

Rebel, who'd been in the group of people surrounding Teak and Senator Kolter, saw the pain in Lizette's eyes, and moved forward, trying to ease the awkward situation without hurting Madeline, who suddenly realized she should have let well enough alone.

"Come now, the music's starting up again," Rebel said, loudly enough so everyone could hear. "So why doesn't everyone dance. Now that the senator's here, and Teak's met him, perhaps we could all enjoy a quadrille," and as she stepped between Lizette and Stuart, raising her hand toward the orchestra, the musicians started tuning their instruments and everyone took the hint, moving away from the door reluctantly but tactfully.

Now it was Madeline's turn to blush as she turned toward Lizette. "Oh, my dear," she apologized frantically, "I never thought . . . It didn't occur to me . . . I'm sorry. I guess because they're my sons I forget at times that they look so much alike." She shook her head. "I didn't mean to. I wouldn't have if I'd only realized. Can you forgive me?"

Lizette was still staring at Stuart, and knew she shouldn't be, so she drew her gaze from him and looked at her mother-in-law, taking Madeline's hands in hers. She could see Madeline was really upset over what she'd done.

"Please," Lizette assured her, "I know you didn't mean anything, and I probably should have said something to you about it, but the subject is so painful to me . . ." She glanced up at Rand, who was directly behind Madeline. "You do understand, don't you?"

Rand Kolter stared down at his daughter-in-law, and for a minute he wasn't sure what he was thinking, except that he was remembering the past a little too vividly. He straightened, brushing the thought aside, and had to tell himself that this was tonight, and had nothing to do with that other night when he'd learned of Stuart's affair with this young woman, who was now his daughter-in-law.

"I guess I can't blame you, Liz," he finally answered. "But you can't avoid everything that reminds you of Bain for the rest of your life."

"And I don't intend to, believe me. But for now I'd rather pick the time and place for the reminders, please. It makes it easier." She squeezed Madeline's hands, then walked away, heading out the door the senator and his wife had just come through.

"Well, I must say," Julia said. "She hasn't changed much, has she?"

Madeline looked at her in surprise. "What do you mean by that?"

"She's still spoiled, stubborn, and looks like she's stuffed into her clothes. No wonder Bain left her."

Stuart's jaw clenched angrily and he wanted to strike back at Julia, but knew if he did there'd be hell to pay.

However, Madeline didn't care. "Good heavens, Julia, is that any way to talk about Liz?" she admonished, her pale blue eyes looking at her other daughter-in-law with disgust. "Why, you should be ashamed of yourself. She's no more spoiled and stubborn than you and I, and you know it. . . . And as far as her weight . . . well, even if she does have a few extra pounds on her, Bain didn't care."

"He isn't back yet, is he?" Julia snapped.

"But he will be, you'll see."

Julia stared at her mother-in-law. "I'm sorry, Mother Kolter," she said, trying not to alienate her mother-in-law too much. After all, Madeline had no idea what she'd gone through back in Washington because of Liz. "But it seems as if she can do anything she wants and everyone's supposed to accept it just like that, without even so much as a by-your-leave. Well, I'll tell you, if Bain decided to leave her, he no doubt had a good reason."

"That's my daughter you're talking about, Julia," Rebel warned. "I'd advise you to watch what you say."

Julia glanced over at blond, violet-eyed Rebel Dante, still so attractive for her age, the filmy pink dress she wore making her look even younger and more lovely. Lizette's mother was as bad as she was, if the truth were fully known,

Julia thought, and she could feel Stuart's body tense, cautioning her to watch her tongue.

"Oh, I'm sorry, Rebel," she apologized. "Please forgive me. I guess I got a little carried away. Mother Kolter's right, I shouldn't have mentioned Lizette's weight, but you see, it's just that I feel so sorry for the poor thing."

"No one has to feel sorry for Liz," Rebel said, her eyes bristling. "She doesn't need anyone's pity. She's been through a horrible ordeal, one you probably couldn't even survive, Julia, but she did make it through, and she'll make it the rest of the way without Bain too. Now, if you don't mind, this isn't a party to celebrate Lizette's coming home, it's a party to say good-bye to my brother and Ann, so why don't you and Stuart go over and join the dancing, and we'll try to forget this whole episode ever happened."

Stuart could have kissed Liz's mother.

"Thank you, Rebel," he said, then looked over at his wife. "Whether you realize it or not, Julia, she had every right to ask us to leave just now, but she was nice about it. So if you'll just keep your mouth shut long enough, we'll join the others to see if we can salvage some of the evening," and he led a very disgruntled Julia off toward the refreshment table, where the guests who weren't dancing were emptying the punch bowl and enjoying the food.

The first thing Stuart did was get a good strong drink; then he and Julia talked to a few acquaintances he was glad had missed the confrontation earlier, finally ending up a short while later on the dance floor. However, all during the next two dances, Julia kept making little snide remarks like she always did, and he wondered if she was doing it for his benefit or her own, because they were always about Liz. Even before all the mess Liz had gotten into, Julia had been good at trying to undermine her. That was one reason he had always hated it when the family got together for holidays and birthdays, because he always had to sit and listen to Julia making nasty remarks to him about Liz and knew he didn't dare defend her. That, and because it hurt so much to have to sit there and watch Liz and Bain obviously so terribly in love and know that Liz could never be his. Now Bain had deserted her, and Stuart wished there was more he could do to ease her pain.

Stuart glanced down at his wife while they danced. He'd hoped that after that horrible scandal in Washington a few years back, when he'd almost lost his Senate seat, that Julia would change, but she hadn't. He had still loved her then in his own way, but it hadn't helped. In one breath she'd tell him she believed him when he said he didn't love Liz, and in the next she'd be accusing and suspicious. In fact, every time the family got together she'd nag at him like hell afterward, telling him she knew he'd been lying to her all along just for the sake of his career. After a while he hadn't even bothered to deny it, and had just let her rave. Why try reassuring someone who didn't want to hear it? She seemed to be enjoying the part of the suffering wife.

That was also about the same time the visits to her bed became fewer. She hadn't come right out and refused, she'd known better than that after what happened in Washington, but there were too many days when she didn't feel well, or some equally simple excuse, and he was glad sometimes that he could spend as much time as he did away from home. That way, she had no reason to complain if he wasn't around to pester her. That was what was so strange about his whole marriage. He was lucky if she suffered his presence in her bed twice a month, and yet if he didn't at least pretend he wanted her favors more often, she'd accuse him of having someone else on the side. Sometimes he wished he could understand her, but understanding Julia would take a genius. He knew she was fanatic about not wanting any more children, so he always tried to be careful, and for years it seemed to be enough, but lately . . .

The music stopped and they joined some other guests, then before long Stuart realized he was being edged out of the conversation, since the guests were mostly women, so having seen a group of men over near the door in a heated talk that looked like it might be political, he excused himself, realizing he wasn't even going to be missed, and walked away, leaving Julia talking with the women about recipes and the new finishing school that was going to be opening in Beaufort in the fall.

When he was about ten feet from the door, however, he suddenly stopped, staring at it, and changed his mind. He didn't want to talk to Heath and the rest of them. Not about politics or anything else. He wanted to find Liz, and since he couldn't see her anywhere in the ballroom, he assumed she hadn't come back in yet. His mind made up, he sauntered slowly toward the door, then slipped through it.

Outside the moon was high, the air balmy and the scent of cape jasmine and honeysuckle filled Lizette's nostrils as she sat on the riverbank beneath the huge oak trees, their branches hung heavy with Spanish moss that kept the moonlight from reaching her. Now and then the smell of the river would overpower the sweet honeysuckle, but she didn't mind. It was all Tonnerre, and full of memories. The whole world was full of memories and there was no way to get away from them, no matter where she went.

She felt a chill run through her and drew her knees up, the filmy gauze overskirt slipping as she tried to tuck it against the satin, and she bit her lip angrily, fighting back the tears. They didn't understand, nobody did, except Stuart perhaps. But then, Stuart always understood.

She'd been sitting here for some time, trying to let the anger and humiliation die a quiet death, and was just ready to stand up and head back toward the house, hoping she could forget what had happened, when she heard a twig snap behind her.

"Liz?"

She turned and looked up at him. "Hello, Stuart."

He closed the space between them and dropped down, facing her. "You weren't crying, were you?"

"It doesn't matter."

"I had no idea Mother'd do that to you."

"I should have realized. After all, she never knew about us."

"I'm sorry, Liz." He reached out and took her hand. "I've missed you. . . . You know I have to see you." He lifted her hand to his lips. "Liz, we could meet where we used to meet."

"You mean it's still there?"

"I was there the other day. I'd hoped . . ."

"I'd thought of that, but I didn't think you'd remember."

"How could I forget?" He reached out, pulling her against him.

"No, Stu, not here," she whispered. "Someone'll see us."

"I have to, Liz, just this once." He kissed her long and hard, then looked into her face, trying to look into her eyes, but it was too dark. All he could see was her vague outline, but it was enough to stir him. Her dress was silky beneath his hands and he could feel the round firmness of her body pushing against the material, and it was a good feeling. "Monday, Liz, meet me there Monday," he whispered against her ear.

She sighed. "What time?"

"I have a meeting at one. It won't take long. I'll be there by four."

"And if something happens?"

"If I don't make it, leave a note under the rock like we used to."

She ran her fingers along his coat lapel, then fingered his black cravat and the ruffled shirt he wore. "I wasn't going to let this happen, Stuart," she said reluctantly.

He took a deep breath. "Do you want it to stop?"

"I need you."

"And I need you." He stood up, pulled her to her feet, and took her in his arms again, the shadows from the moss-laden trees overhead still hiding them. "I'll die a thousand deaths until Monday," he said.

She sighed. "And I a thousand and one."

He kissed her more softly this time; then his arms eased from around her and he walked her back up toward the house, leaving her to walk the last few feet alone, where the risk of being seen together was too great; then, just before Lizette disappeared into the brightly lit ballroom, she glanced back for a moment to where she'd left him standing, near a magnolia tree, and sighed, the strength of his kiss still warming her lips.

The rest of the evening was uneventful for Lizette even though there were times she was forced to talk to Stuart and Julia again, as well as the rest of the Kolters. However, after her talk with Stuart outside and his promise to meet her on Monday afternoon, she didn't care what anyone thought anymore, and each time their eyes met during the rest of the evening, the promise was still there for her to see in his eyes, although no one except Stuart and she was aware of it. Even when everyone was saying good-bye it took just a quick glance of assurance from him, only as their carriage made its way down the drive a little before eleven, Lizette had no idea that one other person had also seen that look of assurance as well as some of the other glances that had been exchanged that evening between Stuart and her, but it wasn't until almost three weeks later that she learned of it.

In the meantime, on Monday afternoon, as he had promised, Stuart met her in the ruins of an old building not far from the river's edge, near the southern tip of the island, but still on Château property. A building that rumor said once had been used by the infamous pirate Teach, and Lizette and Stuart rekindled the forbidden love affair they'd been forced to put an end to when Lizette married Bain because she was pregnant with Stuart's child.

During that time Teak and Ann, with a great many tearful good-byes, said their farewells to family and friends, packed up their clothes, the boys, and Mollie, and sailed from Beaufort on the *White Rose,* a merchantman out of Jamaica, heading for London, promising Loedicia that they wouldn't stay away so long the next time, and Lizette was sad as she stood on the pier with the rest of the family watching them leave. They'd been so good to her and the baby, and never asked any recompense, only it wasn't just that. It was fun having Ann around again, and Liz wondered if Ann was really enjoying her role as a countess and mother as much as she said she was, or was it because being in love with Teak made it all worthwhile?

The thought made her think of Bain and the life they'd had together, and she understood Ann's happiness as she stood quietly watching the ship disappear in the distance, leaving Port Royal Sound. In the days that followed, the Château was so much quieter, with only one little boy to disrupt things, and it took a couple of days for everyone to get over the feeling of loss at their leaving.

But by the middle of the week, things were back to normal again, and life at the Château went on, only not quite as it had before. Lizette really didn't know what to do with herself.

Pretty did a beautiful job taking care of Blythe, so she wasn't needed there, only for an occasional visit or to read to her. Luther had even put wheels on the chair they'd made for Blythe, so it was easier for them to take her from room to room, and he'd fixed it so that when the chair was stationary a block of wood could be put between the wheel and the leg of the chair to keep the wheels from moving. He had even put a seat in a pony cart he'd talked Lizette into buying from one of the neighboring plantations, and he fixed it so Blythe wouldn't fall out; then he'd pull her all over the place so she didn't have to just sit in the yard and watch the river go by anymore.

Aunt Darcy suggested they hitch a pony to it, but Luther wouldn't allow it, and neither would Pretty. They were both

afraid the pony might get skittish and there'd be another
accident.

"Besides, she's light as a feather, that child is," Luther
explained. "I don't minds pullin' her at all."

So Lizette would watch, pleased as could be as Luther
covered the plantation grounds daily with Blythe and her
pony cart in tow. And as for Braxton, he was like a shadow
to Grandpa Roth, only occasionally foregoing being with
him to join his Great-Uncle Heath on an equally exciting
excursion to town or up the river or any of the other places
he had to go.

They did have a few quiet times together in the evening,
though, when Grandpa and Heath were through for the day,
and once in a while he'd include her on one of his jaunts to
the nearby fields. But most of the time it was just a quick
hug and a kiss before trailing off behind someone else so he
could learn something new.

At least Genée was small enough so Lizette could still be
an important part of her life, only since she couldn't nurse
her anymore, even that closeness was gone. All she could do
now was sit with her as much as possible and help teach
Dodee what it was to care for a little one. A task the young
girl learned very quickly.

So Lizette kept busy with other things as best she could to
keep her mind off her problems, only it wasn't easy because
everywhere there were reminders of the fact that she was
going to have to figure out what she was going to do with
her life. She had no income except Bain's, and his father,
being a lawyer, had made sure that even though Bain wasn't
back, she could still have access to it, and she'd even be
allowed to return to the house if she wanted, but she just
couldn't, not yet. It was too soon and she was still at loose
ends, and the only pleasure she seemed to have anymore
was her stolen hours with Stuart, but even that was weighing
on her mind because she was so afraid someone would find
out. That's why when she met him today she'd been glad to
tell him her menses had started, even though it meant their
lovemaking couldn't be complete. All she didn't need was
another questionable pregnancy.

It was Friday afternoon, June 7, and as she rode her
palomino, Diablo, back along the bridle trail that led by the
old pond, her thoughts were running rampant. The seven-
teenth was her birthday, and she thought back to her birth-

day last year and how her life had changed. Only a year, yet
it seemed like a century ago.

Reaching up, she ran her fingers along the white feather
in her green velvet hat, then straightened the jacket of her
riding habit that matched it, making sure there was no sign
she'd had it off. Stuart liked her in green, but so had Bain,
and her lips pursed stubbornly at the thought of him. Suddenly tears filled her eyes. She'd tried not to think of him
too much these past few weeks, but it was difficult.

She maneuvered Diablo around a bend in the path, then
spurred him a little faster. The sooner she got back to the
house, the better. She didn't like being alone because it gave
her too much time to think. Reaching the end of the path,
she reined Diablo onto the dirt lane that went between the
slaves' quarters, then past them to the house and stables,
where she dismounted, turning Diablo over to Luther, who
had just put Blythe's cart back in the carriage house after
taking her for a ride.

This done, she waved to Blythe and Pretty, who were
sitting under the tree in the garden, then headed for the
house to change clothes, and ran into Grandma Dicia in the
foyer.

"Well, you're back a little late, aren't you, dear?" Loedicia
said. "You must have enjoyed the ride."

"It keeps me busy."

"That's all?"

Lizette frowned. "Well, it helps me from getting any
fatter, if that's what you mean."

Loedicia glanced at Lizette's hat, noticing it was at a
slightly different angle than when she'd left, just like the
other day; then she looked down at her riding boots, the toes
showing beneath her skirt. They were badly scuffed.

"That's not what I meant, Liz," she said solemnly. "And I
think maybe it's time we had a talk."

"About what?"

"About you and Stuart," she whispered softly, then raised
her voice. "Come, we'll go into the library."

Lizette was dumbfounded and just stared at her grandmother as Loedicia headed toward the library door, then
stood with it open, waiting for her.

"Liz?" she called.

Lizette's feet moved automatically because her mind wasn't
on what she was doing. It was still echoing Grandma Dicia's

words over and over again. She reached her grandmother, and Loedicia took her arm, pulling her into the library, then shut the door behind them.

Lizette shook her head as if to clear it, then faced Loedicia, finally finding her voice. "What did you say out there, Grandma?" she asked, frowning.

"I said I want to talk to you about Stuart," she answered.

Lizette's eyes were guarded. "What about him?"

"You've been seeing him, haven't you?"

"What do you mean, seeing him?"

"Come now, Liz." Loedicia walked briskly across the floor, the skirt of her crisp pink cotton swishing against her petticoats, and she opened one of the windows to let in some fresh air, then turned to face Lizette, her violet eyes intense, making her hair seem all the grayer, but softening the age lines in her face. "I'm not stupid, you know," she went on as she walked back over to her. "I've seen the signs. I'm just glad no one else saw them."

Lizette stared at her curiously. "I . . . What are you talking about?" she asked.

Dicia shook her head, then looked at Lizette, unwavering. "I'm talking about the way your hair was messed up when you came back from your house that day we visited the Kolters," she answered. "And the way you and Stuart looked at each other at Tonnerre the night of the party, and all the rides on Diablo every day."

"So I like to ride Diablo."

"So you can meet Stuart Kolter?"

"Don't be silly!"

"I'm quite serious, Liz," she replied. "And I want it to stop."

"There's nothing to stop."

"Do I have to spell it out for you, Liz?" Dicia asked. "If so, then I will. You've been having an affair with the man ever since you came back, and it has to end, is that clear?"

Lizette's jaw clenched angrily. "It would be if it were true."

"Don't hedge with me, dear," Loedicia admonished. "It won't work and you know it. You see"—her face softened in compassion for Liz—"I know you were once lovers before, and it's only natural now, with Bain gone—"

"You know what?" Liz was taken completely by surprise. "Who told you we were lovers?"

"Your husband."

"Bain?"

"It was after he'd shot Stuart back in Washington. He was only trying to justify his actions so we wouldn't think the worst of him."

"Oh, I see, instead he let you think the worst of me."

"It was true, wasn't it? You were pregnant with Stuart's baby when you married Bain?"

Lizette swallowed hard, her eyes suddenly misting, and she started to turn, to leave, unable to meet her grandmother's accusing eyes.

"No, don't go, Liz," Loedicia said, grabbing her arm, and she held it tightly. "I don't want us to quarrel, please. I just don't want you hurt."

"It's too late for that, isn't it, Grandma?" Liz answered, her voice breaking as she turned to face her. "The only time I don't hurt anymore is when I'm with Stuart."

"But it isn't right. He has a wife and . . . what of his children, Marie and Adam? What happens to them if people find out?"

"They won't."

"You can't be sure." Loedicia's eyes were pleading. "It isn't worth it, Liz."

Lizette looked at Grandma Dicia, the tears in her eyes blurring them momentarily; then she blinked, clearing them. "Isn't it?" she asked when she could see her grandmother's face again. "What would you know, you've never been without love, Grandma. You've never lain in bed and wished for just a touch, a warm caress, or begged God to let you stop feeling so it wouldn't be so bad. How would you know whether it's worth it or not, you've never been without!"

Loedicia stared at Lizette unhappily and let her words sink in, then shook her head. "But not another woman's husband, Liz."

"He's the only one who cares!"

"Oh, Liz!"

"Please, Grandma, let me be," she pleaded helplessly. "Don't ask me to give up Stuart, I won't, I can't, no more than you could give up Grandpa Roth or Grandpa Quinn. I have to have something to live for, please."

"What of your children? You have them."

"Ah yes, the children." She straightened, sniffing, trying to bring the tears under control. "I have them, yes, I agree, but they're only one part of my life, Grandma. They can't give me what I need, and until someone else comes along to take Bain's place other than Stuart . . . Don't ask it, Grandma, please," she begged, "and don't hate me for it, but I can't let him go."

Loedicia's eyes were steady on Lizette's and an ache filled her breast as she realized that no matter what she said Lizette was going to do as she pleased. Loedicia reached out and took her hand.

"I don't hate you, Liz, I never could," she whispered, knowing she was defeated. "I just hope you won't live to rue the day."

Loedicia was still holding Lizette's hand, and Lizette squeezed it. "Thank you, Grandma," she said affectionately, and once more tears welled up in her eyes. "I love you."

"I love you too," Dicia answered, then watched Lizette open the door, leaving the library to go up and change, and her heart went with her.

Chapter 19

OFF IN THE DISTANCE the sky was gray instead of blue, but Lizette paid little attention as she rode Diablo past the pond and on toward the narrow path between the trees that led to the old ruins. It was Monday afternoon, and all weekend she'd thought over her argument with Grandma Dicia in the library last Friday, then tried to avoid being alone with her again, even though when they were together Dicia didn't bring it up. Yet Lizette wished it had never happened.

She'd been terribly hurt to discover that Bain had told her grandparents about her affair with Stuart, and wondered how they could have kept on loving her all these years. Yet they had, otherwise why would they still let her stay? Even now Grandma hadn't threatened to throw her out if she didn't break things off with Stuart. Maybe she should stop seeing him. After all, just because she hadn't gotten pregnant yet didn't mean she wouldn't, no matter how careful they were. Stuart even said there'd been no guarantee with those funny things he'd been using. Still, the thought of giving him up . . .

Suddenly she realized it wasn't just to have someone love her. It was to have Stuart love her, because with Stuart it was like still having Bain. That's why just the thought of giving him up hurt so much, and as she rode along now, nearing the ruins, and saw his horse tied to a tree waiting, she knew someday she'd have to make a decision, only not today.

Stuart heard her coming and stood in the doorway waiting. Part of the roof on the old building had caved in years ago, and the stone that was left was close to crumbling, yet it was shaded and cool. He stepped from the doorway, his blue frock coat off already, the white shirt he was wearing open at the throat, and he reached up, taking the reins from her, tied Diablo near his own horse, then helped her down.

"Where's my smile?" he teased as his arms went around her.

She smiled, but the smile was forced, and she gazed off at the sky. "There's a storm coming up."

He followed her gaze. "So I see." He kissed her, then put an arm around her, and they walked slowly toward the old ruins. "You worried about the rain?" he asked.

She frowned. "The sky's terribly dark."

"It's at least ten minutes away, maybe longer."

"So how do I explain not getting caught in it?"

"You tell them you found shelter somewhere."

"We could be here for hours."

"Have you ever known of a rainstorm this time of day to stay around very long?"

"You're right, I suppose," she answered, then took another look at the sky.

"Besides, I've got something to tell you," he said, looking back at her to catch her reaction.

"What's that?"

"No, after."

"Now," she pleaded. "Please, Stu, tell me now."

"You're not going to like it, unless . . ."

She stared at him curiously, then leaned back, resting her head on what was left of the old door frame. "Go on."

"I'll be leaving for the state capital in the morning."

"Already?"

"I've been home almost a month."

"Then you're gone." She looked away, watching the leaves on the trees and bushes as the wind began to whip up some; then she looked at the sky, thunder rumbling in the distance. "I almost forgot you'd have to go."

"I want you to go with me," he whispered, and she looked at him startled.

"Go with you?"

"Shhh, just listen." He studied her face as he spoke, his heart pounding erratically. "I could find a place for you up there . . . it wouldn't be that hard. Maybe not right in Columbia, but in the country, and I could see you whenever I could get away."

"What about the children? And Blythe, I can't leave her."

"Bring them with you, if you like. We could be discreet."

"You're serious, aren't you?" she said.

He inhaled, his whole body alive with longing. "Dead

serious," he answered. "Bain may not want you, Liz, but I do, and I'd go to hell and back if it meant I could have you."

She stared at him for a long time, then looked away, watching the trees beginning to sway harder now as the wind grew stronger, and she looked back at the clouds again. They were rolling in fast. Suddenly she shivered as a gust of cold air hit them and went right through the fabric of her satin riding habit, and she clutched her arms.

"It's getting cold."

"Here." He grabbed her arm and ushered her into the building, moving way to the back, to a bed of dried leaves beneath what was left of the roof, and he made her sit down. "Is this better?" he asked, putting his arms about her.

She nodded, beginning to warm some against him, then held her breath, her eyes studying the woods outside. It was growing darker by the minute.

"The horses?" she cried anxiously.

"I'll get them."

He stood up, leaving her sitting alone on the bed of leaves, and picked his way back to the doorway. By now the wind was so strong he could hardly stand against it as he left the doorway and stepped outside, with lightning cracking off in the distance somewhere, the sky lighting up ever few seconds like flashes from a mirrored prism.

Stuart leaned into the wind, moving toward the horses, fighting against it as it seemed to get stronger and stronger; then he turned the back of his head into it, to keep the dirt from the floor of the woods from blowing into his eyes.

Damn nuisance, these summer storms, he thought, then turned sideways a little to look back toward the building, to make sure Liz was all right, only it was just dark enough so he couldn't see well. It was only around four in the afternoon, yet more like twilight. He'd have to hurry.

Reaching out, he grabbed the reins of his horse, then began reaching for Diablo's reins, when suddenly a bolt of lightning crashed through the trees overhead like the shot from a cannon, its fiery ball bouncing around from one limb to another, then exploding into a thousand pieces as it hit a huge limb overhead and Stuart let out a yell, hitting at his horse as he did while his own feet started churning the ground, but it was too late.

As lightning followed lightning, and the screaming wind brought the first drops of rain down on him, Stuart felt the

limb hit the back of his head and he went down to his
knees. Clenching his teeth stubbornly, he pushed against the
ground, trying to get up, but his legs wouldn't work, not the
way he wanted them to, and his eyes, although still open,
were blurred so he could hardly see.

"Liz!" he yelled, trying to be heard above the wind, but
all he got for his trouble was a mouthful of rain. He reached
out, trying to grope his way toward the building, only to
grab a handful of leaves as he realized he'd stumbled onto
the end of the limb that had hit him and was hanging over
the end of its branches.

He blinked, his eyes smarting, and suddenly felt sick, a
wave of nausea sweeping over him; then the last thing he
remembered was crying her name again, and hoping she'd
hear.

Lizette had heard the loud crack of lightning, and she'd
risen to her feet in an instant and now she was standing
looking around, but with the rain and wind it was almost
impossible to see anything at all.

"Stuart!" she called, hands cupping her mouth. There was
no answer. Shielding her eyes against the rain, she made her
way to the doorway, then gasped in horror as she saw a huge
limb on the ground where their horses had been, and Stuart's
horse was gone, while Diablo chomped at his bit, whinnying.
Then she let out a cry as she saw Stuart's vague form
hanging partway through the leaves at the end of the tree
limb, his legs dragging in the mud.

Oblivious of the rain and wind, she ran from the building,
fighting to keep her balance until she reached Stuart, then
dropped down beside him. Reaching out, she touched his
face because it was too dark to see, and with the leaves
half-covering him she couldn't tell. His eyes were shut. She
nudged him gently.

"Stuart!"

There was no answer. She had to do something. Standing
up, the wind still trying to push her over, she made her way to
Diablo and began rubbing his nose, talking to the animal
and trying to soothe him; then, once he quieted, she untied
his reins and led him to where Stuart lay crumbled against
the fallen tree limb.

"Down, boy, down," she ordered. But Diablo just stared
at her for a minute, eyes wild, nostrils flaring.

"Down, boy, please," she begged, and suddenly, sensing

he was needed, the big palomino knelt down hesitantly onto his forelegs and waited for her next command.

It was going to be hard moving the fallen branch without a rope, but it had to be moved. So, grabbing her horse's reins, she tied them to some of the branches where Stuart was hanging; then, "Get up, Diablo, up," she ordered hurriedly.

The horse moved slowly at first, raising his forelegs to stand, struggling against the weight of the branch and the elements; then slowly, a little at a time, the end of the huge limb began to move and cleared the ground by about six inches or more, with Stuart still caught in the leaves and branches.

"Now pull," Liz commanded, as she moved to the other side of the horse, and she led him steadily toward the old ruins with the branch in tow.

It was raining even harder now, and lightning was still exploding all around, yet she kept on until they were at what was left of the door. Stopping the horse, she untied the reins from the branch, tied them around Stuart this time, and made sure they were under his armpits, then once more ordered the horse to move, and Stuart was lifted from the branches, tearing his shirt on the way as she backed the horse into the shelter, until they were under what was left of the roof.

Stuart was groaning as she unfastened the reins from around him and lowered him onto the dry leaves, and she laid him on his back, rainwater from her hat hitting him in the face. She wiped it away with her hand, her own tears mingling with the rain on her cheeks.

"Stuart? Can you hear me?" she pleaded.

His head was hurting like hell and he felt so damn weak he could hardly move, but he'd come to now and was just barely able to talk.

"Liz?"

"You're hurt!"

"My head!"

She lifted his head, then reached out, touching the back of it, and when she drew her hand back it was sticky with blood.

"It's bad, isn't it?" he said.

She found his blue frock coat near where she was sitting, grabbed it, rolled it into a ball, and put it beneath his head when she laid it back down. "I couldn't tell, but at least you're talking," she said, not wanting to scare him.

She rubbed her hand on her skirt, using the wet material to wash it off, then took her hat off and laid it behind her. She tried to make him more comfortable.

"I've got to get you some help."

He started to reach up for her hand, but she saw he was too weak and reached down to meet his instead. His fingers were cold, and she shivered, then glanced over at Diablo, who was making strange snorting noises and pawing the ground.

Looking toward the doorway now, she stared curiously, then cocked her ear at a strange rumbling sound in the distance. It almost sounded like thunder but was too long and even. The rain had begun to let up some and now the dark clouds began to dissipate too; then suddenly, as if someone had pulled away a barrier, the wind began to blow again, stronger than before, and the darkness that had been starting to lift grew darker again, and Lizette was surprised to look over and see Diablo drop down onto his forelegs again and roll over onto his side.

She stared down at Stuart, the hair at the nape of her neck prickling as the weird noise she was hearing grew louder and louder until it was all around them, filling her head, until she clamped her hands over her ears; then she read Stuart's lips.

"Tornado!" he mouthed desperately, and she knew he was right.

With one agonizing sob, she dropped down over Stuart, covering him with her body, one hand shielding his head, the other protecting her own, and she lay for what seemed like an eternity while the world around her sounded like it was exploding with her in the middle of it, and she pressed as hard as she could to keep from being torn off him.

Lizette had no idea how long she'd lain there. Ten seconds? Twenty? A full minute? But now she held her breath, realizing the noise was gone as quickly as it had come, and all she could hear now was the gentle sound of the rain on the leaves and grass around her. Exhaling cautiously, she straightened, then looked down into Stuart's eyes. He was still trying to keep them open, but the fight was almost gone from him.

"Don't . . . don't leave me," he gasped breathlessly. "Use Diablo."

"But how would I get you on?"

"Like . . . like he is."

She stared at the horse for a minute, then understood. But before she could even attempt to leave the ruins, she was going to have to see if there was a path left, and getting to her feet, her knees still trembling, she made her way out from beneath the half-fallen roof and looked around.

Branches were strewn helter-skelter, some trees were uprooted, others broken like twigs, and she stared in amazement at a pitchfork sticking out halfway up the trunk of a pine tree some twenty feet away, as well as a piece from some ship's sail lodged in another a little closer.

Trying to keep from shaking, she moved back beneath the ceiling. It was light again now, but still raining, only not as hard. Walking over to Diablo, who was standing now, she hugged the palomino to help still his fears, then led him to Stuart, making him lie down as he'd done during the tornado.

She helped Stuart slide close enough to reach the animal's back; then, while Diablo stood up, and with Liz helping him, Stuart maneuvered himself around, staying on the saddle, although he wasn't any too steady, until the horse was on his feet, Stuart sitting slumped on his back, and Lizette made sure he was as comfortable as possible.

After retrieving her hat and stuffing it onto her head any old way with the hatpin in it, she grabbed Stuart's bloody, balled-up frock coat, shook it out, put it around him, then searched for his hat. Finding it off in the corner, she plopped it on his head, made sure he wasn't likely to fall off, then led Diablo from the ruins of the building.

Once out in the open, she stopped to look around, but there was still no sign of Stuart's horse. That meant she'd have to walk, so picking up her skirts with one hand, while holding Diablo's reins with the other, she started trudging along the path she'd come down only a short time before, only now it was strewn with leaves, twigs, branches, and anything else that hadn't been nailed down.

Almost two hours later, after keeping Stuart from falling off more times than she could count, and with tears down her face, Lizette passed the pond where they used to race their horses, and started down the last stretch of the bridle path toward the house. Now suddenly a new fear gripped her. The tornado! My God, the house! How far had it reached?

Where had it touched? Had it hit only them, or had it moved upriver to the Château.

She tried to quicken her pace, yet keep Stuart in the saddle, and new tears joined those already there. She had to hurry. Please, God, she prayed, give me strength! Her feet were covered with mud to her ankles, and she kept tripping on her riding skirt, and although the rain had finally stopped, water still dripped in her eyes from her hat and her hair; still she moved on.

"Liz?" Stuart asked breathlessly, his mouth barely moving. "Are . . . are we there yet?"

"Soon, Stuart, soon," she murmured, and only sheer willpower kept her going.

Sometime later, she glanced off ahead to where the bridle path ended and the lane between the slave quarters began, and without having to be told, she knew. Pulling Diablo blindly along, she walked as if in a daze, staring incredulously at the mess that confronted her.

Some of the slave quarters were untouched, flowers still beneath the windows; others weren't even there. Not a board, not a nail, not a stick of furniture, while the rest were scattered from one end of the place to another, and a low wailing moan could be heard hovering over the place as the slaves gathered up the dead and injured who hadn't had time to reach safety.

Lizette's eyes were blurred from her tears, and for a few minutes as she moved forward, her steps faltering, she didn't even want to look, yet knew she had to. Her gaze lifted to beyond the slave quarters, to where the lane reached the back lawn, and she shuddered at the sight. The big oaks that had heralded the lane had been snapped like twigs, with Spanish moss from them blown into and tangled in the gardens, as well as strung along the riverbank, and beyond the oaks stood the Château, or at least what was left of it.

Quickening her pace again, she tugged at Diablo, while ignoring Stuart's mumblings as she drew nearer to what had once been her grandparents' home. One hand moved to her mouth and she bit her knuckles to hold back her sobs.

Only half the house was left, with the stairs open to the sky. The kitchen was completely gone, as were the servants' sleeping quarters, with half the roof in the yard and the rest scattered about the foyer, while the upstairs bedrooms she could see were windowless, only some of the walls standing.

Near what had once been the back terrace, Lizette caught sight of a lone figure, not moving, just standing there as if made from stone. Grandma Dicia! She was staring off toward the river, watching some slaves trying to clean away some of the debris, a blank look on her face.

For the first time since she'd left the ruins, Lizette forgot about Stuart, as she dropped Diablo's reins and stumbled toward her grandmother.

"Grandma!" she shrieked helplessly, her voice cutting through the quiet of the storm's aftermath. "Grandma!"

Loedicia had been miles away, remembering so many things, all of them centered around Roth and the Château, when Lizette's cries began to penetrate into her thoughts, and she turned, watching her granddaughter running across the lawn toward her, trying to avoid falling over the debris.

Lizette finally reached Loedicia and stopped, straightening, her breathing heavy, unsteady. "Grandma!"

Loedicia looked into her face. "You're all right?" she asked, her voice peculiarly expressionless.

"The children?" Lizette asked frantically.

"They're all fine, all of them, dear, even the baby," she answered. "We were all outside visiting, saw it coming, and made it to the cellar in time."

Lizette breathed a sigh of relief, then frowned as Grandma Dicia went on. "All except your grandfather and Braxton, that is. They were on their way back from the mill."

"Oh, God!" Lizette's face was white.

"Don't worry, Braxton's fine," Loedicia assured her calmly.

"And Grandpa?"

"He's in the house. Heath should be calling me soon."

Lizette's heart fell to her stomach as she saw the tears in her grandmother's eyes.

"Grandma?"

Loedicia tried to keep from crying, but it was impossible.

"It came too fast, Liz," she answered, her eyes full of tears. "He was carrying Braxton and running, trying to reach the cellar, only it caught them behind the stables."

Lizette glanced over to where the stables had once been. All that was there was a pile of broken boards.

"He loved that boy, Liz," she went on. "And he threw him on the ground, covering him so he wouldn't be hurt."

"Grandpa's dead?"

"Not yet, no. . . ." Loedicia could hardly talk. "He . . .

his neck's broken and he's bleeding inside. Heath's making him comfortable." She took a handkerchief from the pocket of her dress and wiped her nose. "We didn't even know they were under the rubble until we heard Braxton's crying." Loedicia drew her eyes from Lizette's and stared off toward Diablo, and suddenly Lizette remembered.

"It's Stuart," she said simply. "He's been hurt."

At that moment Heath stepped over some wreckage in the foyer and called to Loedicia.

"Mother?"

Loedicia turned.

"You can go to him now."

Loedicia stared at her son for a minute, noting that his eyes were red as if he'd been crying; then she looked over toward Diablo. "Go find Luther and bring Stuart inside, will you?" she said, remembering that Lizette had said the senator was on her horse. "He's been hurt too," and she walked past Heath, heading for the library, one of the few rooms still intact. The other was the parlor at the front of the house, and the rest of the family was there.

Stopping outside the library door, she stared at it, confused, not wanting to go in, yet knowing she had to. God, it was so hard. Biting back the tears, she started to turn the knob, when Lizette stopped her.

"May I go in for a minute too, Grandma?" she asked.

Loedicia studied her for a minute, then nodded, and they both slipped into the library, closing the door quickly behind them. How incongruous, Loedicia thought as she stood there looking around. Heath said not even a book had been moved out of place. He was right. She bit her lip, then let her gaze move to the far end of the room where Roth lay on a feather mattress, trying to look comfortable. He was staring at the ceiling, his white hair still mussed, and she walked back, Lizette by her side. Then Dicia sat down beside him on the floor and reached out, pushing his hair back off his forehead.

"Hello, love," he whispered softly, his dark eyes studying her face.

She tried to smile. "How do you feel?"

"You really want to know?"

"No."

"Good." He coughed a little, scowling, then sighed and looked up, seeing Lizette. "Liz?" His voice was weak, raspy.

"Yes, Grandpa?"

"You're all right?" he asked.

"Yes, Grandpa."

"And the boy? Braxton's all right too?"

"Yes, Grandpa."

"Good." He sighed. "I'm glad, because I'd hate to think this was all for nothing."

"Oh, Grandpa!" Lizette couldn't stand any more and burst out crying as she ran from the room.

Loedicia took his hand, holding it tightly.

"Liz doesn't understand, does she?" he said.

Loedicia frowned. "Neither do I."

"We went through this already."

"I know."

"Then tell me you love me."

"You know I do."

"I like to hear it."

Loedicia leaned over, kissed him on the lips, then whispered, "I love you."

"That's better." His voice was barely audible. "You're sure Braxton's all right?" he asked.

"Only a few bruises."

"Good." He coughed again. "It hurts, honey," he said, then closed his eyes for a minute and she saw his lips quiver.

She squeezed his hand again, then brought his fingers up to touch her lips.

His eyes opened. "My feet feel funny," he murmured softly, then tried to smile. "Are you ready to say good-bye?"

"No."

"Dicia?"

"You can't go, Roth, I won't let you! I can't lose you, please!" and the tears she'd been holding back began streaming down her face.

"We said we weren't going to cry, remember?"

She nodded, then watched horrified as he suddenly gasped, trying to get his breath, his face contorted in pain.

"Roth?"

"Not yet," he said, half-choking. "Now, don't cry."

"I can't help it."

His dark eyes scanned her face, then captured her eyes with his, and he felt strange, as if his body wasn't attached to his head anymore, the pain that had been so intense only moments ago suddenly overshadowed by the sensation that he was floating.

"Dicia?"

"Roth?"

"Good-bye, love."

"No!"

He coughed, his voice weakening. "Dicia!"

"I love you, Roth, I love you!" she cried, then saw his eyes start to close. "Roth!" They closed all the way and she stared at them for a long time, waiting, but they didn't open again. "Good-bye, love," she finally whispered as she felt his hand go limp in hers, and she knew he was gone.

She stared at him for a long time, dumbfounded, unable to believe it was really happening, and wanting him to open his eyes just once more. Just one more time, only it didn't happen; then slowly she leaned over, resting her head on his chest.

"It was so good, Roth," she murmured tearfully. "So very, very good," and with an agonized sob from deep inside her, she let the pain of loss come in a flood of tears, and cried until there was nothing left inside her but an empty, hollow feeling.

Sometime later, when she finally stepped out of the library and back into the chaotic ruins that had taken her husband's life, Loedicia was once more master of her emotions, the only sign of the pain she was bearing the redness about her eyes. Other than that she was quite composed as she ran into Heath in what was left of the hallway.

He stopped for a minute, staring at her, his own eyes misty with tears. "It's over?" he asked.

"We'll bury him in the field beyond the stables," she answered. "He always loved it there with the wildflowers. You said good-bye?" she asked.

"Before calling you in," Heath said. "He didn't want me there at the end, only you."

She straightened, then glanced about, frowning. "So what did you do with Stuart?" she asked abruptly, changing the subject.

Heath shrugged his shoulders. "What could I do? We set a place for him under the stairs in the foyer."

"Does Julia know he's here?"

"Should I tell her?"

"I don't know." She eyed her son skeptically. "Does Lizette know Julia was visiting when the storm hit?"

He shook his head. "I didn't tell her, did you?"

"I should have, I suppose, but it slipped my mind."

Heath stared at his mother, then reached out and brushed one of her gray hairs back into place. "So what was he doing with Lizette?" he asked.

"You can't guess?"

"Liz?" He frowned, his dark eyes studying his mother curiously, then rubbed his short clipped beard. "How long have you known?"

She straightened wearily. "Too long," she answered; then her gaze rested on the earring in Heath's ear. You'd think a man his age would have tired of the strange memento by now, she thought, but then you'd think a man Roth's age would have tired of her long ago too, but he hadn't. At seventy-three he'd still been such a vital man. She fought to keep the tears from coming again. "So what do we do, Heath?" she asked. "If Julia finds out, the scandal would ruin him, and yet—"

"If Julia finds out what?" Julia asked from behind Heath.

At that moment Luther shouted from the foyer. "I got the senator bedded down beneath the stair, Mr. Heath," he said. "Now what's you want me to do?"

Julia stared at Heath, her eyes puzzled. "The senator?" she asked in disbelief. "The senator?" and she turned abruptly, heading back toward the foyer, while Heath looked at his mother, rolled his eyes disgustedly, then followed Stuart's wife.

Lizette was sitting beside Stuart, oblivious of everyone else in the house. Once she'd made sure the children were all right and were all in the parlor safe and sound, her next concern had been Stuart. She had no idea whatsoever that Julia was anywhere around, since Julia had become ill at the horror of all the damage and let one of the slaves escort her to a quiet place where she had lost the tea and cake Loedicia had fed her just before the storm. However, her stomach was back to normal now and her carriage and driver still intact, which was a miracle in itself, and she'd come into the house to tell the Chapmans that she'd best hurry home to see if the twister had missed Beaufort or not, since she'd left the children at home, when she'd overheard Heath's remark. Now she stepped into the foyer and moved to a spot where she could look under the staircase, only all she could see were a man's feet, minus his boots, and Lizette's back.

"Well, isn't this just lovely!" she said as she stared at them.

Lizette froze, her eyes on Stuart's ashen face, the sound of Julia's voice cutting right through her. She turned slowly and looked at Julia, studying the woman she knew had hated her for so long. "He's been hurt," Lizette said, the surprise at seeing Julia over.

Julia's eyes narrowed suspiciously. "And I presume he was with you at the time."

"Does it really matter?" Lizette's eyes were snapping irritably. "He's hurt badly. He could die."

"Don't be silly." Julia took a step closer, then got a good look at Stuart's face. He did seem rather pale. "What happened?" she asked.

"He was hit on the head by a tree limb."

Lizette went back to her work on Stuart, wiping the sweat from his face. His eyes fluttered and she held her breath, then watched them open, and he looked right at her.

"Liz?" he murmured breathlessly.

She put her finger to his lips. "Shhh," she said, hoping to salvage the moment for him. "Julia's here now, and the doctor'll be here soon, I hope."

He frowned, then looked puzzled. "Julia!"

"Yes, me," Julia said, and stepped forward, then stood looking down at him. "I thought you were at a meeting today."

"I was."

"Oh, I don't doubt that." She glanced at Lizette, then back to Stuart. "It's just that I have a feeling the meeting you were really at wasn't the meeting you were supposed to be at, am I right?"

"Julia, for God's sake!"

"No, Stuart, for my sake, tell me the truth this time."

"I just happened to run into Lizette."

"Hogwash!"

He closed his eyes. His head was hurting like hell and he still felt sick. "All right!" he yelled through clenched teeth, and opened his eyes again, looking right at Julia. "All right, so I was with Liz, but it isn't what you think."

Julia laughed, sneering, then smoothed the skirt of her dark blue traveling suit. "It never is," she answered.

Lizette looked up at her in disgust. "You don't even care that he's hurt, do you?"

"Care? Certainly I care," she answered, and much to Lizette's surprise, she knelt down, feeling Stuart's forehead. "He's getting feverish."

"I know."

"Why were you with him?" she asked as she made sure his collar was loose, then reached down to take his pulse.

"I wanted to talk."

"I don't believe you."

"Then don't."

Julia stared at Stuart, noticing how deep the crow's-feet around his eyes were. He was starting to show his age. "I love him, Lizette," she said simply.

Lizette looked over at Julia and frowned. "But not enough, right?"

"What do you mean?"

"Never mind, Julia," she answered. "You wouldn't understand."

Heath poked his head around the corner. "How's he doing?"

"No good." Lizette wiped his brow again. "He's feverish."

"Maybe I'd better get Mother."

"No," Lizette said. "Grandma's been through enough."

Heath disagreed. "It'll keep her busy. I'll be right back."

He was right, Loedicia had to have something to keep her mind off her sorrow, and trying to keep Stuart alive was just what she needed. She shooed both Lizette and Julia away, then told Heath to go get Mattie. Then the two of them began working on Stuart to lower his fever, leaving Julia to argue with Lizette.

Lizette stood in the ruins of the house her grandparents had once called home, and tears rolled down her cheeks. So much gone, and it had happened so fast. She thought of Grandpa Roth lying dead in the library. He'd sacrificed himself for Braxton and now she was going to have to make sure his sacrifice hadn't been in vain.

Looking down at her dress, she rubbed her hands along the skirt where it was still wet, the blood staining it where she'd wiped her hand.

"Now," Julia said from behind her. "Tell me, Liz, and I want to know the truth. You've been having an affair with Stuart, haven't you?"

Lizette whirled around and stared at her. "Is this just between you and me?" she asked.

Julia glanced about. "I don't see anyone else around, but if you'd rather, we can go down by the river."

"Then I suggest we do."

Lizette stepped over the broken boards on the floor, walked around a smashed flowerpot, and went out onto the walk, heading for the pier down at the river, with Julia right behind her. When she was far enough from the house, where no one would overhear, she turned and looked back, ignoring Julia momentarily as she looked beyond her.

It had stopped raining some time ago, and now the sun was out, low on the horizon, pushing its way through the billowing clouds that were taking over the sky, and it painted everything with a golden glow as if it were mocking the irony of its appearance. She took a deep breath and stared in awe, realizing the power that had been unleashed here today, then sighed and finally looked at Julia, who was watching her curiously.

"Now, you asked me a question," Lizette said, her voice tremulous. "But before I answer, I want to know, Julia, what will you do if the answer's yes?"

"Is it?"

"What will you do?"

"I don't know."

"At least you're honest." Lizette's knees were trembling as she looked directly into Julia's pale blue eyes. When Julia had first asked her the question she'd decided to tell her the truth, but now, studying her curiously, and remembering the simple declaration of love for Stuart Julia had made only a short time before, she began to doubt the wisdom of her decision. Julia was a weak person, but not physically. Physically she was only too thin. Her weakness was her emotions, and Lizette saw the pain in her eyes as she waited for an answer, and in spite of the fact that Lizette knew her sister-in-law couldn't stand her, she suddenly realized she couldn't let Julia know the truth.

"I don't know why you seem to want my answer to be yes, Julia," she said instead, "but no, we're not having an affair, as you call it."

Julia frowned, unsure. "Then why were you with him today?"

"Is it a sin for me to talk to my brother-in-law?"

"It is when he should be at a meeting in Beaufort."

"We happened to run into each other, Julia, that's all," Lizette lied. "He must have finished his meeting early, because I ran into him down the road near the Englers', and asked him to ride with me for a little way so we could talk."

"About what?"

Lizette pursed her lips, knowing that what she was doing had to be. "About Bain," she continued lying. "I asked Stuart to see if there was any way he could have someone try to find out where Bain is and ask him what his plans are so far as the house and everything are concerned. After all, I do have to try to go on with my life. I can't let things just hang as they are."

Julia's frown deepened as she stared at Lizette. "Why would you ask Stuart?"

"Because he has friends in Washington who'd have access to ways of finding Bain."

"Oh." Julia eyed her skeptically. "If you're lying, Liz . . ."

"Why would I lie?"

"For Stuart's sake."

"Then believe the truth for Stuart's sake, will you?" she said. "He's Bain's brother and my friend, and that's all."

Julia still wasn't sure. She'd have to talk to Stuart first, but right now that was impossible. "Then that's your answer?" she asked.

"It's the only one there is."

Julia stared hard at Lizette for a long time, then finally turned and walked away, heading back for the house to see how Stuart was doing, while Lizette watched her, the setting sun making Julia's plain brown hair look amber beneath the small hat she wore, and Lizette knew instinctively that Julia still didn't believe her.

It was late, the house quiet, and yet Lizette couldn't sleep. She figured it had to be close to midnight as she lay on her feather mattress in a corner of the parlor and stared at the broken window only a few feet away. Earlier, shortly before dark, Heath had discovered that the front bedrooms upstairs had barely been touched, and the steps, although exposed to the outdoors, were still sturdy, so the children had been able to go up to their own beds, with Dodee and Genée joining Blythe and Pretty, but the grown-ups had to sleep in the parlor, all but Julia, who had decided to stay to be near Stuart, but sent her carriage and driver back to Beaufort to check on the children. She was bedded down in the foyer, beneath the stairs with her husband.

Rebel and Beau had ridden down earlier from Tonnerre after Loedicia had sent one of the slaves with a message that Roth had been hurt, and when they discovered how extensive the damage was, they tried to get Loedicia to go back upriver with them, only she wouldn't go.

"I can't leave Roth," she insisted, and naturally Heath wouldn't leave her, Darcy wouldn't leave Heath, and Lizette was glad, because she didn't want to go either, even if the place was a mess.

So after helping Heath, Darcy, Loedicia, and Lizette go through the slave quarters, bandaging, soothing, and trying to bring some order to the chaos, Rebel and Beau had finally left for home, just the two of them, with a promise to come back early in the morning, since the tornado had missed Tonnerre, only inflicting some slight wind damage in the fields.

After waving good-bye to her parents, Lizette, tired and weary, had cleaned up in the sewing room beyond the library, where a washstand and water had been set up, washing off the grimy dirt that seemed to cling to her, then put on a nightgown and wrapper she had found earlier in what was left of her room. This done, she had joined everyone else on the parlor floor, only all she'd been doing was tossing and turning for the last hour or so.

She glanced over to where Grandma had been sleeping, then realized her mattress was empty. Moving onto her elbows, she surveyed the room. Grandma must have slipped out when my back was turned, she thought, and, worried about her, Lizette slipped from her own bed, put the heavy satin wrapper on to cover her rather revealing nightgown, then tiptoed from the room as softly as she could so as not to wake Heath and Darcy, who were sleeping peacefully only a few feet away.

It was spooky and rather weird as Lizette stepped into the foyer and looked up at the open sky, so silent and still. Grandpa's body was still in the library and Grandma could be there, but if she knew Grandma Dicia, and she was certain she did, that reasoning would be wrong.

Holding the edge of her nightgown up, Lizette moved stealthily across the foyer and stepped out onto what had once been the terrace, and as she did, she knew her instinct had been right when she saw the figure of a lone woman, her pale nightclothes visible in the darkness. She was near the edge of the pier where the remains of Roth's ship the *Interlude* were still tied. Its hull had been smashed against the piling, its sails were a tangled mess of canvas and rope, the spars were broken, everything twisted, and it lay silently in the river, except for the faint splash of the water flowing by it and against it.

Lizette stood watching Grandma Dicia for a few minutes, then started toward her, being careful not to trip over anything on the lawn and walk that they hadn't gotten out of the way as yet.

"Grandma?" she said as she neared her, and she saw Loedicia take a deep breath, then half-turn, and she held out her hand. Liz took it.

"I'm all right, dear," Loedicia said.

Lizette nodded. "I know, I'm the one who's lonesome."

Loedicia drew her granddaughter to her and held her close, hugging her, then released her, but still held her hand.

"Will you sit with me for a while?" Loedicia asked.

Lizette sat on the cool grass, Loedicia beside her, and both women gazed off toward the water for a long time, neither saying a word, yet each knew what the other was feeling.

"What are you going to do now, Grandma?" Lizette finally asked.

Loedicia sighed. "Who knows? I've lived a long life."

"But it's not over."

"I know." Tears filled Loedicia's eyes and she sighed, leaning her head back to look at the sky filled with stars. "Just like it wasn't over when Quinn died," she went on. "Don't worry, dear, I'm not a foolish old woman who thinks life ends when someone you love dies or goes away."

"Grandma?"

"Yes?"

"Do you think Bain will come back?"

Loedicia glanced over at her. "Do you want him to?"

"Yes."

"What of Stuart?"

"He loves me."

"You love him?"

"In a way, I guess. I don't know." Lizette's hair was down on her shoulders with a ribbon around it and she swung her head back, then brushed it away from her face. "He's so much like Bain, Grandma, and it's so hard," she said softly. "That's always been the trouble." She pulled her knees up, wrapping her arms around them, the call of a night heron diverting her attention for a minute to a nearby tree; then she looked back at her grandmother.

"Does Julia know?" Loedicia asked.

"No. She asked, but I lied."

"Why?"

"It seemed the right thing to do."

There was silence again for a few minutes; then, "Liz, if I go away and leave the Château, will you and the children go with me?" Loedicia asked.

Lizette looked at her, perplexed, then frowned. "Where to?"

"To your brother Cole, where I'm needed. You see, they still haven't found Case yet. Besides, I want to get as far away from here as I can."

"But—"

"No, child." Loedicia turned to Lizette, reaching over, and she touched her arm. "Don't try to get me to change my mind, dear," she said. "It's already made up. I decided hours ago. You see, this place was Roth, the house, the grounds, the people, it was all him." Lizette knew her grandmother was crying now, but still Loedicia went on. "When we bury him, we'll be burying my life with him too, and that's the way I want it. I don't need these reminders, I have my own, and I'll never lose them, just as I still have my reminders of Quinn. No, dear, I can't stay here, I don't want to stay here, not without him, it wouldn't be the same."

"But Texas?"

"Why not? It's a new place, Liz, I can make new memories to add to the old." She squeezed Lizette's hand. "But I don't want to go alone."

"What about Heath?"

She shook her head. "Heath will stay here and rebuild for his father. I knew it the minute Roth died."

"What if Bain comes home and I'm gone?"

"He'll find you if he wants you. And you have no guarantee that he'll even come home. In the meantime, you can make a new life for yourself and the children."

"But it's so far."

"There's a world out there waiting for you, Liz, for us. Will you go with me?"

Lizette felt her grandmother's strong hand on her arm, and she stared at her thoughtfully. It would mean she'd be away from her parents, but she didn't live with them anyway, and she could survive that. But it would mean leaving Stuart. She remembered the look in Julia's eyes today and thought back to the conversation she'd had with Grandma Dicia last week in the library.

"You're not just trying to get me away from Stuart, are you, Grandma?" she asked.

Loedicia released her arm. "Not intentionally, no."

"What of Blythe?"

"What about her?"

"She's crippled."

"But not dead." Loedicia studied Lizette. Her face was shadowed, but from what she could see of it she looked so young. Yet she'd gone through so much. "Don't coddle her, Liz," she told her sternly. "You've survived a lot. She'll survive too. Let her make mistakes and get hurt, it'll only make her stronger."

"When are you leaving?"

"Right after the funeral."

"But there's the house and furniture. What do I do with it?"

"You can't do anything with it, Liz. Not without Bain's knowledge, so it doesn't matter. If and/or when he should decide to show his face in Beaufort, Rand'll take care of things and see that you get any monies coming to you."

Lizette still wasn't sure, and tears filled her eyes. The Château meant as much to her as Tonnerre, and she'd be so far from both. Texas!

"You really think I should, Grandma?" she asked hesitantly.

Loedicia sighed. "Yes, I think you should."

Lizette paused for a minute, then made her decision. "All right then, I'll go," she answered. "Only Pretty and Luther go with me, and Dodee too."

"And Dodee too," Loedicia assured her, then reached out for her granddaughter's hand. "Now, come," and she stood up, pulling Lizette up with her. "I think we'd best get some sleep, dear, because I have a feeling tomorrow's going to be about as bad as today was," and they headed back up the walk arm in arm, with tears in their eyes, toward what was left of the house.

Chapter 20

BAIN'S FACE WAS tanned darker then it had been for a long time as he stood at the rail of the *Sparrow* and watched it plow its way through the rough waves not far from the Hilton Head and Port Royal Sound. It had been a long time since he'd captained a ship, but he'd easily swung into the routine. Cuba was far behind him now, as was Elena de Córdoba, and he grimaced, hoping his stupidity in turning to her in anger hadn't lost him the one women he'd ever loved.

If only he hadn't been so blind jealous. He lifted his head, studying the sky, his gray eyes straining to catch some sight of land on the horizon. The weather had been testy the past few days, and although the sea was still choppy, not a cloud marred the sky.

He continued to stand on deck and thought back over his last sight of Elena standing on the dock in Havana with Eric beside her, and Don Emilio only a few feet away. Don Emilio! The name was like music to his ears now, because even though he'd convinced himself that Lizette had been telling the truth after all, when Don Emilio told him that Sancho hadn't been dead when he'd left, and that de Córdoba had confessed to lying about his involvement with Lizette, it had made his decision even sweeter, and he'd been so anxious to leave that he hadn't even bothered trying to pick up a cargo to make it more profitable for the men. Instead, he'd planned to pay them out of his pocket, and he was glad they'd stuck by him, but then, they knew that sailing for him wasn't a risk.

Bain frowned, wondering how long Elena and Eric were going to last. Well, at least Eric knew Bain would find something for him to do if he ever tired of Elena and decided to quit Havana. But then, maybe he wouldn't, who knows? He could really be in love with Elena. If that were the case, Bain rather pitied Eric because now that he wasn't blinded by anger and frustration Bain could really see Elena for what she was. Just what Eric had called her, a scheming little witch, and his frown turned to a smile as he thought of Eric trying to tame her and keep her satisfied.

Suddenly he straightened, his gaze settling on one small spot on the horizon, and he lifted the spyglass he'd been holding to his eye to get a better look. It was the Hilton Head, all right, and he shouted to the helmsman, then yelled for Waggs. Eric's first mate had stayed with Bain, and it didn't take Bain long to realize why Eric had always counted on him so much. He was a captain's joy to watch aboard ship, and ready at hand for anything Bain might want him to do. After giving him his orders, Bain took one last look in the spyglass, then went down to his cabin to change clothes, since the shirt he was wearing was covered with grime from the past two days.

Bain had taken over Eric's cabin now, and after he'd washed, he went through one of the trunks, pulled out a white shirt, and slipped it on. A short time later, his insides fluttering wildly with apprehension, he came back up on deck somewhat neater than he'd looked when he'd gone down, and he saw that the helmsman was beginning to head the *Sparrow* into the sound.

After rounding the northern shores of the Hilton Head, Bain gave the helmsman instructions to keep to the northern side of the sound, and they sailed past Phillips Island and St. Helena, then avoided the mouth of the sound that led to Beaufort and started sailing toward the river, past Parry Island, when Bain suddenly lifted the spyglass to his eye again and started scanning the shoreline.

"Something's wrong, Waggs," he said to his first mate, who'd joined him just seconds before, and Waggs lifted his hand to shade his eyes, squinting, to see if he could catch what Bain meant. A frown creased his forehead. "Look," Bain went on. "To the right there," and he handed the spyglass to Waggs. "You've been to Beaufort enough times. Where're the trees that stood on the hill over there, and there isn't a house on the beach."

Waggs followed the shoreline, his frown deepening, then took the spyglass down and looked at Bain. "They're there, sir," he said, his voice solemn. "Shattered to pieces. Look down the beach further. Looks like a few people around, picking things up."

Once more the spyglass moved to Bain's eye. Waggs was right. Bain let the spyglass sweep over the terrain, then his jaw tightened, eyes hardening as he saw more trees uprooted. There'd be a house here, none there, occasionally part of a ship sticking out of the sand somewhere, or even caught in the trees.

The *Sparrow* had cut sail now and they were moving slower as they finally cleared Parry Island and started up the Broad River at the southern tip of Port Royal. The landscape was the same. Trees uprooted, sailboats, rowboats, and ship's parts beached on the shore, with torn pieces from several buildings here and there.

The Englers' plantation house was right at the very tip of the island where it could overlook the waterway separating Parry Island from Port Royal, and as Bain looked through the spyglass, he'd swear he saw part of its roof hanging with the Spanish moss in an oak tree at the edge of the water.

Then it struck him. There'd been a storm the other night that had been heading up the coast and could have moved inland. He spotted what was left of a sofa he knew had once sat in the Englers' parlor and was now floating at the water's edge, the colorful flowers of the upholstery brilliant in the morning sunlight, and he shivered, lowering the spyglass as he turned toward Waggs.

"Tornado?" he asked, his face troubled.

Waggs nodded. "Had to be. It wasn't no hurricane or we'd have been in it."

Waggs watched Bain's eyes grow intense as the ship sailed farther upriver, leaving Parry Island and the tip of Port Royal behind, and he knew what the captain was thinking.

Suddenly Bain strode to the other side of the deck and Waggs saw that a small one-masted sailboat with a crew of two was approaching, and he saw Bain lean over, cupping his mouth to call.

"Ho! The boat!" he yelled as loud as he could.

The men handling her both looked over, the one at the tiller waving. "Somethin' we can do?" he called.

Bain shaded his eyes, squinting, but didn't recognize the man. "What happened?" he shouted.

The boatman nodded. "Tornado, day before yesterday.

Hit the Englers and Chapmans, then jumped the river to the north at Hoggs Neck!"

Bain felt his stomach give a lurch as the sailboat continued moving and there was no way to ask anything more. He straightened and joined Waggs again.

"You hear?" he asked.

"What're you gonna do?"

"Keep sailing. If they're not there we'll go on up to Tonnerre," but as the *Sparrow* finally drew near the Château, Bain had the strange feeling she would be there.

Maybe it was because he could see some of the slaves near the edge of the river cleaning things up, or maybe it was because he just sensed that no matter what happened, Roth wouldn't desert the place, and where her grandparents were, he'd find Lizette. Whatever it was, something inside told him he had to find her here. And the children. My God, how he missed them.

They were at least five hundred feet from the pier yet when he caught his first glimpse of the house, and his mouth went dry. It looked like some sort of battle scene, and his gaze moved from the house to the stables that were no more, then stopped at the end of the pier, and he called for Waggs to cut sail, as he saw the remains of the *Interlude* still lashed to the piling and knew they wouldn't be able to get close enough to dock.

"We'll have to row ashore," he said, then took the spyglass and tried to get a better look at the place as the men began furling the sails and lowering the anchor, while on shore, in the field of wildflowers between the river and the lane that led to the cotton mill, Lizette stood beside Grandma Dicia, her gaze on the mound of earth covering Grandpa Roth's body, and her eyes were so blurred with tears she could hardly even see it. The service had been over for at least fifteen minutes, and everyone except her, Grandma Dicia, and Braxton had gone back to the house already, but Braxton hadn't wanted to leave just yet.

He knew what death was. At least they'd tried to explain it to him, but he hadn't liked the part about Grandpa being put into the ground and they'd tried everything they could to reassure him. It wasn't until Grandma Dicia explained that Grandpa Roth had wanted to be among the wildflowers, however, that he'd finally relented and said it would be all right. Only now, as Lizette wiped the tears from her eyes and glanced over at him standing solemnly in front of Grandma Dicia, she had the strangest feeling that Grandpa Roth wasn't going to stay with the wildflowers for very long, but would be right beside Braxton, wherever he went, for the rest of the boy's life.

Lizette looked from her son, dressed in his good summer suit, with a hat covering his blond curls, to Grandma Dicia's face, and a pang of hurt went through her. Grandma looked so sad.

Loedicia, sensing Lizette's eyes on her, turned toward her granddaughter and sighed. "Well, I guess we really should join the others back at the house now, don't you think?" she said. Her eyes were still bloodshot from all the crying she'd done, but she was holding up much better than even Lizette had expected.

Lizette looked down at Braxton. "Are you ready to leave, son?" she asked.

He bit his lower lip, took one last look at the grave, then turned to say something to his mother, when he caught sight of something out of the corner of his eye, and instead, he frowned curiously and stared off behind her downriver, past the pier.

"Look!" he said, his gray eyes squinting beneath the broad-brimmed hat they'd made him wear.

Lizette looked off downriver and a scowl creased her forehead. "Grandma?"

"It's not the *Raven*, yet . . . Oh, my God, Liz, it's the *Sparrow*," she gasped as she made out the outline of the ship.

Lizette's face went white. "It can't be."

"But it is. Look!" and she pointed toward the house to where Heath was heading back toward them, with Rebel close behind. "Here come Heath and your mother, they've seen it too."

Lizette couldn't move. Her feet were rooted to the ground as she looked at her uncle and mother hurrying toward them.

"Is it Bain?" she asked breathlessly when they were only a few feet away.

Rebel smiled. "Heath thinks so. It's the *Sparrow*, all right, and he's sure he caught sight of Bain on board."

"It couldn't be. He said—"

"Forget what he said," Heath cut in. "Come on now, I saw they were lowering a boat."

"No," she said stubbornly, and stood her ground. "Even if it is Bain, there's no certainty that he came to see me. The children are here too, you know."

"But, Liz . . . " Rebel pleaded.

"No matter." Lizette was insistent. "I'm not going to make a fool of myself and go running down to meet him just to have him insult me in front of everyone. I've been through enough shame."

"She's right, Heath," Loedicia said, understanding. "So maybe it's best if the rest of us meet him first; then if he wants Lizette, he can come to her." Loedicia reached down and took Braxton's hand. "I think your father's home, Brax," she said quite calmly. "Would you like to go see him?" and Braxton, who had been watching the ship diligently, let out a cry and began tugging her with him back toward the house and the pier, half-jumping, half-running.

Suddenly he stopped and stared back at Lizette. "Aren't you coming, Mama?" he yelled.

She shook her head. "Not just now, Brax. There are a few things I want to say to Grandpa yet. You go on ahead. I'll be there in a minute," and there were tears in Lizette's eyes as she watched her son trying to run toward the river with his great-grandmother in tow, followed by his Great-Uncle Heath and his grandmother.

Bain hadn't taken his eyes from the shore ever since getting into the longboat, and the last few hundred yards of water was the longest stretch he'd ever seen. His eyes scanned the pier, but he didn't see Lizette.

There were her mother, her uncle, her grandmother, and a number of people behind them on the lawn closer to the house, and he shaded his eyes, trying to pick them out, and was amazed to see his parents, Felicia and Alex, his brother, Stuart, and his wife, as well as a great many neighbors and friends.

His hand dropped hesitantly, and he frowned, puzzled. At first when he'd seen all the activity, he thought everyone was cleaning up, but now, as he stared at them . . . They were all dressed in black!

The gooseflesh rose on his arms, the nape of his neck prickled, and tears came to his eyes. They were having a funeral, but where was Lizette? Fear gripped him and he almost stood up in the boat; then he saw Braxton push out from behind Lizette's mother, Rebel Dante, and start waving enthusiastically. His heart skipped a beat. But where was Lizette? He waved at Braxton, and tried to smile as best he

could, then looked off toward the house, where he spotted
Pretty standing beside Blythe's chair, and there was a smile
on Blythe's face that warmed his heart, making him swallow
hard. Beside her was a young black girl holding a baby in
her arms. He frowned, wondering, then bit his lip. But
where the hell was Lizette?

Anxious now, yet fearing what he might find, he ordered
the men to row in at a spot near the pier that was clear of
debris; then before the men even had a chance to tie up, he
leapt from the boat, grabbing the ladder at the side of the
pilings and climbed up, sticking his head over the top, looking right into Braxton's face.

"Papa!" Braxton cried, and Heath had to hold him back
to let Bain reach the platform; then he let go and Bain
scooped Braxton up in his arms, hugging him so tight Braxton started to laugh.

Bain's arms eased from around the boy, and he drew his
head back, looking into Braxton's face. Good Lord, how
he'd grown.

Bain smiled. "I missed you," he said simply.

Braxton's face grew sober. "I missed you too," he said.

Bain studied him for a second. "Where's your mother?"
he asked.

Braxton's eyes shifted their gaze from his father's face to
the field. "She's with Grandpa," he answered, and Bain's
face went white as he glanced over and saw the trampled
ground and the mound of dirt, where a woman in black was
standing. "Grandpa Roth went to heaven," Braxton went
on, "and we had to put him in the ground, but he's not
really there, only his bones is, and—"

"Braxton!" Rebel cut in, stopping him. "You're scaring
your father." She saw the frightened look in Bain's eyes.
"She's standing over by Grandpa's grave," she explained,
and saw the relief in Bain's eyes; then he frowned.

He looked at Heath. "Your father's dead?" he asked.

"He was killed in the tornado," Heath answered, then
explained what had happened while they all started walking
toward where Blythe was sitting watching anxiously.

"I'm sorry, Heath," Bain said when Heath was finished,
then glanced at Loedicia, who'd been walking along with
them. "Grandma Dicia . . . I wish I knew what to say."
He'd been carrying Braxton all the way and hugged him
tighter. "I thank him for saving my son."

"He loved him," Loedicia answered, and Bain nodded, then turned his attention to Blythe.

"Well, young lady," he said, setting Braxton down, and he knelt beside her, reaching up to push a curl back from her face.

She was wearing a small pleated cap of white organdy, and he was surprised, because unlike most mothers, Lizette had always insisted her children weren't going to wear those ridiculous hot caps all day like other children. She'd said it was an old custom that her mother and grandmother had never kept, and she wouldn't either. However, Blythe looked pretty in it, with her fair hair curling at the sides, and he assumed she'd put it on just for the funeral.

He was at eye level with her now, and she leaned toward him just enough so he could hug her.

"I missed you too," he whispered.

She kissed his cheek soundly. "I told Mama you'd get over your mad," she said, holding him tightly. "Only I was hoping I'd be walking by the time you got home."

He drew back, looking into her eyes. "Well, now I can help you, can't I?"

She smiled. "I'm glad. And you can teach the baby to walk when she's big enough, too," she said, and turned to Dodee. "Show her to Papa, Dodee," she insisted, reaching toward the young black girl who was holding the baby, and Bain stood up, standing motionless as the black girl walked over and lifted the baby off her shoulder, turning Genée so her father could see her.

"A girl?" he asked, staring at Genée, and Rebel reached out, pushing the baby's bonnet higher so Bain could see her face.

"Genée, meet your father," Rebel introduced him, and Bain swallowed hard, just staring.

"Genée?" he said, then reached out, touching her face.

Genée grabbed his finger and held on, trying to pull it to her mouth to chew on it, and her big eyes looked directly at him. Her eyes were blue, or were they purple? It was hard to tell, but she was beautiful, a few chestnut hairs peeking out from beneath her little cap.

Bain reached out and took her from the black girl, held her for a few minutes, studying her face, then handed her back and looked over to where the others were standing. They all looked like spectators at some kind of an exhibition, and he flushed self-consciously as his gaze sifted over his parents, and Stuart, and a number of other people, including Darcy Chapman and Lizette's father, Beau Dante; then he looked off across the field to where Rebel said his wife was, and he straightened nervously.

"I guess I'd better go see Liz now," he announced, his voice breaking with emotion, and Loedicia watched him start across the lawn toward the field where Lizette stood silently at her grandfather's grave, and she turned to all the others.

"I think maybe it'd be best if we all went on into the parlor for coffee and tea, Heath, don't you think?" she said. "You and Rebel round up everyone so Bain and Liz can have some privacy," and a few minutes later, when Lizette looked back toward the Château, all she could see was Bain heading toward her, and tears filled her eyes.

Bain's eyes had been on Lizette all the way across the lawn and the field, and now he stopped a few feet from her, staring.

"Liz?"

She'd been watching him too, and she sniffed, trying to hold back the tears. "Bain?"

He continued to stare at her, but didn't move. "I'm sorry about Grandpa Roth," he said, using the obvious opening, and she tried to be cordial.

"Thank you."

There was another silence; then, "The baby's just beautiful," he said.

She frowned. "You really think so?"

"Yes."

There was silence again; then finally he closed the gap between them and stood looking down at her.

"Dammit, Liz, I'm trying to say I'm sorry," he blurted. "I've been a pigheaded fool and an unmitigated ass, and I'm asking you to forgive me. Will you?"

She stared at him, the tears rolling down her cheeks now, and she couldn't find her voice.

Reaching out, Bain touched her face and his eyes were pleading as his fingers wiped away the tears. "Please, love," he begged. "I've made a horrible mistake." His voice was anguished, tears rimming his own eyes. "Forgive me, please?"

She closed her eyes, trying to ignore the touch of his hand on her cheek and the familiar response it was bringing to her, then straightened stubbornly and opened her eyes again. The tears were still there, but so was anger. If he thought . . .

"You really expect me to forgive you, don't you?" she said as she brushed his hand from her face. "Just like that."

"I've been hoping."

"Why?" she snapped, and her eyes were blazing. "Why should I? What's in it for me?"

"What do you mean?"

"Just what I said." She straightened boldly. "What do I get out of it, Bain? Surely you didn't come back because you love me. What happened, did she get tired of you, or did you run out of money?"

"Neither. But I guess I deserve that, don't I?"

"You guess?" She was fuming. "You deserve more than that, Bain Kolter, and you know it. I should kill you," she yelled through clenched teeth. "And if you think you're just going to come crawling back into my life and hurt me again . . . It isn't that easy, Bain!"

"I didn't say it would be. Look, Liz." He had to convince her. "I admit I made a mistake, and a big one, but I do love you."

"Since when?"

"I always have."

"Then why didn't you trust me?"

"I don't know."

"Well, I do," and she stared at him, unwavering. "Because you wanted Elena de Córdoba, that's why . . . you wanted to sleep with that little witch!"

"No, I wanted you!"

"Then why did you run to her?"

"Because I thought you betrayed me."

"I told you I didn't."

"I know."

There was silence again for a few seconds; then, "You made love to her, didn't you?" she asked.

He hesitated. "No."

"I'm not stupid, Bain!"

"I didn't make love to her, I used her, Lizette!"

"You used her?"

"Yes, used her because you weren't there." He reached out and took her by the shoulders, forcing her to look up at him. "There was no tenderness in what I gave her, Liz, none," he said. "No warmth, no love . . . she was just a woman who was there."

"You expect me to believe that?"

"It's true." His hands dropped from her shoulders. "I couldn't make love to her, Liz. I tried, I wanted to get even with you, and I tried, but all I did was go through the motions like some kind of animal."

She stared at him, her eyes guarded, the thought of his body covering Elena's making her cringe. "Do you know how you hurt me, Bain?" she asked viciously, and there were tears in her eyes again. "Elena did nothing but torture me when I was on board the *Piranha,* telling me how you'd made love to her when you were on that stupid island . . . what's its name . . . ?"

"You mean Barlovento? I didn't make love to her then."

"It doesn't matter, not anymore. The point is, you did make love to her in London, didn't you, and it's just what she wanted."

"I told you—"

"I know." She shook her head. "But it isn't that easy to forget, Bain. I needed you, and you went to someone else."

"And I've paid for it."

"Paid? You've paid?" She laughed bitterly. "How have you paid? I'm the one who's paid, Bain, not you," she went on. "I'm the one who had to sleep in an empty bed and live down the humiliation of having my husband leave me for another woman! I'm the one who had to watch people look at Genée and wonder. And you say you've paid?"

"I have, Liz. I've had to live without you."

"Oh, aren't you funny."

"I didn't mean it to be funny. I'm sorry."

"You're sorry?" The tears ran freely down her cheeks. "So am I, Bain, because I don't know if I can forgive you."

He straightened, studying her face. She'd always looked so beautiful in black, with her eyes like fiery emeralds, her hair as dark as her clothes, and he wanted to take her in his arms and hold her close to make the hurt go away, but knew that to try now would be useless.

"Liz, I need you," he begged softly.

She bit her lip trying to keep from crying. "But I don't need you, not anymore, Bain, don't you see?" she said. "Grandma and I are taking the children with us to Texas to see Cole, and I don't need you anymore. I can find a life for myself out there with someone who'll trust me, someone who'll love me and believe in me." The tears were coming again even though she didn't want them to. "We've got the wagon all ready, everything's packed, we were going to leave right after the service. . . ."

"You mean today?"

"Yes, today, and now you had to show up!"

He glanced back toward the house, where the stable used to be, and saw all the carriages lined up, only one wasn't a carriage. It was a farm wagon, and it was full of trunks, bric-a-brac, a chair, and some big boxes with Lizette's palomino, Diablo, tied to the back.

He turned back to Lizette and felt as if he were drowning. He couldn't lose her.

"You can't go, Liz, you just can't," he cried breathlessly. "I won't let you."

"I already promised Grandma. Besides, there's nothing for me here."

"I'm here now."

"I know, only don't you see, I'll still have it all to live down. I can just hear them," and she mocked the ladies in town, her voice caustic and cruel. " 'Did you know, dear, she actually took him back, and why he returned I'll never know, it was probably the money, or the children, it certainly couldn't be her.' " She wiped her nose and sniffed, talking in her own voice again. "No, I couldn't stay here, Bain, especially if I took you back, I just couldn't."

"Then I'll come with you."

"You'll what?"

"I'll go with you." He reached out and took her face in his hands, gazing deep into her tear-filled eyes, his own eyes alive with longing. "Don't you see, Liz?" he whispered huskily. "We can make a new start together where no one except family knows us. Where you won't have to live anything down or be humiliated or . . ."

He was holding her face gently and she didn't know what to say as she looked directly into his eyes. How much she loved him, but could she forget? Could she forgive?

"I don't know," she answered hesitantly. "I just don't know."

"I do," he finished, and he leaned down just enough so his lips were touching hers, and she wanted to die. He kissed her softly, tenderly, her face still in his hands, and she quivered clear to her toes; then he drew his head back. "Life without you is hell, Liz," he murmured. "And I can't do it anymore. You've got to say yes."

She stared at him, face flushed, cheeks warm, her whole body aching, and for the first time in months she couldn't lie to herself anymore. She wanted him and needed him so badly.

"I guess I can try," she said hesitantly. "I'll try, Bain, I will, but I don't know. There's been so much."

His arms went around her and he pulled her close. "Then you do forgive me? You will forgive me?"

"If I can. I don't know."

"It'll work out, Liz, you'll see," he said anxiously, and kissed her long and hard, and Grandma Dicia, watching from what used to be the back terrace, sighed. Looks like I'll have to go to Texas alone, she thought silently, but was surprised only minutes later when Lizette and Bain walked back to the house and informed her that he was going too.

"But your things?" she asked. "What'll you do for clothes? We were leaving today. Beau rode into Beaufort for us yesterday and booked passage for us on a ship heading for New Orleans."

"We can still leave today, Grandma Dicia," Bain said. "Because I've got a better idea. We'll put the wagon on the *Sparrow*, sail down to the gulf, closer to the Texas border than New Orleans, and save all that time. And money too."

She studied Bain for a few minutes, then looked at Lizette. "Are you sure?" she asked. "I don't want the two of you to go just to please an old lady."

"In the first place, you're not old, Grandma," Lizette said. "And in the second place, we want it this way." She looked at Bain, tears still close to the surface, but they were under control. "I told him I'd forgive him, and I'm going to try, but I could never do it here. There are too many reasons why, but out there it will be like starting over."

"Only one thing bothers me, Grandma Dicia," Bain said, and his eyes looked troubled. "I thought people had to turn Catholic and give up their American citizenship in order to settle in Texas."

Loedicia smiled, then winked. "They do ordinarily," she said. "But Cole ran into a man who didn't make a go of his land and he bought him out, no questions asked. The man was just anxious to leave, and Cole says there are others out there like that too, doing the same thing. I guess the authorities are mostly near cities, and they don't keep too close an eye on the frontier, especially where the Indians are. But, you see, Cole's friendly with the Comanche, so he doesn't mind it out on the plains."

"But is it safe?"

"Nowhere's safe, really, Bain, you should know that," she said, and looked off toward the field where the wildflowers were, then sighed, and there were tears in her eyes. "We thought the Château was safe too, didn't we? But come, let's go tell the children and the others. At least you'll all get to say good-bye. And, oh yes," she went on as she put an arm through Lizette's arm, the other arm through Bain's, leading them into the foyer and on toward the parlor, where tea was being served to the guests who'd attended the funeral services for Roth. "And I think you'd best make arrangements with your father, Bain. The house'll have to be sold, the furniture . . ."

Bain glanced over Loedicia's head at his wife and he smiled. Lizette tried to smile back, but it wasn't easy.

The rest of the morning was strained for everyone as Bain greeted all the guests, trying to act as if nothing had happened, and now he could see what Lizette meant. To try to stay here would be foolish indeed. The atmosphere was too tense, and everyone was staring at them so curiously, making him all too aware of what he had done to Lizette by not believing in her, and he was more than glad they'd be leaving Beaufort and Port Royal. It was for the best. His father wasn't very pleased, though, and tried to talk him out of it, as did his mother and Felicia, but whenever he'd glanced over at Lizette, watching her trying to keep her dignity in spite of all the snide looks, he knew he couldn't disappoint her.

Lizette watched Bain furtively as he talked to everyone, trying to convince them that there'd been nothing unusual about his arrival today, only she was certain everyone knew differently by the looks she was getting, and the only thing that kept her from telling them all off was the fact that after today she wouldn't have to look at their faces anymore. That, and the fact that she didn't want to hurt Grandma Dicia by creating a scene at Grandpa Roth's funeral. After all, most of the people from Port Royal were here since they were all Roth's old friends, and at least half of the population of Beaufort, as well as Rachel Grantham from River Oaks, who'd created scenes enough already with her sobbing and carrying on as if it had been her husband who'd died. Lizette was glad Grandma Dicia wouldn't have to put up with Rachel anymore, once they were gone.

Lizette stood beside Blythe and sipped at a cup of tea as she looked about the parlor, then let her gaze fall on Bain, who was talking to Julia, his sister Felicia, and her husband Alex, and she frowned, wondering where Stuart was. She hadn't really had a chance to talk to him since her decision to leave. Julia had stayed by his side every minute during that first night he'd been injured, as well as the next day until she'd left with him for their home on the outskirts of Beaufort.

However, the head injury hadn't been as severe as they'd thought at first, and although the gash hadn't healed all the way as yet, it had healed enough so that he was able to come back to attend the funeral. Lizette started surveying the room, looking for him, then stiffened as she heard his voice from behind her, close to her ear.

"We have to talk," Stuart said, his voice low and furtive.

She turned slowly, looking into his eyes, and there was no way she could refuse. "The library," she answered simply, then turned back toward the crowded room.

Bain was still talking with his brother-in-law, sister, and Julia, and no one seemed to be watching her, so Lizette excused herself quietly to Blythe, telling her she'd be back in a few minutes, then made her way toward the door, trying to look inconspicuous, and setting her teacup down on a stand on the way.

Stuart was already in the library when she walked in, only instead of walking directly to him, she moved to her right toward Roth's desk.

Stuart started walking toward her.

"No," she said, holding a hand out to stop him. "That's far enough, Stu, please."

He stopped, but his eyes were dark, unsettled. "Why, Liz?" he asked.

She stared at him, trying to ignore any feelings she might have for him. "Because I love him."

"What about Texas?"

"Texas?"

"You were planning to leave even before Bain showed up. Why?"

"Because I couldn't go to Columbia with you, Stu," she answered. "It was an impossible dream."

"So now I have to live a nightmare without you, is that it?"

"I'm sorry."

"So am I." He closed the space between them, then reached up, cupping her face in his hands.

She'd been wearing a hat earlier during the funeral, but now her hair was uncovered and he drank in its beauty, remembering what it was like to bury his face in it, then let his lips caress her neck while he marveled at the way her soft body yielded to him, bringing him pleasures he'd never found in any other woman's arms. She was so lovely and he had to say good-bye to her again, and this time it would really be for good, he knew, and he sighed.

"Does Bain know about us?" he asked as he lifted his head, looking deep into her eyes.

"No."

"But you'll tell him."

"I don't know."

He took a deep breath, his eyes still boring into hers. "You will, I can see it in your face." His thumb moved up, wiping a tear from the corner of her eyes. "For me?" he asked.

"Yes, for you."

His voice lowered. "We just can't win, can we, Liz?" he murmured softly. "I'm always giving you up."

"I can't help it, Stuart, you know that." She reached up, her hands on his wrists. "I told you I'd hurt you again. I always do, and now I have."

His hands dropped to her shoulders and he frowned, concerned. "Are you sure you're doing the right thing, though, Liz?" he asked. "He could leave you again."

"And you could never really be mine. Not the way I'd need you to be, could you? So I'll try to forgive him, hope to God I can, and take my chances, because I do love him, Stu. I always have and I always will, in spite of what I feel for you."

"Then you do care?"

"You know I do. Somehow you and Bain are all mixed up together for me, though, and it's been so hard."

He was still holding her shoulders. "May I kiss you good-bye?"

She nodded, and he bent down, pulling her to him at the same time, and his lips covered hers hungrily, as if he wanted to devour her. It would be the last, and he had to savor every moment, every second, because it would never happen again.

There were tears in Lizette's eyes as she drew away from him, then sighed breathlessly.

"Good-bye, Stuart," she whispered. "May God be with you," and she wrenched free of his arms, hurried to the door, opened it, then left the room, her eyes shut as she closed the door firmly behind her. When she opened them again, she was staring directly into Grandma Dicia's face.

"I was coming to get you," Loedicia said as she stood quietly watching her granddaughter. "Bain's been looking for you."

Lizette flushed. "I . . ."

"Did he take it well?" Loedicia asked.

Lizette looked at her curiously. "You knew?"

"I saw the two of you slip away from the others. That's why I came after you." Loedicia's eyes softened. "Is it over?"

"Yes."

"It isn't easy to be in love with two men at the same time, is it?"

"Is that what it is, Grandma?"

"Isn't it?"

Lizette stared at her grandmother for a few minutes, then sighed. "Shall we go find Bain?"

Loedicia watched Lizette straighten, made sure there were no more tears in her eyes, then the two of them joined the rest of the family in the parlor, where the guests were slowly starting to leave.

When the last carriage had gone, all except the Dantes, Bain's parents, and Stuart and Julia, Bain, with Heath, Stuart, and the slaves helping, began clearing the remains of the *Interlude* away from the pier, and shortly after lunch they were able to bring the *Sparrow* into the dock, drop anchor, tie up, and start loading the things from the wagon aboard, including the wagon itself, which was lashed to the deck near the bow, while Diablo and the horses that were to pull the wagon were also brought aboard and joined Amigo in the hold.

Even the children were excited as the last few things were taken aboard, and Blythe, who they thought might be petrified, was in her glory as they tied her into her chair, then fastened it down securely to some wooden braces Bain had nailed into place on the deck so she could watch everything going on, while Braxton, who had sailed on the *Interlude* dozens of times with Grandpa Roth, was pacing the ship from one end to the other, making sure the men were all doing their jobs, as if he were the captain's mate, if not the captain himself.

By late afternoon the ship was ready, enough provisions were put on board to last them until they reached Savannah, where Bain would try to pick up a cargo to sell when they reached their destination, which was a small port city he knew of near the Texas border, and they all stood on board saying good-bye.

Hands were shaken, there were hugs and kisses all around with promises to write, then those who weren't going made their way down the gangplank and stood on the pier watching them cast off.

Lizette stood beside Bain, who was shouting orders to his men in the rigging, and as the men working the capstan strained, lifting the anchor until it cleared the water, and the last rope was cast off, Lizette glanced toward the pier, where everyone was standing watching them leave, and her gaze rested on Stuart for a moment, a sadness filling her. If only Julia could be to Stuart what he needed, but then somehow she knew he'd survive. Perhaps because he was a senator, and it seemed like politicians always survived somehow. She saw his lips move silently. He was saying good-bye. Her hand went up, and she waved hesitantly, then blew a kiss out over the water as the sails began to unfurl, catching the wind.

The big ship heaved roughly in the water, pulling away from the pier, creaking and groaning as it did; then it lurched into midstream, and while Lizette stood watching, unaware that Bain was no longer calling orders to his men but watching the people on the pier, she saw Stuart pretend to catch the kiss, put it to his lips, then blow it back to her.

Bain was standing a short distance from Lizette, and he frowned as he watched this byplay between his wife and his brother. However, the only indication that he had seen anything was the tightening of his jaw and the hard look creeping into his eyes. Instead, he went back to his work, checking the sails and giving orders to the helmsman, and as the sails slapped fitfully, each new sail filling rapidly, the *Sparrow* began to pick up speed, then headed downriver toward the sound and the open sea.

Later that evening after the children were settled in their cabins for the night, having enjoyed their first meal aboard ship, the *Sparrow* moved steadily along through the dark night, following the coastline south, all sails full, and Lizette stood in the captain's cabin waiting for Bain.

Her hair was loose around her shoulders, she'd brushed it till it shone, and she was naked beneath a wrapper of deep green satin that matched her eyes. She moved to the window, ducking her head so she wouldn't hit the overhead lantern, then pulled back the curtain and gazed out.

Bain's cabin was at the stern of the ship and all she could see were the rolling furrows of the wake the ship was leaving as they whitecapped in the moonlight, along with a few stars overhead. Other than that, everything was dark. She frowned. Bain had been in such a strange mood tonight. Almost as if he were angry with her, and her stomach began to flutter at the horrible thought that maybe he was changing his mind and would leave her again when they reached Texas.

She'd been wondering about it ever since she'd helped put the children to bed in the other cabins with Pretty and Dodee, and now suddenly she turned as she heard the sound of the door opening behind her.

Bain was restless and a little uneasy as he stepped into the cabin, and he stopped for a minute, staring at her curiously, then shut the door.

"I see you're ready for bed," he said, and his voice had a harshness to it she hadn't heard earlier.

"Didn't you want me to be?"

"It all depends."

She watched him anxiously. "What's that supposed to mean?"

"You're not the only one who has something to forgive, are you, Liz?" he said after a few minutes.

She inhaled sharply, then tried to stay calm. "I . . . I don't understand."

"You don't understand?" He looked disgusted. "I saw the kiss you threw Stuart this afternoon, Liz," he said heatedly. "So don't tell me you don't understand. How long has it been going on this time—since before or after you were kidnapped?"

She'd been afraid of this. "Only since you refused to come home with me," she answered, and her eyes grew cold. "You had Elena, Bain, and I had no one!"

"So you turned to Stuart again!"

"That's right, I turned to Stuart again, and for the same reason I turned to him the first time," she retorted. "Because you deserted me. After all, how long did you expect me to go on without someone to love, Bain?" Her eyes were blazing as she confronted him, anger her only defense. "Or wasn't I supposed to have anyone, was that it? It was all right for you to go whoring around with Elena, but fat old Lizette was supposed to just stay home and take care of the children like a good little mother until you decided you'd had enough, was that it? Well, I'm human too!"

Her words cut deep.

"Yes, I turned to Stuart, Bain," she went on. "Because I knew he loved me. You knew it too, we've both known it for a long time, that's why we always kept our distance from him and Julia, even though neither of us would ever come right out and say it. Only I didn't ask him to become my lover again, Bain, it was something that just happened. I needed you and you weren't there. Stuart was."

"But he's my brother!"

"And if it had been someone else?"

Bain's eyes bored into hers. He wanted to lash out at her, hit her, do anything to stop her, but knew she was right. What did it matter whom she'd turned to? What did matter was that she wouldn't have had to turn to anyone if he'd only believed her.

"I'm sorry, Bain," she said, her voice breaking. "I'll sleep in another cabin," and she walked over, starting to gather the dress she'd taken off and some of her other things.

"No!" He closed the space between them and took the things from her hands, tossing them back on the chair. "You'll stay here," he demanded.

"But you don't want me."

"Did I say that?"

"You said—"

"To hell with what I said." He reached down, grabbed her hand, and pulled her to the bed, making her sit on it. "Now, take that thing off," he ordered her, his eyes on the wrapper, and she eyed him skeptically. "I said take it off," and he started pulling the shirt from his pants while he watched her untie the sash around her waist; then she let the wrapper fall open, and flushed crimson under his gaze.

She watched apprehensively as his pants came off, then his Wellington boots, followed closely by his underwear, and she took a deep breath as he straightened and stood staring at her.

"You don't have it off yet," he said, and his gaze rested on the wrapper still covering her shoulders.

Reaching out, he grabbed her hands, pulled her to her feet, and began peeling the satiny fabric down her arms while he held her against him.

"Bain?"

His face was only inches away, his eyes holding hers captive, as if she were mesmerized.

"I thought you were ready for bed," he said as he let the wrapper fall to the floor at their feet, and she trembled as she felt his hands, free of the wrapper now, slide up her arms, then move to her back and begin to caress her.

"I am," she whispered breathlessly. "But nothing's been settled."

"Hasn't it?" His hands stopped caressing her momentarily and he studied her face, the flickering light from the lantern that hung above the table in the cabin giving her skin a tawny hue. "I drove you into his arms just as surely as if I'd stood there and handed you to him," he said after a few seconds. "And I have only myself to blame for that. As far as forgiveness goes, I know you hate knowing I was with Elena as much as I hate knowing you were with Stuart, but if you can forgive, so can I, only I'm going to make you forget him once and for all, Liz, you can count on that, because I'm going to fill you with so much love there'll never be room for him in your life ever again. Not tonight, or any other time," and he kissed her long and hard, his body responding to her as if she were a glass of heady wine, and he felt warm and giddy inside.

Suddenly he pulled back from her, his lips leaving hers, and he stared at her, marveling at the glow on her face that had replaced the anger and frustration of moments before.

"Only one thing," he said warily, and his voice was strained as she stared at him. "You're not pregnant again, are you, Liz?"

He saw anger forming in her eyes again, and took a deep breath, then relaxed as he watched it subside. He had every right to know, Lizette told herself silently, and sighed.

"No, that I can assure you, Bain. I'm not pregnant again," she answered. "My menses ended last Saturday, and I was never with him again."

"Thank God," he whispered fervently, then reached up, cupping the side of her head in his hand. "It's so good to hold you again, Liz," he said huskily. "I've missed you so," and as he kissed her and drew her to him, then gently moved with her, lowering her onto the bed, he began to make love to her as he'd been wanting to for so long now. To feel flesh beneath his hands, not bone, and feel warmth in his heart, not anger, knowing that when he kissed her he'd feel it deep down inside, like a sweet caress. And Liz opened to him passionately, letting him love her, and coax her, until finally, in the warmth of the love they'd always shared and remembered from before, the pain and bitterness of the past few months was washed away. They were whole again, one again, their hearts and bodies surrendering again, and as Bain looked into her eyes, kissed her lips gently, then entered her, bringing with his entry the promise of what lay ahead for them both, up on deck Loedicia stood alone at the rail near the bow of the ship watching some clouds chase the moon, and she sighed.

She was running away, and she knew it, but didn't care. Although it was the first time she'd run away from anything since that cold rainy night almost fifty years ago in Boston when she'd run away from her uncle's home so she wouldn't have to marry Lord Varrick. A loose hair blew into her face, and she brushed it aside. Her hair was gray now, she thought. How quickly the years go by. That was the trouble, she wasn't young anymore, and running away was the only way she knew to fight back.

There were too many memories in Port Royal. Too many things she wanted to forget. Not Roth, nor her life with him—those memories would always be with her, just like the special memories she had of Quinn. But she knew she would never face a day at the Château without Roth beside her and feel alive again. So her only recourse was to run, and as far away as she could.

She watched the clouds finally catch the moon, covering it so no light shone through, glanced over for a minute to another part of the sky where there were no clouds and the stars shone brightly, and thought of Bain and Lizette. They were running away too. Away from all the hurt and anger of the past year, away from Stuart and all the memories.

She sighed again, pulled the shawl she was wearing tighter around her, then turned and headed toward the gangway to go down to her cabin. There were tears in her eyes now. Tears for the life she'd once had and was being forced to give up, and tears for what might lie ahead, and as she disappeared belowdecks, wondering what the future would hold for them this time, the *Sparrow* sailed on through the starry night, the helmsman steering a course for Texas.

About the Author

The granddaughter of an old-time vaudevillian, Mrs. Shiplett was born and raised in Ohio. She is married and lives in the city of Mentor-on-the-Lake. She has four daughters and several grandchildren and enjoys living an active outdoor life.

𝄌

PASSION RIDES THE PAST

☐ **TO LOVE A ROGUE by Valerie Sherwood.** Raile Cameron, a renegade gunrunner, lovingly rescues the sensuous and charming Lorraine London from indentured servitude in Revolutionary America. Lorraine fights his wild and teasing embraces, as they sail the stormy Caribbean seas, until finally she surrenders to fiery passion. (400518—$4.50)

☐ **WINDS OF BETRAYAL by June Lund Shiplett.** She was caught between two passionate men—and her own wild desire. Beautiful Lizette Kolter deeply loves her husband Bain Kolter, but the strong and virile free-booter, Sancho de Cordoba, seeks revenge on Bain by making her his prisoner of love. She was one man's lawful wife, but another's lawless desire. (150376—$3.95)

☐ **HIGHLAND SUNSET by Joan Wolf.** She surrendered to the power of his passion . . . and her own undeniable desire. When beautiful, dark-haired Vanessa Maclan met Edward Romney, Earl of Linton, she told herself she should hate this strong and handsome English lord. But it was not hate but hunger that this man of so much power and passion woke within the Highland beauty. (400488—$3.95)